Robert Dodsley, William Carew Hazlitt, Richard Morris

A select collection of old English plays

Robert Dodsley, William Carew Hazlitt, Richard Morris

A select collection of old English plays

ISBN/EAN: 9783742862525

Manufactured in Europe, USA, Canada, Australia, Japa

Cover: Foto ©Andreas Hilbeck / pixelio.de

Manufactured and distributed by brebook publishing software
(www.brebook.com)

Robert Dodsley, William Carew Hazlitt, Richard Morris

A select collection of old English plays

A SELECT COLLECTION

OF

OLD ENGLISH PLAYS.

ORIGINALLY PUBLISHED BY ROBERT DODSLEY
IN THE YEAR 1744.

FOURTH EDITION,

NOW FIRST CHRONOLOGICALLY ARRANGED, REVISED AND ENLARGED
WITH THE NOTES OF ALL THE COMMENTATORS
AND NEW NOTES

BY

W. CAREW HAZLITT.

VOLUME THE THIRD.

LONDON:
REEVES AND TURNER, 196 STRAND
AND 185 FLEET STREET.
1874.

NEW CUSTOM.

VOL. III.   A

A New Enterlude, no lesse wittie then pleasant, entituled new Custome, deuised of late, and for diuerse causes nowe set forthe, neuer before this tyme imprinted. 1573. [Col.] *Imprinted at London, in Fleete strete, by William How for Abraham Veale, dwelling in Paules churche-yarde at the signe of the Lambe.* 4to, B. L.

DODSLEY'S PREFACE.

I HAVE not been able to discover who was the author of this piece. But I think it is one of the most remarkable of our ancient moralities, as it was wrote purposely to vindicate and promote the Reformation. It was printed in 1573, and contrived so that four people might act it; this was frequently done for the convenience of such as were disposed to divert or improve themselves, by representing these kinds of entertainments in their own houses.

[The authorship of "New Custom" remains undiscovered. It is a piece which may have been written a few years before it was printed, and is one of the dramatic efforts in furtherance of the Reformation. At the same time, there is no apparent foundation for the hypothesis that the morality was in existence any great length of time before the date of publication.]

THE PLAYERS' NAMES IN THIS INTERLUDE BE THESE.

The Prologue.
PERVERSE DOCTRINE, *an old Popish Priest.*
IGNORANCE, *another, but elder.*
NEW CUSTOM, *a Minister.*
LIGHT OF THE GOSPEL, *a Minister.*
HYPOCRISY, *an old Woman.*
CRUELTY, *a Ruffler.*[1]
AVARICE, *a Ruffler.*
EDIFICATION, *a Sage.*
ASSURANCE, *a Virtue.*
GOD'S FELICITY, *a Sage.*

FOUR MAY PLAY THIS INTERLUDE.

1. PERVERSE DOCTRINE.

2. { IGNORANCE, HYPOCRISY, *and* EDIFICATION.

3. { NEW CUSTOM. AVARICE. ASSURANCE.

4. { LIGHT OF THE GOSPEL. CRUELTY. GOD'S FELICITY. THE PROLOGUE.

---

[1] A cheating bully, so called in several Acts of Parliament during the reign of King Henry the Eighth.—*S.*

THE PROLOGUE.

All things be not so as in sight they do seem,
Whatsoever they resemble, or whatever men deem.
For if our senses in their own objects us do fail
Sometimes, then our judgment shall but little avail
In some things, as such, where doubt giveth denial
Of them in the best wise to make any trial.
Which saying is evident, as well shall appear
In this little interlude, which we present here ;
Whereby we may learn how grossly we err,
Taking one thing for another, which differ so far,
As good doth from bad.   Example therefore
You may take by these persons, if you mark no
    more.
For the primitive constitution, which was first
    appointed
Even by God himself and by Christ his annointed ;
Confirmed by th' Apostles, and of great antiquity :
See, how it is perverted by man's wicked iniquity,
To be called New Custom or New Constitution,
Surely a name of too much ungodly abusion.
Which our author, indifferently scanning in his
    mind,
In his simple opinion this cause he doth find :
That, by reason of ignorance which beareth great
    sway,
And also stubborn doctrine, which shutteth up the
    way
To all good instruction and knowledge of right :

No marvel it was, though of the truth we were
      ignorant quite.
For truly in such a case the matter was but small
To make the ignorant soul to credit them all,
Whatsoever they said, were it truth or a lie.
For no man able was then to prove them the con-
      trary.
Wherefore their own fancies they set in great price,
Neglecting the true way, like men far unwise.
Making semblant of antiquity in all that they did,
To th' intent that their subtlety by such means
      might be hid.
New Custom also hath he named this matter verily,
In consideration that the people so speaketh com-
      monly,
Confuting the same by reasons most manifest,
Which in consequent order of talk are exprest.
This sense hath our author followed herein, as we
      said,
For other meaning : moreover he will not have it
      denayed,
But diverse may invent much distant from this,
Which in no wise he will have prejudicial to his,
Nor his unto theirs, whatsoever they be,
For many heads, many wits,[1] we do plainly see.
Only he desireth this of the worshipful audience :
To take in good part without all manner offence,
Whatsoever shall be spoken, marking the intent,
Interpreting it no otherwise but as it was meant.
And for us, if of patience you list to attend,
We are ready to declare you the matter to the end.

FINIS PROLOGI.

---

[1] [A common proverb, of which there are varying versions ;
but the original is *quot homines*, &c.]

NEW CUSTOM.

ACTUS I., SCÆNA 1.

PERVERSE DOCTRINE *and* **IGNORANCE** *enter.*

PERV. DOC. It is even so indeed, the world was
    never in so evil a state ;
But this is no time for us of these matters to debate.
It were good we invented some politic way
Our matters to address in good orderly stay.
And for us reason would we looked to ourselves.
Do you not see how these new-fangled prattling
    elves
Prink up so pertly of late in every place,
And go about us ancients flatly to deface ?
As who should say in short time, as well learned
    as we,
As wise to the world, as good they might accounted
    be,
Nay, nay, if many years and grey hairs do know
    no more,
But that every peevish boy hath even as much wit
    in store :
By the mass, then, have I lived too long, and I
    would I were dead,
If I have not more knowledge than a thousand of
    them in my head,

For how should they have learning that were born
    but even now?
As fit a sight it were to see a goose shod or a
    saddled cow,
As to hear the prattling of any such Jack Straw.
For, when he hath all done, I count him but a very
    daw.
As in London not long since, you wot well where,
They rang to a sermon, and we chanced to be there.
Up stert the preacher, I think not past twenty
    years old,
With a sounding voice and audacity bold,
And began to revile at the holy sacrament and
    transubstantiation :
I never heard one knave or other make such a
    declaration.
But, if I had had the boy in a convenient place,
With a good rod or twain, not past one hour's
    space.
I would so have scourged my merchant,[1] that his
    breech should ache,
So long as it is since that he those words spake.
What, young men to be meddlers in divinity? it
    is a goodly sight !
Yet therein now almost is every boy's delight,
No book now in their hands, but all scripture,
    scripture :
Either the whole Bible or the New Testament, you
    may be sure.
The New Testament for them? and then too for
    Coll my dog ![2]

---

[1] *Merchant* was anciently used as we now use the word
chap. See note on "Romeo and Juliet," A. 2, S. 4.—
Steevens.

[2] *Cowle* or rather *coll* [Coll] I suppose to be the name of
the dog.—*Steevens.*

Cowle my dog, I am inclined to believe, means *put a cowl*

This is the old proverb—to cast pearls to an hog.
Give them that which is meet for them, a racket
      and a ball,
Or some other trifle to busy their heads withal:
Playing at quoits or nine-holes,[1] or shooting at
      butts,
There let them be, a God's name, till their hearts
      ache and their guts!
Let us alone with divinity, which are of riper age.
Youth is rash, they say, but old men hath the
      knowledge.
For while they read they know not what, they
      omit the verity,
And that is now the cause so many fall into heresy,
Every man hath his own way, some that and some
      this,
It would almost for anger (sir reverence![2]) make a
      man to piss,
To hear what they talk of in open communication,

---

or hood on a dog, and he will be as learned as a friar : the contempt into which the order had at this period fallen will at least countenance the explanation, if it should not be thought sufficient to prove it. I once was of opinion, that there might be an allusion to the case of one Collins, a crazy man, who seeing a priest hold up the host over his head, lifted up a dog in the same manner, for which both he and the animal were burnt in 1538. See Fox, vol. ii. 436.

My conjecture requires a little explanation. The speaker means to say, "If the New Testament is fit for the use of boys, so likewise is it adapted equally to the conception of *Coll my dog.* The one will understand and make a proper use of it as soon as the other."—*Steevens.* [What will be thought of the preceding note, I hardly know ; the text is the clearer.]

[1] By the Stat. 33 Hen. VIII. c. 9, s. 16, a penalty is imposed on certain persons therein mentioned, who should play at the tables, tennis, dice, cards, bowls, clash, *coyting,* logating, or other unlawful game.

[2] Perhaps a contraction of *save your reverence.*—*Steevens.*

Surely I fear me, Ignorance, this gear will make
    some desolation.
    IGNORANCE. I fear the same also; but as touching
        that whereof you speak full well,
They have revoked divers old heresies out of hell.
As against transubstantiation, purgatory, and the
    mass,
And say that by scripture they cannot be brought
    to pass.
But that which ever hath been a most true and
    constant opinion,
And defended also hitherto by all of our religion,
That I, Ignorance, am the mother of true devo-
    tion,
And Knowledge the author of the contrary affec-
    tion :
They deny it so stoutly as though it were not so ;
But this hath been believed many an hundred year
    ago.
Wherefore it grieveth me not a little that my case
    should so stand,
Thus to be disproved at every prattler's hand.
    PERV. DOC. Yea, doth? then the more unwise
        man you, as I trow,
For they say as much by me, as you well do know.
And shall I then go vex myself at their talk?
No, let them speak so long as their tongues can
    walk.
They shall not grieve me, for why in very sooth
It were folly to endeavour to stop every man's
    mouth.
They have brought in one, a young upstart lad, as
    it appears,
I am sure he hath not been in the realm very many
    years,
With a gathered frock, a polled head and a broad
    hat,

An unshaved beard, a pale face; and he teacheth
    that
All our doings are nought, and hath been many a
    day.
He disalloweth our ceremonies and rites, and
    teacheth another way
To serve God, than that which we do use,
And goeth about the people's minds to seduce.
It is a pestilent knave, he will have priests no
    corner-cap to wear;[1]
Surplices are superstition: beads, paxes, and such
    other gear,
Crosses, bells, candles, oil, bran, salt, spettle, and
    incense,
With censing and singing, he accounts not worth
    three-halfpence,
And cries out on them all (if to repeat them I wist)
Such holy things, wherein our religion doth con-
    sist.
But he commands the service in English to be
    read,

---

[1] Fox, in the third volume of his "Acts and Monu-
ments," p. 131, says: "Over and besides divers other
things touching M. Rogers, this is not to be forgotten, how,
in the daies of King Edward the Sixth, there was a con-
troversie among the Bishops and Clergie *for wearing of
priests caps,* and other attyre belonging to that order.
Master Rogers, being one of that number which never went
otherwise than in *a round cap* during all the time of King
Edward, affirmed that he would not agree to that decree-
ment of uniformitie, but upon this condition, that if they
would needs have such an uniformitie of wearing the cap,
tippet, &c., then it should be decreed withall, that the
papists, for a difference betwixt them and others, should be
constrained to weare upon their sleeves a chalice with an
host upon it.   Whereunto if they would consent, he would
agree to the other, otherwise he would not, he said, consent
to the setting forth of the same, nor ever weare *the cap;*
nor indeed he never did."

And for the Holy Legend [1] the Bible to put in his
    stead,
Every man to look thereon at his list and pleasure,
Every man to study divinity at his convenient
    leisure,
With a thousand new guises more you know as
    well as I.
And to term him by his right name, if I should
    not lie,
It is New Custom, for so they do him call,
Both our sister Hypocrisy, Superstition, Idolatry
    and all.
And truly me-thinketh, they do justly and wisely
    therein,
Since he is so diverse, and so lately crept in.
   IGNORANCE. So they call him indeed, you have
    said right well,
Because he came newly from the devil of hell,
New Custom, quoth you? now a vengeance of his
    new nose,
For bringing in any such unaccustomed glose!
For he hath seduced the people by mighty great
    flocks :
Body of God, it were good to set the knave in the
    stocks.
Or else to whip him for an example to all rogues
    as he,
How they the authors of new heresies be,
Or henceforth do attempt any such strange devise :
Let him keep himself from my hands, if he be wise.
If ever I may take him within my reign,
He is sure to have whipping there for his pain.
For he doth much harm in each place throughout
    the land.

---

[1] I suppose the " Legenda Aurea," the " Golden Legend "
of Jacobus de Voragine.—*Steevens.*

Wherefore, Perverse Doctrine, here needeth your
    hand :
I mean that ye be diligent in any case,
If ye fortune to come, where New Custom is in
    place,
So to use the villain, you know what I mean,
That in all points you may discredit him clean :
And when he begins of anything for to clatter,
Of any controversy of learning or divinity matter,
So to cling fast unto every man's thought,
That his words may seem heresy, and his doings
    but nought.
    PERV. DOC. Tush, let me alone with that, for I
    have not so little wit,
But I have practised this already, and mind also
    to do it.
Yet a further device I have, I think, not amiss.
Hearken to me, Ignorance, for the matter is this :
For the better accomplishing our subtlety pre-
    tended,[1]
It were expedient that both our names were
    amended ;
Ignorance shall be Simplicity, for that comes very
    nigh ;
And for Perverse Doctrine I will be called Sound
    Doctrine, I.
And now that we are both in such sort named,
We may go in any place, and never be blamed.
See then you remember your name, sir Simplicity,
And me at every word Sound Doctrine to be ;
Beware of tripping, but look in mind that you
    bear
Your feigned name, and what before you were.
But who is this that hitherward doth walk ?
Let us stand still, to hear what he will talk.

---

[1] [Intended.]

ACTUS I., SCÆNA 2.

New Custom entereth alone.

NEW CUS. When I consider the ancient times
    before,
That have been these eight hundred years and more,
And those confer with these our later days,
My mind do these displease a thousand ways.
For sure he, that hath both perceived aright,
Will say they differ as darkness doth from light.
For then plain-dealing bare away the prize ;
All things were ruled by men of good advice;
Conscience prevailed much, even everywhere ;
No man deceived his neighbour and eke a thing
    full rare
It was to find a man you might not trust ;
But look what once they promised, they did that
    well and just.
If neighbours were at variance, they ran not straight
    to law :
Daysmen [1] took up the matter, and cost them not
    a straw,
Such delight they had to kill debate and strife ;
And surely even in those days was there more
    godlier life.

---

[1] *i.e.,* Umpires.   So Spenser—

"For what art thou
That makst thyself his *daysman,* to prolong
The vengeance past?"—*Faerie Queene.—S.*

A *days-man,* says Ray, in his "Collection of North
Country Words," p. 25, is "an arbitrator, an umpire or
judge.   For, as Dr Hammond observes in his Annotation
on Heb. x. 25, p. 752, the word *day,* in all languages and
idioms, signifies judgment.   So *man's day,* 1 Cor. iii. 13,
is the judgment of men.   So *diem dicere* in Latin is to im-
plead."

Howbeit men of all ages are wonted to dispraise
The wickedness of time that flourished at their
    days.
As well he may discern, who for that but lightly
    looks,
In every leaf almost of all their books.
For as for Christ our master, what he thought of
    Jews,
And after him th' apostles, I think it is no news.
    PERV. DOC. Hark, Simplicity, he is some
        preacher, I will lay my gown;
He mindeth to make a sermon within this town.
He speaketh honestly yet; but surely, if he rail at
    me,
I may not abide him, by the mass, I promise thee.
    NEW CUS. Paul to the Corinthians plainly doth
        tell,
That their behaviour pleased him not well.
All our forefathers likewise have been offended
With divers faults at their time, that might have
    been amended.
The doctors of the church great fault they did find,
In that men lived not after their mind:
First with the rulers as examples of sin,
Then with the people as continuing therein:
So that of them both this one thing they thought,
That the people was not good, but the rulers were
    nought.
But in comparison of this time of misery,
In those days men lived in perfect felicity.
Saint Paul prophesied that worse times should
    ensue,
In novissimis venient quidam, saith he, this is true,
Following all mischief, ungodliness and evil,
Leaning to all wickedness and doctrine of the devil;
And spake he not of these days, think you, I pray?
The proof is so plain that no man can denay:

For this is sure, that never in any age before
Naughtiness and sin hath been practised more,
Or half so much, or at all, in respect so I say,
And is now (God amend all) at this present day :
Sin now no sin, faults no faults a whit :
O God, seest thou this, and yet wilt suffer it ?
Surely thy mercy is great ; but yet our sins, I fear,
Are so great, that of justice with them thou canst
    not bear.
Adultery no vice, it is a thing so rife,
A stale jest now to lie with another man's wife !
For what is that but dalliance ? Covetousness they
    call
Good husbandry, when one man would fain have
    all.
And eke alike to that is unmerciful extortion,
A sin in sight of God of great abhomination :
For pride, that is now a grace ; for round about
The humble-spirited is termed a fool or a lout.
Whoso will be so drunken, that he scarcely know-
    eth his way,
O, he is a good fellow, so now-a-days they say.
Gluttony is hospitality, while they meat and drink
    spill,
Which would relieve diverse whom famine doth
    kill.
As for all charitable deeds, they be gone, God
    know'th ;
Some pretend lack, but the chief cause is sloth :
A vice most outrageous of all others sure,
Right hateful to God, and contrary to nature.
Scarce blood is punished but even for very shame,
So make they of murther but a trifling game.
O, how many examples of that horrible vice
Do daily among us now spring and arise !
But thanks be to God that such rulers doth send,
Which earnestly study that fault to amend :

As by the sharp punishment of that wicked crime
We may see that committed was but of late time.
God direct their hearts they may always continue
Such just execution on sin to ensue ;
So shall be saved the life of many a man,
And God will withdraw his sore plagues from us
    then.
Theft is but policy, perjury but a face,
Such is now the world, so far men be from grace.
But what shall I say of religion and knowledge
Of God, which hath been indifferent in each age
Before this ? howbeit his faults then it had,
And in some points then was culpable and bad.
Surely this one thing I may say aright :
God hath rejected us away from him quite,
And given us up wholly unto our own thought,
Utterly to destroy us, and bring us to nought :
For do they not follow the inventions of men ?
Look on the primitive church, and tell me then,
Whether they served God in this same wise,
Or whether they followed any other guise ?
For since God's fear decayed, and hypocrisy crept in,
In hope of some gains and lucre to win,
Cruelty bare a stroke, who with fagot and fire
Brought all things to pass that he did desire.
Next avarice spilt all, which, lest it should be spied,
Hypocrisy ensued the matter to hide.
Then brought they in their monsters, their masses,
    their light,
Their torches at noon to darken our sight :
Their popes and their pardons, their purgatories
    for souls :
Their smoking of the church and flinging of coals.
    IGNORANCE. Stay yet a while, and let us hear
      more communication.
    PERV. DOC. I cannot, by God's soul, if I might
      have all this nation.

Shall I suffer a knave thus to rail and prate?
Nay then, I pray God, the devil break my pate!
I will be revenged, ere he depart away—
Ah, sirrah, you have made a fair speak here to-day,
Do you look for any reward for your deed?
It were good to beat thee, till thy head bleed,
Or to scourge thee well-favouredly at a cart's tail,
To teach such an whoreson to blaspheme and rail
At such holy mysteries and matters so high,
As thou speakest of now, and rail'dst at so lately!
    New Cus. What mean ye, sir, or to whom do
        you speak?
Art you minded on me your anger to wreak,
Which have not offended, as far as I know?
    Perv. Doc. I speak to thee, knave; thou art
        mad, I trow.
What meanest thou to rail right now so contemp-
        tuously
At the chiefest secrets of all divinity?
    New Cus. Verily I railed not, so far as I can
        tell,
I spake but advisedly, I know very well;
For I will stand to it, whatsoever I said.
    Perv. Doc. Wilt thou so? but I will make thee
        well apaid,[1]
To recant thy words, I hold thee a pound,
Before thou depart hence out of this ground.
    New Cus. No, that shall you not do, if I die
        therefore.
    Perv. Doc. Thou shalt see anon, go to, prattle
        no more,
But tell me the effect of the words which were said.
    New Cus. To recite them again, I am not
        afraid:

---

[1] Well content. In Psalm lxxxiii. ver. 8, we have—
"And Assur eke is well *apaid*,
With them in league to be."

I said that the mass, and such trumpery as that,
Popery, purgatory, pardons, were flat
Against God's word and primitive constitution,
Crept in through covetousness and superstition
Of late years, through blindness, and men of no
    knowledge;
Even such as have been in every age.
   PERV. DOC. Now, precious whoreson, thou hast
    made a lie;
How canst thou prove that, tell me by and by.
   NEW CUS. It needeth small proof; the effect
    doth appear.
Neither this is any place for to argue here.
And, as for my saying, I hold the negative:
It lieth you upon to prove the affirmative;
To show that such things were used in antiquity,
And then I can easily prove you the contrary.
   PERV. DOC. Standest thou with me on school
    points? dost thou so indeed?
Thou hadst best to prove me whether I can read;
Thinkest thou I have no logic, indeed thinkest
    thou so?
Yes, prinkocks, that I have; for forty years ago
I could smatter in a Duns [1] prettily, I do not jest;
Better I am sure than a hundred of you, whosoever
    is the best.
   NEW CUS. Truly I believe you, for in such fond
    books
You spent idly your time and wearied your looks:
More better it had been in books of holy scripture,
Where as virtue is expressed, and religion pure,
To have passed your youth, as the Bible and such,
Than in these trifles to have dolted so much;

---

[1] *i.e.*, in the theological writings of *Duns Scotus*, who
obtained the title of *Doctor Subtilis.—S.* See also note 25
to "The Revenger's Tragedy."

Not more to have regarded a Duns or a Questionist,
Than you would the words of the holy evangelist.
    PERV. DOC. What, for a child to meddle with
      the Bible ?
    NEW CUS. Yea, sure, more better than so to be
      idle.
    PERV. DOC. Is study then idleness ? that is a
      new term.
    NEW CUS. They say better to be idle than to do
      harm.
    PERV. DOC. What harm doth knowledge ? I
      pray thee, tell me.
    NEW CUS. Knowledge puffeth up, in Saint Paul
      you may see.
    PERV. DOC. Yea, but what knowledge meaneth
      he ? tell me that.
    NEW CUS. Even such knowledge as ye profess
      flat ;
For the truth and the gospel you have in contempt,
And follow such toys as yourselves do invent :
Forsaking God's laws and the apostle's institution
In all your proceedings and matters of religion.
    PERV. DOC. By what speakest thou that, let
      me hear thy judgment ?
    NEW CUS. Not by any guess, but by that which
      is evident.
As for the scriptures, you have abolished clean ;
New fashions you have constitute in religion ; again,
Abuse of the sacraments than hath been to-fore,
Have you brought, and in number have you made
      them more
Than Christ ever made : wherefore show your
      auctority,
Or else have you done to the church great injury.
Th' apostles never taught your transubstantiation
Of bread into flesh, or any such fashion ;
Howbeit they were conversant every day and hour,

And received that sacrament of Christ our Saviour.
You feign also that Peter was bishop of Rome,
And that he first instituted the seat of your Pope-
    dom :
But, perverse nation, how dare you for shame
Your fancies on Christ and th' apostles to frame ?
    PERV. DOC. Marry, avaunt, Jack-sauce and prat-
    tling knave,
I will conjure thy coat, if thou leave not to rave.
With all my heart and a vengeance, come up and
    be nought :
I see we shall have an heretic of thee, as I thought.
These things were approved, ere thou wast born,
    dost thou not see ?
And shall be, when thou art hanged, I warrant thee.
    NEW CUS. Ere I was born ! nay, sure that is
    not true,
For in comparison of me they be but new.
    PERV. DOC. Of thee ! ha, ha, ha ! what, of thee !
    thou art mad.
    NEW CUS. Surely in my sort I am both sober
    and sad.[1]
    PERV. DOC. Why, how old art thou ? tell me, I
    pray thee heartily.
    NEW CUS. Elder than you, I perceive.
    PERV. DOC. What, older than I !
The young knave, by the mass, not fully thirty,
Would be elder than I, that am above sixty !
    NEW CUS. A thousand and a half, that surely
    is my age :
Ask and inquire of all men of knowledge.
    PERV. DOC. A thousand years ? God's precious
    soul, I am out of my wits ;
He is possessed of some devil or of some evil
    sp'rits.

---

[1] [Serious.]

Why, thou art a young knave of that sort, I say,
That brought into this realm but the other day
This new learning and these heresies, and such
    other things mo,
With strange guises invented not long ago.[1]
And I pray thee tell me, is not thy name New
    Custom?
    NEW CUS. Truly so I am called of some,
As of such as want both wit and understanding,
As you do now, I know by your talking:
But woe be to those that make no distinction
Between many things of diverse condition;
As naught to be good, and hot to be cold,
And old to be new, and new to be old.
Wherefore these deceits you daily invent,
The people to seduce unto your advertisement,
While with tales you assay, and with lies you begin,
The truth to deface, and your credit to win.
    PERV. DOC. What is thy name, then? I pray
    thee make declaration.
    NEW CUS. In faith, my name is Primitive Con-
    stitution.
    PERV. DOC. Who? who, *Prava Constitutio?* even
    so I thought,
I wist that it was some such thing of nought.[2]

---

[1] The original copy reads—
    "With strange guises invented *now* long agoe."
But the sense seems to require the negative, which former
editors substituted for *now.*—*C.*

[2] So in *Hamlet :* "The king is *a thing of nothing.*" See
the Notes of Dr Johnson, Dr Farmer, and Mr Steevens
on that passage, edition of Shakspeare, 1778, vol. 10, p.
336. This play on the words was very common.
    Again, in "The Humorous Lieutenant," A. iv. S. 6—
    "Shall, then, that thing that honours thee
    How miserable a thing soever, yet a thing still,
    And, tho' *a thing of nothing,* thy thing ever."
[Dyce's edit. vi. 516.]

Like lettuce,[1] like lips ; a scabb'd horse for a scald
    squire.
    NEW CUS. *Primitive Constitution* I said, if you
    hear,
Such orders as in the primitive church heretofore
Were used, but not now, the more pity therefore.
    PERV. DOC. Ha, ha ! in good time, sir, well
    might you fare, Primitive Constitution,
That is your true name, you say, without all delusion.
Primitive Constitution (quodestow [2]) as much as
    my sleeve !
The devil on him which will such liars believe !
For my part, if I credit such an hairy nowl,[3]
The foul fiend of hell fetch me, body and soul !
    NEW CUS. Truth cannot prevail, where Ignorance
    is in place.
    IGNORANCE. Peace, or I will lay my beads on
    thy face :
Hast thou nothing to rail at but Ignorance, I trow ?
    NEW CUS. You may use me even at your
    pleasure, I know ;
For Perverse Doctrine, that *is* rooted so fast,
That it may not be changed at no heavenly blast,
May not hear the contrary, but beginneth to kick,

---

[1] "*Similes habent labra lactucas.* A thistle is a sallet fit
for an ass's mouth. We use when we would signify that
things happen to people which are suitable to them, or
which they deserve ; as when a dull scholar happens to a
stupid or ignorant master, a froward wife to a peevish husband, &c. *Dignum patella operculum.* Like priest, like
people, and on the contrary. These proverbs are always
taken in the worst sense. *Tal carne, tal cultello,* Ital. Like
flesh, like knife." [See Hazlitt's " Proverbs," &c., 1869, pp.
33, 263.]

[2] [*i.e., Quodest thou,* or saidest thou.]

[3] [Old copy and Dodsley, *mowle.* A hairy nowl is a
member of the reformed faith, as distinguished from the
shaven crowns of the priests.]

Like a jade when he feeleth the spur for to prick.
    PERV. DOC. Yea ! say'st thou so, thou miscreant
      villain ?
A little thing would make me knock out thy brain :
Hence out of my sight away, packing, trudge !
Thou detestable heretic, thou caitiff, thou drudge ;
If I may take thee, it were as good thou were dead,
For even with this portace[1] I will batter thy head.
                  [Exit New Custom.
Though I hang therefore, I care not, I,
So I be revenged on a slave, ere I die.
Sacrament of God ! who hath heard such a knave ?
Who, after he had done at Ignorance to rave,
Perverse Doctrine (quod he) is also rooted so fast,
That he may be changed by no heavenly blast.
No, God's soul, I warrant him, I will see him
      rotten,
Before that my doctrine I shall have forgotten :
Wherefore it behoveth us some counsel to take,
How we the stronger our matters may make,
Against the surprise of this new invasion,
Begun of late by this strange generation,
Of New Custom and his makes;[2] meaning to deface

---

[1] Sometimes written *portas*, or *portos*, *i.e.*, *breviary*—Du
Cange, in *Portiforium.* "*Portuasses*, Mr Tyrwhitt observes
(Notes on Chaucer, ver. 13061), are mentioned among other
prohibited books in the Stat. 3 and 4 Edw. VI. c. 10. And
in the Parliament Roll of 7, Edw. IV. n. 40, there is a peti-
tion, that the robbing of Porteous, Grayell, Manuell, &c.,
should be made felonie without clergy ; to which the King
answered, *La Roy s'avisera.*"
The *portuse* is mentioned in Greene's "History of Fryer
Bacon and Fryer Bungay." [Works by Dyce, 1861, p. 162—]
      "I ll hamper up the match,
  I'll take my *portace* forth, and wed you here."

[2] *Make* is used for *mate* throughout the works of Gower.
Shakspeare likewise, if I am not mistaken, employs it in
one of his sonnets.—*S.*

Our ancient rites and religion, and to place
Their devilish doctrine the Gospel, and so
Our gains to debate, and ourselves to undo.
I think it best therefore that our sister Hypocrisy
Do understand fully of this matter by and by.
Let us go and seek her, the case for to show,
That we her good counsel may speedily know.

    IGNORANCE. I am ready; in following I will
    not be slow.   [*Exeunt.*

ACTUS II., SCENA 1.

LIGHT OF THE GOSPEL *and* NEW CUSTOM *enter.*

    L. OF GOSPEL. Doubt you nothing at all, for
      God will so provide,
Who leaveth not his elect to defend and to guide:
That wherever I come, such grace you may find,
As shall in each point content well your mind,
And admit that they call you New Custom, what
    then?
Attribute that folly to the ignorance of men,
That follow their fancies, and know not the right
Well, you know where I come once, the Light
Of the Gospel, whose beams do glister so clear,
Then, Primitive Constitution, in each place you
    appear;
And as elsewhere you have been, so do not mistrust,
But in this place hereafter be received you must.

    NEW CUS. According to your nature, so do you
      very well
To put me in good hope, bright Light of the Gospel.
And seeing you be true, I may in no wise
Misdeem you the father or author of lies:
For if trust to the gospel do purchase perpetuance
Of life unto him, who therein hath confidence,

What shall the light do, whose beams be so bright,
That in each respect all things else of light
Are but very darkness, and eke terrestrial ?
So the Light of the Gospel overshineth them all.
Wherefore with great comfort I receive your
    counsel,
With hearty thanks unto you, the Light of the
    Gospel.
    L. OF GOSPEL. Do so, and by faith then shall
    you obtain
Whatsoever you desire, the scripture saith plain :
For *quicquid petieritis in nomine meo,*
It must of truth needs be understood so :
That without faith, whatsoever we fortune to crave,
We may not look for it our desire to have.
Faith moveth mountains, so it be pure faith indeed ;
By faith we obtain whatsoever we need.
Then faith shall restore to you more things than
    this,
Believe me, Primitive Constitution, whatsoever is
    amiss.
But where be those reprobates, devoid of all grace,
Who lately misused you, as you said, in this place ?
    NEW CUS. They be suddenly departed, I wot not
    well whither ;
For I left them right now both here together.
They cannot be far hence, I know very well,
Where they be, there is none, if we ask, but can
    tell.
    L. OF GOSPEL. Do you know them again, if you
    meet them aright ?
    NEW CUS. Yea, sir, that I do, even at the first
    sight.
    L. OF GOSPEL. Then let us not tarry, but go
    seek them straight.
    NEW CUS. At hand I am ready on you for to
    wait.   *[Exeunt.*

ACTUS II., SCENA 2.

HYPOCRISY, PERVERSE DOCTRINE, *and*
IGNORANCE *enter.*

HYPOCRISY. Perverse Doctrine, I say, take heed
    in any sort.
That thou never believe whatsoever they report,
Though they of the Gospel never so much do preach,
Every man will not credit whatsoever they teach.
They will not say, *all believe*, when they do not, I
    promise thee :
For that time will never come in this world, trust
    me.
Tush, tush, be thou busied in any case
To discredit their preaching in every place.
If they teach them one thing, then teach thou the
    contrary ;
And if that no scripture for thy place thou have
    ready,
In words that supply, which wanteth in reason,
For ill things applied sometime in good season,
As of better eftsoons do import the weight,
So they be well ordered by good policy and sleight.
Howbeit their doctrine be sound, yet their vices
    find out,
As this is a sloven, or this is a lout :
He speaketh on envy, such a one for need ;
This saith it in words, but he thinketh it not in
    deed.
Upon greater occasion they stick not to rave,
Saying, this is a whoremaster villain, he, an heretic
    knave,
An extortioner, a thief, a traitor, a murtherer,
A covetous person, a common usurer.
This he doth for my mistress his wife's sake, by
    the rood,

The better to maintain and support the French
    hood.[1]
Remember also, that it were a great shame
For thee for to have forgotten thy own name.
Perverse Doctrine, of right, must the truth so per-
    vert,
That he never let it sink into any man's heart :
As far as he can, with diligence withstand,
For ever it behoveth thee to be ready at hand,
To strengthen thine own parts, and disprove other
    doctrine,
Whatsoever shall be taught that is contrary to
    thine :
Still pretend religion, whatsoever you say,
And that shall get thee good credit alway,
Pleasing the multitude with such kind of gear,[2]
As with them, to the which most inclined they are.
Square caps, long gowns, with tippets of silk,
Brave copes in the church, surplices as white as
    milk,
Beads, and such like : all these bear the price.
To these things apply thy attendant device :
And other likewise, which well you do know,
Which all of great holiness do set forth a show.
Though some of them, doubtless, be indifferent,
    what matter !
They furnish our business never the latter.
For these, of antiquity since that they do smell,
Our cause must commend right wonderful well :
And these be the things whereof thou hast need,
The better of thy will and purpose to speed.
Then give thy attendance, and so be sure of this :

---

[1] [See Hazlitt's "Handbook," 1867, p. 129, *v.* costume,
No. 3.   The phrase seems to be used here to signify ex-
pensive foreign fashions generally.]
[2] The 4to reads *grace.*   The alteration by Mr Dodsley.

That I will be ready and never will miss
To assist thee still in working thy purpose,
To th' advancing of thee, and depressing thy foes.
 PERV. DOC. Gramercy, good sister, even with
  all my heart,
For this your good counsel; and for my part,
Whatsoever in this case may be possibly done,
I shall follow your precepts as a natural son.
For the matter so stands, if we look not well about,
That we quite perish all out of doubt,
Unless some such way we take out of hand,
Whereby we may be able our foes to withstand.
And for this cause my brother Ignorance and I,
Lest it should chance us to fall into jeopardy,
Through envy of our names in any man's ear:
For this intent, I say, we did diligently care
Our names to counterfeit in such manner of sort,
That wherever we go we may win good report.
 HYPOCRISY. Of my faith, that is very well done
  indeed!
God send thee a good wit still at thy need.
And that in thy doings such success thou may'st
 find,
That all things may chance to thee after thy mind.
My brother, if thou have ought else for to say,
Speak on, ere that I depart hence away.
 PERV. DOC. Great thanks for your counsel, and
  if ye chance to go thither,
You may meet with Ignorance, to hasten him
 hither.
 HYPOCRISY. Farewell: he shall be here, you
  shall see, even anon.   [*Exit.*
 PERV. DOC. Alack, alack, now my good sister is
  gone,
Whose presence to enjoy is more pleasant unto me,
That any thing whatsoever in the world could be.
Good occasion have I such a sister to embrace,

For by her means I live and enjoy this place.
Which yet I possess as long as I may,
And have heretofore many a fair day.
For since these new heretics, the devil take them
    all,
In all corners began to bark and to bawl
At the Catholic faith and the old religion,
Making of them both but matters of derision ;
Hypocrisy hath so helped at every need,
That but for her hardly were we like for to speed.
For be our case never so nigh driven to the worst,
Though her means by some means take no place at
    the first :
Yet some means doth she find, by some means at
    the length,
That her ways do prevail, and her matters get
    strength.
She can find out a thousand guiles in a trice,
For every purpose a new strong device.
No matter so difficile for man to find out,
No business so dangerous, no person so stout,
But of th' one she is able a solution to make,
And th' other's great peril and mood for to slake.
And in fine, much matter in few words to contain,
She can find out a cloak for every rain.[1]
What person is there, that beareth more sway
In all manner of matters at this present day
Throughout the whole world, though of simple
    degree,
And of small power to sight she seem for to be ?
Consider all trades and conditions of life,
Then shall you perceive that Hypocrisy is rife
To all kind of men and of every age,
So far as their years them therein may give know-
    ledge :

---

[1] A proverb. *Tu hai mantillo di ogni acqua.*—S.

Lo, here a large field, where at length he may walk.
Who list of this matter at the full for to talk.
To declare of what power and of what efficacy,
In every age, country and time is Hypocrisy.
But I may not about such small points now stand :
The affairs they be greater, that I have in hand.
Ignorance is the cause that I so long tarry here,
And behold where the blind buzzard doth appear.
Come on, thou gross-headed knave, thou whoreson
    ass, I say,
Where hast thou been, since we departed to-day ?

Enter IGNORANCE.

IGNORANCE. Where have I been, quod you ?
    marry, even there I was,
Whereas I would have given an hundred pound, by
    the mass,
To have been here ; for never, since the day I was
    born,
Was I so near-hand in pieces for to have been
    torn.
For as I was going up and down in the street,
To see if I could with Hypocrisy meet,
Behold, afar off I began to espy
That heretic New Custom, with another in his
    company.
As soon as they saw me, they hied them apace,
Came towards, and met me full in the face.
I am glad we have found you then, quod this
    heretic knave,
For you and your fellow this day sought we have
In every place, and now cannot you fly ;
And with these words both they came very nigh.
Whereat I so feared, I may tell you plain,
That I thought at that hour I should have been
    slain.

This is he, quod the varlet, of whom I told you of
    late,
An enemy of the truth, and incensed with hate
Against God and his church, and an imp of Hypo-
    crisy,
A foe to the gospel and to true divinity.
Thou liest, heretic, quod I, and nought else could I
    say,
But brake quickly from them, and hither came
    away.
    PERV. DOC. Who is he that was with him, Sim-
    plicity, canst thou tell?
    IGNORANCE. Not I, sure, but some call him the
    Light of the Gospel.
A good personable fellow, and in countenance so
    bright,
That I could not behold him in the visage aright.
    PERV. DOC. God's precious wounds, that slave!
    marry, fie on him, fie!
Body of our Lord, is he come into the country?
I think all the heretics in the world have taken in
    hand
By some solemn oath to pester this land,
With their wicked schisms and abhominable sects,
Now a vengeance on them all, and the devil break
    their necks!
Light of the Gospel! light of a straw! yet what-
    ever he be,
I would he were hanged as high as I can see.
    IGNORANCE. What, have you heard of him be-
    fore this?
    PERV. DOC. Heard of him? yea, that have I
    often, i-wis.
If there be any in the world, it is this whoreson
    thief,
Believe me, Simplicity, that will work us the mis-
    chief.

Hath that same new Jack got him such a mate?
Now with all my heart a pestilence on his pate!
I would they were both hanged fairly together,
Or else were at the devil, I care not much whether.
For since these Genevan doctors came so fast into
    this land,
Since that time it was never merry with England.
First came New Custom, and he gave the onsay.[1]
And sithens things have gone worse every day.
But, Simplicity, dost thou know what is mine
    intent?
    IGNORANCE. Tell me, and I shall know what
    you have meant.
    PERV. DOC. Our matters with Cruelty our friend
    to discuss,
And to hear him, what counsel in this case he will
    give us;
And this is the cause I have tarried for thee,
Because that to him I would have thee go with me,
But see where he cometh with Avarice sadly walking,
Let us listen, if we can, whereof they be talking.

ACTUS II., SCENA 3.

CRUELTY, AVARICE *enter*. PERVERSE DOCTRINE
and IGNORANCE *tarry*.

    CRUELTY. Nay, by God's heart, if I might do
    what I list,
Not one of them all that should 'scape my fist.
His nails,[2] I would plague them one way or another.

---

[1] *i.e.*, The *onset.*—*S.*
[2] *i.e.*, God's nails. So afterwards "By his wounds"—
"His blood"—without repetition of the sacred name by
way of introduction.—*S.*

I would not miss him, no, if he were mine own
    brother.
With small faults I might bear as I saw occasion,
And punish or forgive at mine own discretion,
For I wot that sometime the wisest may fall;
But heresy—fie on that, that is the greatest of all.
Every stocks should be full, every prison and jail:
Some would I beat with rods, some scourge at a
    cart's tail,
Some hoise their heels upward, some beat in a
    sack,
Some manacle their fingers, some bind in the rack.
Some would I starve for hunger, some would I hang
    privily,
Saying, that themselves so died desperately.
Some would I accuse of matters of great weight,
Openly to hang them as trespassers straight.
A thousand mo ways could I tell, and not miss,
Which here in England, I may say to you, I have
    practised ere this,
And trust, by His wounds, Avarice, soon again for
    to try,
Howsoever the world go, before that I die.
    AVARICE. Now I will tell thee, Cruelty, by God's
    sacrament I have swore,
It were pity but thou were hanged before.
    CRUELTY. Ha, ha, ha; I had as lief they were
    hanged as I.
By the mass, there is one thing makes me laugh
    heartily, ha, ha, ha.
    AVARICE. I pray thee what is that?
    CRUELTY. What? ha, ha, ha; I cannot tell for
    laughing, I would never better pastime desire,
Than to hear a dozen of them howling together in
    the fire;
Whose noise, as me-thinketh, I could best compare
To a cry of hounds following after the hare,

Or a rabblement of bandogs barking at a bear;
Ha, ha, ha.
    AVARICE. I beshrew thy knave's fingers with
        my very heart,
The devil will reward thee, whose darling thou
        art.
But sirrah, I pray thee—
If it had chanced me in those days in thy hands to
        have fell,
I think sure thou wouldst have ordered me well.
    CRUELTY. His blood, I would I might have once
        seen that chance,
I would have vexed thee with a vengeance, for old
        acquaintance.
    AVARICE. Why so? I was always thy furderer
        in those days, I am sure.
    CRUELTY. Yea, but what was the cause? thine
        own profit to procure.
For so that thou mightest 'vantage and lucre obtain,
Thou wouldest not stick to bring thine own brother
        to pain.
    AVARICE. Ha, ha, ha; no, nor father and mother,
        if there were ought to be got,
Thou mightest swear, if I could, I would bring
        them to the pot.
Whereof a like history I shall tell thee, Cruelty,
In England, which myself played in the days of
        queen Mary.[1]
Two brothers there were dwelling, young gentle-
        men; but the heir
Had substantial revenues, his stock also was fair;

---

[1] In Fox's third volume of "Ecclesiastical History,"
1630, p. 799, is an account of one Richard Woodman, who
was burnt at Lewes, with nine others, on the 22d of June
1557. The circumstances attending his apprehension resemble those above-mentioned, and seem to be the same
as are alluded to by the author of this morality.

A man of good conscience, and studious of the
　　　Gospel.
Which the other brother perceiving very well,
Persuaded him by all means, since he was so bent,
To be constant in opinion, and not to relent,
Which done, he gave notice to the officers about,
How they should come with search to find his
　　　brother out ;
Who, when he was once in this sort apprehended,
Shortly after his life in the fire he ended.
The other had the most part of all his living—
How say'st, sir knave ? is not this the near way to
　　　thriving ?
　　CRUELTY. O unreasonable Avarice, unsatiable
　　　with gain.
　　AVARICE. What [of] this ?[1] tush, it was but a
　　　merry train.
　　CRUELTY. For lucre's sake his own brother to
　　　betray ?
Hence, Judas, with these doings I cannot away.[2]
　　AVARICE. I was ever with him, still ready at
　　　hand,
Continually suggesting of the house and the land.
And yet to tell you the truth, as indeed the thing is,
Of my conscience I think the best part was his.
　　CRUELTY. By God's glorious wounds, he was
　　　worthy of none ;

----

　　[1] [*i.e.*, What of this ?]

　　[2] An expression of dislike or aversion used by almost
every writer of the times.　Ben Jonson's *Cynthia's Revels*,
A. iv. S. 5—"Of all nymphs i'the court, *I cannot away with
her.*"

　　Poetaster, A. iii. S. 4—"And do not bring your eating
player with you there; *I cannot away with her.*"

　　Bartholomew Fair, A. i. S. 6 — "Good 'faith, I will
eat heartily too, because I will be no Jew, *I could never
away with* that stiff-necked generation."　[Gifford's edit. iv.
400–1.]

But thou to be whipped for thy greedy suggestion.
  AVARICE. Heart of God, man, be the means
     better or worse,
I pass not, I, so it be good for the purse.
Ha, ha, ha !

Enter from behind PERVERSE DOCTRINE *and*
        IGNORANCE.

  PERV. DOC. If you love the purse so well, Avarice,
    as you say indeed,
Then help me with your counsel now at a need.
  AVARICE. What, Perverse Doctrine, and Ignor-
    ance too, were you both so near ?
We had thought at our coming that no man had
    been here.
  IGNORANCE. We have been in this place ever
    since that you stayed,
And we have heard also whatsoever you have said.
  CRUELTY. Welcome both, on my faith, and I am
    glad it was our chance
To meet with you here, Perverse Doctrine and
    Ignorance.
Why, how go'th the world ? me-thinks you be sad.
  PERV. DOC. Marry, God have mercy, but there
    is small cause to be glad :
For except you come speedily with your helping
    hand,
No doubt we shall shortly be banished the land.
  AVARICE. Why so, Perverse Doctrine ?
  CRUELTY. I pray thee, let me understand.
  PERV. DOC. Why so! you know : how, since
    heresy came lately in place,
And New Custom, that vile schismatic, began to
    deface
All our old doings, our service, our rites, that of
    yore

Have been of great price in the old time before :
Ourselves have been enforced almost for to fly
The country, or else covertly in some corner to lie.
 CRUELTY. By the mass, that is true, for I dare
  not appear,
Whosoever would give me twenty pounds lands by
  the year.
 AVARICE, Ha, ha, ha, by God's foot, and I was
  never in better case in my life,
For covetousness with the clergy was never so rife.
Wherefore I have no cause in such sort to be grieved,
Yet I would I could tell, sirs, how you might be
  relieved.
 PERV. DOC. Now, sirrah, to mend up this matter
  withal :
Precious God, it frets me to the very gall.
For now of late that slave, that varlet, that heretic,
  Light of the Gospel,
Is come over the sea, as some credibly tell,
Whom New Custom doth use in all matters as a
  stay,
The most enemy to us in the world alway ;
Whose rancour is such, and so great is his spite,
That no doubt he will straightway banish us quite,
Unless we provide some remedy for the contrary,
And with speed ; this is truth that I tell thee,
  Cruelty.
 CRUELTY. His wounds, heart and blood, is he
  come without any nay ?
 IGNORANCE. Yea verily, for with these eyes I
  saw him to-day.
 CRUELTY. Now I would he were here, I would
  so dress the slave,
That I warrant he should bear me a mark to his
  grave.
First I would buffet him thus, then give him a fall ;
Afterward I would dash out his brains at the wall.

AVARICE. Hold your hands, you rude knave, or
    by God's body I swear,
I will quickly fetch my fist from your ear.
    PERV. DOC. Tush, tush, it avails nought to
    chafen, or to chide,
It were more wisdom with speed some redress to
    provide.
    CRUELTY. Redress? now, by God's guts, I will
    never stay,
Till I find means to rid the beast out of the way.
I will cut him off the slampambs,[1] I hold him a
    crown,
Wheresoever I meet him, in country or town.
    IGNORANCE. What order you will take, it were
    best make relation,
For mo wits, as you know, may do better than one.
    CRUELTY. I will do then whatsoever shall come
    in my head,
I force not, I,[2] so the villain were dead.
    IGNORANCE. And of my furtherance, whatsoever
    I may do, you be sure,
Your good state again, if I can, to procure,
With my uttermost help to suppress yonder rascal,
For, by the mass, you papists I like best of all.
    PERV. DOC. Then can we not do amiss, I conjec-
    ture lightly,
For where as all these come, Perverse Doctrine,
    Avarice, Ignorance and Cruelty :
There goeth the hare,[3] except all good luck go
    away—
But, sirs, it is good, lest your names you descry,

---

[1] [Beat him by stratagem. See Halliwell's Dict. in *v*.]

[2] *i.e.*, I care not. Camden in his "Remains" says, "I
force not of such fooleries." Shakspeare has the same
phrase.—*S.*

[3] [In that direction sets the tide of opinion. This saying
is in Heywood's collection, 1562.]

To transpose them after some other kind,
Else be sure with the people much hatred to find.
As for Perverse Doctrine, Sound Doctrine; for
    Ignorance, Simplicity:
With these colours of late ourselves cloaked have
    we.
    CRUELTY. What then shall I, Cruelty, be called
      in your judgment?
    PERV. DOC. Marry, Justice with Severity, a
      virtue most excellent.
    AVARICE. What will you term Avarice, I pray
      you let me hear?
    PERV. DOC. Even Frugality, for to that virtue
      it cometh most near.
    AVARICE. Content, by his wounds, I; but we
      must look to our feet,
Lest we stumble in these names, whensoever we
    meet.
    PERV. DOC. Yea, see you take heed to that in
      any manner of case,
So may you delude the people in every place.
    CRUELTY. Come then, it is time hence that away
      we depart.
    IGNORANCE. We are ready to follow with a most
      willing heart.
    AVARICE. But, sirs, because we have tarried so
      long,
If you be good fellows, let us depart with a song.
    CRUELTY. I am pleased, and therefore let every
      man
Follow after in order, as well as he can.

The first SONG.

Well handled, by the mass, on every side.
Come, Avarice; for we two will no longer abide.
                [Exit Cruelty and Avarice.

  PERV. Doc. Farewell to you both, and God
   send you success,
Such as may glad us all in your present business.
Now they be departed, and we may not tarry,
For it lieth us upon all to be stirring, by Saint
  Mary.
New Custom prevaileth much everywhere,
But, no matter, they be fools that do give him such
  ear.
Let old custom prevail rather, it is better than new ;
This all will confess, that think scripture is true.
Do as thy fathers have done before thee (quoth he) :
Then shalt thou be certain in the right way to be.
And sure that is better than to follow the train,
That each man inventeth of his own proper brain.
Which hath brought the world to this case, as we
  see,
That every day we hear of some notorious heresy.
Yet all is the Gospel, whatsoever they say.
Well, if it chance that a dog hath a day,
Wo then to New Custom and all his mates, tush,
  tush,
No man the Gospel will esteem then a rush.
What will that other heretic do, Light of the Gospel.
  I pray ?
Dare not once show his face more than we at this
  day.
But come, Ignorance, let us follow after apace,
For we have abiden all too long in this place.
  IGNORANCE. Let us go then, but, by the mass,
   I am vengeance dry,
I pray let us drink at the alehouse hereby.
  PERV. Doc. Content, in faith, thither with speed
   let us hie.

ACTUS III., SCENA 1.

LIGHT OF THE GOSPEL, NEW CUSTOM, PERVERSE DOCTRINE.

    L. OF GOSPEL. They be not this way, as far as I
        can see,
Unless they have hidden themselves up privily.
For in presence of Light of the Gospel and Primi-
        tive Constitution,
Undoubtedly such reprobates can have no habita-
        tion.
    NEW CUS. Verily I do find it so even as you
        have said,
For at your sight they all fly away as dismayed.
Wherefore I have great cause to give you thanks,
        Light
Of the Gospel, that put thus my enemies to flight.
    L. OF GOSPEL. Nay, they be my enemies also,
        that be enemies to you.
Insomuch as your dealings be both virtuous and
        true.
For what is the Gospel else, whereof I am Light,
But truth, equity, verity and right?
They be enemies to God too, and all liars impure,
Insomuch as he is called Verity in the scripture.
And the lying lips, with speakers of vanity,
The Lord himself will revenge with extremity.
But see, what is he that approacheth so nigh?
    NEW CUS. Of whom I told you: it is Perverse
        Doctrine verily.
    L. OF GOSPEL. Then let us a little step out of
        the way,
If haply we may hear what he will say.
    PERV. DOC. Ah, sirrah, by my troth, there is a
        very good vein!

Ignorance hath well lined his cap for the rain !
I could have tarried longer there with a good will,
But, as the proverb saith, it is good to keep still
One head for the reckoning, both sober and wise ;
Wherefore in this thing I have followed that guise.
Ignorance is but a dolt, it is I that must drudge,
For need (they say) maketh the old wife and man
    both to trudge.[1]
Such snares we shall lay for these heretics, I trust,
That New Custom and his fellows shall soon lie in
    the dust.
If Cruelty may prevail, he will never slack,
Till he have brought a thousand of them to a stake.
Avarice hath promised to do what in him lay,
Who hath been in great credit with the world
    alway.
But if Ignorance may get place, there shall we do
    well,
Then adieu all idle heretics and vain talk of the
    gospel !
For me Perverse Doctrine, this shall be my fetch,[2]
To keep constant the minds of all I can catch ;
Lest these glosers sometime they chance to hear
    preaching,
And thereby be converted, and credit their
    teaching.
For I trust shortly to bring it to pass,
That less knowledge of the Gospel shall serve, by
    the mass.
  L. of Gospel. Let us inclose him, that he may
    not fly,
Else will he be gone, when he doth us espy.
O imp of Antichrist, and seed of the devil !

---

[1] [The usual form of the proverb is, "Need maketh the old wife trot."]
[2] [Exertion, effort.]

Born to all wickedness, and nusled[1] in all evil.
   PERV. DOC. Nay, thou stinking heretic, art thou
      there indeed ?
According to thy naughtiness thou must look for
      to speed.
   NEW CUS. God's holy word in no wise can be
      heresy,
Though so you term it never so falsely.
   PERV. DOC. Ye precious whoreson, art thou
      there too ?
I think you have pretended some harm me to do.
Help, help, I say, let me be gone at once,
Else I will smite thee in the face with my fist, by
      God's bones.
   NEW CUS. You must be contented a little
      season to stay :
Light of the Gospel for your profit hath something
      to say.
   PERV. DOC. I will hear none of your preachings,
      I promise you plain ;
For whatever you speak, it is but in vain.
   L. OF GOSPEL. In vain it shall not be spoken,
      I know very well.
For God hath always given such power to his
      gospel,
That wherever or by whom declared it be,
It should redound unto his own honour and glory.
God is glorified in those whom he doth elect,
God is glorified in those also whom he doth reject.
The elect are saved by that in the world they
      believe ;
But the other, because no credence they give
To the truth, cannot be but blameable,
Committing a fault of all faults most damnable.
For, *Si ad eos non venissem*, saith Christ our Saviour,

---

[1] *i.e.,* Nursed, fostered.—*S.*

If I had not come unto them with the word, this
    is sure,
In far better case the unfaithful had been.
For in this one respect they had had no sin.
But where the truth is, and yet there contemned,
Of Christ his own mouth all such are condemned.
Thus the gospel of Christ, be it received or no,
Showeth the glory of God, wheresoever it go.

    PERV. DOC. I were content to abide, and know
        your pleasure:
But for business at this time I have no leisure.

    L. OF GOSPEL. What leisure ought a man at all
        times more to have,
Than to endeavour both his body and soul for to
        save?

    NEW CUS. For that care all other cares we
        must set aside.

    PERV. DOC. Say on, then, for patiently I mind to
        abide.

    L. OF GOSPEL. Not to hear what is spoken is
        only sufficient,
But to put it in practice with sincere intent
Whatsoever is taught us concerning good-doing,
Expressing it plainly in our virtuous living.

    PERV. DOC. Why, what would you have me in
        living express?

    L. OF GOSPEL. Even the gospel, which is nothing
        else, doubtless,
But amendment of life and renouncing of sin:
With displeasure toward yourself for the faults you
        were in.

    PERV. DOC. How shall I displease myself in
        sin, I would know?

    L. OF GOSPEL. In considering that nothing
        bringeth man so low
Out of God's favour, as sin: nothing setteth him
        so high,

As loathing the same, and calling to him for his
    mercy
    PERV. DOC. Verily I am sorry for my forepassed
    demeanour,
But that cannot avail me but little, I am sure.
    L. OF GOSPEL. Why think you so? boldly tell
    me your mind.
    PERV. DOC. Because God's mercy is far enough
    behind.
    L. OF GOSPEL. God's mercy is at hand, if you
    repent faithfully.
    PERV. DOC. I repent my sins, and for them am
    sorry heartily;
But how shall I be sure mercy for to obtain?
    L. OF GOSPEL. Credit me truly, for my words
    are not vain,
I am Light of the Gospel, and have full authority
To pronounce to the penitent forgiveness of
    iniquity,
So that, in asking, you put your assurance to speed :
Then no doubt you have obtained mercy indeed.
    PERV. DOC. This assurance how cometh it,
    declare, I pray you?
    L. OF GOSPEL. In thinking that Christ his words
    and promises are true ;
And as he cannot deceive, so cannot be deceived,
Which faith of all Christians must needs be received.
    PERV. DOC. What thing is faith, I pray you
    recite?
    L. OF GOSPEL. A substance of things not appear-
    ing in sight,
Yet which we look for, for so Saint Paul doth
    define,
To the Hebrews, the eleventh chapter and the first
    line.
    PERV. DOC. How to purchase this faith, I would
    I could tell.

L. OF GOSPEL. Certainly by me also, the Light
    of the Gospel;
For faith cometh by the word, when we read or
    hear,
As by the same Saint Paul it doth plainly appear,
    PERV. DOC. Give me leave then to embrace
    you, I pray you heartily.
    L. OF GOSPEL. With all my very heart, I receive
    you courteously.
    PERV. DOC. To thee I give most humble thanks,
    O God immortal,
That it hath pleased thee me from my wickedness
    to call;
And where as I deserved no mercy, but judgment,
Yet to pour down thy pardon on me most abun-
    dant,
Revoking me from reprobates and members of hell,
To win me in society with the Light of the Gospel.
    L. OF GOSPEL. Stand up, there is somewhat else
    yet behind.
    PERV. DOC. I wholly yield myself to you: use
    me after your mind.
    L. OF GOSPEL. Perverse Doctrine you shall be
    called no more after this,
But Sincere Doctrine, as now I trust your true
    name is.
    PERV. DOC. By God's grace, while I live, I will
    so endeavour,
That my life and my name may accord thus for
    ever.
    L. OF GOSPEL. Then all wicked company you
    must clean forsake,
And fly their society as a toad or a snake.
    PERV. DOC. I abandon them quite, whatsoever
    they be.
    NEW CUS. Well, Sincere Doctrine, hearken also
    unto me,

Whom needs you must follow, if you will do well,
Since you have embraced the Light of the Gospel.
I am not New Custom, as you have been misled,
But am Primitive Constitution, from the very head
Of the church, which is Christ and his disciples all,
And from the fathers, at that time taking original.
By me then you must learn for your own behest,
And for all vocations what is judged the best.
    PERV. DOC. I receive you gladly with thanks for
      your gentleness,
At your hands craving earnestly for my trespass
      forgiveness.
    NEW CUS. It is easily forgiven.
    PERV. DOC. Now as touching my apparel,
      what counsel do you give?
For I see well that, in the constitution primitive,
They used no such garment as I have on here,
But fashioned it after some other manner.
    NEW CUS. So did they truly, I confess it
      indeed;
But in such things a man ought not to take so great
      heed,
For the wearing of a gown, cap, or any other gar-
      ment,
Surely is a matter, as me-seemeth, indifferent,
Howbeit, wise princes, for a difference to be had,
Hath commanded the clergy in such sort to be
      clad;
But he who puts his religion in wearing the thing,
Or thinks himself more holy for the contrary doing,
Shall prove but a fool, of whatever condition
He be, for sure that is but mere superstition.
Other things there be, which have been abused,
Tolerable enough, if well they were used:
Wherefore use your apparel, as is comely and decent,
And not against scripture anywhere in my judg-
      ment.

L. OF GOSPEL. No, sure : for God weigheth not
  (who is a sprite)
Of any vesture or outward appearance a mite,
So the conscience be pure, and to no sin a slave :
That is all which he most gladly would have.
  NEW CUS. Well, these having declared and
    sufficiently taught,
And, I trust, on your part perceived as they ought :
By your patience, I mind to depart for a season.
  L. OF GOSPEL. If your business be so, it is but
    reason.
  NEW CUS. With great thanks unto you, Light
    of the Gospel, for the gentleness I have found,
At your hands, as of due desert I am bound.
  L. OF GOSPEL. The Lord be your guide, whither-
    soever you depart.
  PERV. DOC. Humble thanks, sir, I yield you
    from the bottom of my heart.
Albeit in this part so small be my skill,
That I may not perform them according to my
    will.
  NEW CUS. The peace of God be with you both
    for evermore.   [*Exit.*

EDIFICATION *entereth.*

Wheresoever Light of the Gospel goeth before,
There I, Edification, do follow incontinent,
As unto the same a necessary consequent :
For though the letter always work not that effect,
Yet surely in the congregation of God's elect,
Where the light and force taketh place, there Edi-
    fication
Of all right must I make my habitation.
Endeavour then always me to retain,
So shall your doctrine not be given in vain.
  VOL. III.   D

PERV. DOC. I receive you most gladly, and I
    trust in the Lord,
That for ever hereafter we shall well accord.
    EDIFICATION. I trust so.
    L. OF GOSPEL. Fare you well, now you are not
    alone,
For this small while I must needs be gone.
Here, take at my hands this Testament-book,
And in mine absence therein I pray you earnestly
    look.
    PERV. DOC. Your commandment shall be done,
    with thanks for your counsel.
    L. OF GOSPEL. Then shall ye sure find great
    delight in the gospel.   *[Exit.*

ASSURANCE *entereth.*

Edification without Assurance 'vaileth not much.
Yet where they both do meet, surely their force is
    such,
That to God's kingdom they open the way,
The sweet place of rest and perpetual joy.
For assurance in Christ Jesus without man's further
    merit,
Is fully sufficient God's favour to inherit:
Wherefore Light of the Gospel willed me so,
That to you, Edification, with all speed I should
    go:
So that with Sincere Doctrine we joined in unity,
Might in short time conduct him to God's Perfect
    Felicity.
    PERV. DOC. I embrace you, Assurance, that bliss
    to obtain.
    ASSURANCE. Then be you assured, that you shall
    not be vain;
For if that Christ's words be faithful and just,
God's Perfect Felicity is not far hence, I trust.

GOD'S FELICITY *entereth.*

Verily, where Edification and Assurance in one are
    allied,
God's Felicity is at hand, it may not be denied,
Which he promiseth to such as unfeignedly crave,
With Assurance that certainly the same they shall
    have :
Which Felicity in person here I do represent,
Who by God himself to the faithful am sent,
Prepared for them, as he plainly hath said,
Since the time that the world's foundations were
    laid ;
Wherefore great thanks unto him doubtless you owe,
That it would please him such gifts on you to bestow,
The most precious thing, which man's reason doth
    excel,
No mind can conceive, much less tongue can tell.
    PERV. DOC. To him therefore let us give all
    manner praise,
That beareth such affection to mankind always.
O Lord, thine honour might be great in heaven so
    high.
And throughout the whole earth thy everlasting
    glory.
Give grace to thy people, that after this transitory
Life they may come to thy perfect felicity.
    EDIFICATION. Defend thy church, O Christ, and
    thy holy congregation,
Both here in England and in every other nation.
That we thy truth may attain, and still follow the
    same,
To the salvation of our souls, and glory of thy name.
    ASSURANCE. Preserve our noble queen Eliza-
    beth and her council all,[1]

---

[1] It was a custom at the end of our ancient interludes
and plays to conclude with a solemn prayer for the king or

With thy heavenly grace, sent from thy seat
    supernal.
Grant her and them long to live, her to reign, them
    to see,
What may always be best for the weal-public's
    commodity.[1]

The second SONG.

queen, the council, the parliament, or the nobleman by
whom the players were protected. Many instances are produced by Dr Farmer and Mr Steevens, in their last notes on
the epilogue to "Second Part of Henry IV.," and many
others might be added. See particularly the conclusion of
Fulwell's "Like will to like, quoth the Devil to the Collier," 1368; Wager's "The longer thou livest the more
foole thou art;" "King Darius," and others.—*Reed*.

[1] [Interest.]

RALPH ROISTER DOISTER
A COMEDY

By NICHOLAS UDALL
(1550)

[The only copy known of this admirable comedy, and that deficient of the title, was discovered in 1818, and is at present in the library of Eton College. It was reprinted in 1818, again in 1821 and 1830, and for the fourth time, with a copious account of Udall and his writings, by Mr W. D. Cooper, 1847. It was licensed and probably printed in 1566, but is quoted in Wilson's "Rule of Reason," 1551, before which date it was no doubt not only composed but performed.

"Ralph Roister Doister" is the first regular comedy in our language—a place of honour long held by "Gammer Gurton's Needle," which is an inferior, as well as a later, production.

Since the appearance of Mr Cooper's edition, Mr Furnivall has printed from the Royal MS. the pageant referred to at p. xiii. of Mr Cooper's introduction in one of the Ballad Society's volumes.]

THE PROLOGUE.

What creature is in health, either young or old,
   But some mirth with modesty will be glad to use,
As we in this interlude shall now unfold ?
    Wherein all scurrility we utterly refuse :
    Avoiding such mirth, wherein is abuse :
Knowing nothing more commendable for a man's
      recreation,
Than mirth which is used in an honest fashion.

For mirth prolongeth life, and causeth health ;
    Mirth recreates our spirits, and voideth pensive-
      ness ;
Mirth increaseth amity (not hind'ring our wealth) ;
    Mirth is to be used both of more and less,
    Being mixed with virtue in decent comeliness,
As we trust no good nature can gainsay the same :
Which mirth we intend to use, avoiding all blame.

The wise poets, long time heretofore,
    Under merry comedies secrets did declare,
Wherein was contained very virtuous lore,
    With mysteries and forewarnings very rare.
    Such to write neither Plautus nor Terence did
      spare,
Which among the learned at this day bears the
      bell :
These with such other therein did excel.

Our comedy or interlude, which we intend to play,
 Is named ROISTER DOISTER indeed,
Which against the vain-glorious doth inveigh,
 Whose humour the roisting sort continually doth
  feed.
 Thus, by your patience, we intend to proceed
In this our interlude, by God's leave and grace :
And here I take my leave for a certain space.

FINIS.

DRAMATIS PERSONÆ.[1]

RALPH ROISTER DOISTER,   { *A vain-glorious, cowardly*   *Blockhead.*

MATTHEW MERRYGREEK, *a needy Humorist.*

GAWIN GOODLUCK, *a Merchant.*

TRISTRAM TRUSTY, *Friend of Gawin Goodluck.*

DOBINET DOUGHTY,
HARPAX,   } *Servants of Ralph.*

TRUEPENNY, *Servant of Dame Custance.*

SIM SURESBY, *Captain of a ship of Gawin Goodluck.*

A SCRIVENER.

DAME CHRISTIAN CUSTANCE,   { *A Widow, betrothed to Gawin*   *Goodluck.*

MADGE MUMBLECRUST,
TIBET TALKAPACE,   } *Servants of Dame Custance.*
ANNOT ALIFACE,

---

[1] [Not in the old copy.]

RALPH ROISTER DOISTER.

ACTUS I., SCÆNA 1.

Matthew Merrygreek.   *He entereth singing.*

As long liveth the merry man (they say),
As doth the sorry man, and longer by a day ;
Yet the grasshopper, for all his summer piping,
Starveth in winter with hungry griping :
Therefore another said saw doth men advise,
That they be together both merry and wise.
This lesson must I practise or else, ere long,
With me, Matthew Merrygreek, it will be wrong.
Indeed men so call me ; for, by him that us bought,
Whatever chance betide, I can take no thought.
Yet wisdom would that I did myself bethink,
Where to be provided this day of meat and drink ;
For know ye that, for all this merry note of mine,
He might oppose me now, that should ask where I
    dine.
My living lieth here and there, of God's grace,
Sometime with this good man, sometime in that
    place ;
Sometime Lewis Loiterer biddeth me come near ;
Somewhiles Watkin Waster maketh us good cheer ;
Sometime Davy Diceplayer, when he hath well
    cast,

Maketh revel-rout, as long as it will last ;
Sometime Tom Titivile [1] maketh us a feast ;
Sometime with Sir Hugh Pie I am a bidden guest ;
Sometime at Nichol Neverthrive's I get a sop ;
Sometime I am feasted with Bryan Blinkinsop ;
Sometime I hang on Hankyn Hoddydoddy's sleeve ;
But this day on Ralph Roister Doister's, by his
　　leave.
For truly of all men he is my chief banker,
Both for meat and money, and my chief shoot-
　　anchor. [2]
Forsooth Roister Doister in that he doth say,
And require what ye will, ye shall have no nay.
But now of Roister Doister somewhat to express,
That ye may esteem him after his worthiness,
In these twenty towns, and seek them throughout,
Is not the like stock whereon to graff a lout.
All the day long is he facing and craking [3]
Of his great acts in fighting and fray-making ;
But when Roister Doister is put to his proof,
To keep the Queen's peace [4] is more for his behoof.
If any woman smile, or cast on him an eye,
Up is he to the hard ears in love by and by :
And in all the hot haste must she be his wife,

---

[1] One of the names of the devil in the old morals.—
W. D. Cooper.
[2] [Sheet-anchor.]
[3] Impudently vaunting and boasting.

　　　　　" You preserve
A race of idle people here about you,
Facers and talkers.—*Maids Tragedy,* Act iv., sc. 2.
　　　　　　　　　—*W. D. Cooper.*

[4] In all probability an alteration to mean Elizabeth, in
whose reign the play was printed ; for in act iii., sc. 4, M.
Merrygreek talks of the " arms of Calais " ; and so does R.
Roister, act iv., sc. 7. Calais was lost in 5th Mary, and
the play was quoted by Wilson in 1551, when Edward was
on the throne.—*W. D. Cooper.*

Else farewell his good days, and farewell his life !
Master Ralph Roister Doister is but dead and gone,
Except she on him take some compassion.
Then chief of council must be Matthew Merry-
    greek !
What, if I for marriage to such an one seek ?
Then must I sooth[1] it, whatever it is ;
For what he saith or doth cannot be amiss.
Hold by his yea and nay, be his nown white son :[2]
Praise and rouse him well, and ye have his heart
    won ;
For so well liketh he his own fond fashions,
That he taketh pride of false commendations.
But such sport have I with him, as I would not
    lese,
Though I should be bound to live with bread and
    cheese.
For exalt him and have him as ye lust indeed ;
Yea, to hold his finger in a hole for a need.
I can with a word make him fain or loth ;
I can with as much make him pleased or wroth ;
I can, when I will, make him merry and glad ;
I can, when me lust, make him sorry and sad ;
I can set him in hope, and eke in despair ;
I can make him speak rough, and make him speak
    fair.
But I marvel I see him not all this same day :
I will seek him out.   But lo ! he cometh this way.
I have yond espied him sadly coming,
And in love, for twenty pound, by his gloming.[3]

---

[1] [Affirm, agree to it.]

[2] [*i. e.*, His own white son.] *White boy* is a common expression of endearment in old plays, and to this day white-
headed boy is an expression of fondness in Ireland, though
the locks of the individual to whom it is applied may be
"black as the raven's plume."—*W. D. Cooper.*

[3] [Or glombing, *i.e.*, louring. See Halliwell *v. Glombe.*]

ACTUS I., SCÆNA 2.

RALPH ROISTER DOISTER, MATTHEW MERRYGREEK.

R. ROISTER. Come, death, when thou wilt : I
am weary of my life.

M. MERRY. I told you, I, we should woo another
wife.   [*Aside.*

R. ROYSTER. Why did God make me such a
goodly person ?

M. MERRY. He is in, by the week; we shall
have sport anon.   [*Aside.*

R. ROISTER.   And where is my trusty friend,
Matthew Merrygreek ?

M. MERRY. I will make as I saw him not; he
doth me seek.   [*Aside.*

R. ROISTER. I have him espied, me-thinketh ;
yond is he ;

Ho ! Matthew Merrygreek, my friend, a word
with thee.

M. MERRY. I will not hear him, but make as I
had haste.   [*Aside.*

Farewell, all my good friends, the time away doth
waste ;

And the tide, they say, tarrieth for no man.

R. ROISTER. Thou must with thy good counsel
help me, if thou can.

M. MERRY. God keep thee, worshipful Master
Roister Doister,

And farewell the lusty Master Roister Doister.

R. ROISTER. I must needs speak with thee a
word or twain.

M. MERRY, Within a month or two I will be
here again.

Negligence in great affairs, ye know, may mar all.

R. ROISTER. Attend upon me now, and well reward thee I shall.

M. MERRY. I have take my leave, and the tide is well-spent.

R. ROISTER. I die, except thou help; I pray thee be content.

Do thy part well now, and ask what thou wilt;
For without thy aid my matter is all spilt.

M. MERRY. Then to serve your turn I will some pains take,

And let all mine own affairs alone for your sake.

R. ROISTER. My whole hope and trust resteth only in thee.

M. MERRY. Then can ye not do amiss, whatever it be.

R. ROISTER. Gramercies, Merrygreek, most bound to thee I am.

M. MERRY. But up with that heart, and speak out like a ram;

Ye speak like a capon that had the cough now:
Be of good cheer; anon ye shall do well enou'.

R. ROISTER. Upon thy comfort I will all things well handle.

M. MERRY. So, lo! that is a breast to blow out a candle.[1]

But what is this great matter, I would fain know?
We shall find remedy therefore, I trow.
Do ye lack money? ye know mine old offers:
Ye have always a key to my purse and coffers.

R. ROISTER. I thank thee: had ever man such a friend!

---

[1] Voice.

> "I syng not musycall,
> For my *brest* is decayd."
> —*Armonye of Byrdes.*

Halliwell's "Archaic and Provincial Words."—*W. D. Cooper.*

M. MERRY. Ye give unto me : I must needs to
    you lend.
R. ROISTER. Nay, I have money plenty all things
    to discharge.
M. MERRY (*aside*). That knew I right well,
    when I made offer so large.
R. ROISTER. But it is no such matter.
M. MERRY. What is it, then ?
Are ye in danger of debt [1] to any man ?
If ye be, take no thought, nor be not afraid ;
Let them hardily take thought [2] how they shall be
    paid.
R. ROISTER. Tut, I owe nought.
M. MERRY. What then ? fear ye imprisonment ?
R. ROISTER. No.
M. MERRY. No ; I wist ye offend not so to be
    shent ;
But, if ye had, the Tower could not you so hold,
But to break out at all times ye would be bold.
What is it ? hath any man threatened you to
    beat ?
R. ROISTER. What is he that durst have put me
    in that heat ?
He that beateth me, by His arms, [3] shall well find
That I will not be far from him, nor run behind.
M. MERRY. That thing know all men, ever since
    ye overthrew
The fellow of the lion which Hercules slew.
But what is it then ?
R. ROISTER. Of love I make my moan.
M. MERRY. Ah, this foolish love ! wil't ne'er let
    us alone ?

---

[1] [In danger of debt, *i.e.* in the power of any man on
account of debt.]
[2] [*i.e.* Let *them* consider how, &c.]
[3] [*i.e.* By God's arms.]

But, because ye were refused the last day,
Ye said ye would ne'er more be entangled that way !
I would meddle no more, since I find all so unkind.
   R. ROISTER. Yea, but I cannot so put love out
      of my mind.
   M. MERRY. But is your love, tell me first, in any
      wise
In the way of marriage or of merchandise ?
If it may otherwise than lawful be found,
Ye get none of my help for an hundred pound.
   R. ROISTER. No, by my troth, I would have her
      to my wife.
   M. MERRY. Then are ye a good man, and God
      save your life !
And what or who is she, with whom ye are in love ?
   R. ROISTER. A woman, whom I know not by
      what means to move.
   M. MERRY. Who is it ?
   R. ROISTER. A woman yond.
   M. MERRY. What is her name ?
   R. ROISTER. Her yonder.
   M. MERRY. Whom ?
   R. ROISTER. Mistress, ah—
   M. MERRY. Fy, fy for shame !
Love ye, and know not whom ? but *her yond !* *a
     woman !*
We shall then get you a wife, I cannot tell when.
   R. ROISTER. The fair woman that supped with
      us yesternight ;
And I heard her name twice or thrice, and had it
     right.
   M. MERRY. Yea, ye may see ye ne'er take me to
      good cheer with you :
If ye had, I could have told you her name now.
   R. ROISTER. I was to blame indeed, but the
      next time perchance—
And she dwelleth in this house—

M. MERRY. What, Christian Custance ?

R. ROISTER. Except I have her to my wife, I
I shall run mad.

M. MERRY. Nay, unwise perhaps ; but I warrant
you for mad.[1]

R. ROISTER. I am utterly dead, unless I have
my desire.

M. MERRY. Where be the bellows that blew this
sudden fire ?

R. ROISTER. I hear she is worth a thousand
pound and more.

M. MERRY. Yea, but learn this one lesson of me
afore :

An hundred pound of marriage-money, doubtless,
Is ever thirty pound sterling, or somewhat less ;[2]
So that her thousand pound, if she be thrifty,
Is much near[3] about two hundred and fifty.
Howbeit, wooers and widows are never poor.

R. ROISTER. Is she a widow ? I love her better
therefore.

M. MERRY. But I hear she hath made promise
to another.

R. ROISTER. He shall go without her, and he
were my brother.

M. MERRY. I have heard say, I am right well
advised,

That she hath to Gawin Goodluck promised.

R. ROISTER. What is that Gawin Goodluck ?

M. MERRY. A merchant-man.

R. ROISTER. Shall he speed afore me ? Nay,
sir, by sweet Saint Anne !

---

[1] [I warrant you, as far as madness is concerned. Mr
Cooper proposed to read *from mad ;* but the alteration
appears to me unnecessary.]

[2] [Fortunes are always exaggerated.]

[3] [Nearer.]

Ah, sir ! *Backare*, quod Mortimer to his sow :[1]
I will have her mine own self, I make God a vow ;
For, I tell thee, she is worth a thousand pound.

   M. MERRY. Yet a fitter wife for your maship [2]
     might be found ;
Such a goodly man as you might get one with land,
Besides pounds of gold a thousand and a thousand,
And a thousand and a thousand and a thousand,
And so to the sum of twenty hundred thousand :
Your most goodly personage is worthy of no less.

   R. ROISTER. I am sorry God made me so comely,
     doubtless ;
For that maketh me each where so highly favoured,
And all women on me so enamoured.

   M. MERRY. Enamoured, quod you? have ye
     spied out that?
Ah, sir, marry, now I see you know what is what.
Enamoured, ka?[3] marry, sir, say that again ;
But I thought not ye had marked it so plain.

   R. ROISTER. Yes, each where they gaze all upon
     me, and stare.

   M. MERRY. Yea, malkin, I warrant you, as
     much as they dare.
And ye will not believe what they say in the street,
When your maship passeth by, all such as I meet,
That sometimes I can scarce find what answer to
     make.
Who is this? (saith one) Sir Launcelot du Lake?[4]
Who is this? Great Guy of Warwick, saith another?

---

[1] This was a proverbial expression. See Heywood's
"Proverbs" and "Taming of the Shrew," act ii., sc. 1.
Backare probably means *Back there !* or *Go back !*—*Cooper.*
[The meaning is, clearly enough, that Gawin Goodluck
must retreat from his courtship.]

[2] Your mastership.—*Cooper.*

[3] Quotha.

[4] Some of these are the heroes of romances.—*Cooper.*

No (say I), it is the thirteenth Hercules brother.
Who is this? noble Hector of Troy? saith the third :
No, but of the same nest (say I) it is a bird.
Who is this? great Goliah, Sampson, or Colbrand?
No (say I), but it is a brute of the aly land.[1]
Who is this? great Alexander or Charlemagne?
No, it is the tenth Worthy, say I to them again :
I know not if I said well—

    R. ROISTER. Yes, for so I am.

    M. MERRY. Yea, for there were but nine wor-
        thies, before ye came.

To some others the third Cato I do you call ;[2]
And so, as well as I can, I answer them all.
Sir, I pray you what lord or great gentleman is this?
Master Ralph Roister Doister, dame (say I), i-wis.
O Lord (saith she then), what a goodly man it is !
Would Christ I had such a husband as he is !
O Lord (say some), that the sight of his face we lack !
It is enough for you (say I) to see his back ;
His face is for ladies of high and noble parages,[3]
With whom he hardly 'scapeth great marriages.
With much more than this and much otherwise.

    R. ROISTER. I can thee thank,[4] that thou canst
        such answers devise :

But I perceive thou dost me throughly know.

    M. MERRY. I mark your manners for mine own
        learning, I trow.

But such is your beauty, and such are your acts,
Such is your personage, and such are your facts,[5]

---

[1] [A creature of the same country. *Aly* seems here to
be the same as *alyche*.   See Halliwell, *v.v. alyche* and *alyc.*]

[2] *Tertius è cælo cecidit Cato.* Juv., *Sat.* ii., 40.—*Cooper.*

[3] [Kindred, parentages.]

[4] I give thee thanks.—*Cooper.*

[5] Feats or deeds, from the Latin *factum*, "And rattle
forth his *facts* of war and blood."—Marlowe's "Tambur-
laine the Great," Part I., 1590.—*Cooper.*

That all women, fair and foul, more and less,
They eye you, they lub[1] you, they talk of you doubt-
    less.
Your pleasant look maketh them all merry :
Ye pass not by, but they laugh, till they be weary :
Yea, and money could I have, the truth to tell,
Of many, to bring you that way where they dwell.
    R. ROISTER. Merrygreek, for this thy reporting
      well of me—
    M. MERRY. What should I else, sir? it is my
      duty, pardè.
    R. ROISTER. I promise thou shalt not lack,
      while I have a groat.
    M. MERRY. Faith, sir, and I ne'er had more
      need of a new coat.
    R. ROISTER. Thou shalt have one to-morrow,
      and gold for to spend.
    M. MERRY. Then I trust to bring the day to a
      good end.
For as for mine own part, having money enou',
I could live only with the remembrance of you—
But now to your widow, whom you love so hot—
    R. ROISTER. By Cock, thou sayest truth, I had
      almost forgot.
    M. MERRY. What, if Christian Custance will
      not have you, what?
    R. ROISTER. Have me? yes, I warrant you,
      never doubt of that :
I know she loveth me, but she dare not speak.
    M. MERRY. Indeed, meet it were somebody
      should it break.
    R. ROISTER. She looked on me twenty times
      yesternight,

---

[1] [This word has escaped Nares and others. But it is
merely a colloquialism for *love*, and is in that sense still in
familiar use.]

And laughed so—
 M. MERRY. That she could not sit upright.
 R. ROISTER. No, faith, could she not.
 M. MERRY. No, even such a thing I cast.[1]
 R. ROISTER. But for wooing, thou knowest,
  women are shamefast.
But, and she knew my mind, I know she would be
 glad,
And think it the best chance that ever she had.
 M. MERRY. To her, then, like a man, and be
  bold forth to start :
Wooers never speed well, that have a false heart.
 R. ROISTER. What may I best do ?
 M. MERRY, Sir, remain ye awhile [here] ;[2]
Ere long one or other of her house will appear.
Ye know my mind.
 R. ROISTER. Yea, now hardily let me alone.
 M. MERRY. In the meantime, sir, if you please,
  I will home,
And call your musicians ; for in this your case
It would set you forth, and all your wooing grace,
Ye may not lack your instruments to play and
 sing.
 R. ROISTER. Thou knowest I can do that—
 M. MERRY. As well as anything.
Shall I go call your folks, that we may show a cast ?
 R. ROISTER. Yea, run, I beseech thee, in all
  possible haste,
 M. MERRY. I go.   [*Exeat.*
 R. ROISTER. Yea, for I love singing out of
  measure,
It comforteth my spirits, and doth me great plea-
 sure.

---

 [1] [Guessed.]
 [2] The word "here," which is not in the original, seems
necessary to complete the metre and rhyme.—*Cooper.*

But who cometh forth yond from my sweetheart
  Custance ?
My matter frameth well ; this is a lucky chance.

ACTUS I., SCÆNA 3.

MADGE MUMBLECRUST [1] *spinning on the distaff* :
  TIBET TALKAPACE *sowing* : ANNOT ALYFACE
  knitting : R. ROISTER *behind*.

M. MUMBL. If this distaff were spun, Margery
  Mumblecrust—
TIB. TALK. Where good stale ale is, will drink
  no water, I trust.
M. MUMBL. Dame Custance hath promised us
  good ale and white bread.
TIB. TALK. If she keep not promise, I will be-
  shrew her head.
But it will be stark night, before I shall have done.
R. ROISTER (*aside*). I will stand here awhile,
  and talk with them anon.
I hear them speak of Custance, which doth my heart
  good ;
To hear her name spoken doth even comfort my
  blood.
M. MUMBL. Sit down to your work, Tibet, like
  a good girl.
TIB. TALK. Nurse, meddle you with your spindle
  and your whirl.

---

[1] Jack Mumblecrust is the name of one of the beggars
who dine with Sir Owen Meredith : "Peace ! hear my lady.
Jack Mumblecrust steal no more penny loaves."—*Patient
Grissel*, act iv., sc. 3.   It is also a name given to the widow
Minever by Captain Tucca in Dekker's "Satiromastix."
Madge Mumblecrust is mentioned in the MS. comedy of
"Misogonus," 1577.—*Cooper*.

No haste but good, Madge Mumblecrust ; for whip
    and whur,[1]
The old proverb doth say, never made good fur.
    M. MUMBL. Well, ye will sit down to your work
    anon, I trust.
    TIB. TALK. Soft fire maketh sweet malt,[2] good
    Madge Mumblecrust.
    M. MUMBL. And sweet malt maketh jolly good
    ale for the nonce.
    TIB. TALK. Which will slide down the lane[3]
    without any bones.   [Cuntet.[4]
Old brown-bread crusts must have much good
    mumbling ;
But good ale down your throat hath good easy
    tumbling.
    R. ROISTER (aside). The jolliest wench that ere
    I heard !   Little mouse,
May I not rejoice that she shall dwell in my house ?
    TIB. TALK. So, sirrah,[5] now this gear beginneth
    for to frame.
    M. MUMBL. Thanks to God, though your work
    stand still, your tongue is not lame.
    TIB. TALK. And though your teeth be gone,
    both so sharp and so fine,

---

[1] Scolding. "Whur, to snarl like a dog."—Bailey.

[2] "Soft fier makes swet malt" ; see "The Marriage of
Wit and Wisdom," edited by Halliwell, p. 13.—Cooper.

[3] [The throat, which we still familiarly term red lane.]

[4] Songs introduced in our old plays are often not found
in the printed copies. Some of those in this piece, are,
however, given at the end, and others are introduced in the
body of the play. In the above instance, perhaps, only an
air was to be hummed.—Cooper.

[5] The terms Sirrah and Sir appear to have been frequently applied indifferently both to male and female. In
Whetstone's "Promos and Cassandra," 1578, Grymball says
to his mistress—

"Ah, syr, you woulde belike let my cocke-sparrowes go."—Cooper.

Yet your tongue can renne on pattens as well as
    mine.

    M. MUMBL. Ye were not for nought named Tib
        Talkapace.

    TIB. TALK. Doth my talk grieve you? Alack,
        God save your grace!

    M. MUMBL. I hold a groat, ye will drink anon
        for this gear.

    TIB. TALK. And I will not pray you the stripes
        for me to bear.

    M. MUMBL. I hold a penny, ye will drink with-
        out a cup.

    TIB. TALK. Whereinsoe'er ye drink, I wot ye
        drink all up.

    AN. ALYFACE. By Cock,[1] and well sewed, my
        good Tibet Talkapace.

    TIB. TALK. And e'en as well knit, my nown
        Annot Alyface.

    R. ROISTER (aside). See what a sort she keepeth,
        that must be my wife:

Shall not I, when I have her, lead a merry life?

    TIB. TALK. Welcome, my good wench, and sit
        here by me just.

    AN. ALYFACE. And how doth our old beldame
        here, Madge Mumblecrust?

    TIB. TALK. Chide and find fault, and threaten
        to complain.

    AN. ALYFACE, To make us poor girls shent[2] to
        her is small gain.

    M. MUMBL. I did neither chide, nor complain,
        nor threaten.

    R. ROISTER (aside). It would grieve my heart
        to see one of them beaten.

---

[1] A corruption of the sacred name.

[2] Scolded. It sometimes means *ruined* or *destroyed.*—
Cooper.

M. MUMBL. I did nothing but bid her work, and
    hold her peace.
TIB. TALK. So would I, if you could your clat-
    tering cease ;
But the devil cannot make old trot hold her tongue.
    AN. ALYFACE. Let all these matters pass, and
    we three sing a song :
So shall we pleasantly both the time beguile now,
And eke despatch all our works, ere we can tell
    how.
TIB. TALK. I shrew them that say nay, and that
    shall not be I.
M. MUMBL. And I am well content.
TIB. TALK. Sing on then by and by.
R. ROISTER (*aside*). And I will not away, but
    listen to their song ;
Yet Merrygreek and my folks tarry very long.

Tib., An., and Margery do sing here.[1]

Pipe, merry Annot, &c.
Trilla, Trilla, Trillary.
Work, Tibet ; work, Annot ; work, Margery ;
Sew, Tibet ; knit, Annot ; spin, Margery.
Let us see who will win the victory.

TIB. TALK. This sleeve is not willing to be sewed,
    I trow.
A small thing might make me all in the ground to
    throw.

---

[1] [This song is quoted in "A Pore Helpe," probably
printed many years before "Ralph Roister Doister." See
Hazlitt's "Popular Poetry," ii., 260. It therefore seems
likely that in this, as in other cases, Udall introduced a
song popular at the time, and the composition of some one
else.]

Then they sing again.

Pipe, merry Annot, &c.
Trilla, Trilla, Trillary.
What, Tibet! what, Annot! what, Margery!
Ye sleep, but we do not, that shall we try,
Your fingers be numbed, our work will not lie.

TIB. TALK. If ye do so again—well, I would
   advise you nay:
In good sooth, one stop more, and I make holy-
   day!

They sing the third time.

Pipe, merry Annot, &c.
Trilla, Trilla, Trillary.
Now, Tibbet; now, Annot; now, Margery;
Now whippet apace for the maistry:
But it will not be, our mouth is so dry.

TIB. TALK. Ah, each finger is a thumb to-day,
   me-think:
I care not to let all alone, choose it swim or sink.

They sing the fourth time.

Pipe, merry Annot, &c.
Trilla, Trilla, Trillary.
When, Tibbet? when, Annot? when, Margery?
I will not,—I can not,—no more can I.
Then give we all over, and there let it lie!
                    [*Let her cast down her work.*

TIB. TALK. There it lieth! the worst is but a
   curried coat.
Tut, I am used thereto: I care not a groat.

AN. ALYFACE. Have we done singing since?
    then will I in again:
Here I found you, and here I leave both twain.
                              [*Exeat.*
    M. MUMBL. And I will not be long after.   Tib.
    Talkapace!   [*She discovers R. Roister Doister.*
    TIB. TALK. What is the matter?
    M. MUMBL. Yond stood a man all this space,
And hath heard all that ever we spake together.
    TIB. TALK. Marry, the more lout he for his
    coming hither,
And the less good he can to listen maidens talk.
I care not, and I go bid him hence for to walk:
It were well done to know what he maketh here-
    away.
    R. ROISTER. Now might I speak to them, if I
    wist what to say.   [*Aside.*
    M. MUMBL. Nay, we will go both of's, and see
    what he is.
    R. ROISTER (*coming forward*). One that heard
    all your talk and singing, i-wis.
    TIB. TALK. The more to blame you: a good
    thrifty husband
Would elsewhere have had some better matters in
    hand.
    R. ROISTER. I did it for no harm; but for good
    love I bear
To your dame Mistress Custance I did your talk
    hear.
And, mistress nurse, I will kiss you for acquaint-
    ance.
    M. MUMBL. I come anon, sir.
    TIB. TALK. Faith, I would our dame Custance
Saw this gear.
    M. MUMBL. I must first wipe all clean, yea, I must.
    TIB. TALK. Ill 'chieve it, doting fool, but it must
    be cust.

M. MUMBL. God 'ield you, sir; chad not so
    much, i-chotte not when :
Ne'er since chwas born, chwine,[1] of such a gay
    gentleman.
R. ROISTER. I will kiss you too, maiden, for the
    good will I bear ye.
TIB. TALK. No, forsooth, by your leave, ye shall
    not kiss me.
R. ROISTER. Yes, be not afeard ; I do not dis-
    dain you a whit.
TIB. TALK. Why should I fear you ? I have not
    so little wit ;
Ye are but a man, I know very well.
R. ROISTER. Why, then ?
TIB. TALK. Forsooth, for I will not : I use not
    to kiss men.
R. ROISTER. I would fain kiss you too, good
    maiden, if I might.
TIB. TALK. What should that need ?
R. ROISTER. But to honour you, by this light.
I use to kiss all them that I love, to God I vow.
TIB. TALK. Yea, sir ? I pray you, when did ye
    last kiss your cow ?
R. ROISTER. Ye might be proud to kiss me, if
    ye were wise.
TIB. TALK. What promotion were therein ?
R. ROISTER. Nurse is not so nice.
TIB. TALK. Well, I have not been taught to
    kissing and licking.
R. ROISTER. Yet, I thank you, mistress nurse,
    ye made no sticking.
M. MUMBL. I will not stick for a koss with such
    a man as you.

---

[1] *i.e.,* "I had not so much, I wot not when : never since I
was born, I ween." She here speaks a rustic dialect.—
Cooper.

TIB. TALK. They that lust!—I will again to
my sewing now.

AN. ALYFACE.[1] Tidings, ho! tidings! dame
Custance greeteth you well.

R. ROISTER. Whom? me?

AN. ALYFACE. You, sir? No, sir: I do no
such tale tell.

R. ROISTER. But, and she knew me here!—

AN. ALFYACE. Tibet Talkapace,
Your mistress Custance and mine must speak with
your grace.

TIB. TALK. With me?

AN. ALYFACE. You must come in to her, out of
all doubts.

TIB. TALK. And my work not half-done? a
mischief on all louts!   [*Ex. amb.*

R. ROISTER. Ah, good sweet nurse!

M. MUMBL. Ah, good sweet gentleman!

R. ROISTER. Who?[2]

M. MUMBL. Nay, I cannot tell, sir, but what
thing would you?

R. ROISTER. How doth sweet Custance, my
heart of gold, tell me how?

M. MUMBL. She doth very well, sir, and command[s] me to you.

R. ROISTER. To me?

M. MUMBL. Yea, to you, sir.

R. ROISTER. To me? nurse, tell me plain,
To me?

M. MUMBL. Yea.

R. ROISTER. That word maketh me alive
again.

M. MUMBL. She command[ed] me to one last
day, whoe'er it was.

---

[1] Her re-entrance is not marked.—*Cooper.*
[2] [Orig. reads, *what.*]

R. ROISTER. That was e'en to me and none other,
    by the mass.
M. MUMBL. I cannot tell you surely, but one it
    was.
R. ROISTER. It was I and none other—this
    cometh to good pass.
I promise thee, nurse, I favour her.
    M. MUMBL. E'en so, sir ?
    R. ROISTER. Bid her sue to me for marriage.
    M. MUMBL. E'en so, sir ?
    R. ROISTER. And surely for thy sake she shall
    speed.
    M. MUMBL. E'en so, sir ?
    R. ROISTER. I shall be contented to take her.
    M. MUMBL. E'en so, sir ?
    R. ROISTER. But at thy request and for thy sake.
    M. MUMBL. E'en so, sir ?
    R. ROISTER. And, come, hark in thine ear what
    to say.
    M. MUMBL. E'en so, sir ?
[Here let him tell her a great long tale in her ear.

ACTUS I., SCÆNA IV.

MATTHEW MERRYGREEK, DOBINET DOUGHTY,
    HARPAX, RALPH ROISTER, MARGERY
    MUMBLECRUST.

    M. MERRY. Come on, sirs, apace, and 'quit your-
    selves like men.
Your pains shall be rewarded.
    D. DOUGH. But, I wot not when.
    M. MERRY. Do your master worship, as ye have
    done in time past.
    D. DOUGH. Speak to them : of mine office he
    shall have a cast.

M. MERRY. Harpax, look that thou do well too,
   and thy fellow.
HARPAX. I warrant, if he will mine example
   follow.
M. MERRY. Court'sy, whoresons : duck you and
   crouch at every word.
D. DOUGH. Yes, whether our master speak ear-
   nest or bord.[1]
M. MERRY. For this lieth upon his preferment
   indeed.
D. DOUGH. Oft is he a wooer, but never doth he
   speed.
M. MERRY. But with whom is he now so sadly
   rounding [2] yond ?
D. DOUGH. With *Nobs nicebectur miserere* [3] fond.
M. MERRY. God be at your wedding : be ye
   sped already ?
I did not suppose that your love was so greedy.
I perceive now ye have chose of devotion ;
And joy have ye, lady, of your promotion !
R. ROISTER. Tush, fool, thou art deceived, this
   is not she.
M. MERRY. Well, mock [1] much of her, and keep
   her well, I 'vise ye.
I will take no charge of such a fair piece keeping.
M. MUMBL. What aileth this fellow ? he driveth
   me to weeping.

---

[1] Joke.—*Borde, bourd,* or *boord,* as the word is spelled by
Spenser, means a jest or sport ; from the French *Bourde*—

> " Of old adventures that fell white,
> And some of *bourdes* and ribaudry."
>   —*Lay le Freine.* See *Toone's Glossary.*—*Cooper.*

[2] Seriously whispering—

> "And in his ear him *rounded* close behind."
>   —*Faerie Queene,* Book iii., Canto 10.—*Cooper.*

[3] [Apparently intentional nonsense for *nobis miscebetur
miserere.*]

[4] [For *make.*]

M. MERRY. What, weep on the wedding-day?
be merry, woman :
Though I say it, ye have chose a good gentleman.
  R. ROISTER. Kock's nowns,[1] what meanest thou,
man? tut, a whistle.
  M. MERRY. Ah, sir, be good to her; she is but
a gristle :
Ah, sweet lamb and coney!
  R. ROISTER. Tut, thou art deceived.
  M. MERRY. Weep no more, lady, ye shall be
well received.
Up with some merry noise,[2] sirs, to bring home
the bride!
  R. ROISTER. Gog's arms, knave, art thou mad?
I tell thee thou art wide.
  M. MERRY. Then, ye intend by night to have
her home brought.
  R. ROISTER. I tell thee, no.
  M. MERRY. How then?
  R. ROISTER. 'Tis neither meant ne thought.
  M. MERRY. What shall we then do with her?
  R. ROISTER. Ah, foolish harebrain,
This is not she.
  M. MERRY. No, is [not]. Why, then, unsaid
again!
And what young girl is this with your maship so
bold?
  R. ROISTER. A girl?
  M. MERRY. Yea, I daresay, scarce yet threescore
year old.
  R. ROISTER. This same is the fair widow's
nurse, of whom ye wot.
  M. MERRY. Is she but a nurse of a house?
hence home, old trot!

---

[1] God's wounds.
[2] *Music.* So often used of old.—*Cooper.*

Hence at once !

R. ROISTER. No, no.

M. MERRY. What, an' please your maship,
A nurse talk so homely with one of your worship ?

R. ROISTER. I will have it so ; it is my pleasure
and will.

M. MERRY. Then I am content. Nurse, come
again, tarry still.

R. ROISTER. What, she will help forward this
my suit, for her part.

M. MERRY. Then is't mine own pigsny, and
blessing on my heart !

R. ROISTER. This is our best friend, man.

M. MERRY. Then teach her what to say.

M. MUMBL. I am taught already.

M. MERRY. Then go, make no delay.

R. ROISTER. Yet hark, one word in thine ear.

M. MERRY. Back, sirs, from his tail !

R. ROISTER. Back, villains ; will ye be privy of
my counsel ?

M. MERRY. Back, sirs ! So. I told you afore
ye would be shent.

R. ROISTER. She shall have the first day a whole
peck of argent.

M. MUMBL. A peck ! *Nomine Patris*, have ye
so much spare ?

R. ROISTER. Yea, and a cart-load thereto, or else
were it bare ;
Besides other moveables, household stuff and land.

M. MUMBL. Have ye lands too ?

R. ROISTER. An hundred marks.

M. MERRY. Yea, a thousand.

M. MUMBL. And have ye cattle too ? and sheep
too ?

R. ROISTER. Yea, a few.

M. MERRY. He is ashamed the number of them
to show.

E'en round about him as many thousand sheep goes,
As he and thou, and I too, have fingers and toes.
   M. MUMBL. And how many years old be you?
   R. ROISTER. Forty at least.
   M. MERRY. Yea, and thrice forty to them.
   R. ROISTER. Nay, thou dost jest.
I am not so old: thou misreckonest my years.
   M. MERRY. I know that; but my mind was on
      bullocks and steers.
   M. MUMBL. And what shall I show her your
      mastership's name is?
   R. ROISTER. Nay, she shall make suit, ere she
      know that, i-wis.
   M. MUMBL. Yet let me somewhat know.
   M. MERRY. This is he, understand
That killed the blue spider in Blanchepowder land.
   M. MUMBL. Yea, Jesus, William, zee, law! did
      he zo, law?
   M. MERRY. Yea, and the last elephant that ever
      he saw,
As the beast passed by, he start out of a busk,[1]
And e'en with pure strength of arms plucked out
      his great tusk.
   M. MUMBL. Jesus, *Nomine Patris*, what a thing
      was that!
   R. ROISTER. Yea, but, Merrygreek, one thing
      thou hast forgot.
   M. MERRY. What?
   R. ROISTER. Of th' other elephant.
   M. MERRY. O, him that fled away?
   R. ROISTER. Yea.
   M. MERRY. Yea, he knew that his match was
      in place that day.

---

[1] A copse or bush. See "Tempest," act iv., sc. 1.

    "And every *bosky* bourn from side to side."—*Milton.*
—*Cooper.*

Tut, he bet the King of Crickets on Christmas-day,
That he crept in a hole, and not a word to say.
   M. MUMBL. A sore man, by zembletee.[1]
   M. MERRY. Why, he wrong a club
Once in a fray out of the hand of Belzebub.
   R. ROISTER. And how when Mumfision—
   M. MERRY. O, your costreling
Bore the lantern a-field so before the gozeling——
Nay, that is too long a matter now to be told.
Never ask his name, nurse, I warrant thee, be bold :
He conquered in one day from Rome to Naples,
And won towns, nurse, as fast as thou canst make
     apples.
   M. MUMBL. O Lord ! my heart quaketh for
     fear, he is so sore.
   R. ROISTER. Thou makest her too much afeard,
     Merrygreek ; no more.
This tale would fear my sweetheart Custance
     right evil.
   M. MERRY. Nay, let her take him, nurse, and
     fear not the devil.
But thus is our song dasht—sirs, ye may home
     again.   [*To the music.*
   R. ROISTER. No, shall they not. I charge you
     all here to remain :
The villain slaves !—a whole day, ere they can be
     found !
   M. MERRY. Couch on your marybones, whore-
     sons, down to the ground !
Was it meet he should tarry so long in one place,
Without harmony of music or some solace ?
Whoso hath such bees as your master in his head
Had need to have his spirits with music be fed.
By your mastership's licence—
   R. ROISTER. What is that ? a mote !

---

[1] [Appearance, *quasi* semblety, semblance.]

M. MERRY. No, it was a fowl's feather had light
on your coat.

R. ROISTER. I was nigh no feathers, since I came
from my bed.

M. MERRY. No, sir, it was a hair that was fall
from your head.

R. ROISTER. My men come, when it please
them.

M. MERRY. By your leave—

R. ROISTER. What is that ?

M. MERRY. Your gown was foul spotted with
the foot[1] of a gnat.

R. ROISTER. Their master to offend they are
nothing afeard.

What now ?

M. MERRY. A lousy hair from your mastership's
beard.

And sir, for nurse's sake, pardon this one offence.

OMNES FAMULÆ. We shall not after this show
the like negligence.

R. ROISTER. I pardon you this once ; and, come,
sing ne'er the worse.

M. MERRY. How like you the goodness of this
gentleman, nurse ?

M. MUMBL. God save his mastership, that can
so his men forgive !

And I will hear them sing, ere I go, by his leave.

R. ROISTER. Marry, and thou shalt, wench :
come, we two will dance.

M. MUMBL. Nay, I will by mine own self foot
the song perchance.

R. ROISTER. Go it, sirs, lustily.

[Retires to write a letter.

M. MUMBL. Pipe up a merry note.

---

[1] [Should we not read fute ? See Halliwell in v.]

Let me hear it played, I will foot it for a groat.

[*Cantent.*[1]

R. ROISTER. Now, nurse, take this same letter
here to thy mistress ;
And as my trust is in thee, ply my business.
M. MUMBL. It shall be done.
M. MERRY. Who made it ?
R. ROISTER. I wrote it each whit.
M. MERRY. Then needs it no mending ?
R. ROISTER. No, no.
M. MERRY. No, I know your wit.
R. ROISTER. I warrant it well.
M. MUMBL. It shall be delivered;
But, if ye speed, shall I be considered ?
M. MERRY. Whough ! dost thou doubt of that ?
M. MUMBL. What shall I have ?
M. MERRY. An hundred times more than thou
canst devise to crave.
M. MUMBL. Shall I have some new gear, for my
old is all spent ?
M. MERRY. The worst kitchen wench shall go
in ladies' raiment.
M. MUMBL. Yea ?
M. MERRY. And the worst drudge in the house
shall go better
Than your mistress doth now.
M. MUMBL. Then I trudge with your letter.
R. ROISTER. Now may I repose me : Custance
is mine own.
Let us sing and play homeward, that it may be known.
M. MERRY. But are you sure that your letter is
well enough ?
R. ROISTER. I wrote it myself.
M. MERRY. Then sing we to dinner.

[*Here they sing, and go out singing.*

---

[1] See the second song at the end of the play.—*Cooper.*

ACTUS I., SCÆNA 5.

CHRISTIAN CUSTANCE, MARGERY MUMBLECRUST.

C. CUSTANCE. Who took thee this letter, Mar-
    gery Mumblecrust?
M. MUMBL. A lusty gay bachelor took it me of
    trust,
And if ye seek to him, he will love your doing.
C. CUSTANCE. Yea, but where learned he that
    manner of wooing?
M. MUMBL. If to sue to him you will any pains
    take,
He will have you to his wife (he saith) for my
    sake.
C. CUSTANCE. Some wise gentleman belike: I
    am bespoken.
And I thought verily this had been some token
From my dear spouse,[1] Gawin Goodluck, whom
    when him please,
God luckily send home to both our hearts' ease!
M. MUMBL. A jolly man it is, I wot well by
    report,
And would have you to him for marriage resort.
Best open the writing, and see what it doth speak.
C. CUSTANCE. At this time, nurse, I will neither
    read ne break.
M. MUMBL. He promised to give you a whole
    peck of gold,
C. CUSTANCE. Perchance, [t'will] lack of a pint,
    when it shall be all told.
M. MUMBL. I would take a gay rich husband,
    and I were you.

---

[1] The word *spouse* is here used for *betrothed lover.*—
Cooper.

C. CUSTANCE. In good sooth, Madge, e'en so
    would I, if I were thou.[1]
But no more of this fond talk now; let us go in,
And see thou no more move me folly to begin;
Nor bring me no mo letters for no man's pleasure,
But thou know from whom.
    M. MUMBL. I warrant, ye shall be sure.

ACTUS II., SCÆNA 1.[2]

DOBINET DOUGHTY.

D. DOUGH. Where is the house I go to, before
    or behind?
I know not where nor when, nor how I shall it
    find.
If I had ten men's bodies and legs, and strength,
This trotting that I have must needs lame me at
    length.
And now that my master is new-set on wooing,
I trust there shall none of us find lack of doing:
Two pair of shoes a day will now be too little
To serve me, I must trot to and fro so mickle.
"Go bear me this token;" "carry me this letter;"
Now this is the best way; now that way is better.
"Up before day, sirs, I charge you, an hour or
    twain;
Trudge, do me this message, and bring word quick
    again."
If one miss but a minute, then, "His arms and
    wounds,

---

[1] The idea is borrowed from Alexander's celebrated reply
to Parmenio.—*Cooper.*

[2] A night has passed between the first and second acts.—
Cooper.

I would not have slacked for ten thousand
    pounds !
Nay see, I beseech you, if my most trusty page
Go not now about to hinder my marriage "
So fervent hot wooing, and so far from wiving,
I trow, never was any creature living ;
With every woman is he in some love's-pang ;
Then up to our lute at midnight, *twangledom twang.*
Then twang with our sonnets, and twang with our
    dumps,[1]
And heigho from our heart, as heavy as lead-lumps.
Then to our recorder [2] with *toodleloodle poop,*
As the howlet out of an ivy bush should hoop.
Anon to our gittern,[3] *thrumpledum thrumpledum*
    thrum,
Thrumpledum, thrumpledum, thrumpledum, thrum-
    pledum, thrum.
Of songs and ballads also he is a maker,
And that can he as finely do as Jack Raker ;[4]
Yea, and extempore will he ditties compose ;
Foolish Marsias ne'er made the like, I suppose ;
Yet must we sing them, as good stuff, I undertake,
As for such a pen-man is well fitting to make.
"Ah, for these long nights ! heigho ! when will it
    be day ?
I fear, ere I come, she will be wooed away."
Then, when answer is made, that it may not be,
"O death, why comest thou not ?" by and by
    saith he.

---

[1] A tune : generally a mournful one.
[2] A flageolet.
[3] A lute, or guitar.

    [4] " What have ye of the Lord Dakers ?
       He maketh vs *Jacke Rakers ;*
       He says we are but crakers."
           —Skelton's *Why come ye not to Court !*

See also the same author's " Speke Parrot."—*Cooper.*

But then from his heart to put away sorrow,
He is as far in with some new love next morrow.
But, in the mean season, we trudge and we trot :
From dayspring to midnight I sit not nor rest not.
And now am I sent to dame Christian Custance ;
But I fear it will end with a mock for pastance.[1]
I bring her a ring with a token in a clout,
And by all guess this same is her house out of
　　doubt.
I know it now perfect, I am in my right way ;
And lo ! yond the old nurse that was with us last
　　day.

ACTUS II., SCÆNA 2.

MADGE MUMBLECRUST, DOBINET DOUGHTY.

M. MUMBL. I was ne'er so shoke [1] up afore, since
　　I was born :
That our mistress could not have had chid, I would
　　have sworn.
And I pray God I die, if I meant any harm ;
But for my lifetime this shall be to me a charm.
　　D. DOUGH. God you save and see, nurse ! and
　　　　how is it with you ?
　　M. MUMBL. Marry, a great deal the worse it is
　　　　for such as thou.
　　D. DOUGH. For me ?　Why so ?
　　M. MUMBL. Why, were not thou one of them,
　　　　say,

---

[1] *Passe-temps*, pastime, sport.　So in act iv., sc. vi.—

　　　　"Do ye think, Dame Custance,
　　That in this wooing I have meant ought but *pastance ?*"

Again, act v., scene 2—

　　" Truly, most dear spouse, nought was done but for *pastance.*"
　　　　　　　　　　　　　　　　　　—*Cooper.*

[2] [Shaken.]

That sang and played here with the gentleman
    last day?
    D. DOUGH. Yes, and he would know, if you
    have for him spoken,
And prays you to deliver this ring and token.
    M. MUMBL. Now, by the token that God tokened,
    brother,
I will deliver no token, one nor other.
I have once been so shent for your master's plea-
    sure,
As I will not be again for all his treasure.
    D. DOUGH. He will thank you, woman.
    M. MUMBL. I will none of his thank.
                     [Exit M. Mumbl.[1]
    D. DOUGH. I ween I am a prophet; this gear
    will prove blank.
But what, should I home again without answer go?
It were better go to Rome on my head than so.[2]
I will tarry here this month, but some of the house
Shall take it of me, and then I care not a louse.
But yonder cometh forth a wench or a lad :
If he have not one Lombard's touch,[3] my luck is
    bad.

ACTUS II., SCÆNA 3.

TRUEPENNY, D. DOUGH., TIBET T., ANNOT AL.

TRUEPENNY. I am clean lost for lack of merry
    company;
We 'gree not half well within, our wenches and I :

---

    [1] [In the original, D. Doughty is made to go out.]
    [2] [Perhaps a sort of allusion to the proverb, To go to Rome
with a mortar on one's head.]
    [3] A Lombard's touchstone, to try gold and silver. See
" Richard III.," act iv., sc. 2.—*Cooper.*

They will command like mistresses, they will
    forbid ;
If they be not served, Truepenny must be chid.
Let them be as merry now, as ye can desire :
With turning of a hand our mirth lieth in the
    mire.
I cannot skill of such changeable mettle,
There is nothing with them but, In dock, out
    nettle.[1]
  D. DOUGH. Whether is it better that I speak to
    him first,
Or he first to me ?   It is good to cast the worst.
If I begin first, he will smell all my purpose :
Otherwise I shall not need anything to disclose.
                           [Aside.

  TRUEPENNY. What boy have we yonder ?   I
    will see what he is.
  D. DOUGH. He cometh to me.   It is hereabout,
    i-wis.   *[Aside.*
  TRUEPENNY. Wouldest thou ought, friend, that
    thou lookest so about ?
  D. DOUGH. Yea ; but whether ye can help me
    or no, I doubt.
I seek to one Mistress Custance house here dwelling.
  TRUEPENNY. It is my mistress ye seek to, by
    your telling.
  D. DOUGH. Is there any of that name here but
    she ?
  TRUEPENNY. Not one in all the whole town
    that I know, pardè.
  D. DOUGH. A widow she is, I trow.
  TRUEPENNY. And what, and she be ?
  D. DOUGH. But ensured to an husband ?
  TRUEPENNY. Yea, so think we.

---

[1] A proverbial expression, relating to a still common
practice.—*Cooper.*

D. DOUGH. And I dwell with her husband that
trusteth to be.

TRUEPENNY. In faith, then must thou needs be
welcome to me.

Let us, for acquaintance, shake hands together,
And, whate'er thou be, heartily welcome hither.

TIB. TALK.[1] Well, Truepenny, never but flinging?

AN. ALYFACE. And frisking?

TRUEPENNY. Well, Tibet and Annot, still
swinging and whisking?

TIB. TALK. But ye roil abroad.

AN. ALYFACE. In the street everywhere.

TRUEPENNY. Where are ye twain? in chambers,
when ye meet me there?

But come hither, fools: I have one now by the
hand,
Servant to him that must be our mistress' husband;
Bid him welcome.

AN. ALYFACE. To me truly he is welcome.

TIB. TALK. Forsooth and, as I may say, heartily
welcome.

D. DOUGH. I thank you, mistress maids.

AN. ALYFACE. I hope we shall better know.

TIB. TALK. And when will our new master
come?

D. DOUGH. Shortly, I trow.

TIB. TALK. I would it were to-morrow; for, till
he resort,

Our mistress, being a widow, hath small comfort:
And I heard our nurse speak of an husband to-
day,
Ready for our mistress; a rich man and a gay.
And we shall go in our French hoods every day:
In our silk cassocks (I warrant you) fresh and gay;

---

[1] Tib and Annot would seem to enter here.—*Cooper.*

In our trick ferdegews and billiments of gold ;
Brave in our suits of change, seven double fold.
Then shall ye see Tibet, sirs, tread the moss so
    trim ;
Nay, why said I tread ? ye shall see her glide and
    swim ;
Not lumperdy-clumperdy, like our spaniel Rig.
  TRUEPENNY. Marry, then, prick-me-dainty; come,
    toast me a fig.
Who shall then know our Tib Talkapace, trow ye ?
  AN. ALYFACE. And why not Annot Alyface as
    fine as she ?
  TRUEPENNY. And what, had Tom Truepenny a
    father or none ?
  AN. ALYFACE. Then our pretty new-come-man
    will look to be one.
  TRUEPENNY. We four, I trust, shall be a jolly
    merry knot.
Shall we sing a fit [1] to welcome our friend, Annot ?
  AN. ALYFACE. Perchance, he cannot sing.
  D. DOUGH. I am at all assays.
  TIB. TALK. By Cock, and the better welcome to
    us always.

Here they sing :

A thing very fit
For them that have wit,
And are fellows knit,
Servants in one house to be ;
As fast for to sit,
And not oft to flit,
Nor vary a whit,
But lovingly to agree.

---

[1] A fit usually means the division of a ballad, but here it
is to be understood as a song.—*Cooper.*

No man complaining,
No other disdaining,
For loss or for gaining.
But fellows or friends to be;
No grudge remaining,
No work refraining,
Nor help restraining,
But lovingly to agree.

No man for despite,
By word or by write,
His fellow to twite,
But further in honesty;
No good turns entwite,
Nor old sores recite,
But let all go quite,
And lovingly to agree.

After drudgery,
When they be weary,
Then to be merry,
To laugh and sing they be free;
With chip and cherry,
Heigh derry derry,
Trill on the bery,
And lovingly to agree.

TIB. TALK. Will you now in with us unto our
   mistress go?
D. DOUGH. I have first for my master an errand
   or two.
But I have here from him a token and a ring;
They shall have most thank of her, that first doth
   it bring.
TIB. TALK. Marry, that will I.

TRUEPENNY. See, and Tibet snatch not now !

TIB. TALK. And why may not I, sir, get thanks
as well as you ?   [*Exit.*

AN. ALYFACE. Yet get ye not all, we will go
with you both,

And have part of your thanks, be ye never so loth.
         [*Exit omnes.*

D. DOUGH. So my hands are rid of it, I care for
no more.

I may now return home : so durst I not afore.
         [*Exit.*

ACTUS II., SCÆNA 4.

C. CUSTANCE, TIBET, ANNOT ALYFACE, TRUEPENNY.

C. CUSTANCE. Nay, come forth all three ; and
come hither, pretty maid :

Will not so many forewarnings make you afraid ?

TIB. TALK. Yes, forsooth.

C. CUSTANCE. But still be a runner up and
down ?

Still be a bringer of tidings and tokens to town ?

TIB. TALK. No, forsooth, mistress.

C. CUSTANCE. Is all your delight and joy

In whisking and ramping abroad, like a Tom-boy ?

TIB. TALK. Forsooth, these were there too, Annot
and Truepenny.

TRUEPENNY. Yea, but ye alone took it, ye cannot deny.

AN. ALYFACE. Yea, that ye did.

TIB. TALK. But, if I had not, ye twain would.

C. CUSTANCE. You great calf, ye should have
more wit, so ye should.   [*To Truep.*

But why should any of you take such things in
hand ?

TIB. TALK. Because it came from him that must
    be your husband.
C. CUSTANCE. How do ye know that?
TIB. TALK. Forsooth, the boy did say so.
C. CUSTANCE. What was his name?
AN. ALYFACE. We asked not.
C. CUSTANCE. No, did [ye not?]
AN. ALYFACE. He is not far gone, of likelihood.
TRUEPENNY. I will see.
C. CUSTANCE. If thou canst find him in the
    street, bring him to me.
TRUEPENNY. Yes.   [*Exeat.*
C. CUSTANCE. Well, ye naughty girls, if ever I
    perceive
That henceforth you do letters or tokens receive,
To bring unto me from any person or place,
Except ye first show me the party face to face,
Either thou, or thou, full truly abi'[1] thou shalt.
    TIB. TALK. Pardon this, and the next time
        powder me in salt.
    C. CUSTANCE. I shall make all girls by you
        twain to beware.
    TIB. TALK. If I ever offend again, do not me spare.
But if ever I see that false boy any more,
By your mistresship's licence, I tell you afore,
I will rather have my coat twenty times swinged,
Than on the naughty wag not to be avenged.
    C. CUSTANCE. Good wenches would not so ramp
        abroad idly,
But keep within doors, and ply their work ear-
    nestly.
If one would speak with me, that is a man likely,
Ye shall have right good thank to bring me word
        quickly;

---

[1] *i.e.*, *Abide* the consequences, rue, or suffer for. See "A
Midsummer Night's Dream," act iii., sc. 2.—*Cooper.*

But otherwise with messages to come in post,
From henceforth I promise you shall be to your cost.
Get you into your work.

    TIB. AND ANNOT. Yes, forsooth.

    C. CUSTANCE. Hence, both twain.
And let me see you play me such a part again !

[Ex. Tib. and Annot.

    TRUEPENNY (re-entering). Mistress, I have run
      past the far end of the street,
Yet can I not yonder crafty boy see nor meet.

    C. CUSTANCE. No !

    TRUEPENNY. Yet I looked as far beyond the people
As one may see out of the top of Paul's steeple.

    C. CUSTANCE. Hence, in at doors, and let me no
      more be vext !

    TRUEPENNY. Forgive me this one fault, and lay
      on for the next.[1]

    C. CUSTANCE. Now will I in too, for I think, so
      God me mend,
This will prove some foolish matter in the end.

[Exeat.

ACTUS III., SCÆNA 1.

MATTHEW MERRYGREEK.

    M. MERRY. Now say this again : he hath some-
      what to doing
Which followeth the trace of one that is wooing ;
Specially that hath no more wit in his head,
Than my cousin Roister Doister withal is led.
I am sent in all haste to espy and to mark,
How our letters and tokens are likely to wark.

---

[1] Truepenny goes out here, but the old copy omits his
exit.—Cooper.

Master Roister Doister must have answer in haste,
For he loveth not to spend much labour in waste.
Now as for Christian Custance, by this light,
Though she had not her troth to Gawin Goodluck
    plight,
Yet rather than with such a loutish dolt to marry,
I daresay would live a poor life solitary.
But fain would I speak with Custance, if I wist how,
To laugh at the matter.   Yond cometh one forth
    now.

ACTUS III., SCÆNA 2.

TIBET.   M. MERRYGREEK (*aside*).

TIB. TALK. Ah! that I might but once in my
    life have a sight
Of him who made us all so ill-shent! By this light,
He should never escape, if I had him by the ear,
But even from his head I would it bite or tear.
Yea, and if one of them were not enou',
I would bite them both off, I make God avow.
    M. MERRY. What is he, whom this little mouse
      doth so threaten?   [*Aside.*
    TIB. TALK. I would teach him, I trow, to make
      girls shent or beaten.
    M. MERRY. I will call her. Maid, with whom
      are ye so hasty?
    TIB. TALK. Not with you, sir, but with a little
      wage-pasty;
A deceiver of folks by subtle craft and guile.
    M. MERRY. I know where she is : Dobinet hath
      wrought some wile.
    TIB. TALK. He brought a ring and token,
      which he said was sent
From our dame's husband, but I wot well I was
    shent;

For it liked her as well (to tell you no lies)
As water in a[1] ship, or salt cast in her eyes :
And yet, whence it came, neither we nor she can tell.
   M. MERRY. We shall have sport anon : I like
     this very well.   *[Aside.*
And dwell ye here with mistress Custance, fair maid ?
   TIB. TALK. Yea, marry do I, sir : what would
     ye have said ?
   M. MERRY. A little message unto her, by word
     of mouth.
   TIB. TALK. No messages, by your leave, nor
     tokens forsooth.
   M. MERRY. Then help me to speak with her.
   TIB. TALK. With a good will that.
Here she cometh forth.   Now speak—ye know
     best what.
   C. CUSTANCE. None other life with you, maid,
     but abroad to skip ?
   TIB. TALK. Forsooth, here is one would speak
     with your mistresship.
   C. CUSTANCE. Ah, have ye been learning of mo
     messages now ?
   TIB. TALK. I would not hear his mind, but bad
     him show it to you.
   C. CUSTANCE. In at doors !
   TIB. TALK. I am gone.   *[Exit.*
   M. MERRY. Dame Custance, God ye save !
   C. CUSTANCE. Welcome, friend Merrygreek :
     and what thing would ye have ?
   M. MERRY. I am come to you a little matter to
     break.
   C. CUSTANCE. But see it be honest, else better
     not to speak.
   M. MERRY. How feel ye yourself affected here
     of late ?

---

[1] [Original, *her.*]

C. CUSTANCE. I feel no manner change, but after
    the old rate.
But whereby do ye mean?
    M. MERRY. Concerning marriage.
Doth not love lade you?
    C. CUSTANCE. I feel no such carriage.
    M. MERRY. Do ye feel no pangs of dotage?
    Answer me right.
    C. CUSTANCE. I doat so, that I make but one
    sleep all the night.
But what need all these words? .
    M. MERRY. O Jesus! will ye see
What dissembling creatures these same women be?
                            [*Aside.*
The gentleman ye wot of, whom ye do so love,
That ye would fain marry him, if he durst it move,
Among other rich widows which are of him glad,
Lest ye for lesing of him perchance might run
    mad,
Is now contented that, upon your suit making,
Ye be as one in election of taking.
    C. CUSTANCE. What a tale is this! That I wot
    of! Whom I love!
    M. MERRY. Yea, and he is as loving a worm
    again as a dove.
E'en of very pity he is willing you to take,
Because ye shall not destroy yourself for his sake.
    C. CUSTANCE. Marry, God 'ield[1] his maship!
    whatever he be,
It is gentmanly spoken.
    M. MERRY. Is it not, trow ye?
If ye have the grace now to offer yourself, ye
    speed.
    C. CUSTANCE. As much as though I did; this
    time it shall not need.

---

[1] [Shield.]

But what gentleman is it, I pray you tell me plain,
That wooeth so finely ?

    M. MERRY. Lo, where ye be again !
As though ye knew him not !

    C. CUSTANCE. Tush ! ye speak in jest.

    M. MERRY. Nay, sure the party is in good
      knacking earnest,
And have you he will (he saith) and have you he
      must.

    C. CUSTANCE. I am promised during my life,
      that is just. ·

    M. MERRY. Marry, so thinketh he—unto him
      alone.

    C. CUSTANCE. No creature hath my faith and
      troth but one,
That is Gawin Goodluck : and if it be not he,
He hath no title this way, whatever he be,
For I know none to whom I have such words
      spoken.

    M. MERRY. Ye know him not, you, by his letter
      and token ?

    C. CUSTANCE. Indeed true it is, that a letter I
      have,
But I never read it yet, as God me save.

    M. MERRY. Ye a woman ? and your letter so
      long unread !

    C. CUSTANCE. Ye may thereby know what haste
      I have to wed.
But now, who is it for my hand ? I know by
      guess.

    M. MERRY. Ah ! well, I say—

    C. CUSTANCE. It is Roister Doister, doubtless.

    M. MERRY. Will ye never leave this dissimula-
      tion ?
Ye know him not ?

    C. CUSTANCE. But by imagination ;
For no man there is, but a very dolt and lout,

That to woo a widow would so go about.
He shall never have me his wife, while he do live.
  M. MERRY. Then will he have you if he may,
    so mot I thrive ;
And he biddeth you send him word by me,
That ye humbly beseech him ye may his wife be,
And that there shall be no let in you nor mistrust,
But to be wedded on Sunday next, if he lust ;
And biddeth you to look for him.
  C. CUSTANCE. Doth he bid so ?
  M. MERRY. When he cometh, ask him whether
    he did or no ?
  C. CUSTANCE. Go say, that I bid him keep him
    warm at home,
For, if he come abroad, he shall cough me a mome.[1]
My mind was vexed, I 'shrew his head, sottish
    dolt.
  M. MERRY. He hath in his head—
  C. CUSTANCE. As much brain as a burbolt.[2]
  M. MERRY. Well, dame Custance, if he hear
    you thus play choploge.[3]
  C. CUSTANCE. What will he ?
  M. MERRY. Play the devil in the horologe.[4]
  C. CUSTANCE. I defy him, lout.
  M. MERRY. Shall I tell him what ye say ?

---

[1] A fool or blockhead. See act v., scenes 2 and 5.
"Cough me a fool" is common in old plays.—*Cooper.*

[2] A birdbolt, a short, thick arrow, with a blunt head,
chiefly made use of to kill rooks. It appears to have been
looked upon as an emblem of dulness. So in Marston's
"What you Will," 1607—

> " Ignorance should shoot
> His gross-knobb'd *bird-bolt.*"

[3] [Chop-logic.]

> 4 " The divell is in th' *orloge,* the houres to trye :
> Searche houres by the sun, the devylls dyall will lie."
>   —Heywood's *Proverbs.*

—*Cooper.*

C. CUSTANCE. Yea, and add whatsoever thou
    canst, I thee pray,
And I will avouch it, whatsoever it be.
    M. MERRY. Then let me alone; we will laugh
    well, ye shall see:
It will not be long, ere he will hither resort.
    C. CUSTANCE. Let him come when him lust, I
    wish no better sport.
Fare ye well: I will in, and read my great letter:
I shall to my wooer make answer the better.

                              [*Exeat.*

ACTUS III., SCÆNA 3.

MATTHEW MERRYGREEK.

M. MERRY. Now that the whole answer in my
    device doth rest,
I shall paint out our wooer in colours of the best,
And all that I say shall be on Custance's mouth,
She is author of all that I shall speak, forsooth.
But yonder cometh Roister Doister now in a trance.

[Enter R. ROISTER.]

R. ROISTER. Juno send me this day good luck
    and good chance!
I cannot but come see how Merrygreek doth speed.
    M. MERRY. I will not see him, but give him a
    jut[1] indeed.
I cry your mastership mercy!
    R. ROISTER. And whither now?
    M. MERRY. As fast as I could run, sir, in post
    against you.
But why speak ye so faintly, or why are ye so sad?

---

[1] A jostle.

R. ROISTER. Thou knowest the proverb—be-
    cause I cannot be had.
Hast thou spoken with this woman?
    M. MERRY. Yea, that I have.
    R. ROISTER. And what, will this gear be?
    M. MERRY. No, so God me save.
    R. ROISTER. Hast thou a flat answer?
    M. MERRY. Nay, a sharp answer.
    R. ROISTER. What?
    M. MERRY. Ye shall not (she saith), by her will,
      marry her cat.
Ye are such a calf, such an ass, such a block,
Such a lilburn, such a hobil, such a lobcock;
And because ye should come to her at no season,
She despised your maship out of all reason.
"Beware what ye say (ko I) of such a gentleman!"
"Nay, I fear him not (ko she), do the best he
      can."
He vaunteth himself for a man of prowess great,
Whereas a good gander, I dare say, may him
      beat.
And where he is louted [1] and laughed to scorn,
For the veriest dolt that ever was born:
And veriest lubber, sloven and beast,
Living in this world from the west to the east;
Yet of himself hath he such opinion,
That in all the world is not the like minion.
He thinketh each woman to be brought in dotage
With the only sight of his goodly personage:
Yet none that will have him: we do him lout
      and flock,
And make him among us our common sporting-
      stock;
And so would I now (ko she), save only because—

---

[1] Mocked or devised for a lout. See "First Part of Henry
VI.," act iv., scene 3.—*Cooper.*

"Better nay (ko I)."   "I lust not meddle with
    daws."
" Ye are happy (ko I) that ye are a woman :
This would cost you your life, in case ye were a
    man."
    R. ROISTER. Yea, an hundred thousand pound
    should not save her life.
    M. MERRY. No, but that ye woo her to have
    her to your wife ;
But I could not stop her mouth.
    R. ROISTER. Heigho, alas !
    M. MERRY. Be of good cheer, man, and let the
    world pass.[1]
    R. ROISTER. What shall I do or say, now that it
    will not be ?
    M. MERRY. Ye shall have choice of a thousand
    as good as she ;
And ye must pardon her ; it is for lack of wit.
    R. ROISTER. Yea, for were not I an husband for
    her fit ?
Well, what should I now do ?
    M. MERRY. I'faith, I cannot tell.
    R. ROISTER. I will go home, and die.
    M. MERRY. Then shall I bid toll the bell ?
    R. ROISTER. No.
    M. MERRY. God have mercy on your soul : ah,
    good gentleman,
That e'er you should thus die for an unkind woman !
Will ye drink once, ere ye go ?
    R. ROISTER. No, no, I will none.
    M. MERRY. How feels your soul to God ?
    R. ROISTER. I am nigh-gone.

---

[1] A proverbial expression of heedless jollity. See the
Induction to the "Taming of the Shrew," where *Sly* ex-
claims : "*Paucas pallabris ; let the world slide ; Sessa !*"—
Cooper.

M. MERRY. And shall we hence straight?

R. ROISTER. Yea.

M. MERRY. *Placebo dilexi.* [*ut infra.*[1]

Master Roister Doister will straight go home, and
    die.

R. ROISTER. Heigho, alas! the pangs of death
    my heart do break.

M. MERRY. Hold your peace, for shame, sir! a
    dead man may not speak

Ne quando. What mourners and what torches shall
    we have?

R. ROISTER. None.

M. MERRY. *Dirige.* He will go darkling to his
    grave:

Neque lux, neque crux, neque mourners, *neque* clink,
He will steal to heaven, unknowing to God, I think.
A porta inferi. Who shall your goods possess?

R. ROISTER. Thou shalt be my sector,[2] and have
    all, more or less.

M. MERRY. *Requiem æternam.* Now, God re-
    ward your mastership,

And I will cry halfpenny-dole for your worship,
Come forth, sirs; hear the doleful news I shall you
    tell. [*Evocat servos milites.*
Our good master here will no longer with us dwell,
But in spite of Custance, which hath him wearied,
Let us see his maship solemnly buried:
And while some piece of his soul is yet him within,
Some part of his funerals let us here begin.
Audivi vocem. All men take heed by this one gen-
    tleman,
How you set your love upon an unkind woman:
For these women be all such mad, peevish elves,
They will not be won, except to please themselves.

---

[1] See the Psalmody at the end of the Comedy. —*Cooper.*
[2] Executor.

But, in faith, Custance, if ever ye come in hell,
Master Roister Doister shall serve you as well—
And will ye needs go from us thus in very deed?
　R. ROISTER. Yea, in good sadness.
　M. MERRY. Now Jesus Christ be your speed.
Good night, Roger, old knave! farewell, Roger, old
　　knave!
Good night, Roger, old knave, knave knap!
　　　　　　　　　　　　　　　[*ut infra.*[1]

Pray for the late master Roister Doister's soul,
And come forth, parish clerk; let the passing-bell
　　toll.　　　　　　　　　[*Ad servos milites.*
Pray for your master, sirs; and for him ring a peal.
He was your right good master, while he was in
　　heal.
　R. ROISTER. *Qui Lazarum.*
Heigho!
　M. MERRY. Dead men go not so fast *in Para-*
disum.
　R. ROISTER. Heigho!
　M. MERRY. Soft, hear what I have cast.
　R. ROISTER. I will hear nothing, I am past.
　M. MERRY. Whough, wellaway!
Ye may tarry one hour, and hear what I shall say.
Ye were best, sir, for awhile to revive again,
And quite them, ere ye go.
　R. ROISTER. Trowest thou so?
　M. MERRY. Yea, plain.
　R. ROISTER. How may I revive, being now so
　　far past?
　M. MERRY. I will rub your temples, and fet you
　　again at last.
　R. ROISTER. It will not be possible.
　M. MERRY. Yes, for twenty pound.
　R. ROISTER. Arms! what dost thou?

---

[1] See the end of the Comedy.—*Cooper.*

M. MERRY. Fet you again out of your sound.[1]
By this cross, ye were nigh gone indeed; I might
     feel
Your soul departing within an inch of your heel.
Now follow my counsel—
     R. ROISTER. What is it?
     M. MERRY. If I were you,
Custance should eft seek to me, ere I would bow.
     R. ROISTER. Well, as thou wilt have me, even
          so will I do.
     M. MERRY. Then shall ye revive again for an
          hour or two.
     R. ROISTER. As thou wilt: I am content, for a
          little space.
     M. MERRY. Good hap is not hasty: yet in space
          cometh grace.
To speak with Custance yourself should be very
     well;
What good thereof may come, nor I nor you can
     tell.
But now the matter standeth upon your marriage,
Ye must now take unto you a lusty carriage.[2]
Ye may not speak with a faint heart to Custance.
But with a lusty breast[3] and countenance,
That she may know she hath to answer to a man.
     R. ROISTER. Yes, I can do that as well as any
          can.
     M. MERRY. Then, because ye must Custance
          face to face woo,
Let us see how to behave yourself ye can do.
Ye must have a portly brag after your estate.
     R. ROISTER. Tush, I can handle that after the
          best rate.
     M. MERRY. Well done; so, lo! up, man, with
          your head and chin!

---

[1] [Swoon.]   [2] [Original, *courage*.]   [3] Voice.

Up with that snout, man : so lo ! now ye begin.
So, that is somewhat like ; but, pranky-coat, nay
    when ?
That is a lusty brute ! hands unto your side, man :
So, lo ! now is it even as it should be ;
That is somewhat like for a man of your degree.
Then must ye stately go, jetting up and down.[1]
Tut ! can ye no better shake the tail of your gown ?
There, lo ! such a lusty brag it is ye must make.
    R. ROISTER. To come behind, and make curts'y,[2]
      thou must some pains take.
    M. MERRY. Else were I much to blame.   I
      thank your mastership ;
The Lord one day all-to begrime you with worship.
Back, Sir Sauce ! let gentlefolks have elbow-room.
'Void, sirs, see ye not Master Roister Doister come ?
Make place, my masters—
    R. ROISTER. Thou jostlest now too nigh.
    M. MERRY. Back, all rude louts.
    R. ROISTER. Tush.
    M. MERRY. I cry your maship mercy.
Hoiday ! if fair fine Mistress Custance saw you now,
Ralph Roister Doister were her own, I warrant you.
    R. ROISTER. Ne'er a *master* by your girdle ?
    M. MERRY. Your good Mastership's
Mastership were her own mistresship's mistres-
    ship's.
Ye were take up for hawks ; ye were gone, ye were
    gone :
But now one other thing more yet I think upon.
    R. ROISTER. Show what it is.
    M. MERRY. A wooer, be he never so poor,
Must play and sing before his best-beloved's door.

---

[1] Walking with an air or swing.
[2] Formerly applied to any kind of obeisance, either of
man or woman.—*Cooper.*

How much more then you?
  R. ROISTER. Thou speakest well, out of doubt.
And perchance that would make her the sooner
    come out.[1]
Go call my musicians; bid them hie apace.
  M. MERRY. I will be here with them, ere ye can
    say *trey ace.*   [*Exeat.*
  R. ROISTER. This was well said of Merrygreek,
    I 'low his wit,
Before my sweetheart's door we will have a fit,
That, if my love come forth, I may with her talk:
I doubt not but this gear shall on my side walk.
But lo! how well Merrygreek is returned since.
  M. MERRY.[2] There hath grown no grass on my
    heel, since I went hence:
Lo! here have I brought that shall make you
    pastance.
  R. ROISTER. Come, sirs, let us sing, to win my
    dear love Custance.   [*Cantent.*[3]
  M. MERRY. Lo, where she cometh! some coun-
    tenance to her make;
And ye shall hear me be plain with her for your
    sake.

ACTUS III., SCÆNA 4.

CUSTANCE, MERRYGREEK, ROISTER DOISTER.

  C. CUSTANCE. What gauding and fooling is this
    afore my door?
  M. MERRY. May not folks be honest, pray you,
    though they be poor?

---

[1] [Original gives this line to Merrygreek.]
[2] The re-entry is not marked in the old copy.—*Cooper.*
[3] See the fourth song at the end of the Comedy.—*Cooper.*

C. CUSTANCE. As that thing may be true, so rich
    folks may be fools.
R. ROISTER. Her talk is as fine as she had learned
    in schools.
M. MERRY. Look partly toward her, and draw
    a little near.   [*Aside.*
C. CUSTANCE. Get ye home, idle folks.
M. MERRY. Why may not we be here?
Nay, and ye will haze, haze;[1] otherwise, I tell you
    plain,
And ye will not haze, then give us our gear again.
    C. CUSTANCE. Indeed, I have of yours much
    gay things, God save all.
    R. ROISTER. Speak gently unto her, and let her
    take all.   [*Aside.*
    M. MERRY. Ye are too tender-hearted. Shall
    she make us daws?   [*Aside.*
Nay, dame, I will be plain with you in my friend's
    cause.
    R. ROISTER. Let all this pass, sweetheart, and
    accept my service.
    C. CUSTANCE. I will not be served with a fool
    in no wise.
When I choose an husband, I hope to take a man.
    M. MERRY. And where will ye find one which
    can do that he can?
Now this man toward you being so kind,
Why not make him an answer somewhat to his
    mind?
    C. CUSTANCE. I sent him a full answer by you,
    did I not?
    M. MERRY. And I reported it.
    C. CUSTANCE. Nay, I must speak it again.
    R. ROISTER. No, no, he told it all.
    M. MERRY. Was I not meetly plain?

---

[3] *i.e.*, If you will have us, have us.—*Cooper.*

R. ROISTER. Yes.
M. MERRY. But I would not tell all ; for, faith,
    if I had,
With you, dame Custance, ere this hour it had
    been bad ;
And not without cause : for this goodly personage
Meant no less than to join with you in marriage.
    C. CUSTANCE. Let him waste no more labour nor
    suit about me.
    M. MERRY. Ye know not where your preferment
    lieth, I see ;
He sendeth you such a token, ring and letter.
    C. CUSTANCE. Marry, here it is ; ye never saw a
    better.
    M. MERRY. Let us see your letter.
    C. CUSTANCE. Hold ! read it if ye can :
And see what letter it is to win a woman.
    M. MERRY. [*reads :*]

To mine own dear coney, bird, sweetheart, and pigsny,
Good Mistress Custance, present these by and by.

Of this superscription do ye blame the style ?
    C. CUSTANCE. With the rest, as good stuff as ye
    read a great while.
    M. MERRY. [*reads :*]

" Sweet Mistress, where as I love you nothing at all,
Regarding your substance and riches chief of all ;
For your personage, beauty, demeanour and wit,
I commend me unto you never a whit.
Sorry to hear report of your good welfare,
For, (as I hear say) such your conditions are,
That ye be worthy favour of no living man :
To be abhorred of every honest man.
To be taken for a woman inclined to vice ;
Nothing at all to virtue giving her due price.
Wherefore concerning marriage ye are thought

Such a fine paragon as ne'er honest man bought.
And now by these presents I do you advertise,
That I am minded to marry you in no wise.
For your goods and substance, I could be content
To take you as ye are. If ye mind to be my wife,
Ye shall be assured, for the time of my life,
I will keep ye right well from good raiment and fare ;
Ye shall not be kept but in sorrow and care.
Ye shall in no wise live at your own liberty ;
Do and say what ye lust, ye shall never please me ;
But when ye are merry, I will be all sad ;
When ye are sorry, I will be very glad.
When ye seek your heart's ease, I will be unkind ;
At no time in me shall ye much gentleness find ;
But all things contrary to your will and mind
Shall be done : otherwise I will not be behind
To speak. And as for all them that would do you
　　wrong,
I will so help and maintain, ye shall not live long.
Nor any foolish dolt shall cumber you, but I ;
I, whoe'er say nay, will stick by you, till I die.
Thus, good Mistress Custance, the Lord you save
　　and keep
From me, Roister Doister, whether I wake or sleep,
Who favoureth you no less (ye may be bold)
Than this letter purporteth, which ye have unfold."[1]

C. CUSTANCE. How, by this letter of love ? is it
　　not fine ?

R. ROISTER. By the Arms of Calais, it is none
　　of mine.

M. MERRY. Fie ! you are foul to blame ; this is
　　your own hand.

---

[1] This is the passage quoted by T. Wilson in his "Rule of
Reason, conteinyng the arte of Logique," printed by Grafton
in 1551.—*Cooper*.

C. CUSTANCE. Might not a woman be proud of
such an husband?

M. MERRY. Ah, that ye would in a letter show
such despite!

R. ROISTER. O, I would I had him here, the
which did it indite!

M. MERRY. Why, ye made it yourself, ye told
me, by this light!

R. ROISTER. Yea, I meant I wrote it mine own
self yesternight.

C. CUSTANCE. I-wis, sir, I would not have sent
you such a mock.

R. ROISTER. Ye may so take it; but I meant it
not so, by Cock.

M. MERRY. Who can blame this woman to fume,
and fret, and rage?
Tut, tut, yourself now have marred your own mar-
riage.   [*Aside*.
Well yet, Mistress Custance, if ye can this remit;
This gentleman otherwise may your love requite.

C. CUSTANCE. No, God be with you both, and
seek no more to me.   [*Exit*.

R. ROISTER. Wough! she is gone for ever, I
shall her no more see.

M. MERRY. What, weep? Fie for shame! And
blubber? For manhood's sake!
Never let your foe so much pleasure of you take.
Rather play the man's part, and do love refrain:
If she despise you, e'en despise ye her again.

R. ROISTER. By Goss[1] and for thy sake, I defy
her indeed!

M. MERRY. Yea, and perchance that way ye
shall much sooner speed;
For one mad property these women have, in fay,[2]

---

[1] [Jesus.]

[2] In faith: from the French, *foy.*—*Cooper.*

When ye will, they will not: will not ye? then
    will they.
Ah, foolish woman! ah, most unlucky Custance!
Ah, unfortunate woman! ah, peevish Custance,
Art thou to thine harms so obstinately bent,
That thou canst not see where lieth thine high
    preferment?
Canst thou not lub dis man, which could lub dee so
    well?
Art thou so much thine own foe?
    R. ROISTER. Thou dost the truth tell.
    M. MERRY. Well, I lament.
    R. ROISTER. So do I.
    M. MERRY. Wherefore?
    R. ROISTER. For this thing,
Because she is gone.
    M. MERRY. I mourn for another thing.
    R. ROISTER. What is it, Merrygreek, wherefore
    thou dost grief take?
    M. MERRY. That I am not a woman myself, for
    your sake.
I would have you myself, and a straw for yond
    Gill,
And mock much of you, though it were against
    my will.
I would not, I warrant you, fall in such a rage,
As so to refuse such a goodly personage.
    R. ROISTER. In faith, I heartily thank thee,
    Merrygreek.
    M. MERRY. And I were a woman ——
    R. ROISTER. Thou wouldest to me seek.
    M. MERRY. For, though I say it, a goodly per-
    son ye be.
    R. ROISTER. No, no.
    M. MERRY. Yes, a goodly man, as e'er I did see.
    R. ROISTER. No, I am a poor homely man, as
    God made me.

M. MERRY. By the faith that I owe to God, sir,
    but ye be.
Would I might, for your sake, spend a thousand
    pound land.
    R. ROISTER. I daresay thou wouldest have me
    to thy husband.
    M. MERRY. Yea, and I were the fairest lady in
    the shire,
And knew you as I know you, and see you now
    here—
Well, I say no more—
    R. ROISTER. Gramercies, with all my heart.
    M. MERRY. But, since that cannot be, will ye
    play a wise part?
    R. ROISTER. How should I?
    M. MERRY. Refrain from Custance a while now,
And I warrant her soon right glad to seek to you.
Ye shall see her anon come on her knees creeping,
And pray you to be good to her, salt tears weeping.
    R. ROISTER. But what, and she come not?
    M. MERRY. In faith, then, farewell she.
Or else, if ye be wroth, ye may avenged be.
    R. ROISTER. By Cock's precious potstick, and
    e'en so I shall;
I will utterly destroy her, and house and all.
But I would be avenged in the mean space,
On that vile scribbler, that did my wooing disgrace,
    M. MERRY. Scribbler, ko you? Indeed, he is
    worthy no less.
I will call him to you, and ye bid me, doubtless.
    R. ROISTER. Yes, for although he had as many
    lives
As a thousand widows and a thousand wives,
As a thousand lions and a thousand rats,
A thousand wolves and a thousand cats,
A thousand bulls and a thousand calves,
And a thousand legions divided in halves,

He shall never 'scape death on my sword's point,
Though I should be torn therefore joint by joint.
    M. MERRY. Nay, if ye will kill him, I will not
        fet him,
I will not in so much extremity set him.
He may yet amend, sir, and be an honest man ;
Therefore pardon him, good soul, as much as ye
    can.
    R. ROISTER. Well, for thy sake, this once with
        his life he shall pass ;
But I will hew him all to pieces, by the mass—
    M. MERRY. Nay, faith, ye shall promise that he
        shall no harm have,
Else I will not fet him.
    R. ROISTER. I shall, so God me save !
But I may chide him a good.[1]
    M. MERRY. Yea, that do hardily.
    R. ROISTER. Go then.
    M. MERRY. I return, and bring him to you by
        and by.[2]   [*Ex.*

ACTUS III., SCÆNA V.

ROISTER DOISTER, MATTHEW MERRYGREEK.

R. ROISTER. What is a gentleman, but his word
    and his promise ?
I must now save this villain's life in any wise ;
And yet at him already my hands do tickle,

---

[1] In earnest—heartily. So in Marlow's "Rich Jew of
Malta," 1633, act ii., sc. 3 [sign. E 2, *verso*]—

> "I have laugh'd *a good* to see the cripples
> Goe limping home to Christendome on stilts."—*Cooper.*

[2] This expression, though now generally used to denote
some little lapse of time, formerly signified *immediately.* It
is so used still in the North of England.—*Cooper.*

I shall unneth [1] hold them, they will be so fickle.
But lo, and Merrygreek have not brought him sens! [2]

    M. MERRY. Nay, I would I had of my purse
      paid fortypence.
    SCRIVENER. So would I too : but it needed not
      that stound. [3]
    M. MERRY. But the gentman had rather spent
      five thousand pound ;
For it disgraced him at least five times as much.

[Enter SCRIVENER at one side.]

    SCRIVENER. He disgraced himself, his loutish-
      ness is such.
    R. ROISTER. How long they stand prating. (To
      Merry.) Why com'st thou not away ?
    M. MERRY (to Scriv.) Come now to himself, and
      hark what he will say.
    SCRIVENER. I am not afraid in his presence to
      appear.
    R. ROISTER. Art thou come, fellow ?
    SCRIVENER. How think you ? Am I not here ?
    R. ROISTER. What hindrance hast thou done
      me, and what villainy !
    SCRIVENER. It hath come of thyself, if thou hast
      had any.
    R. ROISTER. All the stock thou comest of, later
      or rather, [4]
From thy first father's grandfather's father's father,
Nor all that shall come of thee, to the world's end,

---

[1] With difficulty—scarcely. See "Second Part of Henry
the Sixth," act ii., sc. 4.—Cooper.

[2] [Since.] The re-entrance of Merrygreek is not marked
in the old copy.—Cooper.

[3] [Time.]

[4] Earlier. Rath, for early, occurs in Chaucer and in
Milton.—Cooper.

Though to three score generations they descend,
Can be able to make a just recompense
For this trespass of thine and this one offence.
    SCRIVENER. Wherein ?
    R. ROISTER. Did not you make me a letter,
       brother ?
    SCRIVENER. Pay the like hire, I will make you
       such an other.
    R. ROISTER. Nay, see, and these whoreson Phari-
       sees and Scribes
Do not get their living by polling[1] and bribes.
If it were not for shame ——
    M. MERRY. Nay, hold thy hands still.[2]
Why, did ye not promise that ye would not him
       spill ?[3]
    SCRIVENER. Let him not spare me.
    R. ROISTER. Why, wilt thou strike me again ?
    SCRIVENER. Ye shall have as good as ye bring
       of me, that is plain.
    M. MERRY. I cannot blame him, sir, though your
       blows would him grieve ;
For he knoweth present death to ensue of all ye give.
    R. ROISTER. Well, this man for once hath pur-
       chased thy pardon.
    SCRIVENER. And what say ye to me ? or else I
       will be gone.
    R. ROISTER. I say, the letter thou madest me
       was not good.
    SCRIVENER. Then did ye wrong copy it, of like-
       lihood.

---

[1] Plundering—

      "Which *polls* and pills the poor in piteous wise."
—*Cooper.*   —*Faerie Queene,* Book v., canto 2.

[2] [In the old copy this half-line is wrongly given to the
Scrivener.]

[3] Destroy.   See "King Lear," act iii., scene 2.—*Cooper.*

R. ROISTER. Yes, out of thy copy, word for
    word, I it wrote.
SCRIVENER. Then was it as you prayed to have
    it, I wot:
But in reading and pointing there was made some
    fault.
R. ROISTER. I wot not; but it made all my
    matter to halt.
SCRIVENER. How say you, is this mine original,
    or no?
R. ROISTER. The self same that I wrote out of,
    so mot I go.
SCRIVENER. Look you on your own fist, and I
    will look on this.
And let this man be judge, whether I read amiss.

To mine own dear coney, bird, sweetheart, and pigsny,
Good Mistress Custance, present these by and by.

How now? doth not this superscription agree?
R. ROISTER. Read that is within, and there ye
    shall the fault see.
SCRIVENER.

" Sweet Mistress, whereas I love you; nothing at
    all
Regarding your riches and substance; chief of all
For your personage, beauty, demeanour and wit,
I commend me unto you; never a whit
Sorry to hear report of your good welfare :
For (as I hear say) such your conditions are,
That ye be worthy favour; of no living man
To be abhorred; of every honest man
To be taken for a woman inclined to vice
Nothing at all; to virtue giving her due price.
Wherefore, concerning marriage, ye are thought
Such a fine paragon as ne'er honest man bought.
And now, by these presents, I do you advertise

That I am minded to marry you ; in no wise
For your goods and substance ; I can be content
To take you as ye are.   If ye will be my wife,
Ye shall be assured for the time of my life
I will keep ye right well : from good raiment and
    fare
Ye shall not be kept : but in sorrow and care
Ye shall in no wise live ; at your own liberty
Do and say what ye lust ; ye shall never please me,
But when ye are merry ; I will be all sad,
When ye are sorry ; I will be very glad,
When ye seek your heart's ease ; I will be unkind
At no time ; in me shall ye much gentleness find.
But all things contrary to your will and mind
Shall be done otherwise.   I will not be behind
To speak ; and as for all they that would do you
    wrong
(I will so help and maintain ye) shall not live long,
Nor any foolish dolt shall cumber you ; but I—
I, whoe'er say nay, will stick by you till I die.
Thus, good Mistress Custance, the Lord you save
    and keep !
From me, Roister Doister, whether I wake or sleep,
Who favoureth you no less (ye may be bold)
Than this letter purporteth, which ye have unfold."

Now, sir, what default can ye find in this letter ?
   R. ROISTER. Of truth, in my mind, there can-
     not be a better.
   SCRIVENER. Then was the fault in reading, and
     not in writing,
No, nor, I dare say, in the form of inditing.
But who read this letter, that it sounded so nought ?
   M. MERRY. I read it indeed.
   SCRIVENER. Ye read it not as ye ought.
   R. ROISTER. Why, thou wretched villain, was all
     this same fault in thee ?

M. MERRY. I knock your costard,[1] if ye offer to
  strike me.
R. ROISTER. Strikest thou indeed, and I offer
  but in jest?
M. MERRY. Yea, and rap ye again, except ye
  can sit in rest.
And I will no longer tarry here, me believe.
  R. ROISTER. What, wilt thou be angry, and I
  do thee forgive?
Fare thou well, scribbler; I cry thee mercy indeed.
  SCRIVENER. Fare ye well, bibbler, and worthily
  may ye speed.
  R. ROISTER. If it were another than thou, it
  were a knave.
M. MERRY. Ye are another yourself, sir, the
  Lord us both save;
Albeit in this matter I must your pardon crave.
Alas! would ye wish in me the wit that ye have?
But, as for my fault, I can quickly amend:
I will show Custance it was I that did offend.
  R. ROISTER. By so doing her anger may be
  reformed.
  M. MERRY. But if by no entreaty she will be
  turned,
Then set light by her, and be as testy as she,
And do your force upon her with extremity.
  R. ROISTER. Come on therefore; let us go home
  in sadness.
  M. MERRY. That if force shall need, all may be
  in readiness.[2]
And as for this letter, hardily let all go;
We will know, whe'er she refuse you for that or no.
                              [Exeant amb.

---

[1] Head.
[2] [It seems a question, whether this line does not belong
to Ralph Roister.]

ACTUS IV., SCÆNA 1.

SIM. SURESBY.

SIM. SURE. Is there any man but I, Sim.
    Suresby, alone,
That would have taken such an enterprise him
    upon ;
In such an outrageous tempest as this was,
Such a dangerous gulf of the sea to pass?
I think verily Neptune's mighty godship
Was angry with some that was in our ship,
And but for the honesty which in me he found,
I think for the other's sake we had been drown'd.
But fie on that servant which, for his master's
    wealth,[1]
Will stick for to hazard both his life and his health.
My master Gawin Goodluck after me a day,
Because of the weather, thought best his ship to
    stay ;
And now that I have the rough surges so well passed,
God grant I may find all things safe here at last.
Then will I think all my travail well-spent.
Now, the first point whereof my master hath me
    sent,
Is to salute dame Christian Custance, his wife
Espoused, whom he tendreth no less than his life.
I must see how it is with her, well or wrong,
And whether for him she doth not now think long.
Then to other friends I have a message or tway ;
And then so to return and meet him on the way.
Now will I go knock, that I may dispatch with
    speed ;
But lo ! forth cometh herself happily indeed.

---

[1] Welfare. Udall uses the word in this sense in his
letter to the Cornish men.—*Cooper.*

ACTUS IV., SCÆNA 2.

CHRISTIAN CUSTANCE, SIM. SURESBY.

C. CUSTANCE. I come to see if any more stirring
be here.
But what stranger is this, which doth to me ap-
pear ?
SIM. SURESBY. I will speak to her. Dame, the
Lord you save and see !
C. CUSTANCE. What, friend Sim. Suresby. For-
sooth, right welcome ye be.
How doth mine own Gawin Goodluck, I pray thee
tell ?
SIM. SURE. When he knoweth of your health,
he will be perfect well.
C. CUSTANCE. If he have perfect health, I am
as I would be.
SIM. SURE. Such news will please him well.
This is as it should be.
C. CUSTANCE. I think now long for him.
SIM. SURE. And he as long for you.
C. CUSTANCE. When will he be at home ?
SIM. SURE. His heart is here e'en now;
His body cometh after.
C. CUSTANCE. I would see that fain.
SIM. SURE. As fast as wind and sail can carry it
a-main.
But what two men are yond coming hitherwards ?
C. CUSTANCE. Now I shrew their best Christ-
mas cheeks both togetherward.

ACTUS IV., SCÆNA 3.

CHRISTIAN CUSTANCE, SIM. SURESBY, RALPH
ROISTER, MATTHEW MERRYGREEK, TRUEPENNY.

C. CUSTANCE. What mean these lewd fellows
  thus to trouble me still?
Sim. Suresby here, perchance, shall thereof deem
  some ill,
And shall suspect in me some point of naughtiness,
And they come hitherward.   [*Aside.*
SIM. SURE. What is their business?
C. CUSTANCE. I have nought to them, nor they
  to me, in sadness.[1]
SIM. SURE. Let us hearken them; somewhat
  there is, I fear it.
R. ROISTER. I will speak out aloud best, that
  she may hear it.
M. MERRY. Nay, alas! ye may so fear her out
  of her wit.
R. ROISTER. By the cross of my sword, I will
  hurt her no whit.
M. MERRY. Will ye do no harm indeed? Shall
  I trust your word?
R. ROISTER. By Roister Doister's faith, I will
  speak but in bord.[2]
SIM. SURE. Let us hearken them: somewhat
  there is, I fear it.
R. ROISTER. I will speak out aloud, I care not
  who hear it.—
Sirs, see that my harness, my target and my shield
Be made as bright now, as when I was last in field:
As white, as I should to war again to-morrow;

---

[1] In seriousness.   [2] In jest.

For sick shall I be, but I work some folk sorrow.
Therefore see that all shine as bright as Saint
    George,
Or as doth a key, newly come from the smith's
    forge.
I would have my sword and harness to shine so
    bright,
That I might therewith dim mine enemies' sight :
I would have it cast beams as fast, I tell you plain,
As doth the glitt'ring grass after a shower of rain.
And see that, in case I should need to come to
    arming,
All things may be ready at a minute's warning.
For such chance may chance in an hour : do ye
    hear ?
    M. MERRY. As perchance shall not chance again
    in seven year.
    R. ROISTER. Now, draw ye near to her, and
    hear what shall be said.
    M. MERRY. But I would not have you make
    her too much afraid.
    R. ROISTER. Well found, sweet wife, (I trust)
    for all this your sour look.
    C. CUSTANCE. Wife ! Why call ye me wife ?
    SIM. SURE (*aside*). Wife ! This gear goeth a-
    crook.
    M. MERRY. Nay, Mistress Custance, I warrant
    you our letter
Is not as we read e'en now, but much better ;
And where ye half stomached[1] this gentleman afore
For this same letter, ye will love him now therefore ;
Nor it is not this letter, though ye were a queen,
That should break marriage between you twain, I
    ween.

---

[1] Disliked or resented. See " Antony and Cleopatra," act
iii., scene 4.—*Cooper.*

C. CUSTANCE. I did not refuse him for the let-
    ter's sake.

R. ROISTER. Then ye are content me for your
    husband to take.

C. CUSTANCE. You for my husband to take!
Nothing less truly?

R. ROISTER. Yea, say so, sweet spouse, afore
    strangers hardily.

M. MERRY. And though I have here his letter of
    love with me,
Yet his rings and tokens he sent keep safe with ye.

C. CUSTANCE. A mischief take his tokens, and
    him, and thee too!
But what prate I with fools? Have I nought else
    to do?
Come in with me, Sim. Suresby, to take some re-
    past.

SIM. SURE. I must, ere I drink, by your leave,
    go in all haste
To a place or two with earnest letters of his.

C. CUSTANCE. Then come drink here with me.

SIM. SURE. I thank you.

C. CUSTANCE. Do not miss.
You shall have a token to your master with you.

SIM. SURE. No tokens this time, gramercies.
    God be with you.   [*Exeat.*

C. CUSTANCE. Surely, this fellow misdeemeth
    some ill in me;
Which thing, but God help, will go near to spill
    me.

R. ROISTER. Yea, farewell, fellow, and tell thy
    master Goodluck,
That he cometh too late of this blossom to pluck.
Let him keep him there still, or at least-wise make
    no haste;
As for his labour hither he shall spend in waste.
His betters be in place now.

M. MERRY. As long as it will hold.

C. CUSTANCE (*aside*). I will be even with thee,
  thou beast, thou may'st be bold.

R. ROISTER. Will ye have us then ?

C. CUSTANCE. I will never have thee.

R. ROISTER. Then will I have you.

C. CUSTANCE. No, the devil shall have thee.
I have gotten this hour more shame and harm by
  thee,
Than all thy life-days thou canst do me honesty.

  M. MERRY. Why, now may ye see what it com'th
  to in the end,
To make a deadly foe of your most loving friend :
And i-wis this letter, if ye would hear it now—

  C. CUSTANCE. I will hear none of it.

  M. MERRY. In faith, ['t]would ravish you.

  C. CUSTANCE. He hath stained my name for
  ever, this is clear.

  R. ROISTER. I can make all as well in an hour.

  M. MERRY. As ten year.
How say ye, will ye have him ?

  C. CUSTANCE. No.

  M. MERRY. Will ye take him—

  C. CUSTANCE. I defy him.

  M. MERRY. At my word ?

  C. CUSTANCE. A shame take him !
Waste no more wind, for it will never be.

  M. MERRY. This one fault with twain shall be
  mended, ye shall see.
Gentle Mistress Custance now, good Mistress
  Custance,
Honey Mistress Custance now, sweet Mistress
  Custance,
Golden Mistress Custance now, white Mistress
  Custance,
Silken Mistress Custance now, fair Mistress Cus-
  tance.

C. CUSTANCE. Faith, rather than to marry with
    such a doltish lout,
I would match myself with a beggar, out of doubt.
    M. MERRY. Then I can say no more; to speed
    we are not like,
Except ye rap out a rag of your rhetoric.
    C. CUSTANCE. Speak not of winning me; for it
    shall never be so.
    R. ROISTER. Yes, dame, I will have you, whether
    ye will or no.
I command you to love me! wherefore should ye
    not?
Is not my love to you chafing and burning hot?
    M. MERRY. To her! that is well said.
    R. ROISTER. Shall I so break my brain,[1]
To doat upon you, and ye not love us again?
    M. MERRY. Well said yet.
    C. CUSTANCE. Go to, thou goose.
    R. ROISTER. I say, Kit Custance,
In case ye will not haze, well; better yes, per-
    chance.
    C. CUSTANCE. Avaunt, losel![2] pick thee hence!
    M. MERRY. Well, sir, ye perceive,
For all your kind offer, she will not you receive.
    R. ROISTER. Then a straw for her, and a straw
    for her again:
She shall not be my wife, would she never so fain;
No, and though she would be at ten thousand
    pound cost.
    M. MERRY. Lo, dame, ye may see what an hus-
    band ye have lost.

---

[1] So in "The Maid's Metamorphosis," 1600: "In vain,
I fear, *I beat my brains* about." These expressions have the
same signification as the "*Cudgel thy brains no more about
it*," of the *First Gravedigger* in "Hamlet."—*Cooper.*

[2] A pitiful, worthless fellow. See "Winter's Tale,"
act ii., sc. 3.—*Cooper.*

C. CUSTANCE. Yea, no force ;[1] a jewel much
    better lost than found.
M. MERRY. Ah, ye will not believe how this
    doth my heart wound.
How should a marriage between you be toward,
If both parties draw back, and become so froward ?
R. ROISTER. Nay, dame, I will fire thee out of
    thy house, [though I die ;[2]]
And destroy thee and all thine, and that by and by.
M. MERRY. Nay, for the passion of God, sir, do
    not so.
R. ROISTER. Yes, except she will say yea to that
    she said no.
C. CUSTANCE. And what, be there no officers,
    trow we, in town,
To check idle loiterers, bragging up and down ?
Where be they by whom vagabonds should be
    represt,
That poor silly widows might live in peace and rest?
Shall I never rid thee out of my company ?
I will call for help.   What, ho ! come forth, True-
    penny !
TRUEPENNY.[3] Anon. What is your will, Mis-
    tress ?   Did ye call me ?
C. CUSTANCE. Yea : go, run apace, and, as fast
    as may be,
Pray Tristram Trusty, my most assured friend,
To be here by and by, that he may me defend.
TRUEPENNY. That message so quickly shall be
    done, by God's grace,
That at my return ye shall say, I went apace.
                        [*Exeat.*

---

[1] No matter.

[2] These words, not in the old copy, are necessary for the
rhyme.—*Cooper.*

[3] His entrance is not marked in the original.—*Cooper.*

C. CUSTANCE. Then shall we see, I trow, whether
    ye shall do me harm.
R. ROISTER. Yes, in faith, Kit, I shall thee and
    thine so charm,
That all women incarnate by thee may beware.
    C. CUSTANCE. Nay, as for charming me, come
    hither if thou dare.
I shall clout thee, till thou stink, both thee and thy
    train,
And coil [1] thee mine own hands, and send thee
    home again.
    R. ROISTER. Yea, say'st thou me that, dame ?
    Dost thou me threaten ?
Go we, I will see whether I shall be beaten.
    M. MERRY. Nay, for the paishe [2] of God, let me
    now treat peace ;
For bloodshed will there be, in case this strife in-
    crease.
Ah, good dame Custance, take better way with you !
    C. CUSTANCE. Let him do his worst !
    M. MERRY. Yield in time.
    R. ROISTER. Come hence, thou !

                    [*Exeant Roister and Merry.*

ACTUS IV., SCÆNA 4.

CHRISTIAN CUSTANCE, ANNOT ALYFACE, TIBET
    TALKAPACE, M. MUMBLECRUST.

C. CUSTANCE. So, sirrah ! If I should not with
    him take this way,

---

[1] Cuff. In Tim Bobbin's "Glossary of the Lancashire
Dialect," a *coil* is explained by "a lump raised on the head
by a blow." See also Brockett's "Glossary of North Country
Words."—*Cooper.*
[2] [Passion.]

I should not be rid of him, I think, till doom's day.
I will call forth my folks, that without any mocks,
If he come again, we may give him raps and knocks.
Madge Mumblecrust, come forth, and Tibet Talk-
    apace ;
Yea, and come forth too, Mistress Annot Alyface.
    AN. ALYFACE. I come.
    TIB. TALK. And I am here.
    M. MUMBL. And I am here too, at length.
    C. CUSTANCE. Like warriors, if need be, ye
        must show your strength.
The man that this day hath thus beguiled you
Is Ralph Roister Doister, whom ye know well enou';
The most lout and dastard that ever on ground trod.
    TIB. TALK. I see all folk mock him, when he
        goeth abroad.
    C. CUSTANCE. What, pretty maid, will ye talk
        when I speak ?
    TIB. TALK. No, forsooth, good mistress.
    C. CUSTANCE. Will ye my tale break ?
He threateneth to come hither with all his force to
        fight ;
I charge you, if he come, on him with all your
        might :
    M. MUMBL. I with my distaff will reach him one
        rap.
    TIB. TALK. And I with my new broom will
        sweep him one swap ;
And then with our great club I will reach him one rap.
And I with our skimmer will fling him one flap.
    TIB. TALK. Then Truepenny's fire-fork will him
        shrewdly fray :
And you with the spit may drive him quite away.
    C. CUSTANCE. Go, make all ready, that it may
        be e'en so.
    TIB. TALK. For my part, I shrew them that last
        about it go.   [Exeant.

ACTUS IV., SCÆNA 5.

CHRISTIAN CUSTANCE, TRUEPENNY, TRISTRAM
TRUSTY.

C. CUSTANCE. Truepenny did promise me to
    run a great pace,
My friend Tristram Trusty to fet into this place.
Indeed he dwelleth hence a good start, I confess ;
But yet a quick messenger might twice since, as I
    guess,
Have gone and come again. Ah ! yond I spy him
    now.
TRUEPENNY (*To T. Trusty*). Ye are a slow goer,
    sir, I make God a vow ;
My Mistress Custance will in me put all the blame ;
Your legs be longer than mine : come apace, for
    shame.
C. CUSTANCE. I can[1] thee thank, Truepenny ;
    thou hast done right well.
TRUEPENNY. Mistress, since I went, no grass
    hath grown on my heel :
But Master Tristram Trusty here maketh no speed.
C. CUSTANCE. That he came at all, I thank him
    in very deed ;
For now have I need of the help of some wise man.
T. TRUSTY. Then may I be gone again, for none
    such I am.
TRUEPENNY. Ye may be by your going ; for no
    Alderman
Can go, I dare say, a sadder[2] pace than ye can.
C. CUSTANCE. Truepenny, get thee in ; thou
    shalt among them know,
How to use thyself like a proper man, I trow.

---

[1] *I can.* See *ante.*   [2] Slower, graver.

TRUEPENNY. I go.   [*Exit.*

C. CUSTANCE. Now, Tristram Trusty, I thank
    you right much :

For at my first sending to come ye never grutch.

T. TRUSTY. Dame Custance, God ye save ; and
    while my life shall last,

For my friend Goodluck's sake ye shall not send
    in waste.

C. CUSTANCE. He shall give you thanks.

T. TRUSTY. I will do much for his sake.

C. CUSTANCE. But alack ! I fear great dis-
    pleasure shall he take.

T. TRUSTY. Wherefore ?

C. CUSTANCE. For a foolish matter.

T. TRUSTY. What is your cause ?

C. CUSTANCE. I am ill accumbred with a couple
    of daws.

T. TRUSTY. Nay, weep not, woman ; but tell me
    what your cause is.

As concerning my friend is anything amiss ?

C. CUSTANCE. No, not on my part ; but here
    was Sim. Suresby—

T. TRUSTY. He was with me, and told me so.

C. CUSTANCE. And he stood by,

While Ralph Roister Doister, with help of Merry-
    greek,

For promise of marriage did unto me seek.

T. TRUSTY. And had ye made any promise
    before them twain ?

C. CUSTANCE. No, I had rather be torn in
    pieces and slain.

No man hath my faith and troth but Gawin
    Goodluck,

And that before Suresby did I say, and there stuck ;

But of certain letters there were such words
    spoken—

T. TRUSTY. He told me that too.

C. CUSTANCE. And of a ring and token;
That Suresby, I spied, did more than half suspect,
That I my faith to Gawin Goodluck did reject.
　　T. TRUSTY. But was there no such matter, Dame
　　　Custance, indeed?
　　C. CUSTANCE. If ever my head thought it, God
　　　send me ill speed!
Wherefore, I beseech you, with me to be a witness,
That in all my life I never intended thing less.
And what a brainsick fool Ralph Roister Doister
　　　is,
Yourself knows well enough.
　　T. TRUSTY. Ye say full true, i-wis.
　　C. CUSTANCE. Because to be his wife I ne grant
　　　nor apply,
Hither will he come, he sweareth, by and by,
To kill both me and mine, and beat down my
　　　house flat;
Therefore I pray your aid.
　　T. TRUSTY. I warrant you that.
　　C. CUSTANCE. Have I so many years lived a
　　　sober life,
And showed myself honest: maid, widow, and
　　　wife,
And now to be abused in such a vile sort?
To see how poor widow live, all void of comfort!
　　T. TRUSTY. I warrant him do you no harm
　　　nor wrong at all.
　　C. CUSTANCE. No, but Matthew Merrygreek
　　　doth me most appal;
That he would join himself with such a wretched
　　　lout.
　　T. TRUSTY. He doth it for a jest, I know him
　　　out of doubt.
And here cometh Merrygreek?
　　C. CUSTANCE. Then shall we hear his mind.

ACTUS IV., SCÆNA 6.

MERRYGREEK, CHRISTIAN CUSTANCE, TRIST. TRUSTY.

M. MERRY. Custance and Trusty both, I do you
  here well find.
C. CUSTANCE. Ah! Matthew Merrygreek, ye
  have used me well!
M. MERRY. Now, for altogether,[1] ye must your
  answer tell.
Will ye have this man, woman, or else will ye
  not?
Else will he come, never boar so brim,[2] nor toast
  so hot.
C. CUSTANCE. But why join ye with him?
T. TRUSTY. For mirth?
C. CUSTANCE. Or else in sadness?
M. MERRY. The more fond of you both: hardily
  the matter guess.
T. TRUSTY. Lo, how say ye, dame?
M. MERRY. Why, do ye think, dame Custance,
That in this wooing I have meant ought but
  pastance?
C. CUSTANCE. Much things ye spake, I wot, to
  maintain his dotage.
M. MERRY. But well might ye judge, I spake it
  all in mockage;
For why is Roister Doister a fit husband for you?
T. TRUSTY. I dare say ye never thought it.
M. MERRY. No, to God I vow.

---

[1] Now, once for all.
[2] *i.e.*, So fierce.   A sow at certain seasons is said *to go to
brim—*

> "They foughten *breme* as it were bolles two."
—*Cooper.*   Chaucer, *Knight's Tale*, line 1701.

And did not I know afore of the insurance
Between Gawin Goodluck and Christian Custance?
And did not I for the nonce, by my conveyance,
Read his letter in a wrong sense for dalliance?
That if you could have take it up at the first bound,
We should thereat such a sport and pastime have
 found,
That all the whole town should have been the
 merrier.
 C. CUSTANCE. Ill ache your heads both! I was
 never wearier,
Nor never more vexed since the first day I was born.
 T. TRUSTY. But very well I wist, he here did
 all in scorn.
 C. CUSTANCE. But I feared thereof to take dis-
 honesty.
 M. MERRY. This should both have made sport,
 and showed your honesty;
And Goodluck, I dare swear, your wit therein
 would 'low.[1]
 T. TRUSTY. Yea, being no worse than we know
 it to be now.
 M. MERRY. And nothing yet too late: for, when
 I come to him,
Hither will he repair with a sheep's look full grim,
By plain force and violence to drive you to yield.
 C. CUSTANCE. If ye two bid me, we will with
 him pitch a field,
I and my maids together.
 M. MERRY. Let us see; be bold!
 C. CUSTANCE. Ye shall see women's war.
 T. TRUSTY. That fight will I behold.
 M. MERRY. If occasion serve, taking his part
 full brim,
I will strike at you, but the rap shall light on him.

---

[1] Allow.

When we first appear—
  C. CUSTANCE. Then will I run away,
As though I were afeard.
  T. TRUSTY. Do you that part well play,
And I will sue for peace.
  M. MERRY. And I will set him on ;
Then will he look as fierce as a Cotsold lion.[1]
  T. TRUSTY. But when goest thou for him ?
  M. MERRY. That do I very now.
  C. CUSTANCE. Ye shall find us here.
  M. MERRY. Well, God have mercy on you.
                                    [Exit.
  T. TRUSTY. There is no cause of fear ; the least
    boy in the street—
  C. CUSTANCE. Nay, the least girl I have, will
    make him take his feet.
But, hark ! me-think they make preparation.
  T. TRUSTY. No force, it will be a good recreation.
  C. CUSTANCE. I will stand within, and step forth
    speedily,
And so make as though I ran away dreadfully.

ACTUS IV., SCÆNA 7.

R. ROISTER, M. MERRYGREEK, C. CUSTANCE, D.
DOUGHTY, HARPAX, TRISTRAM TRUSTY.

  R. ROISTER. Now, sirs, keep your 'ray, and see
    your hearts be stout.
But where be these caitiffs ? Me-think they dare
    not rout.[2]

---

[1] A sheep. Cotswold (pronounced Cotsold) is an old word
for a sheepcote. Hence the name of the hills in Gloucester-
shire.—*Cooper.*

[2] To assemble. It is used by Bacon in his " History of
Henry the Seventh," p. 68, fol. 1629.—*Cooper.*

How sayest thou, Merrygreek? What doth Kit
    Custance say?
  M. MERRY. I am loth to tell you.
  R. ROISTER. Tush, speak, man. Yea or nay?
  M. MERRY. Forsooth, sir, I have spoken for you
    all that I can;
But if ye win her, ye must e'en play the man:
E'en to fight it out ye must a man's heart take.
  R. ROISTER. Yes, they shall know, as[1] thou
    knowest, I have a stomach.
  M. MERRY. A stomach (quod you), yea, as good
    as e'er man had.
  R. ROISTER. I trow, they shall find and feel that
    I am a lad.
  M. MERRY. By this cross, I have seen you eat
    your meat as well
As any that e'er I have seen of, or heard tell.
A stomach, quod you? He that will that deny,
I know was never at dinner in your company.
  R. ROISTER. Nay, the stomach of a man it is,
    that I mean.
  M. MERRY. Nay, the stomach of an horse or a
    dog, I ween.
  R. ROISTER. Nay, a man's stomach with a weapon,
    mean I.
  M. MERRY. Ten men can scarce match you with
    a spoon in a pie.
  R. ROISTER. Nay, the stomach of a man to try
    in strife.
  M. MERRY. I never saw your stomach cloyed
    yet in my life.
  R. ROISTER. Tush, I mean in strife or fighting
    to try.
  M. MERRY. We shall see how ye will strike now,
    being angry.

---

[1] [Old copy, *and.*]

R. ROISTER. Have at thy pate then, and save
    thy head, if thou may.
M. MERRY. Nay, then, have at your pate again,
    by this day.
R. ROISTER. Nay, thou mayest not strike at me
    again in no wise.
M. MERRY. I cannot in fight make to you such
    warrantise :
But as for your foes here let them the bargain [1] by.
R. ROISTER. Nay, as for [that,] they shall every
    mother's child die.
And in this my fume a little thing might make me
To beat down house and all, and else the devil
    take me.
M. MERRY. If I were as ye be, by Gog's dear
    mother,
I would not leave one stone upon another.
Though she would redeem it with twenty thousand
    pounds.
R. ROISTER. It shall be even so, by his lily
    wounds !
M. MERRY. Be not at one with her [2] upon any
    amends.
R. ROISTER. No, though she make to me never
    so many friends.
Not if all the world for her would undertake :
No, not God himself neither shall not her peace
    make.
On therefore, march forward !   Soft, stay a while
    yet.
M. MERRY. On !
R. ROISTER. Tarry.
M. MERRY. Forth !
R. ROISTER. Back.

---

[1] [Abide by the bargain.]
[2] *i.e.*, Be not reconciled to her.—*Cooper.*

M. MERRY. On !
R. ROISTER. Soft.   Now forward set.

Enter C. CUSTANCE.

C. CUSTANCE. What business have we here ?
    Out, alas, alas !
R. ROISTER. Ha, ha, ha, ha, ha !
Didst thou see that, Merrygreek, how afraid she was ?
Didst thou see how she fled apace out of my sight ?
Ah, good sweet Custance ! I pity her, by this light.
    M. MERRY. That tender heart of yours will mar
        altogether ;
Thus will ye be turned with wagging of a feather.
    R. ROISTER. On, sirs, keep your 'ray.
    M. MERRY. On forth, while this gear is hot.
    R. ROISTER. Soft, the Arms of Calais, I have
        one thing forgot.
    M. MERRY. What lack we now ?
    R. ROISTER. Retire, or else we be all slain.
    M. MERRY. Back, for the pash of God ! back,
        sirs, back again !
What is the great matter ?
    R. ROISTER. This hasty forth-going
Had almost brought us all to utter undoing ;
It made me forget a thing most necessary.
    M. MERRY. Well remembered of a captain, by
        Saint Mary.
    R. ROISTER. It is a thing must be had.
    M. MERRY. Let us have it then.
    R. ROISTER. But I wot not where or how.
    M. MERRY. Then wot not I when.
But what is it ?
    R. ROISTER. Of a chief thing I am to seek.
    M. MERRY. Tut, so will ye be, when ye have
        studied a week.   [*Aside.*
But tell me what it is ?

R. ROISTER. I lack yet an headpiece.
M. MERRY. The kitchen collocavit the best hens
    to grease ;
Run, fet it, Dobinet, and come at once withal,
And bring with thee my potgun,[1] hanging by the
    wall.[2]
I have seen your head with it, full many a time,
Covered as safe as it had been with a scrine :
And I warrant it save your head from any stroke,
Except perchance to be amazed with the smoke :
I warrant your head therewith, except for the mist,
As safe as if it were fast locked up in a chist.
And lo, here our Dobinet cometh with it now.
    D. DOUGH. It will cover me to the shoulders
    well enou'.
    M. MERRY. Let me see it on.
    R. ROISTER. In faith, it doth meetly well.
    M. MERRY. There can be no fitter thing. Now
    ye must us tell
What to do.
    R. ROISTER. Now forth in 'ray, sirs, and stop
    no more.
    M. MERRY. Now, Saint George to borrow ![3]
    Drum, dub-a-dub afore.
    T. TRUSTY. What mean you to do, sir ? Com-
    mit manslaughter ?
    R. ROISTER. To kill forty such is a matter of
    laughter.
    T. TRUSTY. And who is it, sir, whom ye intend
    thus to spill ?

---

[1] A small gun, perhaps a corruption of *popgun.—Cooper*.

[2] The exit and re-entry of Dobinet are not marked in the old copy.—*Cooper*.

[3] To protect or guard. In " Richard II.," act i., sc. 3, the expression is—

    " Mine innocency and Saint George to thrive ! "—*Cooper*.

R. ROISTER. Foolish Custance here forceth me
    against my will
T. TRUSTY. And is there no mean your extreme
    wrath to slake?
She shall some amends unto your good maship
    make.
R. ROISTER. I will none amends.
T. TRUSTY. Is her offence so sore?
M. MERRY. And he were a lout, she could have
    done no more.
She hath call'd him fool, and 'dressed him like a
    fool,
Mocked him like a fool, used him like a fool.
    T. TRUSTY. Well, yet the Sheriff, the Justice or
        Constable,
Her misdemeanour to punish might be able.
    R. ROISTER. No, sir, I mine own self will, in
        this present cause,
Be Sheriff and Justice, and whole Judge of the
    laws.
This matter to amend all officers be I shall:
Constable, Bailiff, Sergeant—
    M. MERRY. And hangman, and all.   [Aside.
    T. TRUSTY. Yet a noble courage and the heart
        of a man
Should more honour win by bearing with a woman.
Therefore take the law, and let her answer thereto.
    R. ROISTER. Merrygreek, the best way were
        even so to do.
What honour should it be with a woman to fight?
    M. MERRY. And what, then, will ye thus forego
        and lese your right?
    R. ROISTER. Nay, I will take the law on her
        withouten grace.
    T. TRUSTY. Or, if your maship could pardon this
        one trespass—
I pray you, forgive her.

R. ROISTER. Hoh !
M. MERRY. Tush, tush, sir, do not.
T. TRUSTY. Be good master to her.
R. ROISTER. Hoh !
M. MERRY. Tush, I say, do not.
And what ! shall your people here return straight
    home ?
R. ROISTER. Yea, levy the camp, sirs, and hence
    again each one.
But be still in readiness, if I hap to call ;[1]
I cannot tell what sudden chance may befall.
    M. MERRY. Do not off your harness, sirs, I you
    advise,
At the least for this fortnight, in no manner wise.
Perchance in an hour, when all ye think least,
Our master's appetite to fight will be best.
But soft, ere ye go, have once at Custance house.
    R. ROISTER. Soft, what wilt thou do ?
    M. MERRY. Once discharge my arquebus ;
And for my heart's ease, have once more with my
    potgun.
    R. ROISTER. Hold thy hands ! else is all our
    purpose clean fordone.
M. MERRY. And it cost me my life !
R. ROISTER. I say, thou shalt not.
M. MERRY. By the matt,[2] but I will have once
    more with hail-shot.
I will have some pennyworth ; I will not lese all.

---

[1] T. Trusty is the prefix to this and the following line in
the old copy, but it must be an error.—*Cooper.*
[2] [Put for *mass,* as *Gog* for *God,* &c.]

ACTUS IV., SCÆNA 8.

M. MERRYGREEK, C. CUSTANCE, R. ROYSTER, TIB. T., AN. ALYFACE, M. MUMBLECRUST, TRUEPENNY, DOBINET DOUGHTY, HARPAX.

Two drums with their Ensigns.

C. CUSTANCE. What caitiffs are those, that so shake my house-wall?

M. MERRY. Ah, sirrah now Custance, if ye had so much wit,

I would see you ask pardon, and yourselves submit.

C. CUSTANCE. Have I still this ado with a couple of fools?

M. MERRY. Hear ye what she saith?

C. CUSTANCE. Maidens, come forth with your tools,

In a ray.

M. MERRY. Dubba-dub, sirrah!

R. ROISTER. In a ray!

They come suddenly on us.

M. MERRY. Dub-a-dub-dub!

R. ROISTER. In a ray!

That ever I was born! we are taken tardy.

M. MERRY. Now, sirs, quit yourselves like tall men and hardy.

C. CUSTANCE. On afore, Truepenny! Hold thine own, Annot!

On toward them, Tibet, for scape us they cannot!

Come forth, Madge Mumblecrust! so, stand fast together.

M. MERRY. God send us a fair day!

R. ROYSTER. See, they march on hither.

TIB. TALK. But, mistress—

C. CUSTANCE. What say'st thou?

TIB. TALK. Shall I go fet our goose?

C. CUSTANCE. What to do?

TIB. TALK. To yonder Captain I will turn her loose.

And she gape and hiss at him, as she doth at me,
I durst jeopard my hand she will make him flee.[1]

C. CUSTANCE. On forward!

R. ROISTER. They come.

M. MERRY. Stand!

R. ROISTER. Hold!

M. MERRY. Keep!

R. ROISTER. There!

M. MERRY. Strike!

R. ROISTER. Take heed!

C. CUSTANCE. Well said, Truepenny!

TRUEPENNY. Ah, whoresons!

C. CUSTANCE. Well done, indeed!

M. MERRY. Hold thine own, Harpax! Down with them, Dobinet!

C. CUSTANCE. Now, Madge; there, Annot; now stick them, Tibet!

TIB. TALK. All my chief quarrel is to this same little knave,

That beguiled me last day; nothing shall him save.

D. DOUGH. Down with this little quean, that hath at me such spite!

Save you from her, master, it is a very sprite.

C. CUSTANCE. I myself will mounsire grand captain undertake.

---

[1] [An idea perhaps borrowed from the interlude of "Thersites," where we have the ludicrous incident of the snail. Udall has drawn Ralph Roister Doister somewhat on the model of "Thersites," except that in Roister Doister the man's good nature and singleness of character win our regard, whereas the other is a contemptible braggart without any redeeming trait.]

R. ROISTER. They win ground!

M. MERRY. Save yourself, sir, for God's sake!

R. ROISTER. Out, alas! I am slain; help!

M. MERRY. Save yourself!

R. ROISTER. Alas!

M. MERRY. Nay, then, have at you, mistress.

R. ROISTER. Thou hittest me, alas!

M. MERRY. I will strike at Custance here.

R. ROISTER. Thou hittest me!

M. MERRY. (*aside.*) So I will.

Nay, mistress Custance.

R. ROISTER. Alas! thou hittest me still.

Hold!

M. MERRY. Save yourself, sir!

R. ROISTER. Help! out alas! I am slain.

M. MERRY. Truce, hold your hands! truce, for
a pissing while or twain.[1]

Now, how say you, Custance, for saving of your life,
Will ye yield, and grant to be this gentleman's wife?

C. CUSTANCE. Ye told me he loved me; call ye
this love?

M. MERRY. He loved a while, even like a turtle-
dove.

C. CUSTANCE. Gay love, God save it! so soon
hot, so soon cold.

M. MERRY. I am sorry for you: he could love
you yet, so he could.

R. ROISTER. Nay, by Cock's precious, she shall
be none of mine.

M. MERRY. Why so?

R. ROISTER. Come away, by the matt, she is
mankine.[2]

---

[1] See "Two Gentlemen of Verona," act. iv., scene 4.—
Cooper.

[2] *Mankind* is used by Shakespeare and other writers of his
time as an adjective, in the sense of masculine.—*Cooper.*

I durst adventure the loss of my right hand.
If she did not slee her other husband.
And see, if she prepare not again to fight!

M. MERRY. What, then, Saint George to bor-
row, our Lady's knight?

R. ROISTER. Slee else whom she will, by Gog, she
shall not slee me.

M. MERRY. How then?

R. ROISTER. Rather than to be slain, I will flee.

C. CUSTANCE. To it again, my knightesses! down
with them all!

R. ROISTER. Away, away, away! she will else
kill us all.

M. MERRY. Nay, stick to it, like an hardy man
and a tall.

R. ROISTER. O bones, thou hittest me! Away,
or else die we shall.

M. MERRY. Away, for the pash of our sweet
Lord Jesus Christ!

C. CUSTANCE. Away, lout and lubber, or I
shall be thy priest!   [*Exeant Om.*[1]

So this field is ours; we have driven them all away.

TIB. TALK. Thanks to God, mistress, ye have
had a fair day.

C. CUSTANCE. Well, now go ye in, and make
yourself some good cheer.

OMNES PARITER.   We go.

T. TRUSTY. Ah, sir! what a field we have had
here.

C. CUSTANCE. Friend Tristram, I pray you be a
witness with me.

T. TRUSTY. Dame Custance, I shall depose for
your honesty.

---

[1] So in the old copy, but Ralph, Mat., Dob., and Harpax,
only go out; lower down, the *exeat* of course applies to T.
Trusty.—*Cooper.*

And now fare ye well, except something else ye
    would.
   C. CUSTANCE. Not now, but when I need to
    send, I will be bold.   *[Exeat.*
I thank you for these pains. And now I will get
    me in.
Now Roister Doister will no more wooing begin.
                          [Ex.

ACTUS V., SCÆNA 1.

GAWIN GOODLUCK, SIM. SURESBY.

   G. GOOD. Sim. Suresby, my trusty man, now ad-
    vise thee well,
And see that no false surmises thou me tell.
Was there such ado about Custance, of a truth?
   SIM. SURE. To report that I heard and saw to
    me is ruth;
But both my duty, and name, and property,[1]
Warneth me to you to show fidelity.
It may be well enough, and I wish it so to be,
She may herself discharge, and try her honesty;
Yet their claim to her, me-thought, was very large,
For with letters, rings, and tokens they did her
    charge.
Which when I heard and saw, I would none to
    you bring.
   G. GOOD. No, by Saint Mary, I allow thee [2] in
    that thing.
Ah sirrah! now I see truth in the proverb old:
All things that shineth is not by and by pure gold.

---

  [1] [Peculiar place or function.]
  [2] *i.e.,* I approve of your conduct. See "Second Part of
Henry IV.," act iv., sc. 2; "King Lear," act ii., sc. 4; and
Romans, c. xiv., v. 22.—*Cooper.*

If any do live a woman of honesty,
I would have sworn Christian Custance had been
    she.
    Sim. Sure. Sir, though I to you be a servant
    true and just,
Yet do not ye therefore your faithful spouse mis-
    trust;
But examine the matter, and if ye shall it find
To be all well, be not ye for my words unkind.
    G. Good. I shall do that is right, and as I see
    cause why.
But here cometh Custance forth; we shall know
    by and by.

ACTUS V., SCÆNA 2.

C. Custance, Gawin Goodluck, Sim. Suresby.

    C. Custance. I come forth to see and hearken
    for news good;
For about this hour is the time, of likelihood,
That Gawin Goodluck, by the sayings of Suresby,
Would be at home; and lo! yond I see him, I.
What, Gawin Goodluck! the only hope of my life,
Welcome home, and kiss me your true espoused
    wife.
    G. Good. Nay, soft, dame Custance; I must
    first, by your licence,
See whether all things be clear in your conscience.
I hear of your doings to me very strange.
    C. Custance. What! fear ye that my faith to-
    wards you should change?
    G. Good. I must needs mistrust ye be elsewhere
    entangled,
For I hear that certain men with you have wrangled

About the promise of marriage by you to them
    made.
    C. CUSTANCE. Could any man's report therein
    your mind persuade !
    G. GOOD. Well, you must therein declare your-
    self to stand clear,
Else I and you, dame Custance, may not join this
    year.
    C. CUSTANCE. Then would I were dead, and
    fair laid in my grave.
Ah ! Suresby, is this the honesty that ye have,
To hurt me with your report, not knowing the
    thing ?
    SIM. SURE. If ye be honest, my words can hurt
    you nothing ;
But what I heard and saw, I might not but report,
    C. CUSTANCE. Ah, Lord, help poor widows,
    destitute of comfort !
Truly, most dear spouse, nought was done but for
    pastance.
    G. GOOD. But such kind of sporting is homely
    daliance.
    C. CUSTANCE. If ye knew the truth, ye would
    take all in good part.
    G. GOOD. By your leave, I am not half well-
    skilled in that art.
    C. CUSTANCE. It was none but Roister Doister,
    that foolish mome.
    G. GOOD. Yea, Custance, better (they say) a bad
    excuse than none.
    C. CUSTANCE. Why, Tristram Trusty, sir, your
    true and faithful friend,
Was privy both to the beginning and the end.
Let him be the judge, and for me testify.
    G. GOOD. I will the more credit that he shall
    verify ;
And because I will the truth know, e'en as it is,

I will to him myself, and know all without miss.
Come on, Sim. Suresby, that before my friend thou
    may
Avouch thee the same words, which thou did'st to
    me say.   *[Exeant.*

ACTUS V., SCÆNA 3.

CHRISTIAN CUSTANCE.

C. CUSTANCE. O Lord ! how necessary it is now
    of days,
That each body live uprightly all manner ways ;
For let never so little a gap be open,
And be sure of this, the worst shall be spoken.
How innocent stand I in this for deed or thought,
And yet see what mistrust towards me it hath
    wrought.
But thou, Lord, knowest all folks' thoughts, and
    eke intents ;
And thou art the deliverer of all innocents.
Thou didst help the advoutress,[1] that she might be
    amended ;
Much more then help, Lord, that never ill intended.
Thou didst help Susanna, wrongfully accused,
And no less dost thou see, Lord, how I am now
    abused.
Thou didst help Hester, when she should have
    died ;
Help also, good Lord, that my truth may be tried.
Yet, if Gawin Goodluck with Tristram Trusty
    speak,

---

[1] Adulteress, from the old French *advoultrer*. In Cart-
wright's " Ordinary," act iv., sc. 5, the *Constable* says, " I'll
look there shall be no *advoutry* in my ward."—*Cooper.*

I trust of ill-report the force shall be but weak ;
And lo ! yond they come, sadly talking together :
I will abide, and not shrink for their coming hither.

ACTUS V., SCÆNA 4.

GAWIN GOODLUCK, TRISTRAM TRUSTY, C. CUSTANCE, SIM. SURESBY.

G. GOOD. And was it none other than ye to me
  report ?
T. TRUSTY. No ; and here were ye wished, to
  have seen the sport.
G. GOOD. Would I had, rather than half of that
  in my purse.
SIM. SURE. And I do much rejoice the matter
  was no worse.
And like as to open it I was to you faithful,
So of Dame Custance honest truth I am joyful.
For God forfend that I should hurt her by false
  report.
G. GOOD. Well, I will no longer hold her in dis-
  comfort.
C. CUSTANCE. Now come they hitherward : I
  trust all shall be well.
G. GOOD. Sweet Custance, neither heart can
  think, nor tongue tell,
How much I joy in your constant fidelity.
Come now, kiss me, the pearl of perfect honesty.
C. CUSTANCE. God let me no longer to continue
  in life,
Than I shall towards you continue a true wife.
G. GOOD. Well, now to make you for this some
  part of amends,
I shall desire first you, and then such of our friends
As shall to you seem best, to sup at home with me,

Where at your fought field we shall laugh and
    merry be.
  SIM. SURE. And, mistress, I beseech you take
    with me no grief : [1]
I did a true man's part, not wishing your repreef.
  C. CUSTANCE. Though hasty reports, through
    surmises growing,
May of poor innocents be utter overthrowing,
Yet because to thy master thou hast a true heart,
And I know mine own truth, I forgive thee for my
    part.
  G. GOOD. Go we all to my house, and of this
    gear no more.
Go, prepare all things, Sim. Suresby ; hence, run
    afore.
  SIM. SURE. I go.   [Ex.
  G. GOOD. Good. But who cometh yond ? Master
    Merrygreek ?
  C. CUSTANCE. Roister Doister's champion ; I
    shrew his best cheek.
  T. TRUSTY. Roister Doister's self, your wooer, is
    with him too.
Surely some thing there is with us they have to do.

ACTUS V., SCÆNA 5.

M. MERRYGREEK, RALPH ROISTER [*to them*], GAWIN
  GOODLUCK, TRISTRAM TRUSTY, C. CUSTANCE.

  M. MERRY. Yonder I see Gawin Goodluck, to
    whom lieth my message.
I will first salute him after his long voyage,
And then make all things well concerning your
    behalf.

---

[1] *i.e.*, Bear me no ill-will.

R. ROISTER. Yea, for the pash of God.

M. MERRY. Hence ! out of sight, ye calf,
Till I have spoke with them, and then I will you
    fet.

R. ROISTER. In God's name.[1]

M. MERRY. What, master Gawin Goodluck,
    well-met ;
And from your long voyage I bid you right wel-
    come home.

G. GOOD. I thank you.

M. MERRY. I come to you from an honest mome,

G. GOOD. Who is that ?

M. MERRY. Roister Doister, that doughty kite.

C. CUSTANCE. Fie ! I can scarce abide ye should
    his name recite.

M. MERRY. Ye must take him to favour, and
    pardon all past ;
He heareth of your return, and is full ill aghast.

G. GOOD. I am right well content he have with
    us some cheer.

C. CUSTANCE. Fie upon him, beast ! then will
    not I be there.

G. GOOD. Why, Custance, do ye hate him more
    than ye love me ?

C. CUSTANCE. But for your mind, sir, where he
    were, would I not be.

T. TRUSTY. He would make us all laugh.

M. MERRY. Ye ne'er had better sport.

G. GOOD. I pray you, sweet Custance, let him
    to us resort.

C. CUSTANCE. To your will I assent.

M. MERRY. Why, such a fool it is,
As no man for good pastime would forego or miss.

G. GOOD. Fet him to go with us.

M. MERRY. He will be a glad man.   [*Ex.*

---

[1] With these words R. Roister evidently retires.—*Cooper.*

T. TRUSTY. We must, to make us mirth, main-
tain him [1] all we can.
And lo, yond' he cometh, and Merrygreek with
him.
C. CUSTANCE. At his first entrance, ye shall see
I will him trim.
But first let us hearken the gentleman's wise talk.
T. TRUSTY. I pray you, mark, if ever ye saw
crane so stalk.

ACTUS V., SCÆNA 6.

R. ROISTER, M. MERRYGREEK, C. CUSTANCE, G.
GOODLUCK, T. TRUSTY, D. DOUGHTY, HARPAX.

R. ROISTER. May I then be bold ?
M. MERRY. I warrant you on my word.
They say they shall be sick, but ye be at their
board.
R. ROISTER. They were not angry, then ?
M. MERRY. Yes, at first, and made strange ;
But when I said your anger to favour should
change,
And therewith had commended you accordingly,
They were all in love with your maship by and by ;
And cried you mercy, that they had done you
wrong.
R. ROISTER. For why no man, woman, nor child
can hate me long.
M. MERRY. We fear (quod they) he will be
avenged one day ;

---

[1] Encourage him. So in the epistle to Gabriel Harvey,
prefixed to Spenser's "Shepherd's Calendar": "The Right
Worshipfull Maister Philip Sidney is a speciall favourer and
maintainer of all kinde of learning."—*Cooper.*

Then for a penny give all our lives we may.

    R. ROISTER. Said they so indeed?

    M. MERRY. Did they? yea, even with one
    voice.

He will forgive all (quod I). O, how they did
    rejoice!

    R. ROISTER. Ha, ha, ha!

    M. MERRY. Go fet him (say they), while he is in
    good mood;

For have his anger who lust, we will not, by the rood!

    R. ROISTER. I pray God that it be all true, that
    thou hast me told,

And that she fight no more.

    M. MERRY. I warrant you; be bold.

To them, and salute them.

    R. ROISTER. Sirs, I greet you all well.

    OMNES. Your mastership is welcome.

    C. CUSTANCE. Saving my quarrel,

For sure I will put you up into the Exchequer.

    M. MERRY. Why so? Better nay. Wherefore?

    C. CUSTANCE. For an usurer.

    R. ROISTER. I am no usurer, good mistress, by
    His arms.

    M. MERRY. When took he gain of money, to any
    man's harms?

    C. CUSTANCE. Yes, a foul usurer he is, ye shall
    see else.

    R. ROISTER. Did'st not thou promise she would
    pick no mo quarrels?   *[To Merr.*

    C. CUSTANCE. He will lend no blows, but he
    have in recompense

Fifteen for one, which is too much of conscience.

    R. ROISTER. Ah dame! by the ancient law of
    arms, a man

Hath no honour to foil his hands on a woman.

    C. CUSTANCE. And where other usurers take
    their gains yearly,

This man is angry, but he have his by and by.
   G. GOOD. Sir, do not for her sake bear me your
     displeasure.
   M. MERRY. Well, he shall with you talk thereof
     more at leisure.
Upon your good usage he will now shake your hand.
   R. ROISTER. And much heartily welcome from a
     strange land.
   M. MERRY. Be not afeard, Gawin, to let him
     shake your fist.
   G. GOOD. O, the most honest gentleman that
     e'er I wist.
I do beseech your maship to take pain to sup with us.
   M. MERRY. He shall not say you nay, (and I
     too by Jesus,)
Because ye shall be friends, and let all quarrels pass.
   R. ROISTER. I will be as good friends with them
     as e'er I was.
   M. MERRY. Then, let me fet your quire, that we
     may have a song.
   R. ROISTER. Go.
   G. GOOD. I have heard no melody all this year
     long.
   M. MERRY.[1] Come on, sirs, quickly.
   R. ROISTER. Sing on, sirs, for my friend's sake.
   D. DOUGH. Call ye these your friends?
   R. ROISTER. Sing on, and no mo words make.
                    [*Here they sing.*
   G. GOOD. The Lord preserve our most noble
     Queen of renown,[2]

---

[1] The exit and re-entry are not marked.—*Cooper.*

[2] [It seems probable that this prayer at the end was intended for Queen Elizabeth, not for her predecessor. The
original prayer, if there was one, on the first presentation of
the comedy, may have been suppressed in favour of one to
suit the new circumstances.]

And her virtues reward with the heavenly crown.
   C. CUSTANCE. The Lord strengthen her most
     excellent Majesty,
Long to reign over us in all prosperity.
   T. TRUSTY. That her godly proceedings, the
     faith to defend,
He may stablish and maintain through to the end.
   M. MERRY. God grant her, as she doth, the Gos-
     pel to protect,
Learning and virtue to advance, and vice to correct.
   R. ROISTER. God grant her loving subjects both
     the mind and grace
Her most godly proceedings worthily to embrace.
   HARPAX. Her highness most worthy coun-
     cillors God prosper,
With honour and love all men to minister.
   OMNES. God grant the nobility her to serve and
     love,
With all the common'ty, as doth them behove !
            AMEN.[1]

Certain Songs [2] to be sung by those which shall
    use this Comedy or Interlude.

The Second Song.

Who so to marry a minion wife,[3]
Hath had good chance and hap,

---

[1] Ancient interludes frequently ended with a prayer,
which it was the custom of the players to deliver kneeling.
—*Cooper.*

[2] These are the songs referred to in the body of the
Comedy.

[3] A *pet* or *darling* wife.—*Cooper.*

Must love her and cherish her all his life,
  And dandle her in his lap,

If she will fare well, if she will go gay,
  A good husband ever still,
Whatever she lust to do or to say,
  Must let her have her own will,

About what affairs soever he go,
  He must show her all his mind,
None of his counsels she may be kept fro,
  Else is he a man unkind.

The Fourth Song.

I mun be married a Sunday;
I mun be married a Sunday;
Whosoever shall come that way,
I mun be married a Sunday.

Roister Doister is my name;
Roister Doister is my name;
A lusty brute I am the same;
I mun be married a Sunday.

Christian Custance have I found;
Christian Custance have I found;
A widow worth a thousand pound:
I mun be married a Sunday.

Custance is as sweet as honey;
Custance is as sweet as honey;
I her lamb, and she my coney;
I mun be married a Sunday.

When we shall make our wedding feast,
When we shall make our wedding feast,
There shall be cheer for man and beast;
I mun be married a Sunday.
    I mun be married a Sunday, &c.

The Psalmody.

Placebo dilexi.
Master Roister Doister will straight go home and die,
Our Lord Jesus Christ his soul have mercy upon:
Thus you see, to-day a man, to-morrow John.[1]
Yet, saving for a woman's extreme cruelty,
He might have lived yet a month, or two, or three;
But in spite of Custance, which hath him wearied,
His maship shall be worshipfully buried.
And while some piece of his soul is yet him within,
Some part of his funeral let us here begin.
Dirige.   He will go darkling[2] *to his grave;*
Neque lux, neque crux, nisi solum clink;
Never genman so went toward heaven, I think.
Yet, sirs, as ye will the bliss of heaven win,
When he cometh to the grave, lay him softly in;
And all men take heed by this one gentleman,
How you set your love upon an unkind woman;
For these women be all such mad peevish elves,
They will not be won, except it please themselves.
But, in faith, Custance, if ever ye come in hell,
Master Roister Doister shall serve you as well.

Good night, Roger, old knave; farewell, Roger, old
    knave;
Good night, Roger, old knave; knave, knap.
Ne quando.   Audivi vocem.   Requiem æternam.

---

[1] [Query, *Sir John, i.e.,* the priest, to say the requiem.
See Hazlitt's "Proverbs," p. 414.]
[2] ["So out went the candle, and we were left darkling,"
"King Lear," i. 4 ; Dyce's 2d edit. vii. 269.]

*The Peal of bells rung by the parish Clerk and
Roister Doister's four men.*

The first Bell, a Triple. When died he? When
    died he?
The second. We have him! We have him!
The third. Roister Doister! Roister Doister!
The fourth Bell. He cometh! He cometh!
The great Bell. Our own! Our own!

FINIS.

GAMMER GURTON'S NEEDLE.

*A Ryght Pithy, Pleasaunt, and merie Comedie: Intytuled
Gammer gurtons Needle: Played on Stage not longe ago
in Christes Colledge in Cambridge. Made by Mr S. Mr.
of Art. Imprynted at London, in Fleetestreat beneth the
Conduit at the signe of S. John Euangelist, by Thomas
Colwell. 1575. 4º. Black letter.*

There was a second edition, 4to, 1661, which is of no
value.

[I found this introduction to "Gammer Gurton's
Needle" among some collections made by my father
about twenty years ago for a similar purpose, and as it
was much fuller than that previously printed, it has
been substituted. I have, however, introduced a few
additions from the Memoirs of Still in the "Athenæ
Cantabrigienses," ii., 467, and the "Proceedings of the
Suffolk Institute of Archæology," iii., 130, the latter
kindly communicated to me by Mr Joseph Bryant, of
Cheshunt.—W. C. H.]

PREFACE.

JOHN STILL, the reputed author of this play, was the only son of William Still, Esq. of Grantham, in Lincolnshire, and was born in or about 1543. In 1559 he matriculated as a pensioner in Christ's College, Cambridge, proceeded B.A. in 1561–2, and was elected M.A. in 1565. In 1570 he was presented to the rectory of St Martin Outwich, London, and in the same year proceeded B.D. On the 30th July 1571, Archbishop Parker collated Still to the rectory of Hadleigh, in Suffolk, and in 1572 the primate, to whom he was chaplain, appointed him, with Dr Watts, Joint-Dean of Bocking. Other church preferments followed in quick succession; but this is perhaps scarcely a place for entering at large into biographical particulars, more especially as the authorship of the drama is a little uncertain. We must content ourselves with noting his gradual rise from the deanery of Bocking to the canonry at Westminster, the mastership of St John's College, Cambridge, the vice-chancellorship of the university on two occasions, the mastership of Trinity College, Cambridge, and finally, the bishopric of Bath and Wells, to which last dignity he was named 16 January 1592-3. He died at the episcopal palace at Wells, February 26, 1607-8, and was buried, on the 4th April following, in the cathedral, where a handsome monument was erected to his memory. He was twice married, and left behind him several children. His excellent character is attested by Sir John Harington, who says that he was a man "to whom I never came but I grew more religious, and from whom I never went but I parted more instructed." The comedy of "Gammer Gurton's Needle," the only dramatic product of his pen of which we have any knowledge, was "played on stage, in Christ's College, Cambridge," in the year 1566, and the following entry from the bursars' books of that college, on the occasion, manifests that the authorities applied themselves to its production with spirit. "Item, for the Carpenters setting upp the Scaffold at the plaie xxd.[1]" At this time, Mr Still was twenty-three years old; but an entry in the registers of the Stationers' Company, under the year 1563, is considered by Mr Collier to have very possible reference to the present comedy, and, in this case, the young clergyman would have begun, and ended, his authorship ere he was nineteen: "Received of Thomas Colwell for his lycense for pryntinge of a play intituled Dyccon of Bedlam, iiijd." There is no such play, Mr Collier points out, as "Dyccon of Bedlam," but Diccon of Bedlam is

---

[1] ["Proceedings of the Suffolk Institute," iii., 130.]

a principal character in "Gammer Gurton's Needle;"
and it is further to be observed that Thomas Colwell is
the same publisher, "at the sygne of S. John Evangelist,
beneth the Conduit in Fleetestreat," by whom the earliest
known edition of the present comedy was produced.
The circumstance, after all, is as inconclusive as the
fact is immaterial. The true subject of regret is, not
that we cannot determine precisely whether Still wrote
comedy when he was nineteen, or when he was twenty-
three, but that having written one play so well, he did not
write more. Had he so elected to do, indeed, the See of
Bath and Wells might not have seen the name of Still
in its *Catena Episcoporum*, but the other prelate would,
doubtless, have done his duty, and English readers
would have been amused with further Gammer Gurtons.

" Gammer Gurton's Needle," acted at Christ's College,
Cambridge, in 1566, "has," writes Mr Collier, "this
peculiarity belonging to it, that it is the first existing
play acted at either university; and it is a singular coin-
cidence, that the author of the comedy so represented
should be the very person who, many years afterwards,
when he had become Vice-Chancellor of Cambridge,
was called upon to remonstrate with the Ministers of
Queen Elizabeth against having an English play performed before her at that university, as unbefitting its
learning, dignity, and character."[1] Of the play itself
Hazlitt writes : " It is a regular comedy in five acts,
built on the circumstance of an old woman having lost

---

[1] "Annals of the Stage," ii. 463.

her needle, which throws the whole village into confusion, till it is at last providentially found sticking in an
unlucky part of Hodge's dress. This must evidently
have happened at a time when the manufacturers of
Sheffield and Birmingham had not reached the height
of perfection which they have at present done. Suppose that there is only one sewing-needle in a parish,
that the owner, a diligent, notable old dame, loses it;
that a mischief-making wag sets it about that another
old woman has stolen this valuable instrument of household industry; that strict search is made in-doors for it
in vain, and that then the incensed parties sally forth
to scold it out in the open air, till words end in blows,
and the affair is referred over to higher authorities; and
we shall have an exact idea (though perhaps not so
lively a one) of what passes in this authentic document
between Gammer Gurton and her gossip Dame Chat;
Diccon, the bedlam (the causer of these harms); Hodge,
Gammer Gurton's servant; Tib, her maid; Cock, her
prentice boy; Doll; Scapethrift; Master Baillie, his
master; Doctor Rat, the curate; and Gib the cat, who
may be fairly reckoned one of the *dramatis personæ*,
and performs no mean part." "Such," observes the
same critic, further on, characterising the comedy, "Such
was the wit, such was the mirth of our ancestors—
homely, but hearty; coarse, perhaps, but kindly; let
no man despise it; for "evil to him that evil thinks."
To think it poor and beneath notice, because it is not
just like ours, is the same sort of hypercriticism that
was exercised by the person who refused to read some

old books because they were " such very poor spelling."
The meagreness of their literary or their bodily fare
was at least relished by themselves ; and this is better
than a surfeit or an indigestion. It is refreshing to look
out of ourselves sometimes, not to be always holding
the glass to our own peerless perfections ; and as there
is a dead wall which always intercepts the prospect of
the future from our view (all that we can see beyond it
is the heavens), it is as well to direct our eyes now and
then without scorn to the page of history, and repulsed
in our attempts to penetrate the secrets of the next six
thousand years, not to turn our backs on old long syne.[1]

This entertaining old piece is mentioned in "Histrio-
mastix," 1610, act ii. (sign. C. 3), under the title of
" Mother Gurton's Needle," and in burlesque it is there
called " a Tragedy."

The present edition of " Gammer Gurton's Needle "
is printed from that of 1575.

---

[1] " Lectures on the Dramatic Literature of the Age of
Elizabeth," 1820, p. 208.

THE NAMES OF THE SPEAKERS IN THIS COMEDY.

DICCON[1] *the Bedlam.*[2]	DAME CHAT.
HODGE, *Gammer Gurton's Servant.*	DOCTOR RAT, *the Curate.*
TIB, *Gammer Gurton's Maid.*	MASTER BAILY.
	DOLL, *Dame Chat's Maid.*
GAMMER GURTON.	SCAPETHRIFT, *Master Baily's Servant.*
COCK, *Gammer Gurton's Boy.*	Mutes.

---

[1] The ancient abbreviation of Richard.

[2] After the dissolution of the religious houses where the poor of every denomination were provided for, there was for many years no settled or fixed provision made to supply the want of that care, which those bodies appear always to have taken of their distressed brethren. In consequence of this neglect, the idle and dissolute were suffered to wander about the country, assuming such characters as they imagined were most likely to insure success to their frauds, and security from detection. Among other disguises, many affected madness, and were distinguished by the name of *Bedlam Beggars.* These are mentioned by Edgar in " King Lear : "—

> " The country gives me proof and precedent,
> Of bedlam beggars who, with roaring voices,
> Strike in their numbed and mortified bare arms,
> Pins, wooden pricks, nails, sprigs of rosemary,
> And with this horrible object from low farms,
> Poor pelting villages, sheepcotes, and mills,
> Sometime with lunatic bans, sometimes with prayers,
> Enforce their charity."

In Dekker's " Belman of London " [1608] all the different species of beggars are enumerated. Amongst the rest mentioned "Tom of Bedlam's" band of madcaps, otherwise called Poor Tom's flock of wild geese or hair-brains, are called Abraham men. An Abraham man is afterwards described in this manner: "Of all the mad rascalls (that are of this wing) the *Abraham-man* is the most phantastick. The fellow (quoth this old lady of the Lake vnto me) that sat halfe naked (at table to day) from the girdle vpward, is the best *Abraham-man* that euer came to my house, & the notablest villaine: he sweares he hath bin in bedlam, and will talke frantickly of purpose: you see pinns stuck in sundry places of his naked flesh, especially in his armes, which paine hee gladly puts himselfe to (beeing indeede no torment at all, his skin is either so dead with some fowle disease, or so hardened with weather) onley to make you beleeue he is out of his wits: he calls himselfe by the name of *Poore Tom*, and comming neere any body cryes out, Poore Tom is a cold. Of these *Abraham-men*, some be exceeding mery, and doe nothing but sing songs, fashioned out of their owne braines, some will dance; others will doe nothing but either laugh or weepe; others are dogged, and are sullen both in looke and speech, that, spying but small company in a house, they boldly and bluntly enter, compelling the seruants through feare to giue them what they demaund, which is commonly *bacon*, or something that will yielde ready mony." [Edit. 1608, sign. D 2.] Of this respectable fraternity Diccon seems to have been a member. Massinger mentions them in "A New Way to Pay Old Debts," act ii., sc. 1: "Aro they padders, or *Abraham-men*, that are your consorts?"

PROLOGUE.

As Gammer Gurton, with many a wide stitch,
Sat piecing and patching of Hodge her man's breech,
By chance or misfortune, as she her gear toss'd,
In Hodge leather breeches her needle she lost.
When Diccon the Bedlam had heard by report,
That good Gammer Gurton was robbed in this sort,
He quietly persuaded with her in that stound,
Dame Chat, her dear gossip, this needle had found.
Yet knew she no more of this matter (alas),
Than knoweth Tom our clerk what the priest
    saith at mass.
Hereof there ensued so fearful a fray,
Mas. Doctor was sent for, these gossips to stay ;
Because he was curate and esteemed full wise,
Who found that he sought not, by Diccon's device.
When all things were tumbled and clean out of
    fashion,
Whether it were by fortune, or some other con-
    stellation,
Suddenly the needle Hodge found by the pricking,
And drew it out of his buttock, where he found it
    sticking.
Their hearts then at rest with perfect security,
With a pot of good nale they struck up their
    plaudity.

THE FIRST ACT.

THE FIRST SCENE.

DICCON. Many a mile have I walked divers and
 sundry ways,
And many a good man's house have I been at in
 my days,
Many a gossip's cup in my time have I tasted,
And many a broach and spit have I both turned
 and basted,
Many a piece of bacon have I had out of their
 balks,[1]
In running over the country with long and weary
 walks.
Yet came my foot never within those door cheeks,
To seek flesh or fish, garlick, onions, or leeks,
That ever I saw a sort in such a plight,[2]

---

[1] The summer beam or dorman.   Poles laid over a stable
or other building.—Ray's "Collection of English Words,"
p. 167.
[2] *A sort* is a company.   So in Jonson's "Every man out
of his Humour," act ii., sc. 3: "I speak it not gloriously,
nor out of affectation, but there's he and the count Frugale,

As here within this house appeareth to my sight,
There is howling and scowling, all cast in a dump,
With whewling and puling, as though they had
    lost a trump.
Sighing and sobbing, they weep and they wail.
I marvel in my mind what the devil they ail.
The old trot sits groaning with alas and alas,[1]
And Tib wrings her hands and takes on in worse
    case.
With poor Cock their boy, they be driven in such
    fits,

signior Illustre, signior Luculento, and *a sort* of them," &c.
Also, in Nash's "Pierce Pennilesse," 1592, p. 6, "I know a
great *sort* of good fellows that would venture," &c. Again,
in the "Vocacyon of Johan Bale," 1533: "In parell of
pyrates, robbers, and murthirors, and a great *sort* more."
And in Skelton's Works, edit. 1736, p. 136—

> "Another *sorte* of sluttes
> Some brought walnutes."

See also Dr Johnson and Mr Steevens's Notes on Shakspeare, Vol. III. p. 69.

[1] An old *trot* or *trat*, Dr Grey says, signifies a decrepid old
woman or an old drab. In which sense it is used in Gawin
Douglas' Virgil, B. iv. p. 96, 97—

> "Out on the *old trat* agit wyffe or dame."

And p. 122, 39 :

> "Thus saith *Dido*, and the tother with that,
> Hyit or furth with slow pase like *ane trot*."

And Shakspeare; "Why give her gold enough, and marry
him to a puppet, aglet baby, or an *old trot* with ne'er a
tooth in her head" (*Taming of the Shrew*, act i., sc. 5 ;
Critical Notes on Shakspeare, Vol. I. p. 118.) It is also used
by Churchyard—

> "Away young Frie that gives leawd counsel, nowe,
> Awale *old trotts*, that sets young flesh to sale," &c.
> —*Challenge*, 1593, p. 250.

And by Gascoigne :

> "Goe : that gunne pouder consume the old *trotte* / "
> —*Supposes*, act iii., sc. 5. [Hazlitt's edit. i. 230.]

Again, in Nash's "Lenten Stuff," 1599: "A cage or

I fear me the folks be not well in their wits.
Ask them what they ail, or who brought them in
    this stay?
They answer not at all, but alack and wellaway.
When I saw it booted not, out at doors I hied me,
And caught a slip of bacon, when I saw none spied
    me,
Which I intend not far hence, unless my purpose
    fail,
Shall serve me for a shoeing horn to draw on two
    pots of ale.[1]

THE FIRST ACT.

THE SECOND SCENE.

HODGE, DICCON.

HODGE. See, so cham arrayed[2] with dabbling in
    the dirt!
She that set me to ditching, ich would she had the
    squirt.

---

pigeon house, roomsome enough to comprehend her, and
the toothless *trot* her nurse, who was her only chat mate
and chamber maid," &c.

    See also Mr Steevens's Notes on Shakspeare, Vol. II. p. 93.

[1] So in Nash's "Pierce Pennilesse," p. 23, "we have
generall rules and injunctions as good as printed precepts,
or statutes set downe by acte of parliament, that goe from
drunkard to drunkard as still to keepe your first man, not
to leave anie flockes in the bottom of the cup, to knock the
glasse on your thumbe when you have done, to have some
shooring horne to pull on your wine, as a rasher of the coles,
or a redde herring." Again in Nash's "Lenten Stuff,"
1599, "which being double roasted, and dried as it is, not
only sucks up all the rheumatick inundations, but is a
shoeing horn for a pint of wine overplus."

[2] [Soiled.]

Was never poor soul that such a life had ?
Gog's bones, this vilthy glay has dress'd me too
    bad.
Gog's soul, see how this stuff tears !
Ich were better to be a bearward, and set to keep
    bears.
By the mass, here is a gash, a shameful hole in-
    deed,
And one stitch tear further, a man may thrust in
    his head.
   DICCON. By my father's soul, Hodge, if I should
    now be sworn,
I cannot choose but say thy breech is foul betorn.
But the next remedy in such a case and hap
Is to planch [1] on a piece as broad as thy cap.
   HODGE. Gog's soul, man, 'tis not yet two days
    fully ended,
Since my dame Gurton (cham sure) these breeches
    amended.
But cham made such a drudge to trudge at every
    need,
Chwold rend it, though it were stiched with sturdy
    packthread.
   DICCON. Hodge, let thy breeches go, and speak
    and tell me soon,
What devil aileth Gammer Gurton, and Tib her
    maid to frown.
   HODGE. Tush, man, th' art deceived, 'tis their
    daily look :

---

[1] A *planch* is a plank of wood. To *planch* therefore is a
verb formed from it. See "Measure for Measure," Vol. II.,
edit. 1778, p. 106.—*S.*
   The above note but ill explains its meaning; the word
will be better illustrated by the following description of the
fortification of Ypres by Holinshed : "It was fensed with a
mighty rampire and a thicke hedge, trimlie *planshed*, and
woond with thornes," &c.—*Chron.* 2. 759. *Ed.* 1807.—*O. G.*

They cow'r [1] so over the coals, their eyes be blear'd
    with smoke.
    DICCON. Nay, by the mass, I perfectly perceived
       as I came hither,
That either Tib and her dame hath been by the
    ears together,
Or else as great a matter, as thou shalt shortly see.
    HODGE. Now ich beseech our Lord they never
       better agree.
    DICCON. By Gog's soul, there they sit as still as
       stones in the street ;
As though they had been taken with fairies, or else
    with some ill-spreet.
    HODGE. Gog's heart, I durst have laid my cap
       to a crown,
Ch'would learn of some prancome, as soon as ich
    came to town.
    DICCON. Why, Hodge, art thou inspired? or
       didst thou thereof hear ?
    HODGE. Nay, but ich saw such a wonder, as ich
    saw nat this seven year.

---

[1] This is the reading of the first edition, which in all the
subsequent ones is very improperly altered to *cover*. *To
cower*, is to bend, stoop, hang, or lean over. See Beaumont
and Fletcher's " Monsieur Thomas," act. iv., sc. 6, and Nash's
" Pierce Pennilesse," 1592, p. 8.
    Again—

      " He much rejoyst, and *cour'd* it tenderly,
        As chicken newly hatcht, from dreaded destiny."—
              Spenser's *Fairy Queen*, B. ii., c. 8, sc. 9.

    So in Shakspeare's " King Henry VI." Part II. vol. vi.,
p. 362, edit. 1778—

      " The splitting rocks *cowr'd* in the sinking sand."—*S.*

Again—

     " As thus he spake, each bird and beast behold
      Approaching two and two, these *cow'ring* low
      With blandishment, each bird stoop'd on his wing."
            —*Paradise Lost*, B. viii., l. 349.

Tom Tankard's cow (by Gog's bones) she set me
    up her sail,
And flinging about his halse aker,[1] fisking with her
    tail,
As though there had been in her arse a swarm of
    bees ;
And chad not cried tphrowh, whore, shea'd leapt
    out of his lees.
    DICCON. Why, Hodge, lies the cunning in Tom
    Tankard's cow's tail?
    HODGE. Well, ich chave heard some say such
    tokens do not fail.
But ca'st thou not tell, in faith, Diccon, why she
    frowns, or whereat?
Hath no man stolen her ducks or hens, or gelded
    Gib her cat?[2]
    DICCON. What devil can I tell, man, I could not
    have one word,
They gave no more heed to my talk than thou
    wouldst to a lord.
    HODGE. Ich cannot skill but muse, what mar-
    vellous thing it is :
Chill in and know myself what matters are amiss.
    DICCON. Then farewell, Hodge, a while, since
    thou dost inward haste,
For I will into the good wife Chat's, to feel how
    the ale doth taste.

---

[1] I believe we should read *halse anchor*, or *anker*, as it was
anciently spelt; a naval phrase. The *halse* or *halser* was a
particular kind of cable. Shakspeare, in his " Antony and
Cleopatra, has an image similar to this—

> " The brize upon her, like a *cow* in June,
> *Hoists sail and flies.*"—S.

[2] Gib was the name by which all male or ram cats were
distinguished. See Warton's Note on the " First Part of
Henry IV.," act i., sc. 2.

THE FIRST ACT.

THE THIRD SCENE.

HODGE, TIB.

HODGE. Cham aghast, by the mass, ich wot not
  what to do.
Chad need bless me well, before ich go them to.
Perchance some felon sprit may haunt our house
  indeed.
And then chwere but a noddy to venture, where cha'
  no need.
  TIB. Cham worse than mad, by the mass, to be
  at this stay,
Cham chid, cham blam'd, and beaten all th' hours on
  the day.
Lamed and hunger-starved, pricked up all in jags,
Having no patch to hide my back, save a few rotten
  rags.
  HODGE. I say, Tib, if thou be Tib, as I trow
  sure thou be,
What devil make-a-do is this between our dame
  and thee ?
  TIB. Gog's bread, Hodge, thou had a good turn,
  thou wert not here this while.
It had been better for some of us to have been
  hence a mile.
My gammer is so out of course, and frantic all at
  once,
That Cock our boy and I, poor wench, have felt it
  on our bones.
  HODGE. What is the matter, say on, Tib, whereat
  she taketh so on ?
  TIB. She is undone ; she saith (alas) her joy and
  life is gone.

If she hear not of some comfort, she saith she is
    but dead,
Shall never come within her lips one inch of meat
    ne bread.
    HODGE. By'r lady, cham not very glad to see
    her in this dump;
Chold a noble her stool hath fallen, and she hath
    broke her rump.
    TIB. Nay, and that were the worst, we would
    not greatly care,
For bursting[1] of her huckle-bone or breaking of
    her chair,
But greater, greater is her grief, as, Hodge, we
    shall all feel.
    HODGE. Gog's wounds, Tib, my gammer has
    never lost her nee'le?
    TIB. Her nee'le!
    HODGE. Her nee'le?
    TIB. Her nee'le; by him that made me, it is
    true, Hodge, I tell thee.
    HODGE. Gog's sacrament! I would she had lost
    th' heart out of her belly.
The devil or else his dame, they ought her sure a shame,
How a murrion came this chance, (say, Tib) unto
    our dame?

----

[1] *i.e.*, Breaking.   See Note on "King Henry IV.," Part
II., edit. 1778, vol. v., p. 537.—*S.*
    From the following passage, in a letter from Mr Sterne,
dated August 11, 1767, it appears that the word was then
still used in the same sense among the common people in
the north of England.   "My postilion has set me a-ground
for a week, by one of my pistols bursting in his hand, which
he, taking for granted to be quite shot off, he instantly fell
upon his knees, and said, 'Our Father which art in heaven,
hallowed be thy name,' at which, like a good Christian, he
stopped, not remembering any more of it; the affair was
not so bad as he at first thought, for it has only *bursten* two
of his fingers, he says."

TIB. My gammer sat her down on her pes,[1] and
　　bad me reach thy breeches,
And by and by, a vengeance in it, ere she had take
　　two stitches,
To clout a clout upon thine arse, by chance aside
　　she leers,
And Gib our cat in the milk-pan she spied over
　　head and ears.
Ah whore, out these, she cried aloud, and swept
　　the breeches down,
Up went her staff, and out leapt Gib at doors into
　　the town.
And since that time was, never wight could set
　　their eyes upon it.
Gog's malison chave Cock and I bid twenty
　　times light on it.[2]
　　HODGE. And is not then my breeches sewed up,
　　　　to-morrow that I should wear?
　　TIB. No, in faith, Hodge, thy breeches lie, for
　　　　all this never the near.
　　HODGE. Now a vengeance light on all the sort,
　　　　that better should have kept it;
The cat, the house, and Tib our maid, that better
　　should have swept it.
See where she cometh crawling! come on, in
　　twenty devils' way;
Ye have made a fair day's work, have you not,
　　pray you say?

THE FIRST ACT.

THE FOURTH SCENE.

GAMMER, HODGE, TIB, COCK.

GAMMER. Alas, alas, I may well curse and ban

---

[1] [Haunch.　See Halliwell's "Dict. v. Pesate."]
[2] *i.c.*, God's curse.　Glossary to Peter Langtoft.

This day, that ever I saw it, with Gib and the
    milk-pan.
For these and ill luck together, as knoweth Cock
    my boy,
Have stack[1] away my dear nee'le, and robbed me
    of my joy.
My fair long straight nee'le, that was mine only
    treasure,
The first day of my sorrow is, and last end of my
    pleasure.
    HODGE (*aside*). Might ha' kept it, when ye had
    it ; but fools will be fools still :
Lose that is vast in your hands ? ye need not, but
    ye will.
    GAMMER. Go hie thee, Tib, and run, thou whore,
    to the end here of the town.
Didst carry out dust in thy lap ? seek where thou
    pourest it down ;
And as thou sawest me raking in the ashes where
    I mourned,
So see in all the heap of dust thou leave no straw
    unturned.
    TIB. That chall, Gammer, swyth and tite,[2] and
    soon be here again.
    GAMMER. Tib, stoop and look down to the
    ground to it, and take some pain.
    HODGE. Here is a pretty matter, to see this gear
    how it goes :

---

[1] Mr Dodsley, in the former edition, reads *tacke.*

[2] Swiftly and directly—

> Kyng Estmere threwe the harpe asyde
> And *swith* he drew his brand ;
> And Estmere he and Alder yonge,
> Right stiffe in stour can stand.
>   —Percy's *Reliques of Ancient Poetry,*
>   [Ed. 1765] vol. i., p. 75.

Hence *swythe* to Doctor Rat hie thee, that thou were gone.
    —Act iii., sc. 3.

Thou shalt find lying an inch of white tallow candle.
Light it, and bring it *tite* away.
    —Act i., sc. 4.

By Gog's soul, I think you would lose your arse,
    and it were loose.
Your nee'le lost? it is pity you should lack care
    and endless sorrow.
Gog's death, how shall my breeches be sewed?
    Shall I go thus to-morrow?

  GAMMER. Ah, Hodge, Hodge, if that ich could
    find my nee'le, by the reed,
Ch'ould sew thy breeches, ich promise thee, with
    full good double thread,
And set a patch on either knee should last this
    moneths twain,
Now God and good Saint Sithe, I pray to send it
    home [2] again.

  HODGE. Whereto served your hands and eyes,
    but this your nee'le to keep?
What devil had you else to do? ye keep, ich wot,
    no sheep.
Cham fain abroad to dig and delve, in water, mire,
    and clay,
Sossing and possing in the dirt still from day to
    day.
A hundred things that be abroad cham set to see
    them well :
And four of you sit idle at home, and cannot keep
    a nee'le !

  GAMMER. My nee'le, alas, ich lost it, Hodge, what
    time ich me up hasted,
To save milk set up for thee, which Gib our cat
    hath wasted.

  HODGE. The devil he burst both Gib and Tib,
    with all the rest ;
Cham always sure of the worst end, whoever have
    the best.

---

[1] Perhaps a corruption of Saint Swithin.—S.
[2] Mr Dodsley reads, *back again.*

Where ha' you been fidging abroad, since you your
    nee'le lost?
    GAMMER. Within the house, and at the door,
    sitting by this same post;
Where I was looking a long hour, before these
    folks came here;
But, wellaway! all was in vain, my nee'le is never
    the near.
    HODGE. Set me a candle, let me seek, and
    grope wherever it be.
Gog's heart, ye be foolish (ich think), you know it
    not, when you it see.
    GAMMER. Come hither, Cock: what, Cock, I say.
    COCK. How, Gammer?
    GAMMER. Go, hie thee soon, and grope behind
    the old brass pan,
Which thing when thou hast done,
There shalt thou find an old shoe, wherein, if thou
    look well,
Thou shalt find lying an inch of white tallow
    candle;
Light it, and bring it tite away.
    COCK. That shall be done anon.
    GAMMER. Nay, tarry, Hodge, till thou hast light,
    and then we'll seek each one.
    HODGE. Come away, ye whoreson boy, are ye
    asleep? ye must have a crier.
    COCK. Ich cannot get the candle light: here is
    almost no fire.
    HODGE. Chill hold thee a penny, chill make thee
    come, if that ich may catch thine ears.
Art deaf, thou whoreson boy? Cock, I say; why,
    canst not hear?
    GAMMER. Beat him not, Hodge, but help the
    boy, and come you two together.

THE FIRST ACT.

THE FIFTH SCENE.

GAMMER, TIB, COCK, HODGE.

GAMMER. How now, Tib! quick, let's hear what
   news thou hast brought hither?
TIB. Chave tost and tumbled yonder heap over
   and over again,
And winnowed it through my fingers, as men
   would winnow grain;
Not so much as a hen's turd, but in pieces I tare it.
Or whatsoever clod or clay I found, I did not spare
   it.
Looking within and eke without, to find your
   nee'le (alas)
But all in vain and without help your nee'le is
   where it was.
   GAMMER. Alas, my nee'le, we shall never meet!
   adieu, adieu, for aye.
TIB. Not so, Gammer, we might it find, if we
   knew where it lay.
COCK. Gog's cross, Gammer, if ye will laugh,
   look in but at the door,
And see how Hodge lieth trembling and tossing
   amids the flour.
Raking there some fire to find among the ashes dead,
Where there is not one spark so big as a pin's
   head:
At last in a dark corner two sparks he thought he
   sees,
Which were indeed nought else but Gib our cat's
   two eyes.
Puff, quod Hodge, thinking thereby to have fire
   without doubt;

With that Gib shut her two eyes, and so the fire
    was out ;
And by and by them opened, even as they were
    before,
With that the sparks appeared even as they had
    done of yore ;
And even as Hodge blew the fire (as he did think),
Gib, as she felt the blast, straightway began to
    wink ;
Till Hodge fell of swearing, as came best to his
    turn,
The fire was sure bewitch'd, and therefore would
    not burn :
At last Gib up the stairs, among the old posts and
    pins,
And Hodge he hied him after, till broke were both
    his shins :
Cursing and swearing oaths were never of his
    making,
That Gib would fire the house, if that she were
    not taken.
   GAMMER. See, here is all the thought that the
    foolish urchin taketh !
And Tib, me-think, at his elbow almost as merry
    maketh.
This is all the wit ye have, when others make their
    moan :
Come down, Hodge, where art thou? and let the
    cat alone.
   HODGE. Gog's heart, help and come up : Gib in
    her tail hath fire,
And is like to burn all, if she get a little higher.
Come down (quoth you?) nay, then you might
    count me a patch,[1]

---

[1] " This term," says Mr Malone, " came into use from the
name of a celebrated fool. This I learn from Wilson's

The house cometh down on your heads, if it take
   once the thatch.
GAMMER. It is the cat's eyes, fool, that shineth
   in the dark.
HODGE. Hath the cat, do you think, in every
   eye a spark?
GAMMER. No, but they shine as like fire as ever
   man see.
HODGE. By the mass, and she burn all, you sh'
   bear the blame for me.
GAMMER. Come down and help to seek here our
   nee'le, that it were found;
Down, Tib, on *thy* knees, I say, down, Cock, to the
   ground.

' Art of Rhetorique,' 1553 : 'A word making, called of the
Grecians Onomatopiea, is when we make words of our own
mind, such as be derived from the nature of things,' as to
call one *patche,* or cowlson, whom we see to do a thing
foolishly; because these two in their time were notable
fools.

"Probably the dress which the celebrated *patch* wore was
in allusion to his name, patched or parti-coloured. Hence
the stage-fool has ever since been exhibited in a motley
coat. In Rowley's ' When you see me, you know me,
Cardinal Wolsey's fool *Patch* is introduced. Perhaps he
was the original *patch* of whom Wilson speaks."—Note on
" Merchant of Venice," act ii., sc. 5.

In Chaloner's translation of the " Praise of Folly," by
Erasmus, 1549, is the following passage : " And by the
fayeth ye owe to the immortal godds, may any thing to an
indifferent considerer be deemed more happie and blisful
than is this kinde of men whome commonly ye call fooles,
poltes, ideotes, and *paches ?* "

Again, " I have subtraied these my selie *paches,* who not
onelye themselves are ever mery, playing, singing, and
laughyng, but also whatever they doo, are provokers of
others lykewyse to pleasure, sporte, and laughter, as who
sayeth ordeyned herefore by the Godds of theyr benevolence
to recreate the sadnesse of mens lyves."

To God I make a vow, and so to good Saint
    Anne,[1]
A candle shall they have a-piece, get it where I
    can,
If I may my nee'le find in one place or in other.
    HODGE. Now a vengeance on Gib light, on Gib
    and Gib's mother.
And all the generation of cats both far and near.
Look on the ground, whoreson, thinks thou the
    nee'le is here?
    COCK. By my troth, Gammer, me-thought your
    nee'le here I saw,
But when my fingers touch'd it, I felt it was a
    straw.
    TIB. See, Hodge, what's t'is; may it not be
    within it?
    HODGE. Break it, fool, with thy hand, and see,
    and thou canst find it.
    TIB. Nay, break it you, Hodge, according to
    your word.
    HODGE. Gog's sides, fie! it stinks: it is a cat's
    turd:
It were well done to make thee eat it, by the
    mass.
    GAMMER. This matter amendeth not, my nee'le
    is still where it was.
Our candle is at an end, let us all in quite,
And come another time, when we have more light.

---

[1] In all cases of distress, and whenever the assistance of
a superior power was necessary, it was usual with the Roman
Catholics to promise their tutelary saints to light up candles
at their altars, to induce them to be propitious to such
applications as were made to them. The reader will see a
very ridiculous story of this kind in the first volume of
Lord Oxford's " Collection of Voyages," p. 771, quoted in
Dr Grey's " Notes on Shakspeare," vol. i. p. 7. Erasmus
has a story to the same purpose in his " Naufragium."

THE SECOND ACT.

First a SONG.[1]

Back and side go bare, go bare,
  Both foot and hand go cold :
But, belly, God send thee good ale enough,
  Whether it be new or old.

I cannot eat but little meat,
  My stomach is not good;
But sure I think, that I can drink
  With him that wears a hood.[2]
Though I go bare, take ye no care,
  I am nothing a-cold ;
I stuff my skin so full within
  Of jolly good ale and old.
Back and side go bare, go bare,
  Both foot and hand go cold :
But, belly, God send thee good ale enough,
  Whether it be new or old.

I love no roast but a nut-brown toast,[3]
  And a crab laid in the fire.
A little bread shall do me stead :
  Much bread I not desire.

---

[1] [Respecting this song, see Bell's "Songs from the Dramatists," p. 34.]

[2] Alluding to the drunkenness of the Friars.

[3] So in act iii., sc. 4—

  "*A* cup of ale had in his hand, and *a crab* lay in the fire."

Again—

  "Now *a crab* in the fire were worth a good groat,
    That I might quaff with my Captain Tom tospot."
                              —Fulwell's *Like will to Like*, c. 2.

No frost nor snow, no wind, I trow,
  Can hurt me if I would;
I am so wrapt, and thoroughly lapt
  Of jolly good ale and old.
    Back and side go bare, &c.

And Tib my wife, that as her life
  Loveth well good ale to seek,
Full oft drinks she, till ye may see
  The tears run down her cheek;
Then doth she trowl to me the bowl [1]
  Even as a malt-worm should;
And saith, sweet heart, I have take my part
  Of this jolly good ale and old.
    Back and side go bare, &c.

Again—

> " And sometime lurk I in a gossip's bowl,
>   In very likeness of a *roasted crab*."
>   —*Midsummer Night's Dream*, act ii., sc. 1.

Upon this last passage, Mr Steevens has given the following examples of the use of this word—

> " Yet we will have in store *a crab* in the fire,
>   With nut-brown ale."—*Henry V.*, Anon.
> " And sit down in my chaire by my faire Alison,
>   And turn a *crabbe* in the fire as merry as Pope Joan."
>   —Edwards's *Damon and Pithias.*
>
>   " Sitting in a corner turning *crabs*,
>   Or coughing o'er a warmed pot of ale."
>   —*Description of Christmas in Summer's last Will*
>   *and Testament*, by Nash, 1600.

[1] *Trowl*, or *trole the bowl*, was a common phrase in drinking for passing the vessel about, as appears by the following beginning of an old catch—

> " *Trole, trole* the bowl to me,
>   And I will *trole* the same again to thee."

And in this other, in Hilton's Collection—

> " Tom Bouls, Tom Bouls,
>   Seest thou not how merrily this good ale *trowles?*
>   —Sir John Hawkins's *History of Music*, Vol. III., 22.

Now let them drink, till they nod and wink,
    Even as good fellows should do,
They shall not miss to have the bliss
    Good ale doth bring men to ;
And all poor souls that have scoured bowls,
    Or have them lustly troll'd,
God save the lives of them and their wives,
    Whether they be young or old.
      Back and side go bare, &c.

THE FIRST SCENE.

DICCON, HODGE.

DICCON. Well done, by Gog's malt, well sung
    and well said :
Come on, mother Chat, as thou art a [1] true maid,
One fresh pot of ale let's see, to make an end,
Against this cold weather my naked arms [2] to de-
    fend :
This gear it warms the soul : now, wind, blow on
    thy worst,

Again—

    " Sirra Shakebagge, canst thou remember
    Since we *trould the boule* at Sittingburn.
             —*Arden of Feversham,* 1592.

    " Giv't us weele pledge, nor shall a man that lives
    In charity refuse it, I will not be so old
    As not be grac't to honour Cupid, giv't us full.
    When we were young, we could ha *trold* it off.
    Drunke down a Dutchman."
        —Marston's *Parasitaster or The Fowne,* act. v.

    " Now the cups *trole* about to wet the gossips whistles,
    It pours down, I faith, they never think of payment."
        —*A Chast Mayd in Cheap-side,* p. 34.

[1] Add.
[2] See Dekker's Description of an Abraham-man, *supra.*

And let us drink and swill till that our bellies
    burst,
Now were he a wise man, by cunning could define
Which way my journey lieth, or where Diccon
    will dine :
But one good turn I have, be it by night or day,
South, east, north, or west, I am never out of my
    way.
    HODGE. Chim goodly rewarded, cham I not, do
    you think ?
Chad a goodly dinner for all my sweat and swink.[1]
Neither butter, cheese, milk, onions, flesh, nor
    fish,
Save this piece of barley-bread : 'tis a pleasant costly
    dish !
    DICCON. Hail, fellow Hodge, and well[2] to fare
    with thy meat, if you have any :
But by thy words, as I them smelled, thy daintrels
    be not many.
    HODGE. Daintrels, Diccon ! Gog's soul, man, save
    this piece of dry horsebread,

---

[1] *To swink* is to work or labour; as in Spenser's "Fairy
Queen," B. II., cant. vii., st. 8.

    "For which men sweat and *swink* incessantly."

Again in "Comus," l. 293—

    "And the *swinkt* hedger at his supper sat."

Also in Chaucer's "Canterbury Tales," Prol., l. 184—

    "What schulde he studie, make himselven wood,
    Uppon a book in cloystre alway to powre,
    Or *swinke* with his hands, and laboure,
    As Austin byt ? how schal the world be served ?
    Let Austyn have his *swynk* to him reserved."

And in "Pierce Plowman's Vision"—

    "Hermets an heape with hoked staves,
    Wenten to Walsingham, and her wenches after.
    Great loubees and long, that loth were to *swinke*,
    Clothed hem in copes, to be knowen from other."

[2] Will.

Chat bit no bit this livelong day, no crumb come
    in my head :
My guts they yawl, crawl, and all my belly rum-
    bleth,
The puddings cannot lie still, each one over other
    tumbleth.
By Gog's heart, cham so vexed, and in my belly
    penn'd,
Chould one piece were at the spital-house, another
    at the castle's end.
    DICCON. Why, Hodge, was there none at home
      thy dinner for to set ?
    HODGE. Gog's bread, Diccon, ich came too late,
      was nothing there to get :
Gib (a foul fiend might on her light) licked the
    milk-pan so clean ;
See, Diccon, 'twas not so well washed this seven
    year, as ich ween.
A pestilence light on all ill-luck, chad thought yet
    for all this
Of a morsel of bacon behind the door at worst
    should not miss :
But when ich sought a slip to cut, as ich was wont
    to do,
Gog's souls, Diccon, Gib our cat had eat the bacon
    too :
    [*Which bacon Diccon stole, as is declared before.*
    DICCON. Ill-luck, quod he ? marry, swear it,
      Hodge, this day the truth tell,
Thou rose not on thy right side, or else blessed
    thee not well.
Thy milk slopped up ! thy bacon filched ! that was
    too bad luck, Hodge.
    HODGE. Nay, nay, there was a fouler fault, my
      Gammer ga' me the dodge :
Seest not how cham rent and torn, my heels, my
    knees, and my breech ?
VOL. III.   N

Chad thought, as ich sat by the fire, help here and
    there a stitch;
But there ich was pouped indeed.
    DICCON. Why, Hodge?
    HODGE. Boots not, man, to tell,
Cham so drest amongst a sort of fools, chad better
    be in hell,
My Gammer (cham ashamed to say) by God, served
    me not well.
    DICCON. How so, Hodge?
    HODGE. Has she not gone, trowest now thou,
    and lost her nee'le?
    DICCON. Her eel, Hodge! who fished of late?
    that was a dainty dish.
    HODGE. Tush, tush, her nee'le, her nee'le, her
    nee'le, man : 'tis neither flesh nor fish,
A little thing with an hole in the end, as bright as
    any sil'er,
Small, long, sharp at the point, and straight as
    any pillar.
    DICCON. I know not what a devil thou meanest,
    thou bring'st me more in doubt.
    HODGE. Knowest not with what Tom-tailor's
    man sits broaching through a clout?
A nee'le, a nee'le, a nee'le, my Gammer's nee'le is
    gone.
    DICCON. Her nee'le! Hodge, now I smell thee ;
    that was a chance alone :
By the mass, thou hast a shameful loss, and it were
    but for thy breeches.
    HODGE. Gog's soul, man, chould give a crown,
    chad it but three stitches.
    DICCON. How sayest thou, Hodge? what should
    he have, again thy needle got?
    HODGE. By m' father's soul, and chad it, chould
    give him a new groat.
    DICCON. Canst thou keep counsel in this case?

HODGE. Else chwold my tongue were out.

DICCON. Do thou[1] but then by my advice, and
  I will fetch it without doubt.

HODGE. Chill run, chill ride, chill dig, chill
    delve,
Chill toil, chill trudge, shalt see ;
Chill hold, chill draw, chill pull, chill pinch,
  Chill kneel on my bare knee ;
Chill scrape, chill scratch, chill sift, chill seek,
  Chill bow, chill bend, chill sweat,
Chill stoop, chill stour, chill cap, chill kneel,
  Chill creep on hands and feet ;
Chill be thy bondman, Diccon, ich swear by sun
    and moon,
And channot somewhat to stop this gap, cham
    utterly undone.
          [*Pointing behind to his torn breeches.*
DICCON. Why, is there any special cause thou
    takest hereat such sorrow ?

HODGE. Kirstian Clack, Tom Simson's maid, by
    the mass, comes hither to-morrow.
Cham not able to say between us what may hap,
She smiled on me the last Sunday, when ich put off
    my cap.

DICCON. Well, Hodge, this is a matter of weight,
    and must be kept close,
It might else turn to both our costs, as the world
    now goes.[2]

---

[1] Old copy, *than.*

[2] In the 14th of Queen Elizabeth, 1572, an Act of Parliament passed, by which very heavy penalties were inflicted on
all rogues, vagabonds, and sturdy beggars. Among others,
who are therein described and directed to be deemed such,
are idle persons going about feigning themselves to have
knowledge in phisnomie, palmestrie, or other abused sciences,
whereby they bear the people in hand that they can tell their
destinies, deaths, and fortunes, *and such other like fantastical*

Shalt swear to be no blab, Hodge?
   HODGE. Chill, Diccon.
   DICCON. Then go to,
Lay thine hand here, say after me, as thou shalt
     hear me do.
Hast no book?
   HODGE. Cha no book, I.
   DICCON. Then needs must force us both,
Upon my breech to lay thine hand, and there to
     take thine oath.
   HODGE. I, Hodge breechless,
Swear to Diccon rechless
By the cross that I shall kiss,
To keep his counsel close,
And always me to dispose
To work that his pleasure is.
            [Here he kisseth Diccon's breech.
   DICCON. Now, Hodge, see thou take heed,
And do as I thee bid;
For so I judge it meet,
This needle again to win,
There is no shift therein,
But conjure up a spreet.
   HODGE. What the great devil, Diccon, I say?
   DICCON. Yea, in good faith, that is the way,
Fet[1] with some pretty charm.
   HODGE. Soft, Diccon, be not too hasty yet,
By the mass, for ich begin to sweat,
Cham afraid of some[2] harm.
   DICCON. Come hither then, and stir thee not
One inch out of this circle plat,
But stand, as I thee teach.

---

imaginations. This statute seems to be alluded to here by
Diccon, and will serve to confirm the later date of the play;
and at the same time prove the forgery of that assigned to
it by Chetwood.
  [1] Fetched.   [2] Old copy, *syme.*

HODGE. And shall ich be here safe from their
    claws ?
DICCON. The master-devil with his long paws
Here to thee cannot reach—
Now will I settle me to this gear.
    HODGE. I say, Diccon, hear me, hear :
Go softly to this matter.
    DICCON. What devil, man, art afraid of nought ?
    HODGE. Canst not tarry a little thought
Till ich make a courtesy of water ?[1]
    DICCON. Stand still to it, why shouldest thou
    fear him ?
    HODGE. Gog's sides, Diccon, me-think ich hear him,
And tarry, chall mar all.
    DICCON. The matter is no worse than I told it.
    HODGE. By the mass, cham able no longer to
    hold it :
So[2] bad, ich must beray the hall.
    DICCON. Stand to it, Hodge, stir not, you whore-
    son.
What devil, be thine arse-strings brusten ?
Thyself a while but stay,
The devil (I smell him) will be here anon.
    HODGE. Hold him fast, Diccon, cham gone, cham
    gone,
Chill not be at that fray.

THE SECOND ACT.

THE SECOND SCENE.

DICCON, CHAT.

DICCON. Fie, shitten knave, and out upon thee !
Above all other louts, fie on thee !

---

[1] "Ut mulieres solent ad mingendum."—S.   [2] To.

Is not here a cleanly prank?
But thy matter was no better,
Nor thy presence here no sweeter,
To fly I con[1] thee thank.[2]
Here is a matter worthy glosing[3]
Of Gammer Gurton's needle losing,
And a foul piece of wark:
A man, I think, might make a play
And need no word to this they say,
Being but half a clerk.
Soft, let me alone, I will take the charge
This matter further to enlarge
Within a time short;
If ye will mark my toys, and note,
I will give ye leave to cut my throat
If I make no good sport.

----

[1] Can.

[2] I con him no thanks for it, occurs in Shakspeare's "All's Well that Ends Well," and Mr Steevens says it means, "I shall not thank him in studied language." I meet with the same expression in Nash's "Pierce Pennilesse," &c.—

> "I believe he *will con thee little thanks for it.*"

Again, in "Wily Beguiled," 1606—

> "I *con* master Churms *thanks* for this."

Again, in "Anything for a Quiet Life": "He would not trust you with it, I *con* him thanks for it."

Cun or con thanks, says the "Glossary to the Lancashire Dialect," is to *give thanks;* and in that sense only the words appear to be used to this day in the North of England. In Erasmus's "Praise of Folly," by Chaloner, 1549, sig. E 2: "But in the meane while ye ought to *conne me thanke*," &c., and sig. I 4: "Who natheless *conned him as greate thanke*," &c. Again, in Nash's "Pierce Pennilesse," p. 28: "It is well doone 'to practise thy wit, but (I believe) our Lord will *cun thee little* thanke for it.'"

[3] *i.e.*, Glossing or commenting upon. So, in "Pierce Plowman":

> "*Glosed* the Gospel as hem good liked,
>   For covetous of copes construe it as thei wold."

Dame Chat, I say, where be ye within?
  CHAT. Who have we there maketh such a din?
  DICCON. Here is a good fellow maketh no great
    danger.
  CHAT. What, Diccon? come near, ye be no
    stranger:
We be fast set at trump,[1] man, hard by the fire;
Thou shalt set on the king, if thou come a little
    nigher.
  DICCON. Nay, nay, there is no tarrying: I must
    be gone again;
But first for you in counsel[2] I have a word or
    twain.
  CHAT. Come hither, Doll; Doll, sit down and
    play this game,
And as thou sawest me do, see thou do even the
    same:
There is five trumps besides the queen, the hind-
    most thou shalt find her,
Take heed of Sim Glover's wife, she hath an eye
    behind her.
Now, Diccon, say your will.
  DICCON. Nay, soft a little yet,
I would not tell my sister, the matter is so great,
There, I will have you swear by Our Dear Lady
    of Boulogne,[3]

---

[1] Trump was a game played with cards, as will appear by
the following passage of Dekker's "Bellman of London,"
1608, sig. F: "To speak of all the slights used by *Card-
players* in al sorts of Games would but weary you that are
to read, and bee but a thanklesse and unpleasing labour for
me to set them downe. Omitting therefore the deceipts
practised (even in the fairest & most ciuill companies) at
Primero, Saunt, Maw, *Tromp*, and such like games, I will,"
&c. [See Nares, *v. Trump.*]

[2] *i.e.*, In secrecy. See note to the "Merry Wives of
Windsor," edit. 1778, vol. i., p. 228.—*S.*

[3] Our dear Lady of Boulogne is no other than the image

Saint Dunstan and Saint Dominic, with the three
　　Kings of Cologne,[1]
That ye shall keep it secret.
　CHAT. Gog's bread, that will I do,
As secret as mine own thought, by God and the
　　devil too.[2]

---

of the Virgin Mary at Boulogne, which was formerly held
in so much reverence, that it was one of those to which Pil-
grimages used to be made. In Chaucer's "Canterbury
Tales," Prol. 1. 465, describing the "Wife of Bath," he
says—

> "And thries hadde sche ben at Jerusalem.
> Sche hadde passed many a straunge streem.
> At Rome sche hadde ben, and at *Boloyne.*
> In Galice at seynt Jame, and at Coloyne."

The Virgin Mary was the patroness of the town of Boulogne
in a very singular manner, it being holden immediately of
her : "For when King Lewis II., after the decease of Charles
of Burgundy, had taken in Boulogne, anno 1477, as new
Lord of the town (thus John de Serres relateth it), he did
homage without sword or spurs bareheaded, and on his knee,
before the Virgin Mary, offering unto her image an heart of
massie gold, weighing 2000 crowns. He added also this, that
he and his successors, kings after him, should hold the county
of Boulogne of the said Virgin, and do homage unto her
image in the great church of the higher town dedicated to
her name, paying at every change of a vassal an heart of
pure gold of the same weight." — Heylin's "Survey of
France," 1656, p. 193.

[1] The three kings of Cologne are supposed to have been
the wise men who travelled unto our Saviour by the direction of the star. To these kings several writers have given
the names of Gaspar, Melchior, and Balthazar ; but Sir
Thomas Browne, in his "Vulgar Errors," has a whole chapter
concerning them, in which he doubts all the principal facts
in the account of them. See B. vii., c. 8. The celebrated
Thomas Coryat, when at Cologne, took some pains to collect
many circumstances relative to these kings, with which he
hath filled several pages of his book ; and to which those
who are desirous of further information on the subject must
be referred.

[2] Two.

DICCON. Here is Gammer Gurton, your neigh-
　　bour, a sad and heavy wight,
Her goodly fair red cock at home was stole this
　　last night.
CHAT. Gog's soul! her cock with the yellow legs,
　　that nightly crowded [1] so just?
DICCON. That cock is stolen.
CHAT. What, was he fet out of the hen's roost?
DICCON. I cannot tell where the devil he was
　　kept under key or lock,
But Tib hath tickled in Gammer's ear, that you
　　should steal the cock.
CHAT. Have I; strong whore! by bread and
　　salt [2]—
DICCON. What, soft, I say, be still:
Say not one word for all this gear.
CHAT. By the mass, that I will,
I will have the young whore by the head and the
　　old trot by the throat.
DICCON. Not one word, dame Chat, I say, not
　　one word for my coat.
CHAT. Shall such a beggar's brawl [3] as that,
　　thinkest thou, make me a thief?
The pox light on her whore's sides, a pestilence
　　and mischief!

---

[1] A crowd is a small fiddle. Hence the name of *Crowdero*,
in Hudibras. *Crowded* means—made a musical noise.—*S.*

[2] This oath occurs again, act v., sc. 2—

　"Yet shall ye find no other wight save she, *by bread and salt.*"

From the following passage, in Nash's "Lenten Stuff,"
1599, it may be inferred that it was once customary to eat
bread and salt previous to the taking an oath: "Venus, for
Hero was her Priest, and Juno Lucina the Midwife's Goddess, for she was now quickened, and cast away by the cruelty
of Æolus, took *bread and salt,* and eat it, that they would be
smartly revenged on that truculent, windy jailor," &c.

[3] [Brat.]

Come out, thou hungry needy bitch ; O, that my
    nails be short !
  DICCON. Gog's bread, woman, hold your peace,
    this gear will else pass sport ;
I would not for an hundred pound this matter
    should be known
That I am author of this tale, or have abroad it
    blown.
Did ye not swear ye would be ruled, before the tale
    I told ?
I said ye must all secret keep, and ye said sure ye
    would.
  CHAT. Would you suffer, yourself, Diccon, such
    a sort to revile you
With slanderous words to blot your name, and so
    to defile you?
  DICCON. No, good wife Chat, I would be loth
    such drabs should blot my name ;
But yet ye must so order all, that Diccon bear no
    blame.
  CHAT. Go to, then, what is your reed,[1] say on
    your mind, ye shall me rule herein.

---

[1] Counsel or advice. So in act iv., sc. 2—

    "Therefore I *reed* you three, go hence and within keep close."

Again—

    "Well, if ye will be ordered and do by my *reed*."

Again, act v., sc. 2—

    "And where ye sat, he said full certain, if I would follow his *reed*."

Again, in Erasmus's "Praise of Folie," by Chaloner, sig.
D 3 : "Vnles perchaunce some would chuse suche a souldiour
as was Demosthenes, who folowying Archilocus the poetes *rede*,
scarse lookynge his enemies in the face, threw downe his
shelde and ranne awaie, as cowardly a warriour as he was a
wyse oratour."

  The old version of the singing Psalms also begins in this
manner—

    "The man is blest that hath not bent
    To wicked *rede* his ear."

Diccon. Godamercy, dame Chat, in faith thou
      must the gear begin :
It is twenty pound to a goose-turd my Gammer
      will not tarry.
But hitherward she comes as fast as her legs can carry,
To brawl with you about her cock, for well I heard
      Tib say,
The cock was roasted in your house to breakfast
      yesterday :
And when ye had the carcase eaten, the feathers
      ye outflung,
And Doll your maid the legs she hid a foot-deep in
      the dung.
   Chat. O gracious God, my heart it bursts !
   Diccon. Well, rule yourself a space.
And Gammer Gurton, when she cometh anon into
      this place,
Then to the quean let 's see : tell her your mind, and
      spare not.
So shall Diccon blameless be ; and then go to, I
      care not.
   Chat. Then, whore, beware her throat, I can
      abide no longer :
In faith, old witch, it shall be seen which of us two
      be stronger ;
And Diccon, but at your request I would not stay
      one hour.
   Diccon. Well, keep it in, till she be here, and
      then out let it pour.
In the meanwhile get you in, and make no words
      of this ;
More of this matter within this hour to hear you
      shall not miss.
Because I know you are my friend, hide it I could
      not doubtless :
Ye know your harm, see ye be wise about your own
      business.

So fare ye well—
    CHAT. Nay, soft, Diccon, and drink : what, Doll,
      I say,
Bring here a cup of the best ale, let's see, come
    quickly away.

THE SECOND ACT.

THE THIRD SCENE.

HODGE, DICCON.

    DICCON. Ye see, masters, that one end tapp'd of
      this my short device,
Now must we broach t'other too, before the smoke
    arise ;
And by the time they have a while run,
I trust ye need not crave it,
But look what lieth in both their hearts, ye are like
    sure to have it.
    HODGE. Yea, Gog's soul, art alive yet? what
      Diccon, dare ich come?
    DICCON. A man is well hied to trust to thee, I
      will say nothing but mum.
But, and ye come any nearer, I pray you see all be
    sweet.
    HODGE. Tush, man, is Gammer's nee'le found?
      that chould gladly weet.[1]
    DICCON. She may thank thee it is not found,
      for if you had kept thy standing,

---

[1] *i.e.*, Gladly know. So in Shakspeare's "Antony and
Cleopatra," act i., sc. 1—

      "In which I bind,
On pain of punishment, the world to *weete,*
We stand up peerless."

The [form] *weet* is also used by Spenser and Fairfax.

The devil he would have fet it out—ev'n, Hodge,
    at thy commanding.
    HODGE. Gog's heart! and could he tell nothing
      where the nee'le might be found?
    DICCON. Ye foolish dolt, ye were to seek, ere
      we had got our ground;
Therefore his tale so doubtful was, that I could not
    perceive it.
    HODGE. Then ich see well something was said,
      chope one day yet to have it.
But Diccon, Diccon, did not the devil cry, ho, ho,
    ho?[1]
    DICCON. If thou hadst tarried where thou
      stood'st, thou wouldst hove said so.
    HODGE. Durst swear of a book, cheard him
      roar, straight after ich was gone;
But tell me, Diccon, what said the knave, let me
    hear it anon.
    DICCON. The whoreson talked to me, I know
      not well of what:
One while his tongue it ran, and paltered[2] of a cat,

---

[1] In the ancient moralities, and in many of the earliest entertainments of the stage, the devil is introduced as a
character, and it appears to have been customary to bring
him before the audience with this cry of *ho, ho, ho.* See
particularly the " Devil is an Ass," by Ben Jonson, act. i.,
sc. 1. From the following passages in " Wily Beguiled,"
1606, we learn the manner in which the character used to be
dressed :—" Tush! fear not the dodge : I 'll rather put on
my flashing red nose and my flaming face, and come wrapp'd
in a calf's skin, and cry, *ho, ho,*" &c. Again, " I 'll put
me on my great carnation nose, and wrap me in a rowsing
calf's skin suit, and come like some hobgoblin, or some
devil ascended from the grisly pit of hell; and like a
scarbabe make him take his legs: I 'll play the devil, I warrant ye."

[2] To *palter* is, as Dr Johnson explains it, to *shuffle* with
ambiguous expressions. Thus—

Another while he stammered still upon a rat ;
Last of all there was nothing but every word, Chat,
    Chat ;
But this I well perceived, before I would him rid,
Between Chat, and the rat, and the cat, the needle
    is hid :
Now whether Gib our cat hath eat it in her maw,
Or Doctor Rat our curate hath found it in the
    straw,
Or this dame Chat your neighbour hath stolen it,
    God he knoweth,
But by the morrow at this time we shall learn how
    the matter goeth.
    HODGE. Canst not learn to-night, man, seest not
    what is here ?

                [Pointing behind to his torn breeches.
DICCON. 'Tis not possible to make it sooner ap-
    pear.
    HODGE. Allas, Diccon, then chave no shift ; but
    lest ich tarry too long,
[Will] hie me to Sim Glover's shop, there to seek
    for thong,
Therewith this breech to thatch and tie, as ich
    may.
    DICCON. To-morrow, Hodge, if we chance to
    meet, shall see what I will say.

    " And be these juggling fiends no more believ'd,
      That *palter* with us in a double sense."
                     —*Macbeth*, act v., sc. 8.

In confirmation of Dr Johnson's explanation, Mr Steevens
produces the following instances :—

    "Now, fortune, frown, and *palter*, if thou please."
                 —*Marius and Sylla*, 1594.

    " Romans that have spoke the word,
      And will not *palter*."
          .—*Englishmen for my Money*, c. 3.—O.G.

THE SECOND ACT.

THE FOURTH SCENE.

DICCON, GAMMER.

DICCON. Now this gear must forward go, for
    here my Gammer cometh :
Be still a while, and say nothing, make here a little
    romth.[1]
GAMMER. Good lord ! shall never be my luck
    my nee'le again to spy ?
Alas the while, 'tis past my help ; where 'tis, still
    it must lie.
DICCON. Now, Jesus, Gammer Gurton, what
    driveth you to this sadness ?
I fear me, by my conscience, you will sure fall to
    madness.
GAMMER. Who is that? what, Diccon ? cham
    lost, man : fie, fie.
DICCON. Marry, fie on them that be worthy ;
    but what should be your trouble ?
GAMMER. Alas, the more ich think on it, my
    sorrow it waxeth double.
My goodly tossing[2] Spurrier's nee'le[3] chave lost,
    ich wot not where.
DICCON. Your nee'le ! when ?
GAMMER. My nee'le : alas ! ich might full ill it spare,

---

[1] I suppose he means to say a little *room ;* and therefore
retires till Gammer Gurton has uttered her complaint—S.

[2] I imagine this word was formerly used to signify *sharp.*
So in "The Woman's Prize," by Beaumont and Fletcher,
act ii., sc. 4—

    "They heave ye stool on stool, and fling [a-]main pot-lids
    Like massy rocks dart ladles, tossing irons
    And tongs like thunder-bolts, till overlaid
    They fall beneath the weight."

[Dyce's B. and F. vii., 140.]

[3] The ancient spurs were fixed into straps of leather.
Spurriers, of course, would be obliged to use very strong
needles.—S.

As God himself he knoweth, ne'er one beside chave.

    DICCON. If this be all, good Gammer, I warrant
        you all is safe.

    GAMMER. Why, know you any tidings which
        way my nee'le is gone?

    DICCON. Yea, that I do, doubtless, as ye shall
        hear anon,

'A see a thing this matter toucheth within these
        twenty hours,

Even at this gate before my face, by a neighbour
        of yours ;

She stooped me down, and up she took up a
        needle or a pin,

I durst be sworn it was even yours, by all my
        mother's kin.

    GAMMER. It was my nee'le, Diccon, ich wot ;
        for here even by this post

Ich sat, what time as ich up start, and so my nee'le ich
        lost :

Who was it, leve son ?[1] speak, ich pray thee, and
        quickly tell me that.

    DICCON. A subtle quean as any in this town,
        your neighbour here, dame Chat.

    GAMMER. Dame Chat ! Diccon, let me be gone :
        chill thither in post haste.

    DICCON. Take my counsel yet, ere ye go, for
        fear ye walk in waste,

It is a murrain crafty drab, and froward to be
        pleased,

And ye take not the better way, your [2] needle yet
        ye lose :

---

[1] Who was it, dear son? So in the ballad-poem of " Adam
Bell," &c.—

    "Ye myght have asked towres and towne,
      Parkes and forestes plentie,
    None so pleasaunt to my pay, she said ;
      Nor none so *lefe* to me."
              [—Hazlitt's *Popular Poetry*, ii. 160.]

[2] *Our*, first edition.

For when she took it up, even here before your
    doors :
What, soft, dame Chat (quoth I), that same is none
    of yours.
Avaunt (quoth she), sir knave, what pratest thou
    of that I find ?
I would thou hadst kiss'd me I wot where : (she
    meant I know behind)
And home she went as brag as it had been a
    body-louse,[1]
And I after her, as bold as it had been the good-
    man of the house :
But there, and ye had heard her, how she began to
    scold,
The tongue it went on patins, by him that Judas
    sold !
Each other word I was a knave, and you a whore
    of whores,
Because I spake in your behalf, and said the nee'le
    was yours.
    GAMMER. Gog's bread ! and thinks the callet [2]
    thus to keep my nee'le me fro ?

---

[1] "As brisk as a body-louse was formerly proverbial."
See Ray's "Proverbs," 1742, p. 219.

[2] "*Callet*, a lewd woman, a drab." [See Nares, edit.
1859, p. 128.] So in the "Supposes," by Geo. Gascoigne,
act v., sc. 6 : "Come hither, you old *kallat*, you tatling
huswife : that the deuill cut oute your tong."
Again, in Jonson's "Fox," act iv., sc. 3—

    "Why, the callet
    You told me of here I have ta'en disguis'd."

Callett is elsewhere used for stupid, inactive—

    " Bid maudlin lay the cloth, take up the meat ;
    Look how she stirres ; you sullen elfe, you *callett*,
    Is this the haste you make ? "
        —*Englishmen for my Money*, 1631.—*O.G.*

See other instances in Dr Grey's "Notes on Shakspeare,"
vol. ii., p. 41.

DICCON. Let her alone, and she minds none
　　other, but even to dress you so.
GAMMER.　By the mass, chill rather spend the
　　coat that is on my back.
Thinks the false quean by such a sleight,[1] that
　　chill my nee'le lack ?
DICCON. Slip not your gear,[2] I counsel you, but
　　of this take good heed,
Let not be known, I told you of it, how well
　　soever ye speed.
GAMMER. Chill in, Diccon, and clean aporn to
　　take, and set before me ;
And ich may my nee'le once see, chill sure re-
　　member thee.

THE SECOND ACT.

THE FIFTH SCENE.

DICCON. Here will the sport begin, if these two
　　once may meet,
Their cheer, durst lay money, will prove scarcely
　　sweet.
My gammer sure intends to be upon her bones
With staves or with clubs, or else with cobble
　　stones.[3]
Dame Chat on the other side, if she be far behind,
I am right far deceived, she is given to it of kind.[4]
He that may tarry by it a while, and that but short,
I warrant him trust to it, he shall see all the sport.

---

[1] *Slygh.*—First edition.
[2] *Slepe not you gere.*—First edition.
[3] Pebble-stones.　A *cobble* in the north signifies a *pebble*
To *cobble* is to throw stones.　See Ray.—*S.*
[4] By nature.—*S.*

Into the town will I, my friends to visit there,
And hither straight again to see the end of this
    gear.
In the meantime, fellows, pipe up your fiddles : I
    say, take them,[1]
And let your friends hear such mirth as ye can
    make them.

THE THIRD ACT.

THE FIRST SCENE.

HODGE. Sim Glover, yet gramercy ! cham
    meetly well-sped now,
Th 'art even as good a fellow as ever kiss'd a cow.
Here is a thong[2] indeed, by the mass, though ich
    speak it,
Tom Tankard's great bald curtal,[3] I think, could
    not break it.
And when he spied my need to be so straight and
    hard,
Hase lent me here his nawl to set the gib forward.[4]

---

[1] This passage evidently shows that music playing between
the acts was introduced in the earliest of our dramatic
entertainments.

[2] [Altered by Dodsley. Old edition has *thing*.]

[3] *Curtal* is a *small horse;* properly one who hath his
tail *docked or curtailed.* So, in Dekker's "Villanies discovered by Lanthorne and Candlelight," &c., 1620, sig. H. :
"He could shewe more crafty foxes in this wild goose
chase, then there are white foxes in Russia; and more
strange horse-trickes plaide by such riders, then *Bankes his
curtal* did ever practise (whose gambals of the two were the
honester)."

[4] A naval phrase. The gib is the gib-sail. To set a sail,
is also the technical term.—*S.*

As for my gammer's nee'le the flying fiend go wi'
    it,
Chill not now go to the door again with it to meet.
Chould make shift good enough, and chad a candle's
    end :
The chief hole in my breech with these two chill
    amend.

THE THIRD ACT.

THE SECOND SCENE.

GAMMER, HODGE.

GAMMER. How, Hodge! may'st now be glad,
    cha news to tell thee,
Ich know who hase my nee'le, ich trust soon shall
    it see.
    HODGE. The devil thou does ; hast heard, gam-
      mer, indeed, or dost but jest ?
    GAMMER. Tis as true as steel, Hodge.
    HODGE. Why, knowest well where didst lese it ?
    GAMMER. Ich know who found it, and took it
      up: shalt see, ere it be long.
    HODGE. God's mother dear, if that be true, fare-
      well both nawl and thong !
But who hase it, gammer, say ? one chould fain
    hear it disclosed.
    GAMMER. That false vixen, that same dame Chat,
      that counts herself so honest.
    HODGE. Who told you so ?
    GAMMER. That same did Diccon the bedlam,
      which saw it done.
    HODGE. Diccon ! it is a vengeable knave, gam-
      mer, 'tis a bonable [1] whoreson,

---

[1] [Abominable.]

Can do mo things than that, els cham deceived evil :
By the mass, ich saw him of late call up a great black
    devil.
O, the knave cried *ho, ho !* he roared and he thun-
    dered,
And ye 'ad been here, cham sure you 'ld murrainly
    ha' wondered.
    GAMMER. Was not thou afraid, Hodge, to see
      him in this place ?
    HODGE. No, and chad come to me, chould have
      laid him on the face,
Chould have promised him.
    GAMMER. But, Hodge, had he no horns to push?
    HODGE. As long as your two arms. Saw ye
      never Friar Rush
Painted on a cloth with a side-long cow's tail,
And crooked cloven feet, and many a hooked nail?
For all the world (if I should judge) chould reckon
    him his brother :
Look, even what face Friar Rush[1] had, the devil
    had such another.
    GAMMER. Now, Jesus mercy, Hodge, did Diccon
      in him bring ?
    HODGE. Nay, gammer (hear me speak), chill tell
      you a greater thing.
The devil, when Diccon bad him (ich heard him
    wondrous well)
Said plainly (here before us) that dame Chat had
    your nee'le.

---

[1] *Friar Rush* is mentioned in Reginald Scot's "Discoverie
of Witchcraft," 1584, p. 522 : "*Frier Rush* was for all the
world such another fellow as this *Hudgin,* and brought up
even in the same schoole ; to wit, in a kitchen : insomuch
as the selfsame tale is written of the one as of the other
concerning the skullian, which is said to have been slaine, &c.
For the reading whereof I referre you to *Frier Rush* his
storie, or else to John Wierus 'De præstigiis demonum.'"

GAMMER. Then let us go, and ask her wherefore
    she minds to keep it ;
Seeing we know so much, 'twere madness now to
    slip it.
HODGE. Go to her, gammer, see ye not where
    she stands in her doors ?
Bid her give you the nee'le ; 'tis none of hers, but
    yours.

THE THIRD ACT.

THE THIRD SCENE.

GAMMER, CHAT, HODGE.

GAMMER. Dame Chat, ch' ould pray thee fair,
    let me have that is mine,
Chill not these twenty years take one fart that is
    thine ;
Therefore give me mine own, and let me live beside
    thee—
CHAT. Why art thou crept from home hither to
    mine own doors to chide me ?
Hence, doating drab, avaunt, or I shall set thee
    further.
Intends thou and this knave me in my house to
    murther ?
GAMMER. Tush ! gape not so on[1] me, woman :
    shalt not yet eat me,
Nor all the friends thou hast in this shall not en-
    treat me ;
Mine own goods I will have, and ask thee no[2]
    by'r leave :
What, woman, poor folks must have right, though
    the thing you aggrieve.

---

[1] Old copy, no.   [2] Old copy, on.

CHAT. Give thee thy right, and hang thee up,
    with all thy beggar's brood !
What, wilt thou make me a thief, and say I stole
    thy good ?
GAMMER. Chill say nothing (ich warrant thee),
    but that ich can prove it well,
Thou fet my good even from my door, cham able
    this to tell.
CHAT. Did I (old witch) steal ought was thine ?
    how should that thing be known ?
GAMMER. Ich cannot tell, but up thou tookest
    it, as though it had been thine own.
CHAT. Marry, fie on thee, thou old gib, with
    all my very heart.
GAMMER. Nay, fie on thee, thou ramp,[1] thou
    rig,[2] with all that take thy part.
CHAT. A vengeance on those lips that layeth
    such things to my charge.
GAMMER. A vengeance on those callet's hips,
    whose conscience is so large.
CHAT. Come out, hog.
GAMMER. Come out, hog, and let have me right.
CHAT. Thou arrant witch.
GAMMER. Thou bawdy bitch, chill make thee
    curse this night.
CHAT. A bag and a wallet ![3]

---

[1] Gabriel Harvey, in his " Pierces Supererogation,"
1593, speaking of Long Meg of Westminster, says : " Although she were a lusty, bouncing *rampe*, somewhat like
Gallimetta or maid Marian, yet was she not such a roinish
rannel, such a dissolute flirt gillian," &c.

[2] Thou strumpet. See Note on " Antony and Cleopatra,"
Shakspeare, 1778, vol. viii., p. 175.—*S.*
So in Davies's " Scourge of Folly " [1611]—

    " Or wanton *Rigg*, or letcher dissolute,
      Do stand at Powles Crosse in a sheeten sute."—*Reed.*

[3] The accoutrements of an itinerant trull.—*S.*

GAMMER. A cart for a callet !

CHAT. Why, weenest[1] thou thus to prevail?
I hold thee a groat,
I shall patch thy coat.

GAMMER. Thou wert as good kiss my tail ;
Thou slut, thou cut,[2] thou rakes, thou jakes, will
    not shame make thee hide thee?[3]

CHAT. Thou skald, thou bald, thou rotten,[4]
    thou glutton, I will no longer chide thee ;
But I will teach thee to keep home.

GAMMER. Wilt thou, drunken beast?

                        [They fight.

HODGE. Stick to her, gammer, take her by the
    head, chill warrant you this feast.
Smite, I say, gammer,
Bite, I say, gammer ;

---

[1] Thinkest or imaginest.

[2] *Cut* appears to have been an opprobrious term used by the vulgar when they scolded or abused each other. It occurs again, act v., sc. 2 : "That lying *cut* is lost, that she is not swinged and beaten."

A horse is sometimes called *Cut* in our ancient writers, as in the "First Part of Henry IV.," act ii., sc. 1., and Falstaff says : "If I tell thee a lye, spit in my face, and call me *horse*." *Cut* is therefore probably used in the same sense as *horse*, to which it seems to have been synonymous. Several instances of the use of this term are collected by Mr Steevens, in his edition of Shakspeare; see vol. iv., p. 202.

It appears probable to me that the opprobrious epithet *Cut* arose from the practice of cutting the hair of convicted thieves ; which was anciently the custom in England, as appears from the edicts of John de Northampton against adulterers, who thought, with Paulo Migante, that

    "England ne'er would thrive,
    Till all the whores were burnt alive."
        —See Holinshed, vol. 9., 754, Ed. 1807.—*O. G.*

[3] [*Thee* is not in the old copy.]

[4] *i.e.*, Rat. So in one of the Chester Whitsun plays—
    "Here is a *rotten*, there a mouse."—*S.*

I trow ye will be keen ;
Where be your nails ? claw her by the jaws, pull
    me out both her eyen.
Gog's bones, gammer, hold up your head.
    CHAT. I trow, drab, I shall dress thee.
Tarry, thou knave, I hold thee a groat, I shall
    make these hands bless thee. ·
    [GURTON.] Take thou this, old whore, for
    amends, and learn thy tongue well to tame,
And say thou met at this bickering, not thy
    fellow,[1] but thy dame.
    HODGE. Where is the strong stewed whore ?[2]
    chill gi 'r a whore's mark.
Stand out one's way, that ich kill none in the dark.
Up, gammer, and ye be alive, chill fight[3] now for
    us both ;
Come no near me, thou scald callet, to kill thee
    ich were loth.
    CHAT. Art here again, thou hoddypeke ?[4] what,
    Doll, bring me out my spit.
    HODGE. Chill broach thee with this, by
    m' father's soul, chill conjure that foul
    spreet.

---

[1] Not thy equal, but thy mistress.
[2] *i.e.*, Rank strumpet from the stews.—*S.*
[3] *Fygh*—First edition.
[4] *i.e.*, Hodmandod.—*S.*
I find this word used in Nash's " Anatomie of Absurditie,"
1589, sig. B., where it seems intended as synonymous to
cuckold : " But women, through want of wisedome, are
growne to such wantonesse, that uppon no occasion they
will crosse the streete, to have a glaunce of some gallant,
deeming that men by one looke of them shoulde be in love
with them, and will not stick to make an errant over
the way, to purchase a paramour to help at a pinche, who,
under hur husbands, that *hoddy peekes* nose, must have all
the destilling dew of his delicate rose, leaving him onely a
sweet sent, good inough for such a sencelesse sotte."

Let door stand, Cock, why com'st indeed? keep
    door, thou whoreson boy.
    CHAT [*to Doll.*] Stand to it, thou dastard, for
    thine ears ; ise teach the sluttish toy.
    HODGE. Gog's wounds, whore, chill make thee
    avaunt,
Take heed, Cock, pull in the latch.
    CHAT. I' faith, sir loose-breech, had ye tarried,
    ye should have found your match.
    GAMMER. Now 'ware thy throat, losel,[1] thou'se
    pay for all.
    HODGE. Well said, gammer, by my soul.
Hoise her, souse her, bounce her, trounce her, pull
    her throat-hole.
    CHAT. Com'st behind me, thou withered witch?
    and I get once on foot,
Thou'se pay for all, thou old tar-leather, I'll teach
    thee what longs to 't.
Take thee this to make up thy mouth, till time
    thou come by more.
    HODGE. Up, gammer, stand on your feet, where
    is the old whore?

---

[1] A *losel* is a worthless fellow. It is a term of contempt
frequently used by Spenser. It is likewise to be met with
in the "Death of Robert, Earl of Huntington," 1601 :

> "To have the lozels company."

Again, in "The Pinner of Wakefield," 1599 :

> "Peace, prating lozel," &c.

See Mr Steevens's "Notes on Shakspeare," vol. iv., p. 337.
Again, in Hall's "Satires," edit. 1753, p. 78—

> "How his enraged ghost would stamp and stare,
> That Cæsar's throne is turn'd to Peter chayre,
> To see an old shorne *lozel* perched high,
> Crossing beneath a golden canopy."

See Holinshed's "Chron.," edit. 1577, vol. ii., p. 740 ("Five
Days' Pastime," p. 67); "Englishmen for my Money," p. 42 ;
Holinshed, vol. v., p. 208.—*O. G.*

Faith, would chad her by the face, chould crack
    her callet crown.
    GAMMER. Ah, Hodge, Hodge, where was thy
    help, when th' vixen had me down!
    HODGE. By the mass, Gammer, but for my staff,
    Chat had gone nigh to spill you.
Ich think the harlot had not cared, and chad not
    come, to kill you.
But shall we lose our nee'le thus?
    GAMMER. No, Hodge, ich were loth to do so.
Thinkest thou chill take that at her hand? no,
    Hodge, ich tell thee no.
    HODGE. Chould yet this fray were well take up,
    and our own nee'le at home,
'Twill be my chance else some to kill, wherever it
    be or whom.
    GAMMER. We have a parson (Hodge, thou
    knows), a man esteemed wise,
Mast Doctor Rat, chill for him send, and let me
    hear his advice.
He will her shrive [1] for all this gear, and give her
    penance straight.
Wese have our nee'le, else dame Chat comes ne'er
    within heaven-gate.
    HODGE. Yea marry, gammer, that ich think
    best: will you now for him send?
The sooner Doctor Rat be here, the sooner wese
    ha' an end.
And here, gammer, Diccon's devil (as ich remem-
    ber well)
Of Cat and Chat, and Doctor Rat, a felonious tale
    did tell,
Chold you forty pound, that is the way your nee'le
    to get again.

---

[1] Confess.

GAMMER. Chill ha' him straight ; call out the
　　boy, wese make him take the pain.
HODGE. What, Cock, I say, come out ; what
　　devil, can'st not hear ?
COCK.[1] How now, Hodge, how does gammer ?
　　is yet the weather clear ?
What would chave me to do ?
GAMMER. Come hither, Cock, anon.
Hence swith to Doctor Rat hie thee, that thou
　　were gone,
And pray him come speak with me, cham not well
　　at ease :
Shalt have him at his chamber, or else at Mother
　　Bee's,
Else seek him at Hob Filcher's shop ; for, as cheard
　　it reported,
There is the best ale in all the town, and now is
　　most resorted.
COCK. And shall ich bring him with me, gam-
　　mer ?
GAMMER. Yea, by and by, good Cock.
COCK.[2] Shalt see that shall be here anon, else
　　let me have on the dock.
HODGE. Now, gammer, shall we two go in, and
　　tarry for his coming ?
What devil, woman, pluck up your heart, and
　　leave off all this glooming.[3]
Though she were stronger at the first, as ich think
　　ye did find her.
Yet there ye dress'd the drunken sow, what time
　　ye came behind her.[4]

---

[1] *Gammer* in the first edition.
[2] *Hodge* in the first edition.
[3] *i.e.*, Sulky, gloomy looks.　It is still said, in vulgar
language, that a discontented person looks *glum.*—S.
[4] This line is given to Gammer Gurton in the first edition.

GAMMER. Nay, nay, cham sure she lost not all,
    for set them to the beginning,
And ich doubt not, but he will make small boast
    of her winning.

THE THIRD ACT.

THE FOURTH SCENE.

TIB, HODGE, GAMMER, COCK.

TIB. See, gammer, gammer, Gib our cat, cham
    afraid what she aileth,
She stands me gasping behind the door, as though
    her wind her faileth.
Now mot[1] ich doubt what Gib should mean, that
    now she doth so doat.[2]
HODGE. Hold hither, ich hold twenty pound,
    your nee'le is in her throat.
Grope her, ich say, methinks ich feel it; does not
    prick your hand?
GAMMER. Ich can feel nothing.
HODGE. No! ich know that's not within this
    land
A murrainer cat than Gib is, betwixt the Thames
    and Tyne,
Sh'ase as much wit in her head almost as ch'ave in
    mine.
TIB. Faith, sh'ase eaten something, that will
    not easily down,
Whether she gat it at home, or abroad in the
    town,
Ich cannot tell.

---

[1] Old copy, *let.*
[2] That is, appear so mad. *To doat* and *to be mad* were
used as synonymous terms. See Baret's "Alvearie," *v. Dote.*

GAMMER. Alas ! ich fear it be some crooked
    pin,
And then farewell Gib, she is undone and lost, all
    save the skin.
HODGE. 'Tis [1] your nee'le, woman, I say ; Gog's
    soul, give me a knife,
And chill have it out of her maw, or else chall
    lose my life.
GAMMER. What ! nay, Hodge, fie, kill not our
    cat, 'tis all the cats we ha' now.
HODGE. By the mass, dame Chat hase me so
    moved, ich care not what I kill, ma' God a vow.
Go to then, Tib, to this gear, hold up her tail and
    take her,
Chill see what devil is in her guts, chill take the
    pains to rake her.
GAMMER. Rake a cat, Hodge ! what wouldest
    thou do ?
HODGE. What, think'st that cham not able ?
Did not Tom Tankard rake his curtal t'o'er day
    standing in the stable ?
GAMMER. Soft, be content, let 's hear what news
    Cock bringeth from Master Rat.
COCK. Gammer, chave been there as you bad,
    you wot well about what.
'Twill not be long before he come, ich durst swear
    off a book,
He bid you see ye be at home, and there for him
    to look.
GAMMER. Where didst thou find him, boy ? was
    he not where I told thee ?
COCK. Yes, yes, even at Hob Filcher's house, by
    him that bought and sold me :
A cup of ale had in his hand, and a crab lay in the
    fire :

---

[1] Old copy has *Tyb*.

Chad much a-do to go and come, all was so full of
    mire :
And, gammer, one thing I can tell : Hob Filcher's
    nawl was lost,
And Doctor Rat found it again, hard beside the
    door-post.
Ich hold a penny can say something, your nee'le
    again to fet.[1]
  GAMMER. Cham glad to hear so much, Cock,
    then trust he will not let
To help us herein best he can; therefore, till time
    he come,
Let us go in, if there be ought to get, thou shalt
    have some.

THE FOURTH ACT.

THE FIRST SCENE.

DOCTOR RAT, GAMMER GURTON.

DOCTOR RAT. A man were better twenty times
    be a bandog and bark,
Than here among such a sort be parish priest or
    clerk.

---

[1] Fetched. So, in " Cynthia's Revels," act i., sc. 2 :
" Nay, the other is better, exceeds it much : the invention
is farther *fet* too."

Again, in Ascham's " Toxophilus," p. 15 : "And therefore
agaynst a desperate evill began to seeke for a desperate
remedie, which was *fet* from Rome, a shop alwayes open to
any mischief, as you shall perceive in these few leaves, if
you marke them well."

Again, in Lyly's " Euphues," p. 33 : " That far *fet* and
deere bought, is good for ladies."

Where he shall never be at rest one pissing while[1]
    a day,
But he must trudge about the town this way, and
    [then] that way,
Here to a drab, there to a thief, his shoes to tear
    and rent,
And that which is worst of all, at every knave's
    commandment.
I had not sit the space to drink two pots of ale,
But Gammer Gurton's sorry boy was straightway
    at my tail ;
And she was sick, and I must come, to do I wot
    not what :
If once her finger's-end but ache : trudge, call for
    Doctor Rat.
And when I come not at their call, I only thereby
    lose,
For I am sure to lack therefore a tithe-pig or a
    goose.
I warrant you, when truth is known, and told they
    have their tale,
The matter whereabout I come is not worth a half-
    pennyworth of ale :
Yet must I talk so sage and smooth, as though I
    were a gloser
But ere the year come at an end, I shall be sure
    the loser.
What work ye, Gammer Gurton ? know here is your
    friend Doctor Rat.
    GAMMER. Ah ! good master Doctor, 'ch a
    troubled, 'ch a troubled you, 'ch wot well that.

---

[1] A proverbial expression used by Ben Jonson in his
"Magnetic Lady," and by Shakspeare in "The Two Gentlemen of Verona." See Mr Steevens's Note on the latter, and
[Hazlitt's "Proverbs," 1869, p. 127.] It is also to be found
in Nash's "Lenten Stuff," 1599.

DOCTOR RAT. How do ye, woman? be ye lusty,
or be ye not well at ease?

GAMMER. By Gis,[1] master, cham not sick, but
yet chave a disease.

Chad a foul turn now of late, chill tell it you by
gigs.

DOCTOR RAT. Hath your brown cow cast her
calf, or your sandy sow her pigs?

GAMMER. No, but chad been as good they had,
as this, ich wot well.

---

[1] In Shakspeare's "Hamlet," Ophelia sings a song, in
which this adjuration is used—

> "*By gys* and by Saint Charity."

And it is also to be found in Gascoigne's Poems, in Preston's
"Cambyses," and in the comedy of "See me and see me
not," 1618—

> "*By gisse* I swear, were I so fairly wed," &c.

Mr Steevens's note on "Hamlet," in which Mr Steevens
observes, that *Saint Charity* is a known saint among the
Roman Catholics. Spenser mentions her ("Eclog," v.,
255):—

> "Ah dear Lord and sweet *Saint Charity* !"

Again, in "The Downfall of Robert, Earl of Huntington,"
1601—

> "Therefore, sweet master, for *Saint Charity*."
> —Note on *Hamlet*, act iv., sc. 5.

[Dr Bailey supposes, which is very probable, that this
abbreviated or corrupt form of *Jesus* arose from] the letters
I H S being anciently all that was set down to denote that
sacred name on altars, the covers of books, &c.

It occurs also in the following passage of Erasmus's
"Praise of Folie," by Chaloner, 1549:—"Lyke as many
great lordes there be who set so muche by theim, as scant
they can eate theyr meate, or byde a minute without theim,
cherisshyng them (*by iysse*) a little better than thei are
wont to dooe these frounyng philosophers," &c. Sig. G 2.

Again, in "Euphues and his England," 1582, p. 5:—
"Unto whome he replyed, shoaring up his eyes, '*by Jis*,'
soune, I accompt the cheere good which mainteineth health,
and the servauntes honest whome I finde faythfull."

DOCTOR RAT. What is the matter?
GAMMER. Alas, alas, 'ch a lost my good nee'le.
My nee'le, I say, and wot ye what? a drab came
    by, and spied it,
And when I asked her for the same, the filth flatly
    denied it.
DOCTOR RAT. What was she that—
GAMMER. A dame, ich warrant you : she began
    to scold and brawl ;
Alas, alas, come hither, Hodge ; this wretch can tell
    you all.

THE FOURTH ACT.

THE SECOND SCENE.

HODGE, DOCTOR RAT, GAMMER, DICCON, CHAT.

HODGE. Good morrow, Gaffer Vicar.
DOCTOR RAT. Come on, fellow, let us hear.
Thy dame hath said to me, thou knowest of all
    this gear ?
Let 's see what thou canst say.
HODGE. By m' fay, sir, that ye shall,
What matter soever here was done, ich can tell
    your maship :
My Gammer Gurton here, see now,
  Sat her down at this door, see now,
And as she began to stir her, see now,
  Her nee'le fell in the floor, see now,
And while her staff she took, see now,
  At Gib her cat to fling, see now,
Her nee'le was lost in the floor, see now ;
  Is not this a wondrous thing, see now ?
Then came the quean dame Chat, see now,

To ask for her black cup, see now :
And even here at this gate, see now,
  She took that nee'le up, see now,
My gammer then she yede,[1] see now,
  Her nee'le again to bring, see now,
And was caught by the head, see now ;
  Is not this a wondrous thing, see now ?
She tare my gammer's coat, see now,
  And scratched her by the face, see now,
Chad thought sh'ad stopp'd her throat, see now ;
  Is not this a wondrous case, see now ?
When ich saw this, ich was wroth, see now,
  And stert between them twain, see now,
Else ich durst take a book-oath, see now,
  My gammer had been slain, see now.
  GAMMER. This is even the whole matter, as
    Hodge has plainly told.
And chould fain be quiet for my part, that chould.
But help us, good master, beseech ye that ye do,
Else shall we both be beaten, and lose our nee'le
    too.
  DOCTOR RAT. What would ye have me to do ?
    tell me, that I were gone,
I will do the best that I can to set you both at one.
But be ye sure dame Chat hath this your nee'le
    found ?
  GAMMER. Here comes the man, that see her
    take it up off the ground,
Ask him yourself, Master Rat, if ye believe not me,
And help me to my nee'le, for God's sake and
    Saint Charity.[2]

---

[1] i.e., *she went*.

      "For all *i-yede* out at one ere,
      That in that other she did lere."
                —*Romaunt of the Rose.*

The word is also used by Spenser and Fairfax.
  [2] [See a note *supra.*]

DOCTOR RAT. Come near, Diccon, and let us
    hear what thou can express.
Wilt thou be sworn, thou seest dame Chat this
    woman's nee'le have?
DICCON. Nay, by Saint Benet, will I not, then
    might ye think me rave.[1]
GAMMER. Why did'st not thou tell me so even
    here? canst thou for shame deny it?
DICCON. Ay, marry, gammer: but I said I
    would not abide by it.
DOCTOR RAT. Will you say a thing, and not
    stick to it to try it?
DICCON. Stick to it, quoth you, Master Rat?
    marry, sir, I defy it.[2]
Nay, there is many an honest man, when he such
    blasts hath blown
In his friend's ears, he would be loth the same by
    him were known:
If such a toy be used oft among the honesty,[3]
It may [not] beseem a simple man of your and my
    degree.
DOCTOR RAT. Then we be never the nearer, for
    all that you can tell.
DICCON. Yes, marry, sir, if ye will do by mine
    advice and counsel:
If mother Chat see all us here, she ['ll] know how
    the matter goes,
Therefore I reed you three go hence, and within
    keep close;
And I will into dame Chat's house, and so the
    matter use,
That ere ye could go twice to church, I warrant
    you hear news.

---

[1] Baret, in his "Alvearie," explains *rave*, " to talke like
a madde bodie."
[2] I refuse, deny the charge.
[3] [Among the honest sort?]

She shall look well about her, but I durst lay a
    pledge,
Ye shall of gammer's nee'le have shortly better
    knowledge.
    GAMMER. Now, gentle Diccon, do so ; and, good
    sir, let us trudge.
    DOCTOR RAT. By the mass, I may not tarry so
    long to be your judge.
    DICCON. 'Tis but a little while, man : what, take
    so much pain ;
If I hear no news of it, I will come soon here [1]
    again.
    HODGE. Tarry so much, good Master Doctor, of
    your gentleness.
    DOCTOR RAT. Then let us hie inward, and, Dic-
    con, speed thy business.
    DICCON. Now, sirs, do you no more, but keep
    my counsel just,
And Doctor Rat shall thus catch some good, I trust ;
But mother Chat, my gossip, talk first withal I
    must,
For she must be chief captain to lay the Rat in the
    dust.   [*Aside. Exit.*
Good even,[2] dame Chat, in faith, and well-met in
    this place.
    CHAT. Good even, my friend Diccon, whither
    walk ye this pace ?
    DICCON. By my truth, even to you, to learn how
    the world goeth.
Heard ye no more of the other matter, say me
    now, by your troth ?
    CHAT. O yes, Diccon : hear the old whore and
    Hodge that great knave.

---

[1] [Original, *sooner.*]
[2] [This should form the commencement of a new scene,
but it is not so marked.]

But, in faith, I would thou hadst seen : O Lord, I
    drest them brave.
She bare me two or three souses behind in the
    nape of the neck,
Till I made her old weasand to answer again keck.
And Hodge, that dirty bastard, that at her elbow
    stands,
If one pair of legs had not been worth two pair of
    hands,
He had had his beard shaven, if my nails would
    have served,
And not without a cause, for the knave it well
    deserved.
    DICCON. By the mass, I can[1] thee thank, wench,
    thou didst so well acquit thee.
    CHAT. And th' adst seen him, Diccon, it would
    have made thee beshit thee
For laughter : the whoreson dolt at last caught up
    a club,
As though he would have slain the master-devil,
    Belsabub ;
But I set him soon inward.
    DICCON. O Lord ! there is the thing,
That Hodge is so offended, that makes him start
    and fling.
    CHAT. Why, makes the knave any noiling,[2] as
    ye have seen or heard ?
    DICCON. Even now I saw him last, like a mad
    man he far'd,
And sware by heaven and hell, he would a-wreak
    his sorrow,
And leave you never a hen alive by eight of the
    clock to-morrow :

---

[1] So the edition of 1575. See note, *supra*.
[2] [Ado. See Nares, edit. 1859, p. 576.]

Therefore mark what I say, and my words see that
    ye trust,
Your hens be as good as dead, if ye leave them on
    the roost.
    CHAT. The knave dare as well go hang himself,
      as go upon my ground.
    DICCON. Well, yet take heed, I say, I must tell
      you my tale round :
Have you not about your house, behind your fur-
    nace or lead,
A hole where a crafty knave may creep in for
    need ?
    CHAT. Yes, by the mass, a hole broke down
      even within these two days.
    DICCON. Hodge, he intends this same night to
      slip in thereaways.
    CHAT. O Christ, that I were sure of it ! in faith,
      he should have his meed.[1]
    DICCON. Watch well, for the knave will be
      there as sure as is your creed ;
I would spend myself a shilling to have him
    swinged well.
    CHAT. I am as glad as a woman can be of this
      thing to hear tell ;
By Gog's bones, when he cometh, now that I know
    the matter,
He shall sure at the first skip to leap in scalding
    water :
With a worse turn besides : when he will, let him
    come.
    DICCON. I tell you as my sister ; you know
      what meaneth mum.
Now lack I but my doctor to play his part
    again.   [*Aside.*

---

[1] Reward. It is a word used by Spenser, Shakspeare,
and the chief of our ancient writers.

And lo, where he cometh towards, peradventure
    to his pain.   *[Leaves Mother Chat.*
    DOCTOR RAT. What good news, Diccon? fellow,
    is mother Chat at home?
    DICCON. She is, sir, and she is not; but it please
    her to whom:
Yet did I take her tardy, as subtle as she was.
    DOCTOR RAT. The thing that thou went'st for,
    hast thou brought it to pass?
    DICCON. I have done that I have done, be it
    worse, be it better.
And dame Chat at her wits-end I have almost set her.
    DOCTOR RAT. Why, hast thou spied the nee'le:
    quickly, I pray thee tell?
    DICCON. I have spied it in faith, sir, I handled
    myself so well;
And yet the crafty quean had almost take my trump;
But, ere all came to an end, I set her in a dump.
    DOCTOR RAT. How so, I pray thee, Diccon?
    DICCON. Marry, sir, will ye hear?
She was clapp'd down on the backside,[1] by Cock's [2]
    mother dear,
And there she sat sewing a halter or a band,
With no other thing but gammer's needle in her
    hand:
As soon as any knock, if the filth be in doubt,
She needs but once puff, and her candle is out:
Now I, sir, knowing of every door the pin,
Came nicely, and said no word, till time I was
    within,
And there I saw the nee'le, even with these two eyes.
Whoever say the contrary, I will swear he lies.
    DOCTOR RAT. O Diccon, that I was not there
    then in thy stead!

---

[1] At the back of her house.
[2] God's, not the boy Cock's.

DICCON. Well, if ye will be ordered, and do by
    my reed,
I will bring you to a place, as the house stands,
Where ye shall take the drab with the nee'le in
    her hands.
    DOCTOR RAT. For God's sake, do so, Diccon,
    and I will gage my gown,
To give thee a full pot of the best ale in the town.
    DICCON. Follow me but a little, and mark what
    I say,
Lay down your gown beside you, go to, come on
    your way :
See ye not what is here ? a hole wherein ye may
    creep
Into the house, and suddenly unawares among
    them leap ;
There shall ye find the bitch-fox and the nee'le to-
    gether.
Do as I bid you, man, come on your ways hither.
    DOCTOR RAT. Art thou sure, Diccon, the swill-
    tub stands not hereabout ?
    DICCON. I was within myself, man, even now,
    there is no doubt.
Go softly, make no noise, give me your foot, sir
    John,
Here will I wait upon you, till you come out
    anon.   [*D. Rat creeps in.*
    DOCTOR RAT [*calling from within*]. Help, Diccon,
    out alas, I shall be slain among them.
    DICCON. If they give you not the needle, tell
    them that ye will hang them.
Ware that ! how, my wenches, have ye caught the
    fox,
That used to make revel among your hens and
    cocks ?
Save his life yet for his order, though he sustain
    some pain.

Gog's bread, I am afraid they will beat out his
    brain.
  DOCTOR RAT. Woe worth the hour that I came
    here ;
And woe worth him that wrought this gear,
A sort of drabs and queans have me blest,
Was ever creature half so evil drest ?
Whoever it wrought, and first did invent it,
He shall, I warrant him, ere long repent it.
I will spend all I have without my skin,
But he shall be brought to the plight I am in ;
Master Baily, I trow, and he be worth his ears,
Will snaffle these murderers, and all that [with]
    them bears :
I will surely neither bite nor sup,
Till I fetch him hither, this matter to take up.

THE FIFTH ACT.

THE FIRST SCENE.

MASTER BAILY, DOCTOR RAT.

  BAILY. I can perceive none other, I speak it
    from my heart,
But either ye are all in the fault, or else in the
    greatest part.
  DOCTOR RAT. If it be counted his fault, besides
    all his griefs,
When a poor man is spoiled, and beaten among
    thieves,
Then I confess my fault herein at this season :
But I hope you will not judge so much against
    reason.
  BAILY. And methinks by your own tale, of all
    that ye name,

If any played the thief, you were the very same :
The women they did nothing, as your words made
    probation,
But stoutly withstood your forcible invasion.
If that a thief at your window to enter should
    begin,
Would you hold forth your hand, and help to pull
    him in ?
Or would [1] you keep him out ? I pray you answer
    me.
  DOCTOR RAT. Marry, keep him out : and a good
    cause why.
But I am no thief, sir, but an honest learned clerk.
  BAILY. Yea, but who knoweth that, when he
    meets you in the dark ?
I am sure your learning shines not out at your nose.
Was it any marvel, though the poor woman arose,
And start up, being afraid of that was in her purse ?
Me-think you may be glad that your [2] luck was no
    worse.
  DOCTOR RAT. Is not this evil enough, I pray
    you, as you think ?　[*Showing his broken head.*
  BAILY. Yea, but a man in the dark oft [3] chances
    to wink,
As soon he smites his father as any other man,
Because, for lack of light, discern him he ne can.
Might it not have been your luck with a spit to
    have been slain ?
  DOCTOR RAT. I think I am little better, my
    scalp is cloven to the brain :
If there be all the remedy, I know who bears the
    knocks. [4]
  BAILY. By my troth, and well worthy besides
    to kiss the stocks.

---

[1] Orig. *you would.*　　　　[2] Orig. *you.*
[3] [Orig. *of.*]　　　　[4] Orig. *kockes.*

To come in on the back side, when ye might go
    about,
I know none such, unless they long to have their
    brains knock'd out.
    DOCTOR RAT. Well, will you be so good, sir, as
    talk with dame Chat,
And know what she intended, I ask no more but
    that.
    BAILY. Let her be called, fellow, because of
    master doctor,
I warrant in this case, she will be her own proctor:
She will tell her own tale, in metre or in prose,
And bid you seek your remedy, and so go wipe
    your nose.

THE FIFTH ACT.

THE SECOND SCENE.

M. BAILY, CHAT, D. RAT, GAMMER, HODGE,
    DICCON.

    BAILY. Dame Chat, master doctor upon you
    here complaineth,
That you and your maids should him much
    disorder,
And taketh many an oath that no word be feigned,
Laying to your charge, how you thought him to
    murder:
And on his part again, that same man say'th
    furder,
He never offended you in word nor intent;
To hear you answer hereto, we have now for you
    sent.
    CHAT. That I would have murdered him! fie
    on him, wretch!

And evil mought he the for it, our Lord I beseech.
I will swear on all the books that opens and shuts,
He feigneth this tale out of his own guts.
For this seven weeks with me, I am sure, he sat
    not down;
[*To D. Rat.*] Nay, ye have other minions in the
    other end of the town,
Where ye were liker to catch such a blow
Than anywhere else, as far as I know.
    BAILY. Belike then, master doctor, your[1] stripe
      there ye got not.
    DOCTOR RAT. Think you I am so mad, that
      where I was bet, I wot not?[2]
Will ye believe this quean, before she hath
    tried it?
It is not the first deed she hath done, and after-
    ward denied it.
    CHAT. What, man, will you say I broke your
      head?
    DOCTOR RAT. How canst thou prove the
      contrary?
    CHAT. Nay, how provest thou that I did the
      deed.
    DOCTOR RAT. Too plainly, by St Mary.
This proof, I trow, may serve, though I no word
    spoke.   [*Showing his broken head.*
    CHAT. Because thy head is broken, was it I that
      broke?
I saw thee, Rat, I tell thee, not once within this
    fortnight.
    DOCTOR RAT. No, marry, thou sawest me not:
      for why thou hadst no light;

---

[1] Original, *you.*

[2] [Beaten. Here was a note of half a page to explain
and illustrate the meaning of the very common word
wot/]

But I felt thee for all the dark, beshrew thy
    smooth cheeks !
And thou groped me, this will declare any day
    this six weeks.   *[Showing his head.*
    BAILY.   Answer me to this, Master Rat, when
    caught you this harm of yours ?
    DOCTOR RAT. A while ago, sir, God he know-
    eth ; within less than these two hours.
    BAILY. Dame Chat, was there none with you
    (confess, i' faith) about that season ?
What, woman, let it be what it will, 'tis neither
    felony nor treason.
    CHAT. Yes, by my faith, Master Baily, there was
    a knave not far,
Who caught one good filip on the brow with a
    door-bar.
And well was he worthy, as it seemed to me :
But what is that to this man, since this was not he ?
    BAILY.   Who was it, then ? let 's hear.
    DOCTOR RAT. Alas, sir, ask you that ?
Is it not made plain enough by the own mouth of
    dame Chat ?
The time agreeth, my head is broken, her tongue
    cannot lie ;
Only upon a bare nay, she saith it was not I.
    CHAT. No, marry, was it not indeed, ye shall
    hear by this one thing.
This afternoon a friend of mine for good-will gave
    me warning.
And bad me well look to my roost and all my
    capons' pens ;
For if I took not better heed, a knave would have
    my hens.
Then I, to save my goods, took so much pains as
    him to watch ;
And as good fortune served me, it was my chance
    him for to catch.

What strokes he bare away, or other what was his
      gains,
I wot not, but I am sure he had something for his
      pains.
    BAILY. Yet tell'st thou not who it was.
    CHAT. Who it was?   A false thief,
That came like a false fox, my pullen [1] to kill and
      mischief.
    BAILY. But knowest thou not his name?
    CHAT. I know it, but what then?
It was that crafty cullion [2] Hodge, my Gammer
      Gurton's man.
    BAILY. Call me the knave hither, he shall sure
      kiss the stocks.
I shall teach him a lesson for filching hens or cocks.
    DOCTOR RAT. I marvel, Master Baily, so bleared
      be your eyes!

---

[1] Poultry.   So in Fitzherbert's "Boke of Husbandry":
"Gyve thy *poleyn*—meate in the morning," &c.   Again, in
"Your five Gallants," by Middleton: "And to see how piti-
fully the *pullen* will looke, it makes me after relent, and
turne my anger into a quick fire to roast them."
[2] A base, contemptible fellow.   So, in "Tom Tyler and
his Wife," 1661, p. 19—

> "It is an old saying, praise at the parting,
> I think I have made *the cullion* to wring.
> I was not beaten so black and blew,
> But I am sure he has as many new."

In "Wily Beguiled:" "But to say the truth, she had little
reason to take a *cullion* lug loaf, milksop slave, when she
may have a lawyer, a gentleman that stands upon his reputation in the country;" in Massinger's "Guardian," act.
ii., sc. 4—

> "Love live Severino,
> And perish all such *cullions* as repine
> At his new monarchy."

And Bobadil, in Ben Jonson's "Every Man to his Humour," act. iii., sc. 5, when beating Cob, exclaims:

> "You base *cullion*, you."

An egg is not so full of meat, as she is full of
    lies :
When she hath played this prank, to excuse all
    this gear,
She layeth the fault on such a one as I know was
    not there.
    CHAT. Was he not there ? look on his pate ; that
      shall be his witness.
    DOCTOR RAT. I would my head were half so
      whole, I would seek no redress.
    BAILY. God bless you, Gammer Gurton.
    GAMMER. God 'eild [1] ye, master mine.
    BAILY. Thou hast a knave within thy house,
      Hodge, a servant of thine.
They tell me that busy knave is such a filching
    one,
That hen, pig, goose, or capon, thy neighbour can
    have none.
    GAMMER. By God, cham much a-meved to hear
      any such report :
Hodge was not wont, ich trow, to have him in that
    sort.
    CHAT. A thievisher knave is not on-live, more
      filching nor more false ;
Many a truer man than he has hanged up by the
    halse. [2]
And thou his dame of all his theft thou art the sole
    receiver ;
For Hodge to catch, and thou to keep, I never new
    none better.

----

  [1] [Original, *Dylde* ; the compositor having repeated the
d of *God* at the beginning of the following word.   This is
not an uncommon misprint.]

  [2] *Hals*, in the Glossary to Douglas's *Æneid*, is thus explained : " The hawse, the throat, or neck.   A-S. and Isl.
Hals, collum, thence, *to hals* or *hawse*, to embrace, *collo dare
brachia circvm.*"

GAMMER. Sir reverence of your masterdom, and
    you were out a-door,
Chould be so bold, for all her brags, to call her
    arrant whore.
And ich knew Hodge as bad as t' ou, ich wish me
    endless sorrow,
And chould not take the pains to hang him up
    before to-morrow.
    CHAT. What have I stolen from thee or thine,
    thou ill-favor'd old trot?
    GAMMER. A great deal more (by God's blest)
    than chever by thee got,
That thou knowest well, I need not say it.
    BAILY. Stop there, I say,
And tell me here, I pray you, this matter by the
    way :
How chance Hodge is not here? him would I fain
    have had.
    GAMMER. Alas, sir, he 'll be here anon ; a' be
    handled too bad.
    CHAT. Master Baily, sir, ye be not such a fool,
    well I know,
But ye perceive by this lingering there is a pad in
    the straw.
    [*Thinking that Hodge his head was broke, and that
       Gammer would not let him come before them.*
    GAMMER. Chill show you his face, ich warrant
    thee——lo, now where he is !
    BAILY. Come on, fellow ; it is told me thou art
    a shrew,[1] i-wis ;
Thy neighbour's hens thou takest, and plays the
    two-legged fox ;

---

[1] The word *shrew* at present is wholly confined to the
female sex. It here appears to have been equally applied
to the male, and signifies *naught* or *wicked*. See Baret's
"Alvearie," *v. Shrewd.*

Their chickens and their capons too, and now and
    then their cocks.
    HODGE. Ich defy them all that dare it say; cham
      as true as the best.
    BAILY. Wert not thou take within this hour in
      dame Chat's hens'-nest?
    HODGE. Take there! no, master, chould not do't
      for a house full of gold.
    CHAT. Thou, or the devil in thy coat; swear
      this I dare be bold.
    DOCTOR RAT. Swear me no swearing, quean:
      the devil he give thee sorrow:
All is not worth a gnat, thou canst swear till to-
    morrow.
Where is the harm he hath? show it, by God's
    bread,
Ye beat him with a witness, but the stripes light
    on my head.
    HODGE. Beat me! Gog's blessed body, chould
      first, ich trow, have burst thee:
Ich think, and chad my hands loose, callet, chould
    have crust[1] thee.
    CHAT. Thou shitten knave, I trow, thou knowest
      the full weight of my fist.
I am foully deceived, unless thy head and my
    door-bar kissed.
    HODGE. Hold thy chat, whore; thou criest so
      loud, can no man else be heard?
    CHAT. Well, knave, and I had thee alone, I
      would surely rap thy costard.[2]

---

[1] [Crushed.]

[2] The head. So, in "Hickscorner"—
    "I will rap you on the *costard* with my horn."
    —Mr Steevens's Note on *Love's Labour's Lost*, act iii., sc. 1.
Again, in Ben Jonson's "Tale of a Tub," act ii., sc. 2—
    "Do you mutter | sir, snorle this way,
      That I may hear and answer what you say,
      With my school dagger 'bout your *costard*, sir."

BAILY. Sir, answer me to this, Is thy head whole
    or broken ?
CHAT. Yea, Master Baily, blest be every good
    token.
HODGE. Is my head whole ? ich warrant you,
    'tis neither scurvy nor scald :
What, you foul beast, does think 'tis either pild
    or bald ? [1]
Nay, ich thank God, chill not for all that thou
    may'st spend,
That chad one scab on my narse as broad as
    thy finger's end.
  BAILY. Come nearer here.
  HODGE. Yes, that ich dare.
  BAILY. By our lady, here is no harm :
Hodge's head is whole enough, for all dame Chat's
    charm.
  CHAT. By Gog's blest,[2] however the thing he
    cloaks or smolders,
I know the blows he bare away either with head
    or shoulders.
Camest thou not, knave, within this hour, creeping
    into my pens,
And there was caught within my house, groping
    among my hens ?
  HODGE. A plague both on thy hens and thee '
    a cart, whore, a cart !
Chould I were hanged as high as a tree, and ich
    were as false as thou art.
Give my gammer again her washical [1] thou stole
    away in thy lap.
  GAMMER. Yea, Master Baily, there is a thing
    you know not on, mayhap :

---

[1] See Note on "King Henry VI.," Part I. Shakspeare,
1778, vol. vi., p. 192.—*S.*
  [2] Bliss.   [3] A corruption of *what do you call it.*—*S.*

This drab she keeps away my good (the devil he
    might her snare) :
Ich pray you, that ich might have a right action
    on her.
  CHAT. Have I thy good, old filth, or any such
    old sow's ?
I am as true, I would thou knew, as [the] skin
    between thy brows.[1]
  GAMMER. Many a truer hath been hanged,
    though you escape the danger.
  CHAT. Thou shalt answer (by God's pity) for
    this thy foul slander.
  BAILY. Why, what can you charge her withal?
    to say so ye do not well.
  GAMMER. Marry, a vengeance to her heart, the
    whore has stol'n my nee'le.
  CHAT. Thy needle, old witch ! how so ? it were
    alms thy soul to knock ;
So didst thou say the other day, that I had stol'n
    thy cock.
And roasted him to my breakfast, which shall not
    be forgotten :
The devil pull out thy lying tongue, and teeth
    that be so rotten.
  GAMMER. Give me my nee'le ; as for my cock,
    chould be very loth,
That chould here tell he should hang on thy false
    faith and troth.
  BAILY. Your talk is such, I can scarce learn
    who should be most in fault.
  GAMMER. Yet shall ye find no other wight,
    save she, by bread and salt.
  BAILY. Keep ye content a while, see that your
    tongues ye hold ;

---

[1] A proverbial phrase, used also by Dogberry in "Much
ado about Nothing." Shakspeare, 1778, vol. ii., p. 326.—S.

Methinks you should remember, this is no place
    to scold.
How knowest thou, Gammer Gurton, dame Chat
    thy needle had ?
    GAMMER. To name you, sir, the party, chould
    not be very glad.
    BAILY. Yea, but we must needs hear it, and
    therefore say it boldly.
    GAMMER. Such one as told the tale full soberly
    and coldly,
Even he that looked on, will swear on a book,
What time this drunken gossip my fair long nee'le
    up took :
Diccon (Master) the bedlam, cham very sure ye
    know him.
    BAILY. A false knave, by God's pity ! ye were
    but a fool to trow him.
I durst aventure well the price of my best cap,
That when the end is known, all will turn to a jape.[1]
Told he not you that besides she stole your cock
    that tide ?

---

[1] *Jape* is generally used in an obscene sense, as in the
Prologue to "Grim the Collier of Croydon," and in Skelton's Song in Sir John Hawkins's "History of Music,"
vol. iii., p. 6. It here signifies a *jest* or *joke*. So in the
Prologue to Chaucer's "Canterbury Tales," l. 705—

    "Upon a day he gat him more moneie
    Than that the persone gat in monthes tweie.
    And thus with fained flattering and *japes*,
    He made the persone and the peple his apes."

And in "Batman upon Bartholome," 1535, as quoted by
Sir John Hawkins, in his "History of Music," vol. ii.,
p. 125 : "They kepe no counseyll, but they telle all that
they here : sodeinly they laugh, and sodenly they wepe:
alwaye they crye, jangle, and *jape*, uneth they ben stylle
whyle they slepe."

    "Nay, *iape* not with hym, he is no smal fole.
    It is a solemnpne syre and solayne."
        —Skelton's Works, [1843, vol. i., p. 17.]

GAMMER. No, master, no indeed, for then he should have lied ;
My cock is, I thank Christ, safe and well a-fine.
  CHAT. Yea, but that rugged colt, that whore, that Tib of thine,
Said plainly thy cock was stol'n, and in my house was eaten ;
That lying cut is lost, that she is not swinged and beaten.
And yet for all my good name it were a small amends ;
I pick not this gear (hear'st thou) out of my fingers' ends.
But he that heard it told me, who thou of late didst name :
Diccon, whom all men knows, it was the very same.
  BAILY. This is the case ; you lost your nee'le about the doors ;
And she answers again, she hase no cock of yours ;
Thus in your talk and action, from that you do intend,
She is whole five mile wide from that she doth defend.
Will you say she hath your cock ?
  GAMMER, No, marry, sir, that chill not.
  BAILY. Will you confess her nee'le ?
  CHAT. Will I ? no, sir, will I not.
  BAILY. Then there lieth all the matter.
  GAMMER. Soft, master, by the way,
Ye know she could do little, and she could not say nay.
  BAILY. Yea, but he that made one lie about your cock-stealing,
Will not stick to make another, what time lies be in dealing.
I ween the end will prove this brawl did first arise
Upon no other ground but only Diccon's lies.

CHAT. Though some be lies, as you belike have
    espied them :
Yet other some be true, by proof I have well tried
    them.
    BAILY. What other thing beside this, dame
    Chat ?
    CHAT. Marry, sir, even this,
The tale I told before, the self-same tale it was
    his ;
He gave me, like a friend, warning against my
    loss,
Else had my hens be stol'n each one, by God's cross.
He told me Hodge would come, and in he came
    indeed ;
But as the matter chanced, with greater haste than
    speed.
This truth was said, and true was found, as truly
    I report.
    BAILY. If Doctor Rat be not deceived, it was
    of another sort.
    DOCTOR RAT. By God's mother, thou and he be
    a couple of subtle foxes ;
Between you and Hodge I bear away the boxes.
Did not Diccon appoint the place, where thou
    should'st stand to meet him ?
    CHAT. Yes, by the mass ; and, if he came, bad
    me not stick to spite him.
    DOCTOR RAT. God's sacrament ! the villain
    knave hath dress'd us round about ;
He is the cause of all this brawl, that dirty shitten
    lout,
When Gammer Gurton here complained, and made
    a rueful moan,
I heard him swear that you had gotten her needle
    that was gone.
And this to try, he further said, he was full loth :
    howbeit

He was content with small ado to bring me where
    to see it.
And where he sat, he said, full certain, if I would
    follow his reed,
Into your house a privy way he would me guide
    and lead,
And where ye had it in your hands, sewing about
    a clout,
And set me in the back-hole, thereby to find you out:
And whiles I sought a quietness, creeping upon
    my knees,
I found the weight of your door-bar for my reward
    and fees.
Such is the luck that some men gets, while they
    begin to mell,[1]
In setting at one such as were out, minding to
    make all well.
    HODGE. Was not well blest, gammer, to 'scape
      that scour? And chad been there,
Then chad been dress'd, belike, as ill (by the mass)
    as Gaffer Vicar.
    BAILY. Marry, sir, here is a sport alone; I
      looked for such an end;
If Diccon had not play'd the knave, this had been
    soon amend.
My gammer here he made a fool, and dress'd her
    as she was;
And goodwife Chat he set to scold,[2] till both parts[3]
    cried, alas!
And Doctor Rat was not behind, whiles Chat his
    crown did pare;
I would the knave had been stark blind, if Hodge
    had not his share.
    HODGE. Cham meetly well-sped already among's,
      cham dress'd like a colt;

---

[1] *i.e.*, To meddle.—*S.*　　[2] Old copy, *Scole.*　　[3] [Parties.]

And chad not had the better wit, chad been made
    a dolt.
    BAILY. Sir knave, make haste Diccon were
        here ; fetch him, wherever he be.
    CHAT. Fie on the villain, fie, fie, that makes us
        thus agree !
    GAMMER. Fie on him, knave, with all my heart.
        now fie, and fie again !
    DOCTOR RAT. Now fie on him, may I best say,
        whom he hath almost slain.
    BAILY. Lo, where he cometh at hand, belike he
        was not far.
Diccon, here be two or three thy company cannot
    spare.
    DICCON. God bless you, and you may be bless'd,
        so many all at once !
    CHAT. Come, knave, it were a good deed to geld
        thee, by Cock's bones.
Seest not thy handiwork? sir Rat, can ye forbear him?
    DICCON. A vengeance on those hands light, for
        my hands came not near him.
The whoreson priest hath lift the pot in some of
    these alewives' chairs,
That his head would not serve him, belike, to
    come down the stairs.
    BAILY. Nay, soft, thou may'st not play the
        knave, and have this language too ;
If thou thy tongue bridle a while, the better
    may'st thou do.
Confess the truth as I shall ask, and cease a while
    to fable,
And for thy fault, I promise thee, thy handling
    shall be reasonable.
Hast thou not made a lie or two, to set these two
    by the ears ?
    DICCON. What, if I have ? five hundred such
        have I seen within these seven years :

I am sorry for nothing else, but that I see not the
    sport,
Which was between them when they met, as they
    themselves report.
    BAILY. The greatest thing, Master Rat, ye see
    how he is dress'd.
    DICCON. What devil, need he be groping so
    deep in goodwife Chat's hens' nest?
    BAILY. Yea, but it was thy drift to bring him
    into the briars.
    DICCON. God's bread! hath not such an old fool
    wit to save his ears?
He showeth himself herein, ye see, so very a cox,[1]
The cat was not so madly allured by the fox,[2]
To run in the snares was set for him doubtless;
For he leapt in for mice, and this sir John for
    madness.
    DOCTOR RAT. Well, and ye shift no better, ye
    losel lither[3] and lazy,

---

[1] Minsheu, in his Dictionary, 1627 (as quoted by Mr
Tollet, in his "Notes on Shakspeare," vol. v. p. 433, says:
"Natural ideots and fools have and still do accustome themselves to weare in their cappes cockes feathers, or a hat
with a necke and head of a cock on the top," &c. From
this circumstance Diccon probably calls Dr Rat *a cox;*
that is, *a coxcomb, an idiot.*

[2] See the "History of Reynard the Fox," chap. vii., edit.
1701.—S.

[3] [Wicked.] *Lither* is used sometimes for *weak* or *limber,*
at other times *lean or pale.* Several examples of the former
are collected by Mr Steevens ("Notes on Shakspeare," vol.
vi., p. 263).
    Again, in "Euphues and his England," 1582, p. 24:
"For as they that angle for the tortoys, having once caught
him, are driven into such a *lythernesse,* that they loose all
their spirites, being benummed so," &c. Of the latter, the
following will serve as a proof (Erasmus's "Praise of
Folie," Chaloner's translation, 1549, sig. F 2) : "Or at lest
hyre some younge Phaon for mede to dooe the thyng, still
daube theyr *lither* chekes with peintyng," &c.

I will go near for this to make ye leap at a daisy.[1]
In the king's name, Master Baily, I charge you
    set him fast.

    DICCON. What ! fast at cards or fast on sleep ?
    it is the thing I did last.

    DOCTOR RAT. Nay, fast in fetters, false varlet,
    according to thy deeds.

    BAILY. Master Doctor, there is no remedy, I
    must entreat you needs
Some other kind of punishment.

    DOCTOR RAT. Nay, by All-Hallows,
His punishment, if I may judge, shall be nought
    else but the gallows.

    BAILY. That were too sore ; a spiritual man
    to be so extreme !

    DOCTOR RAT. Is he worthy any better, sir ?
    how do you judge and deem ?

    BAILY. I grant him worthy punishment, but
    in no wise so great.

    GAMMER. It is a shame, ich tell you plain, for
    such false knaves entreat.
He has almost undone us all, that is as true as
    steel.
And yet for all this great ado, cham never the
    near my nee'le.

    BAILY. Can'st thou not say anything to that,
    Diccon, with least or most ?

    DICCON. Yea, marry, sir, thus much I can say
    well, the nee'le is lost.

    BAILY. Nay, canst not thou tell which way that
    needle may be found ?

---

[1] [An apparent reference to the story told in one of the
early jest-books of a fellow who was led to execution, and
who, when on the gallows, instead of a neck-verse, cried
out, "Have at you daisy that grows yonder!" and leapt
off the ladder. See "Pasquil's Jests," 1604, repr. Hazlitt,
p. 48.]

DICCON. No, by my fay, sir, though I might
    have an hundred pound.
HODGE. Thou liar lickdish, didst not say the
    nee'le would be gotten?
DICCON. No, Hodge; by the same token you
    were that time beshitten,
For fear of hobgoblin—you wot well what I mean,
As long as it is since, I fear me yet ye be scarce clean.
    BAILY. Well, Master Rat, you must both learn
    and teach us to forgive,
Since Diccon hath confession made, and is so clean
    shreve:
If ye to me consent to amend this heavy chance,
I will enjoin him here some open kind of penance:
Of this condition—where ye know my fee is twenty
    pence
For the bloodshed, I am agreed with you here to
    dispense;
Ye shall go quit, so that ye grant the matter now
    to run,
To end with mirth among us all, even as it was
    begun.
    CHAT. Say yea, Master Vicar, and he shall sure
    confess to be your debtor,
And all we that be here present will love you much
    the better.
    DOCTOR RAT. My part is the worst; but since
    you all hereon agree,
Go even to, Master Baily, let it be so for me.
    BAILY. How say'st thou, Diccon, art content
    this shall on me depend?
    DICCON. Go to, Master Baily, say on your
    mind, I know ye are my friend.
    BAILY. Then mark ye well; to recompense
    this thy former action,
Because thou hast offended all, to make them satis-
    faction,

Before their faces here kneel down, and as I shall
    thee teach,
For thou shalt take an oath of Hodge's leather
    breech ;
First for Master Doctor, upon pain of his curse,
Where he will pay for all, thou never draw thy
    purse :
And when ye meet at one pot, he shall have the
    first pull ;
And thou shalt never offer him the cup, but it be
    full.
To goodwife Chat thou shalt be sworn, even on
    the same wise,
If she refuse thy money once, never to offer it twice.
Thou shalt be bound by the same here, as thou
    dost take it :
When thou may'st drink of free cost, thou never
    forsake it.
For Gammer Gurton's sake, again sworn shalt thou
    be,
To help her to her needle again, if it do lie in thee ;
And likewise be bound, by the virtue of that,
To be of good a-bearing to Gib her great cat.
Last of all for Hodge, the oath to scan,
Thou shalt never take him for fine gentleman.
    HODGE. Come on, fellow Diccon, chall be even
      with thee now.
    BAILY. Thou wilt not stick to do this, Diccon,
      I trow ?
    DICCON. No, by my father's skin, my hand down
      I lay it ;
Look, as I have promised, I will not denay it ;
But, Hodge, take good heed now, thou do not be-
    shit me.
        [And give him a good blow on the buttock.
    HODGE. Gog's heart, thou false villain, dost thou
      bite me ?

BAILY. What, Hodge, doth he hurt thee, ere
    ever he be begin?
HODGE. He thrust me into the buttock with a
    bodkin or a pin,   [*He discovers the needle.*
I say, gammer, gammer!
GAMMER. How now, Hodge, how now!
HODGE. God's malt, gammer Gurton——
GAMMER. Thou art mad, ich trow.
HODGE. Will you see the devil, gammer?
GAMMER. The devil, son! God bless us.
HODGE. Chould, [if] ich were hanged, gammer.
GAMMER. Marry, see, ye might dress us.
HODGE. Chave it, by the mass, gammer.
GAMMER. What, not my nee'le, Hodge?
HODGE. Your nee'le, gammer, your nee'le.
GAMMER. No, fie, dost but dodge.
HODGE. Ch' a found your nee'le, gammer, here
    in my hand be it.
GAMMER. For all the loves on earth,[1] Hodge, let
    me see it.
HODGE. Soft, gammer.

---

[1] For the love of God, of heaven, or anything sacred, are
adjurations frequently used at this day, and appear likewise
to have been so at the time this play was written. From
the indiscriminate use of them, it became customary on very
earnest occasions to request *of all loves,* or *for all the loves on
earth.* Of these modes of expression, Mr Steevens hath produced the following examples: "Conjuring his wife *of all
loves* to prepare cheer fitting."—"Honest Whore," part 1.

    "Desire him *of all loves* to come over quickly."
                —Plautus's *Menæchmi,* 1595.

    "I pray thee *for all loves* be thou my mynde sens I am thyne"
                —*Acolastus,* 1540.

    "Mrs Arden desired him *of all loves* to come back
againe." —Holinshed's *Chronicle,* p. 1064. — "Notes on
Shakspeare," vol. i., p. 279.
    Again—
        "Speak *of all loves.*"
        —*Midsummer Night's Dream,* act. ii., sc. 3.

GAMMER. Good Hodge.

HODGE. Soft, ich say, tarry a while.

GAMMER. Nay, sweet Hodge, say truth, and not
me beguile.

HODGE. Cham sure on it; ich warrant you, it
goes no more astray.

GAMMER. Hodge, when I speak so fair, wilt still
say me nay?

HODGE. Go near the light, gammer, 'tis well in
faith, good luck:

Ch' was almost undone, 'twas so far in my buttock.

GAMMER. 'Tis mine own dear nee'le, Hodge,
sikerly [1] I wot.

HODGE. Cham I not a good son, gammer, cham
I not?

GAMMER. Christ's blessing light on thee, hast
made me for ever.

HODGE, Ich knew that ich must find it, else
chould a' had it never.

CHAT. By my troth, gossip Gurton, I am even
as glad,

As though I mine own self as good a turn had.

BAILY. And I by my conscience, to see it so
come forth,

Rejoice so much at it, as three needles be worth.

DOCTOR RAT. I am no whit sorry to see you so
rejoice.

DICCON. Nor I much the gladder for all this noise.

Yet say, gramercy, Diccon, for springing of the
game.

GAMMER. Gramercy, Diccon, twenty times! O,
how glad cham!

---

[1] Securely or certainly. So in Chaucer's "Troilus and
Cressida," Book iii., l. 833—

"The drede of lesing makith him, that he
May in no parfite *sikernesse* ybe."

If that chould do so much, your masterdom to come
 hither,
Master Rat, goodwife Chat, and Diccon together ;
Cha but one halfpenny, as far as ich know it,
And chill not rest this night, till ich bestow it.
If ever ye love me, let us go in and drink.
 BAILY. I am content, if the rest think as I
 think.
Master Rat, it shall be best for you if we so do,
Then shall you warm you and dress yourself too.
 DICCON. Soft, sirs, take us with you, the com-
 pany shall be the more ;
As proud comes behind, they say, as any goes be-
 fore.
But now, my good masters, since we must be gone,
And leave you behind us here all alone :
Since at our last ending thus merry we be,
For Gammer Gurton's needle sake, let us have a
 plaudite.

FINIS.

THE TRIAL OF TREASURE.

VOL. III.

R

EDITION.

*A New and Mery Enterlude called the Triall of Treasure,
newly set foorth, and neuer before this tyme imprinted.*

THE NAMES OF THE PLAYERS.

First, STURDINESS, CONTENTATION, VISITATION, TIME.
The Second, LUST, SAPIENCE, CONSOLATION.
The Third, the PREFACE, JUST, PLEASURE, GREEDY-GUT.
The Fourth, ELATION; TRUST, a Woman; and
TREASURE, a Woman.
The Fifth, INCLINATION, the Vice.

Imprinted at Londö in Paules Churcheyarde, at the
signe of the Lucrece, by Thomas Purfoote.   1567.   4º.
Black letter.

MR HALLIWELL'S PREFACE.[1]

THE interlude, presented to the modern reader for the first time in the following pages, was printed from a copy formerly in the possession of Steevens, the eminent Shaksperian critic, before it was noticed that a copy in the British Museum contained several variations and superior readings.[2] These were the more important, settling in some places the distribution of the speeches with greater accuracy than they were arranged in the exemplar we used. Perhaps, indeed, this may in some measure have arisen from the one last mentioned having

---

[1] [To the former edition. Printed for the Percy Society, 1849.]

[2] These have all been adopted in the present reprint. The *variations* exhibited in the Percy Society's text should be rather called mistakes of the transcriber, and two whole lines were omitted.]

been what booksellers technically term "cropped," but we have noticed all variations of importance in the notes, and some of them seem incompatible with any supposition, except that there were two different impressions in the same year,[1] or that the Museum copy had been corrected while the work was in the press.

Mr Collier conjectures that the "Trial of Treasure" was written some years before it was printed, but subsequently to the composition of "Lusty Juventus," which is, he says, "mentioned in it."   But it appears to me that the allusion to "Lusty Juventus" [p. 263], is merely a generic proverbial title, and has no reference whatever to the old play so called.   Mr Collier ("Hist. Dram. Poet." ii., 330), has given a brief analysis of the interlude now reprinted.

December 21, 1849.

---

[1] The Museum copy has a woodcut on the back of the title-page, which is wanting in the other copy, a circumstance which appears to confirm this opinion.

THE TRIAL OF TREASURE.

Do all things to edify the Congregation.

DIOGENES, which used a barrel for his house,
Being fled from his father to the city of Athens,
Comforted himself much in beholding the mouse,
Which desired neither castle nor hold for her
    defence ;
Concerning sustentation she made no difference,
But ate whatsoever to her did befall,
And, touching her apparel, she had least care of
    all ;
This poor mouse's property noted Diogenes,
Which oftentimes also he would have in sight,
And though he were disciple unto Antisthenes,
Yet he learned of the mouse as much as he
    might ;
In the science of 'sophy he had great delight,
But concerning his state and outward condition,
The most can declare, if you make inquisition.
On a time he chanced accompanied to be
With Alexander, which stood between him and
    the sun :
What requirest thou to have, Diogenes (quod he) ?
Is there any thing that by me may be done ?

I pray thee stand aside, and make a little room
(Quod Diogenes), that the sun upon me may
　　shine,
Nought else require I of that that is thine.
He used to say, that as servants be obedient
To their bodily masters, being in subjection,
Even so evil men, that are not content,
Are subjects and slaves to their lusts and affection ;
This lesson unto us may be a direction
Which way our inclination to bridle and subdue,
Namely, if we labour the same to eschew.
Thus see you how little this philosopher esteemed
The abundant possessions of this mundane treasure,
Which yet, notwithstanding, at these days is
　　deemed
To be the original and fountain of pleasure ;
This causeth lust to reign without measure,
To the which men are subjects, Diogenes doth
　　say,
Yet both lust and treasure in time weareth away.
A philosopher is he that wisdom doth love,
Which before Pythagoras wise men were named.
Now, Diogenes being wise, this doth approve
That some men of this age ought as fools to be
　　blamed.
For where the one with treasure-lack his life
　　framed,
The other travail, care, and labour with greedi-
　　ness
The same by all means to enjoy and possess.
As lust with the lusts converteth to dust,
And leaveth of force his pleasant prosperity,
So treasure in time is turned to rust,
As St James, in his epistle, showeth the verity ;
Hereof we purpose to speak without temerity,
Therefore our matter is named the *Trial of Treasure*,
Which time doth expel with all mundane pleasure.

Both merry and short we purpose to be,
And therefore require your pardon and patience ;
We trust in our matter nothing you shall see,
That to the godly may give any offence ;
Though the style be barbarous, not fined with
    eloquence,
Yet our author desireth your gentle acceptation,
And we the players likewise with all humiliation.

Enter LUST, *like a gallant, singing this song.*

> *Heigho, care away, let the world pass,*
> *For I am as lusty as ever I was ;*
> *In flowers I flourish as blossoms in May,*
> *Heigho, care away ; heigho, care away !*

LUST. What the devil ailed me to sing thus ?
I cry you mercy, by my faith, for ent'ring :
Most like I have ridden on the flying Pegasus,
Or in Cock Lorel's barge I have been a vent'ring.
Sing ? why, I would sing, if it were to do again,
With Orpheus and Amphion I went to school :
What ! lads must be lively attending on the train
Of Lady Delectation, which is no small fool.
Hey rouse, fill all the pots in the house ;
Tush, man, in good fellowship let us be merry.
Look up like a man, or it is not worth a louse :
Heigho, troly ; hey, dery, dery,
Ha, pleasant Youth and lusty Juventus,
In faith, it is good to be merry this May :
For of man's living here there is no point endentus,[1]
Therefore a little mirth is worth much sorrow,
    some say.

---

[1] [Probably for the sake of the rhyme, instead of *entendu*,
understood.]

Enter JUST.

But remember ye not the wise man's sentence ?
It is better in the house of mourning to be
Than in the house of laughter, where folly hath
    residence,
For lightness with wisdom cannot agree ;
Though many have pleasure in foolish phantasy,
Ensuing [1] their inclination and lust,
Yet much better is the life of one that is just.
    LUST. Sir, in this you seem against me to inveigh.
    JUST. Nothing but reason, I think, I do say.
    LUST. Marry, you shall have a nightcap for
    making the reason.
Friend, have you not a piece of stock-fish to sell ?
I would you had a dish of buttered peason.
By my faith, your communication likes me well,
But, I beseech you, tell me, is not your name
    Just ?
    JUST. Yes, forsooth.
    LUST. And my name, thou shalt understand, is
    Lust,
And according thereto I am lusty indeed ;
But, I think, thou hast drunk of Morpheus seed.
Thou goest like a dromedary, dreamy and drowsy ;
I hold twenty pound the knave is lousy !
    JUST. Mine apparel is not like unto thine,
Disguised and jagged, of sundry fashion ;
Howbeit, it is not gold always that doth shine,
But corrupting copper of small valuation ;
Too horrible besides is thy operation,
Nothing more odious unto the just,
Than the beastly desires of inordinate lust.
    LUST. It is a shameful thing, as Cicero doth
    say,

---

[1] [Following.]

That a man his own acts should praise and com-
    mend ;
Hypocrites accustom the like, day by day,
Checking other men, when they do offend.
    JUST. Yea, but it is an hard thing, saith the
      philosopher,
For a foolish man to have his manners reprehended;
And even at this day it is come so far,
God grant, for his mercy, it may be amended !
For tell a man friendly now of his fault,
Being blasphemy, pride, or vile fornication,
He will be as presumptuous as Haman the halt,
And repay with revenge or else defamation :
Thus few men a friendly monition will bear,
But stoutly persist and maintain their ill ;
And in noblemen's houses truly I do fear,
There are too many have such forward will.
    LUST. Wounds and hearts,[1] who can abide this ?
Nay, ye vile villain, I will dress you therefore ;
Your lazy bones I pretend [2] so to bless,
That you shall have small lust to prate any more.
    JUST. Behold the image of incipient fools !
There['re] not a few even now of thy property ;
Until you be put into poverty's schools
Ye will not forsake this foolish insolency.
    LUST. Nay, soft, with thee I have not made an
      end.   *[Draw out his sword.*
    JUST. The just against lust must always con-
      tend,
Therefore I propose to wrestle with thee [*put it vp*],
Who shall have the victory, straightway we shall
    see.
    LUST. When thou wilt; by his flesh, I shall
    hold the wag.

---

[1] [*i.e.*, God's wounds and hearts ; the orig. has *hartes.*]
[2] [Intend.]

    [Wrestle, and let LUST *seem to have the better*
      at the first.

JUST. I know that Lust useth not little to brag.

LUST. Thou shalt find me as mighty as Samson
  the strong.

JUST. Yea, the battle of lust endureth long.

LUST. Wounds and flesh! I was almost down
  on my back;

But yet I will wrestle, till my bones crack.

             [Stay, and then speak.

JUST. The end of thy presumption now doth
  appear.

LUST. Yet do what thou canst, I will not lie
  here;

No, by his wounds, you old doting knave!

        [Cast him, and let him arise again.

Thinkest thou that Lust will be made a slave?

I shall meet you in Smithfield, or else other-where,

By his flesh and blood, I will thee not forbear!

JUST. Not of my power I do thee expel,

But by the might of his sprit that dwelleth in me:

Inordinate lust with the just may not dwell,

And therefore may not I accompany thee.

LUST. Well, goodman Just, it is no matter,

But, in faith, I pretend not with thee to flatter;

Though from thy company depart I must,

I shall live as much in wealthiness, I trust.

      [Go out.   He must drive him out.

JUST. Where most wealth is, and most delectation,

There Lust is commonly of most estimation;

For whereas wealth wanteth, idleness doth slake,

For where idleness is, Lust parteth the stake.

                [Pause.

Thus have you seen the conflict of the just,

Which all good men ought to use and frequent;

For horrible are the fruits of inordinate lust,

Which in some case resembleth Hydra the serpent,
Whose head being cut off, another riseth incon-
      tinent :
So, one of Lust's cogitations being cut away,
There riseth up another, yea, many, we may say.
It is requisite therefore that every degree
Against this his lust both strive and contend ;
And though, at the first, he seem sturdy to be,
The Lord will convince [1] him for you in the end.
Your cause unto him therefore wholly commend,
Labouring to avoid all inordinate lust,
And to practice in life to live after the Just.
           [Go out.   Enter Inclination, the Vice.
   INC. I can remember since Noe's ship
Was made, and builded on Salisbury Plain ;
The same year the weathercock of Paul's caught
      the pip.
So that Bow-bell was like much woe to sustain.
I can remember, I am so old,
Since Paradise gates were watched by night ;
And when that Vulcanus was made a cuckold,
Among the great gods I appeared in sight.
Nay, for all you smiling, I tell you true.
No, no, ye will not know me now ;
The mighty on the earth I do subdue.
Tush, if you will give me leave, I 'll tell ye how ;
Now, in good faith, I care not greatly,
Although I declare my daily increase ;
But then these gentlewomen will be angry,
Therefore I think best to hold my peace :
Nay, I beseech you, let the matter stay,
For I would not for twenty pounds come in their
      hands ;
For if there should chance to be but one Dalila,
By the mass, they would bind me in Samson's bands !

---

[1] [Conquer.]

But what, mean I first with them to begin,
Seeing that in all men I do remain ?
Because that first I remained Eve within,
And after her Adam, and so forth to Cain.
I perceive by your looks my name ye would know ;
Why, you are not ignorant of that, I dare say ;
It is I that do guide the bent of your bow,
And ruleth your actions also day by day ;
Forsooth, I am called Natural Inclination,
Which bred in old Adam's fostred bones ;
So that I am proper to his generation,
I will not away with casting of stones !
I make the stoutest to bow and bend :
Again, when I lust, I make men stand upright ;
From the lowest to the highest I do ascend,
Drawing them to things of natural might.

Enter LUST *and* STURDINESS, *singing this song.*

> *Where is the knave that so did rave ?*
> *O, that we could him find,*
> *We would him make for fear to quake,*
> *That lout of lobbish kind.*
> *My name is Lust, and let him trust*
> *That I will have redress ;*
> *For thou and I will make him fly,*
> *Mine old friend Sturdiness.*

LUST. Where is now that valiant Hercules ?
For all his brags, he is now run away.
    STURD. (*braggingly.*) By the guts of Goliah,
        it is best for his ease,
For he was like for the pottage to pay.
    INC. Cock's soul ! what bragging knaves have
        we here ?
Come ye to convince the mightiest conqueror ?
It was I, that before you now doth appear,

Which brought to confusion both Hector and
    Alexander :
Look on this leg, ye prating slaves,
I remember since it was no greater than a tree ;
At that time I had a couple of knaves,
Much like unto you, that waited on me.
   LUST. Cock's precious soul, let us conquer the
    knave.
   STURD. By his flesh and sides, a good courage
    I have ;
Stand you, therefore, a little aside,
And ye shall see me quickly abate the fool's pride.
     *[Draw out the sword; make him put it up; and
       then strike him. Look in your spectacles.*
   INC. Nay, I dare not, I, if thou lookest so big ;
What, should such a boar fight with a pig !
Put up thy sword, man, we will agree ;
So, lo ! do so much as bear that for me.
   STURD. Nay, by his heart then, I will you dress.
   INC. Be good in thine office, gentle friend
    Sturdiness ;
For though thou and I do seem to contend,
Yet we are, and must be, friends till the end.
   STURD. Come, give me thy hand, I beshrew
    thy heart.
   INC. Nay, you must take all things in good part ;
Who standeth yonder ? Captain Lust ?
   STURD. Yea, marry.
   INC. No remedy then, to him go I must.
You have forgot, I dare say, your old friend In-
    clination ;
But let us renew acquaintance again, for Cock's
    passion !
   LUST. Why, man, our acquaintance hath been
    of old ;
I am yours at commandment, therefore be bold ;
For Lust can do nothing without Inclination,

Chiefly in matters concerning a pleasant vocation.
   INC. Indeed Lust may be taken for a thing
     indifferent,
Except Inclination be joined thereunto;
But when that I once have revealed my intent,
As I will men to work, so commonly they do.
   LUST. Ye have heard of the combat between me
     and Just?
   INC. Yea, marry, I heard say that you lay in the
     dust.
   LUST. What say ye?
   INC. Neither one word nor other, ye may me
     trust.
   Lust. Of mine honesty, my company he utterly
     refused,
And in wrestling with me he gave me the foil,
Saying that I had myself and other abused,
Leading men in perplexity and marvellous toil.
   STURD. By Gog's wounds, if we had found him
     here,
We should, by his flesh, have abated his cheer.
   INC. I perceive, Sturdiness, thou art no fool;
Tell me of fellowship, where wentest thou to school?
   STURD. What, to read or write?
   INC. Nay, to swear and fight:
For I think thou canst neither write, read, nor spell;
But in swearing and fighting thou dost excel.
   STURD. Thou knowest that I am joined with Lust,
And sturdy by nature I am in like case.
What, let the world wag: all cannot be just,
Some must natural inclination embrace.
   LUST. All men just? no, I remember the sen-
     tence of Tully,
That no man is just that feared death, poverty, or
     pain,
Which I do fear all, and that marvellously;
For fortune is variable, I do perceive plain,

And notwithstanding that Felix possessed great
    gain,
Yet when Paul preached of the judgment-day.
He trembled for fear, and bad him go away.
  INC. Doth such passions often trouble your
    mind ?
  LUST. Nay, not often, but sometime I do them
    find ;
But then, to the intent to drive them away,
I either go to sleep, or else to some play.
  STURD. By Gog's precious heart, even so do I :
But sometime they cumber me pestilently.
  INC. Well, Master Lust, such dumps to eschew,
My advice and request you must needs ensue :
That is, to become disciple to doctor Epicurus,
And then you shall have mirth by measure and
    overplus ;
Tush, I know a couple companions in store
That were marvellous meet for you evermore ;
I wish you were known, you, unto them.
  LUST. Well, then, call them in.
  INC. Here they come, each of them in a knave's
    skin.

Enter ELATION *and* GREEDY-GUT.   *They sing.*

      With lust to live is our delight,
        In high estate and dignity;
      Seeing that the Just put us to flight,
        Let them alone in misery.

STURD. Nay, they be lusty lads, I tell ye.
  ELA. What, Inclination ! methought I did smell
    thee :
Give me thy hand, ere we further go.
  INC. Now, welcome in faith, and Greedy-gut
    also ;

But, sirs, are none of you both acquainted with
   Lust?
  LUST. Yes, that they have been both of them,
   I trust;
Welcome, sirs, in faith, welcome unto me.
  ELA. By my troth, I am glad your mastership
   to see
In health and prosperity, as presently you be.
  GRE. Bom fay, zo am I wod all my heart.
  INC. This cow-bellied knave doth come from
   the cart;
Ise teach you to speak, I hold you a pound!
Curchy, lob, curchy down to the ground.
  GRE. Che can make curchy well enou'.
  INC. Lower, old knave, or I'll make ye to bow
The great-bellied lout methink cannot bend
Yes, so, lo, he beginneth to amend.
  LUST. Well, sirs, now I remember Æsop's advice,
Which he gave to the Samies[1] against king Crœsus;[2]
Therefore it is good to be witty and wise,
And being in liberty to keep me still thus,
I cannot abide a life that is dolorous,
And seeing that my name is properly Lust,
I hate the conversation of the just.
  INC. Well, Master Lust, first join you to me, In-
   clination.
Next here with Sturdiness you must you acquaint;
Turn you about, and embrace Elation;
And that wealth may increase without any re-
   straint,
Join you with Greedy-gut here in our presence,
That all these in you may have prosperous influence.
                  [Bow to the ground.
  LUST. Out, alas! what a sudden passion is this!
I am so taken, that I cannot stand;

---

[1] [Samians.]   [2] [Original has Crassus.]

The cramp, the cramp, hath touched me, i-wis ;
I shall die without remedy now out of hand.
   GRE. By my matins cheese, our master is sick.
   INC. Stand back, Nicol-noddy, with the pudding-
      prick,
More brains in thy skin than wit in thy brain,
Such Greedy-gut in faith would be flain !
This cramp doth signify nothing in effect :
None of all your counsels he will now reject,
And therefore fear not to make full declaration.
But how he is bowed by me Inclination.
   STURD. Then fear not the force of these that be
      just,
But labour yourself to advance and augment ;
Be jocund and lively, sith your name is Lust,
And then you shall easily obtain your intent.
   ELA. Esteem yourself always equal with the best,
And seek for promotion, power, and dignity ;
It is good when men may live as they lust,
And unto the just bear hate and malignity.
   GRE. O zur, ye must be greedy to catch and to
      claw.
   INC. Well said, Greedy-gut, as wise as a daw !
   GRE. Eat up, at a mouthful, houses and lands.
   INC. There 's a vengeable mouth to—
                     [Gape, and the Vice gape.
   GRE. Never fear God, nor the governor's law,
But gripe, gripe, gripe greedily all that cometh in
      your hands.
By the mass, but Hugh Howlet is pestilent witty,
What guttish greediness the whoreson can teach !
That thou art not erected, in faith, it is pity,
As high as three trees and a halter will reach.
   LUST. Marry, sirs, but your counsels hath set me
      on fire !
Hey, lusty lad, how fresh am I now !
Lead me, Inclination, to have my desire,
   VOL. III.   s

And then at thy request I will ever bend and bow.
  INC. He that bendeth to follow his own inclina-
    tion,
Must needs live a wicked and vile conversation,
But so, Master Lust, I will lead you to a place,
Where you shall have pleasure enough in short
    space.
  LUST. Yea, but shall not this company go thither?
  INC. Yes, marry, we four will all go together ;
But Sturdiness shall tarry to face out the matter,
If Just peradventure against you shall clatter.
  STURD. By the mass, and well said, but first let
    us sing.
  INC. I must tune my pipes first of all by drink-
    ing.
  ELA. Tush, what then? I pray thee help us a
    part.
  INC. Yes, I will sing the treble with all my
    heart.

They sing.

> *Lust shall be led by Inclination*
> *To Carnal Cogitation ;*
> *Where Lust is wholly led by me,*
> *He must fall to cupidity ;*
> *For carnal cares shall him assail,*
> *And speedily they shall prevail ;*
> *I, Sturdiness, will face it out*
> *In his cause, sturdy, stiff and stout.*
> *Then Greedy-gut shall make him eat*
> *Both house and lands like bread and meat ;*
> *Elation shall puff him high*
> *For to aspire above the sky ;*
> *Then natural and lordly Lust*
> *Shall with his power despise the Just.*

  ELA. Our song is ended, hast thou other in store?

INC. I shall not have done this half hour and
　　more.
Yet I will, now I remember.　Come in, Lust ;
That I go before, is but needful and just.
You shall be now led by me Inclination
To reason and talk with Carnal Cogitation.
　　STURD. Is there more vanity underneath the sun,
Than to be inclined after this sort ?
Well, Lust doth now as other have done,
Yea, and do day by day, esteeming it a sport ;
This Lust is the image of all wicked men,
Which in seeking the world have all delectation ;
They regard not God, nor his commandments ten,
But are wholly led by their own inclination.
First, to inculcate with Carnal Cogitation,
And after to the desire of all worldly treasure,
Which alone they esteem the fulness of pleasure.
With Elation or Pride he is also associate,
Which puffeth up his senses with presumption
　　pestilent ;
Then Greedy-gut maketh them continually to grate
On the mock of this world, which he thinketh per-
　　manent.
I, Sturdiness, to hear out all things am bent :
Thus see you how men, that are led by their lust,
Dissent from the virtuous, goodly and just.
　　　　　[*Go out.　Enter* JUST *and* SAPIENCE.
　　SAP. The advice of Aristippus have in your mind,
Which willed me to seek such things as be perma-
　　nent,
And not such as are of a vanishing kind,
For the one with the other is not equivalent.
Be circumspect, therefore, foreseeing and sapient,
For treasures here gotten are uncertain and vain,
But treasures of the mind do continually remain.
　　JUST. This is the mind of Musonus, also I re-
　　member,

Like as presently you have advertised me,
For the which I cannot but thankfully render
Such commendations as is requisite to be ;
And as your name is Sapience, thus much I see,
That on heavenly wisdom you do depend,
And not on as time doth bring to an end.
   SAP. Truth indeed, and therefore, your name
      being Just,
With me and my documents must be associate ;
Where, contrary, such as are led by their lust,
To incline evil are always appropriate :
They have not, as you have, battle and combat
Against the cogitations that inwardly spring,
But rather are obedient unto the same thing :
And this is the occasion that men are so ambitious
And so foolish, led by the lust of their brain :
Sometime to covet, sometime to be vicious ;
Sometime the counsel of the wise to disdain ;
Sometime to climb till they fall down again ;
Sometime to usurp the possessions of other ;
Sometime to disobey both father and mother.
   JUST. Alas, what availeth it riches to enjoy,
Though as much in comparison as Crœsus the
      king ?
What helpeth it to have Helen in Troy,
If the conscience of man continually sting ?
Elation and Pride no commodity doth bring,
But is often known the forerunner of shame,
And the blot of immortal memory and fame.

Enter INCLINATION, *the Vice.*

   INC. Now, by my halidom, it is alone a :
Better sport in my life I never saw,
It is trim, I tell you, to dance with John and
      Jone a,
We pass not a point for God nor his law :

But Lust is lusty, and full of porridge :
Cogitation and he in one bed doth lie.
When here is Master Just, with his cank'red cour-
    age,
What, and old doting Sapience ! then I am dressed, I.
So often already Just hath me restrained,
That I dare not entice him any more,
For through Sapience he hath me clearly disdained,
That my courage is spent, and I have no more.
                      [*Make as going back.*

   SAP. Nay, soft, sir, we must talk with you, ere
    ye go.
   INC. I cannot tarry at this time, the truth is so.
   JUST. Nay, there is no remedy ; with you we
    must talk.
   INC. By the body of me, I hold best that I walk,
Or else learn to speak language another while,
And so I may happen the knaves to beguile,
   JUST. Turn back, ere you go, we have somewhat
    to say.
   INC. Non point parle françois, non, par ma foy.
   SAP. To deceive us now himself he doth prepare.
   INC. Ick en can ghene english spreken von waer.
Body of me, let me go, or else I shall piss :
I-wis, Master Just, you have loved me ere this ;
Therefore now be ruled after my counsel,
And godly things for your commodity I shall you
    tell.
   SAP. Let him that is just not lightly ensue
His vile inclination and carnal concupiscence,
But let him rather contend the same to subdue ;
And chiefly those that have knowledge of Sapience :
Therefore to bridle this lust do your diligence,
His crafty provocations utterly to restrain,
That Just may live, while life doth remain.
   INC. Goodman Hobal, speak you in earnest ?
What dost thou say, shall the Just bridle me ?

No, no, brother Snaps, do the worst and thy best,
I will not be bridled of him nor of thee.
   Just. Seeing Sapience consisteth in heavenly
      document,
And that heavenly document consisteth in Sapience,
To bridle this wretch I cannot but consent,
Sith I of his purpose have had oft intelligence.
   Inc. Yet again [to] bridle it doth not prevail;
I will not be bridled of the best of you both.
See you this gear? here's one will make you to
      quail;
Stand back! to kill you, Master Just, I would be
      loth!
You have been so burned and fried of late,
That it were pity to hurt you any more.
Back, I say, or my dagger shall about your pate,
By the mass, but I will, sir, I'll make your bones
      sore.   [*Struggle two or three times.*
   Just. I will bridle thee, beast, for all thy brag-
      ging.
   Inc. In faith, goodman Just, I'll hold ye wag-
      ging;
Nay, brother, ye shall find me a curst colt to bridle,
Nay, in faith, better yet I will make thee to
      struggle.
   Sap. Never leave him, but ensue the counsel of
      Sapience.
   Just. Lo, now, I have brought him under obedi-
      ence.   [*Bridle him.*
   Inc. Not so obedient as thou thinkest me to
      have;
Nay, brother, ye shall find me a coltish knave:
We-he-he, it is good for you to hold fast,
For I will kick and winch, while the life doth last.
   Sap. Thou shalt kick indeed, but no victory
      win;
Neither to conquer the Just to ungodliness nor sin.

INC. O yes, O yes, I will make a proclamation.
JUST. What shall that be ?
INC. If ye will give me leave, then you shall see.
O yes ! is there any man or woman that hath lost
A gambolling gelding with a grey tail ?
Let him come to the crier, and pay for his cost,
And he will tell him tidings without any fail.

    SAP. To the intent that you may him sharply
      restrain,
Let him not enjoy so much of the rein.
                        [*Bridle him shorter.*

    INC. Cock's soul, now the snaffle cutteth my lip,
I would this lubberly knave had the pip !
I shall leap no hedges while this bridle is on,
Out, alas ! I think it will fret me to the bone.

    SAP. Thus should every man, that will be called
      Just,
Bridle and subdue his beastly inclination,
That he in the end may obtain perfect trust,
The messenger of God to give sight to salvation.

    JUST. That trust to obtain with him I have
      struggled.

    SAP. Then let us depart, and leave this beast
      bridled.   [*Go out both.*

    INC. May the devil go with you and his dun
      dame !
Such horse-masters will make a colt quickly tame ;
I would he were hanged that this snaffle did make,
It maketh my chaps so shamefully to ache ;
Ye have no pity on me, you, I see, by your
      laughing ;
I care not greatly, if I fall to gambolling ;
We-he-he-he-he-he, come aloft, I say,
Beware the horse-heels, I advise you stand away ;
The rein of my bridle is tied so short,
That I cannot make you any more sport.
But though I be bridled now of the Just,

I doubt not but I shall be unbridled by Lust,
And let not Just think but I will rebel,
Although he bridle me ten times all well ;
Though Nature saith one doom with a croch,
It will not lie long, but incontinent approach ;
Even so, though that I be bridled a while,
The colt will at length the courser beguile.

Enter GREEDY-GUT *running, and catch a fall.*

GRE. Chill run, I, as fast as I can,
Zurs, did none of you zee a man ?
Cham zent in haste from my Master Lust,
So that Inclination needs come to him must.
  INC. Where is he now ? I pray thee, tell me.
  GRE. Why, what have we here ? Jesus, benedicite !
I hold twenty pound it is Balaam's ass !
Nay 'tis a colt, I see his tail, by the mass !
  INC. Am I a colt ? nay, thou liest like a knave,
Somewhat for thy labour now shalt thou have.
  GRE. Hobal, ho, lousy jade, must ye kick ?
  INC. Whoever saw such a desperate Dick ?
Why Greedy-gut, do'st thou not know Inclination ?
  GRE. Body of me, who hath drest thee of that
    fashion ?
Thou art bridled for biting now indeed,
Sirrah, Master Lust would have thee make
    speed.
  INC. I am bridled, I, even as thou do'st see,
Therefore desire him to come and help me.
But what is the matter, that he for me sent ?
  GRE. Marry, together with Greediness now he
    is bent ;
He hath had long talk with Carnal Cogitation,
And is set on fire by the means of Elation,
So that he is so lusty, he cannot abide,
Therefore one or other for him must be spied.

INC. Well, Greedy-gut, I pray thee, go and make
    haste.
GRE. Tush, fear not, chill spend no time in waste.
INC. I had rather than forty pence that he were
    come ;
If I be bridled long, I shall be undone.
So sharp is this snaffle, called Restraint,
That it maketh me sweat I am so faint :
Hark ! I hear the voice of my Master Lust ;
Now I shall be unbridled shortly, I trust.

Enter LUST.

LUST. Cock's precious wounds, here hath been
    villainy.
INC. Eh, they have used me with too much
    villainy,
That old knave Sapience so counselled Just ;
But let me be unbridled, good Master Lust.
                      [*Unbridle him.*
LUST. Lo, now thou art unbridled, be of good
    cheer.
INC. By'r Lady, I am glad I have gotten thus
    clear.
But hark you, Master Lust, if I may do you
    pleasure,
Whisper, whisper,
LUST.   She is called Treasure.[1]
O, my heart is on fire, till she come in place.
INC. O Master Lust, she hath an amiable face ;[2]
A tricker, a trimmer, in faith that she is,
The goddess of wealth, prosperity, and bliss.

---

[1] [In the original the hemistich, *She is called Treasure,* is
assigned to Inclination.]
[2] This speech is not assigned to *Inclination* in the
original.—*Halliwell* (*Additional Notes*).

Lust. But think you that this minion long en-
dure shall ?

Inc. For ever and ever, man, she is immortal.
There be many other; but she exceedeth them all.

Lust. What be they, have you their names in
store ?

Inc. Yea, hark, in your ear [*whispers*], and
many other more.

Lust. Sith that the apple of Paris before me is
cast,
And that I may deliver the same where I will,
I would Prometheus were here to help me hold fast,
That I might have a fore-wit with me ever still.
Pallas, I consider, in science hath skill,
But Juno and Venus good will do I bear ;
Therefore to give the apple I know not where.

Inc. Be counsell'd by me, and give it Lady
Treasure.
It shall be for your commodity in the end without
measure,
For having the company of this minion lass,
You shall never want the society of Pallas ;
Juno, nor yet the armipotent Mars,
Can not resist your strength, be they never so
fierce ;
And as for Venus, you shall have [her] at pleasure,
For she is bought and sold always with Treasure ;
She of her power hath whole countries conquered,
The most noble champions by her hath been mur-
thered ;
Acon for her sake was stoned to death.
Tush, innumerable at this day spend their breath,
Some hang or be hanged, they love her so well,
She is the great goddess, it is true that I tell.

Lust. Which way should I work of her to have
a sight ?

Inc. I, Inclination, will lead you thither right ;

But we must have Greedy-gut and also Elation.
   LUST. They are at the house of Carnal Cogita-
   tion.
   INC. Whither I would wish that we might depart;
I will lead you thither with all my heart.

Enter JUST, TRUST, *and* CONTENTATION.

TRUST, *a woman plainly* [*apparelled,*] *and* CON-
TENTATION *kneel down and sing, she have a crown.*

      So happy is the state of those
        That walk upright and just,
      That thou, Lord, dost thy face disclose
        By perfect hope and trust.
      Their inclination thou dost stay,
        And sendeth them Sapience,
      That they should serve, and eke obey,
        Thy high magnificence.
      And sendest Contentation,
        That we in thee may rest.
      Therefore all adoration
        To thee pertaineth best.

   JUST. God careth for his, as the prophet doth
     say,
And preserveth them under his merciful wings ;
Namely the just, that his will do obey,
Observing his holy commandment in all things ;
Not for our sake or for our deservings,
But for his own sake openly to declare,
That all men on earth ought to live in his fear.
   TRUST. How God hath blessed you, all men may
     see ;
For first at your entrance you conquered Lust,
Not by your power, but by might of the deity,
As all persons ought to do that be just.
Then through Sapience, which God did you send,

You bridled that brutish beast Inclination,
And also ordered you with Contentation.
   CONT. Those that are contented with their voca-
     tion
Be thankful to God; this is a true consequent;
And those that be thankful in their conversation,
Cannot but please the Lord God omnipotent;
But those that be sturdy, proud, and disobedient,
The Ruler of all rulers will them confound,
And rot their remembrance off from the ground.
   JUST. When Solon was asked of Crœsus the
     king,
What man was most happy in this vale terrestrial,
To the end he seemeth to attribute that thing
When men be associate with treasures celestial,
Before the end can no man judge, he doth say,
That any man is happy that here beareth breath,
But then by his end prettily judge we may.
Thus true happiness consisteth, saith he, after death.
If this be a truth, as undoubtedly it is,
What men are more foolish, wretched, and miser-
     able,
Than those that in these treasures accompt 'their
     whole bliss?
Being infect with ambition, that sickness incurable;
Ah, wicked Adrastia, thou goddess deceivable,
Thus to pluck from men the sense of their mind,
So that no contentation therein they can find.
   TRUST. The treasure of this world we may well
     compare
To Circes the witch with her crafty cautility,
Wherewith many men's minds so poisoned are,
That quite they are carried into all fidelity;
They are conjured indeed, and bewitched so sore,
That treasure is their trust, joy and delight.
True trust is expelled, they pass not therefore,
And against contentation they continually fight.

But though wicked men follow their lust,
Crying, on earth is our felicity and pleasure,
Yet God doth so guide the hearts of the just,
That they respect chiefly the celestial treasure.
    CONT. Alas! should we not have that estimation
Which God hath prepared for his dear elect?
Should not our minds rest in full contentation,
Having trust in this treasure, most high in respect?
St Paul, whom the Lord so high did erect,
Saith: It passeth the sense of our memory and
    mind,
Much less can our outward eyes the same find,
And as for treasures which men possess here,
Through fickleness of fortune soon fadeth away;
The greatest of renown and most worthy peer
Sometime falleth in the end to misery and decay.
Record of Dionysius, a king of much fame,
Of the valiant Alexander and Cæsar the strong.
Record of Tarquinius, which Superbus had to name,
And of Heliogabalus, that ministered with wrong;
If I should recite all, I should stand very long,
But these be sufficient plainly to approve,
How soon by uncertainty this treasure doth remove.
    JUST. It is true; therefore a mind well content
Is great riches, as the wise King Solomon doth say.
We have seen of late days this canker pestilent
Corrupting our realm to our great decay—
Ambition, I mean, which chiefly did reign
Among those that should be examples to others;
We saw how their brethren they did disdain,
And burned with fire the child with the mother;
It is often seen that such monsters ambitious,
As spare not to spill the blood of the innocent,
Will not greatly stick to become seditious,
The determination of God thereby to prevent.
God grant every one of us earnestly to repent,
And not to set our minds on this fading treasure,

But rather wish and will to do the Lord's pleasure.
  TRUST. O ye emperors, potentates, and princes
    of renown,
Learn of Just with Trust yourselves to associate.
That like as your vocation by right doth ask the
    crown,
And also due obedience, being the appointed
    magistrate,
So rule that at the last you may be resuscitate,
And reign with the Almighty with perfect con-
    tinuance,
Receiving double crowns for your godly governance.
Ye noblemen, whom God hath furnished with
    fame,
Be mindful to walk in the ways of the Just,
Add virtue evermore to your honourable name,
And be not overcome of concupiscence or lust.
Flee from love of treasure, catch hold of me, Trust ;
And then double felicity at the last you shall
    possess,
And in all earthly doings God shall give you
    success.
Ye poor men and commons, walk well in your
    vocation,
Banish lust and desire, which is not convenient ;
Let trust work in you a full contentation,
Considering that it leadeth to treasures more
    excellent,
For these are uncertain, but they are most per-
    manent.
Your necessity supply with virtue and trust,
And then shall you enjoy your crown among the
    just
  JUST. As I, being properly nominate Just,
Am here associate with Contentation,
So have I my whole felicity in Trust,
Who illumineth mine eyes to see my salvation.

TRUST. Fear ye not, shortly you shall have
   consolation,
If I were once grown in you to perfection,
Even thus goeth it always with the children of
   election.
   JUST. I will depart now ; will ye go with me,
   Trust ?
   TRUST. Yea, I must always associate the Just.
   CONT. A psalm of thanksgiving first let us sing,
To the laud and praise of the immortal King.
      [*Here, if you will, sing " the man is blest
        that feareth God," &c.—Go out.*]

Enter INCLINATION, *laughing.*

INC. Lust (quod he) ; now in faith he is lusty,
Lady Treasure and he hath made a match ;
He thinketh that I were marvellous trusty,
Because I teach him to claw and to catch,
And nowadays amity doth therein consist ;
He that can flatter shall be well beloved ;
But he that saith, *thus* and *thus, saith Christ,*
Shall as an enemy be openly reproved.
Friendship, yea, friendship consisteth now in adula-
   tion ;
Speak fair and please the lust of thy lord,
I warrant thee be had in great estimation,
When those that tell truth shall be abhorr'd.
Ah, unhappy Lingua, whither wilt thou ren ?
Take heed, I advise thee, lest thou be shent ;
If ye chance to tell any tales of these gentlewomen,
With flesh-hooks and nails you are like to be rent ;
Nay, for the passion of me be not so moved,
And I will please you incontinent again.
Above all treasures you are worthy to be loved,
Because you do no men deride nor disdain ;
You do not contemn the simple and poor ;

You be not high-minded, proud, and presumptuous,
Neither wanton nor wily you be nevermore,
But gentle, loving modesty, and virtuous,
Behold how a lie can please some folks' diet,
O[r] pacify their minds marvellous well!
All hist, I warrant ye, so they [be] in quiet.
How to please you hereafter now I can tell :
Hark, I hear Lust and my Lady Treasure,
They are given to solace, singing and pleasure.

Enter LUST *and* TREASURE, *a woman finely
appareled.*

LUST. Ah, amorous lady, of beautiful face,
Thou art heartily welcome into this place ;
My heart is inclined to thee, Lady Treasure,
My love is insatiate, it keepeth no measure.
TREAS. It is I, Master Lust, that will you advance ;
Treasure it is that things doth enhance :
Upon me set your whole affection and lust,
And pass not a point for the ways of the Just.
Treasure is a pleasure, bear that in mind ;
Both trusty and true ye shall me always find.
INC. As trusty as is a quick eel by the tail !
[*Aside.*
What, Lady Treasure, welcome without fail ;
To be better acquainted with you once I trust,
But I dare not in the presence of my Master Lust.
[TREAS.] Ye are welcome, sir, heartily ; what !
be of good courage ;
Drawer, let us have a pint of white wine and
borage,
LUST. Wherefore, I pray thee tell ?
INC. Marry, methink you are not well.
LUST. Not well ? who can a better life crave,
Than to possess such a lady as I have ?
Is there any wealth not contained in Treasure

Ah, lady, I love thee, in faith, out of measure.
  Inc. It is out of measure indeed, as you say,
And even so most men love her at this day;
O, she is a minion of amorous hue,
Her peer in my days yet I never knew.
Old (quod you): I am an old knave, I tell ye,
Nay, never laugh at the matter, for doubtless I
    smell ye;
She passeth Juno, Ceres, and Pallas,
More beautiful than ever dame Venus was,
Othea in sapience she doth exceed,
And Diana in dignity, of whom we do read;
What should fair Helen once named be,
She excelleth all these, Master Lust, believe me.
  Lust. How say you, is not this an eloquent lad?
  Treas. That you have such a servant, truly I am
    glad.
  Inc. Ha, ha, now indeed I can you not blame,
For women of all degrees are glad of the same;
They that flatter and speak them fair,
Shall be their sons, and peradventure their heir.
  Lust. You told me of a brother you had, Lady
    Treasure.
  Treas. Yea, sir, that I have; his name is called
    Pleasure;
And seeing you enjoy me now at your will,
Right soon, I am sure, he will come you until.
  Lust. Truly of him I would fain have a sight,
For because that in pleasure I have marvellous
    delight.
  Inc. Then honesty and profit you may bid good
    night.   [*Aside.*
  Lust. What say'st thou?
  Inc. I say he will shortly appear in sight;
I know by his singing the same is he,
[*Aside*] The misbegotten Orpheus I think that he
    be.
  VOL. III.   T

Enter PLEASURE, *singing this song.*

O happy days and pleasant plays,
Wherein I do delight-a;
I do pretend, till my life's end,
To live still in such plight-a.

INC. Master Pleasure, I perceive you be of good
cheer.

PLEAS. What, Inclination, old lad, art thou here?

INC. Yea, sir, and Lady Treasure your sister,
also.

PLEAS. Body of me, then unto her I will go.
What, sister, I am glad to meet with you here.

TREAS. Welcome unto me, mine own brother
dear.
Master Lust, this is my brother, of whom I told;
He is pleasant and lusty, as you may behold.

LUST. Gentleman (I pray you), is your name
Master Pleasure?

PLEAS. Yea, sir, and I am brother to Lady Treasure.

LUST. And are you contented to accompany me?

PLEAS. Whereas she is resident, I must needs
be;
Treasure doth Pleasure commonly precede.[1]
But the one is with the other, they have both so
decreed.

INC. Marry, now you are well indeed, Master
Lust;
This is better, I trow, than the life of the just:
They be compelled to possess contentation,
Having no treasure but trust of salvation.
But my lady your mistress—my mistress, I would
say,

---

[1] [Original has *proceed.*]

She worketh, you may see, to keep you from decay.
    LUST. O, madam, in you is all my delight,
And in your brother Pleasure, both day and night.
The *Trial of Treasure* this is indeed,
I perceive that she is a true friend at need;
For I have proved her, according as Thales doth say,
And I perceive that her beauty cannot decay.
    TREAS. Always with you I will be resident,
So that your life shall be most excellent.
    PLEAS. Yea, sir, and me Pleasure also you shall
        have,
So that none other thing there needeth to crave;
I will replenish your heart with delight,
And I will be always with Treasure in sight.
But if you desire to enjoy me at your will,
My sister you must have in reputation still;
And then, as her treasure is certain and excellent,
My pleasure shall be both perfect and permanent.
Credit not those, sir, that talk that and this,
Saying that in two consisteth no bliss.
But let experience your mind ever move,
And see if all men us two do not love.
    INC. [*aside.*] Love? yes, they love you indeed,
        without a doubt,
Which shutteth some of them God's kingdom with-
        out.
They love you so well, that their God they do hate,
As time hath declared to us even of late.
But he that on such things his study doth cast,
Shall be sure to be deceived at the last.
    LUST. What dost thou say?
    INC. Of Treasure, forsooth, ye must ever hold fast,
For if you should chance to lose Lady Treasure,
Then farewell in post this gentleman Pleasure.
    LUST. My love to them both cannot be express'd,
And especially, my lady, you I love best.
    TREAS. If you love me, as you do profess,

Be sure you shall want no kind of wealthiness.
  PLEAS. And if you have wealthiness at your
    own will,
Then will I Pleasure remain with you still.
  INC. [*aside.*] You are both as constant as snow
    in the sun,
Which from snow to water through melting doth
    run ;
But worldly-wise men cannot conceive that :
To hunt for such mice they learn of the cat.
  LUST. My lady is amorous, and full of favour.
  INC. [*aside.*] I may say to you she hath an ill-
    favoured savour.
  LUST. What sayest thou ?
  INC. I say she is loving and of gentle behaviour.
  TREAS. And so I will continue still, be you sure.
  PLEAS. And I in like case, while your life doth
    endure.
  LUST. Ah trusty Treasure ! ah pleasant Plea-
    sure !
All wealth I possess now without measure ;
And seeing that the same shall firmly remain,
To help me sing a song will you take the pain ?
  TREAS. Even with all my heart, begin when ye
    will.
  INC. [*aside.*] To it, and I will either help or stand
    still.

Sing this Song.

Am I not in blessed case,
   Treasure and Pleasure to possess ?
I would not wish no better place,
   If I may still have wealthiness :
And to enjoy in perfect peace
   My lady, lady.
My pleasant pleasure shall increase,
   My dear lady.

Helen may not compared be,
  Nor Cressida that was so bright ;
These cannot stain the shine of thee,
  Nor yet Minerva of great might.
Thou passest Venus far away,
    Lady, lady,
Love thee I will both night and day,
    My dear lady.

My mouse, my nobs, and coney sweet,
  My hope and joy, my whole delight ;
Dame Nature may fall at thy feet,
  And may yield to thee her crown of right.
I will thy body now embrace,
    Lady, lady ;
And kiss thy sweet and pleasant face,
    My dear lady.

Enter GOD'S VISITATION.

VISIT. I am God's minister, called Visitation,
Which divers and many ways you may understand ;
Sometime I bring sickness ; sometime perturbation ;
Sometime trouble and misery throughout the land ;
Sometime I signify God's wrath to be at hand ;
Sometime a forerunner of destruction imminent,
But an executor of pain I am at this present.
Thou insipient fool, that hast followed thy lust,
Disdaining the doctrine declared by Sapience,
In Treasure and Pleasure hath been thy trust,
Which thou thoughtest should remain ever in thy
    presence :
Thou never rememb'red'st Thales his sentence,
Who willeth men in all things to keep a measure,
Especially in love to uncertainty of treasure ;
Even now I am come from visiting the Just,
Because God beginneth first with his elect ;
But he is so associated and comforted with Trust,

That no kind of impatience his soul can infect.
Contentation in such sort his race doth direct,
That he is contented with God's operation,
Comfortably embracing me his Visitation ;
But now I am come to vex thee with pain,
Which makest Treasure thy castle and rock :
Thou shall know that both she and Pleasure is
    vain,
And that the Almighty thou canst not mock.
Anguish and grief into thee I do cast,
With pain in thy members continually.
Now thou hast pain, thy pleasure cannot last,
But I will expel him incontinently.

    Lust. O Cock's heart ! what a pestilence is this !
Depart from me, I say, hence, God's Visitation !
Help, help, Lady Treasure, thou goddess of bliss !
At thy hands let me have some consolation.

    Treas. I will remain with you, be out of doubt.

    Inc. Will ye be packing, you ill-favoured lout ?

    Visit. Presently, indeed from him thou shalt
    not go,
And why ? because God's will hath not deter-
    mined so ;
But in time thou, Treasure, shalt be turned to rust.
And as for Pleasure he shall now attend on the
    Just.

    Lust. Gog's wounds ! these pangs increase ever-
    more.

    Inc. And my little finger is spitefully sore ;
You will not believe how my heel doth ache.

    Treas. (to Visitation). Nay, let me alone,
    your part I will take.
(To Lust) Be of good comfort, while I here remain ;
For Pleasure and he shall be parted in twain.

    Visit. It is not meet that he should be partici-
    pate with Lust,
But rather virtuous, godly and just.

Lust. Remain with me still, Master Pleasure, I
    say.

Pleas. Nay, there is no remedy; I must away;
For where God doth punition and pain,
I Pleasure in no case cannot remain.

Visit. I could in like case separate thy treasure,
But God doth admonish thee by losing thy pleasure.
        [*Go out* Visitation *and* Pleasure.

Inc. Farewell, in the devil's name, old lousy
    lout,
That my master will die I stand in great doubt.
Ho, ho, ho, how is it with you, Master Lust?

Lust. By the flesh of Goliah, yet Treasure is
    my trust,
Though Pleasure be gone, and I live in pain,
I doubt not but Treasure will fetch him again.

Treas. Yea, that I will, fear not, and with you
    remain.

Inc. The property of rich men undoubtedly he
    hath,
Which think with money to pacify God's wrath,
And health at their pleasure to buy and to sell.
How is Master Lust, are you anything well?

Lust. Against this Visitation my heart doth
    rebel.
Gog's wounds! shall I still in these pangs remain?

Treas. Fear you not, Master Lust, I will help
    you again,
Treasure in physic exceedeth Galenus:
Tush! there is no physician but we shall have with
    us;
To the ease of your body they will you bring,
And therefore I pray you despair in no thing;
Put your trust always in me Lady Treasure,
And I will restore you again unto Pleasure,
For I am the goddess that therein hath power,
Which shall remain perfect unto the last hour.

Inc. Yea, yea, Master Lust, be as merry as you
    may ;
Let Treasure be your trust, whosoever say nay.

Enter Time.

Time. The ancient Greeks have called me
    Chronos,
Which in our vulgar tongue signifieth Time ;
I am ent'red in presently for a certain purpose—
Even to turn Treasure to rust and to slime,
And Lust, which hath long disdained the Just,
Ensuing his filthy and vile inclination,
Shall immediately be turned to dust,
To the example of all the whole congregation ;
For Time bringeth both these matters to pass,
As experience hath taught in every age,
And you shall behold the same in this glass,
As a document both profitable and sage.
Both Lust and Treasure come forth with speed
Into the shop of the most mighty God,
There shall you be beaten to powder indeed,
And for your abusion feel his scourge and rod.
    Inc. By Saint Mary ! then they have made a
    wise match,
I pretend therefore to leap over the hatch :
Nay, let me depart, sirs ; stop me not, I say,
For I must remain, though both these decay.
                         [*Go out.*
    Lust. Lust from the beginning frequented hath
    been,
And shall I now turn to nothing for thee ?
    Treas. Treasure in all ages hath been beloved,
And shall she from the earth by thee be removed ?
    Time. You know that all such things are subject
    to time ;
Therefore me to withstand is no reason nor rhyme ;

For like as all things in time their beginning had,
So must all things in time vanish and fade.
    LUST. Gog's wounds, let Treasure remain still
      with me.
    TREAS. Yea, let me continue still in my dignity.
    TIME. Nay, I must carry you into Vulcan's fire,
Where you shall be tried unto the uttermost.
Seeing Lust against Trust did daily conspire,
To dust he shall turn for all his great boast !
Both of you shall have one rigorous host ;
Come therefore with speed, Time cannot tarry :
To the end of your felicity I will you carry.
    TREAS. If there be no remedy, then there is no
      shift.
    LUST. He must needs go, that is driven by the
      devil's drift ;
Ah ! Cock's precious sides, what fortune is this !
Whither go I now, to misery or bliss ?   [*Go out.*

Enter JUST, *leading* INCLINATION *in his bridle*
shackled.

    INC. We—he, he, he, he ! ware the horse-heels,
      I say ;
I would the rein were loose, that I might run
    away.
    JUST. Nay, sith thou wilt not spare against me
      to rebel,
I will not spare, by God's grace, thee to bridle :
All men may see how vile Inclination
Spareth not to put the just to vexation ;
Even so may all men learn of me again,
Thy beastly desires to bridle and restrain.
    INC. Marry, sir, I am bridled indeed, as you
      say,
And shackled, I think, for running away ;
This snaffle is sharp indeed for the nonce,

And these shackles do chafe my legs to the bones ;
And yet will I provoke, spurn and prick,
Rebel, repugn, lash out and kick.
We-he !—
    JUST.   In the jade's name, are ye so fresh ?
This gear, I suppose, will pluck down your flesh.
Nay, soft, thou shalt have a little more pain,
For somewhat shorter now I will tie thy rein.

Enter TRUST *and* CONSOLATION.

    TRUST. Most blessed and happy, I say, are the
        just,
Even because they restrain their own inclination ;
Thou, therefore, that hast made thy treasure of
        trust,
Behold, I have brought thee here Consolation.
    JUST. Now blessed be God of his mercy and
        grace,
With all my heart and soul I do you embrace.
    CON. Consolation is my name, even as Trust
        hath said,
Which is joy or comfort in this life transitory ;
He that possesseth me is of nothing afraid,
But hath a most quiet and peaceable memory.
For I, through Trust, doth show thee the glory
That God hath prepared for them beforehand.
Wherein at the last they shall perfectly stand.
    TRUST. Receive this crown of felicity now at
        this space,
Which shall be made richer at the celestial place.
    INC. By'r lady, I would I had such a gay crown.
    JUST. Now praised be God for this riches of re-
        nown ;
Felicity, in this world, the just doth enjoy.
    [INC. *aside.*] Namely, when the devil can them
        not annoy.

[Just.] The Lord's work this is, who be praised
    for ever,
Who grant us in his laws still to persever.
    Con. Amen, amen !—God give us delight
In his holy covenant both day and night.
    Trust. Our matter is almost brought to an end,
Saving that Inclination in prison must be shut.
Just, carry him forth, that useth to contend,
And see that surely enough he be put.
    Just. That shall be done shortly, by God's grace.
    Inc. What, soft, I say, me-think ye go a shame-
    ful pace ;
Was there ever poor colt thus handled before ?
Fie upon it, my legs be unreasonably sore ;
Well, yet I will rebel, yea, and rebel again,
And though a thousand times you shouldest me re-
    strain.   [*Lead him out.*

Enter TIME, *with a similitude of dust and rust.*

    Time. Behold here, how Lust is converted into
    dust ;
This is his image, his wealth and prosperity ;
And Treasure in like case is turned to rust,
Whereof this example showeth the verity.
The *Trial of Treasure* this is, no doubt,
Let all men take heed that trust in the same,
Considering what things I Time bring about,
And quench out the ungodly, their memory and
    fame.
Enter JUST.

    Just. Why, and is Lust and Treasure converted
    to this ?
    Time. Yea, forsooth.
    Just. What foolish man in them would put trust,
If this be the final end of their bliss ?
Much better I commend the life of the just.

Con. So it is, no doubt, for they have consola-
    tion,
Possessing felicity even in this place ;
I mean, through trust and hope of salvation,
Which setteth out to us God's mercy and grace.
    Just. Let all men consider this good erudition,
And not to put confidence in Lust nor Treasure ;
By these two examples receive admonition,
And also of the sudden banishment of Pleasure.
    Time. Remember that Time turneth all things
    about :
Time is the touchstone the just for to try.
But whereas Lust and Treasure in time is come to
    nought,
Just, possessing Trust, remaineth constantly.
So that as I Time have revealed their infamy,
So have I showed the consolation and gain,
That the just shall receive that justly do reign.
    Con. We will now no longer trouble this
    audience,
Sith somewhat tedious to you we have been ;
Beseeching you to bear all things with patience,
And remember the examples that you have seen.
God grant them to flourish lively and green,
That some of us the better therefore may be,
Amen, amen ! I beseech the blessed Trinity.

Pray for all Estates.

Take heed in time, and note this well,
Be ruled always by counsel.

Learn of the just to lead thy life,
Being free from envy, wrath, and strife :
Presumption, pride, and covetousness,
With all other ungodliness.

Learn of them always to obey
The Lord's precepts, from day to day,
That thou mayest walk, as he doth will,
And labour thy fond affects to kill.

Always subdue thy beastly lust,
And in the Lord put hope and trust ;
Bridle thine inclination
By godly conversation.

The counsel of the wise embrace,
The fool's advice do then deface.
Which fast and pray with good delight,
That Adam may be killed quite.

That joy in us may still increase,
That God the Lord may give us peace,
That we may be content with Trust
To have our crown among the just.

LIKE WILL TO LIKE.

EDITIONS.

An Enterlude Intituled Like wil to like quod the Deuel to the Colier, very godly and ful of pleasant mirth. Wherin is declared not onely what punishment followeth those that wil rather followe licentious liuing, then to esteeme & followe good councel: and what great benefits and commodities they receiue that apply them vnto vertuous liuing and good exercises. Made by Vlpian Fulwel. Imprinted at Lōdon at the long shop adioyning vnto S. Mildreds Churche in the Pultrie by Iohn Allde. Anno Domini 1568. 4°. Black letter.

A Pleasant Interlude, &c. London. Printed by Edward Allde, &c. 1587. 4o. Black letter.

A copy of the latter is among Garrick's books at the Museum.

Of another production by this writer, not of a dramatic character, an account will be found in Mr Collier's "Bibliographical Catalogue," 1865. "Like will to Like" was Fulwell's only performance in this direction, and is now first reprinted from a copy of the 4to of 1568 in the Malone collection at Oxford. Both editions are of the highest rarity.

THE NAMES OF THE PLAYERS.

Five may easily play this Interlude.

THE PROLOGUE, TOM TOSSPOT, HANKIN HANGMAN, TOM COLLIER.	} *For one.*	LUCIFER, RALPH ROISTER, GOOD FAME, SEVERITY.	} *For one.*	
HANCE, VIRTUOUS LIFE, GOD'S PROMISE, CUTHBERT CUTPURSE.	} *For one.*	PHILIP FLEMING, PIERCE PICKPURSE, HONOUR.	} *For another.*	
		NICHOL NEWFANGLE, *the Vice.*		

VOL. III   υ

THE PROLOGUE.

CICERO in his book *De Amicitia* these words
    doth express,
Saying nothing is more desirous than like is unto
    like ;
Whose words are most true and of a certainty
    doubtless :
For the virtuous do not the virtuous' company
    mislike.
But the vicious do the virtuous' company eschew :
And like will unto like, this is most true.
It is not my meaning your ears for to weary,
With hearkening what is the 'ffect of our matter :
But our pretence [1] is to move you to be merry,
Merrily to speak, meaning no man to flatter.
The name of this matter, as I said whilere,
Is, Like will to Like, quoth the Devil to the Collier.
Sith pithy proverbs in our English tongue doth
    abound,
Our author thought good such a one for to choose,
As may show good example, and mirth may eke
    be found,
But no lascivious toys he purposeth for to use.
Herein, as it were in a glass, see you may
The advancement of virtue, of vice the decay :
To what ruin ruffians and roisters are brought ;
You may here see of them the final end :

---

[1] [Intention.]

Begging is the best, though that end be nought ;
But hanging is worse, if they do not amend.
The virtuous life is brought to honour and dignity :
And at the last to everlasting eternity.
And because divers men of divers minds be,
Some do matters of mirth and pastime require :
Other some are delighted with matters of gravity,
To please all men is our author's chief desire.
Wherefore mirth with measure to sadness [1] is an-
    nexed :
Desiring that none here at our matter will be
    perplexed.
Thus, as I said, I will be short and brief,
Because from this dump you shall relieved be :
And the Devil with the collier, the thief that seeks
    the thief,
Shall soon make you merry, so shortly you shall see ;
And sith mirth for sadness is a sauce most sweet,
Take mirth then with measure, that best sauceth it.

---

[1] [Seriousness.]

LIKE WILL TO LIKE.

NEW. Ha, ha, ha, ha ! now like unto like : it will
    be none other,
Stoop, gentle knave, and take up your brother.
Why, is it so ? and is it even so indeed ?
Why then may I say God send us good speed !
And is every one here so greatly unkind,
That I am no sooner out of sight, but quite out of
    mind ?
Marry, this will make a man even weep for woe,
That on such a sudden no man will let me know,
Sith men be so dangerous[1] now at this day :
Yet are women kind worms, I dare well say.
How say you, woman? you that stand in the angle,
Were you never acquainted with Nichol Newfangle?
Then I see Nichol Newfangle is quite forgot,
Yet you will know me anon, I dare jeopard a groat.
Nichol Newfangle is my name, do you not me
    know ?

---

[1] [Suspicious.]

My whole education to you I shall show.
For first, before I was born, I remember very well,
That my grandsire and I made a journey into hell ;
Where I was bound prentice before my nativity
To Lucifer himself, such was my agility.
All kinds of sciences he taught unto me :
That unto the maintenances of pride might best
    agree.
I learn'd to make gowns with long sleeves and
    wings :
I learn'd to make ruffs like calves' chitterlings,
Caps, hats, coats, with all kind of apparels,
And especially breeches as big as good barrels.
Shoes, boots, buskins, with many pretty toys :
All kind of garments for men, women, and boys.
Know you me now ? I thought that at the last !
All acquaintance from Nichol Newfangle is not
    pass'd.
Nichol Newfangle was and is, and ever shall be :
And there are but few that are not acquainted
    with me.
For so soon as my prenticehood was once come out,
I went by and by the whole world about.
  [*Here the* DEVIL *entereth in, but he speaketh not yet.*
Sancte benedicite, whom have we here ?
Tom Tumbler, or else some dancing bear ?
Body of me, it were best go no near :[1]
For ought that I see, it is my godfather Lucifer,
Whose prentice I have been this many a day :
But no more words but mum : you shall hear
    what he will say.
        [*This name* LUCIFER *must be written on his*
          back and in his breast.
  LU. Ho ! mine own boy, I am glad that thou art
    here !

---

[1] [Nearer.]

NEW. He speaketh to you, sir, I pray you come
near.   [*Pointing to one standing by.*
LU. Nay, thou art even he, of whom I am well
apaid.
NEW. Then speak aloof,[1] for to come nigh I
am afraid.
LU. Why so, my boy? as though thou diddest
never see me.
NEW. Yes, godfather, but I am afraid it is now,
as ofttimes it is with thee ;
For if my dame and thou hast been tumbling by
the ears,
As oftentimes you do, like a couple of great bears,
Thou carest not whom thou killest in thy raging
mind.
Dost thou not remember, since thou didst bruise
me behind ?
This hole in thy fury didst thou disclose,
That now may a tent be put in, so big as thy nose.
This was, when my dame called thee bottle-nosed
knave,
But I am like to carry the mark to my grave.
    LU. O my good boy, be not afraid,
For no such thing hath happened, as thou hast said.
But come to me, my boy, and bless thee I will,
And see that my precepts thou do fulfil.
NEW. Well, godfather, if you will say ought to
me in this case,
Speak, for in faith I mean not to kneel to that ill
face.
If our Lady of Walsingham had no fairer nose and
visage,
By the mass, they were fools that would go to her .
on pilgrimage.
LU. Well, boy, it shall not greatly skill,

---

[1] [In the old copy, *aloof of.*]

Whether thou stand, or whether thou kneel :
Thou knowest what sciences I have thee taught,
Which are able to bring the world to naught.
For thou knowest that through pride from heaven
  I was cast,
Even unto hell, wherefore see thou make haste.
Such pride through new fashions in men's hearts
  to show
That those, that use it, may have the likc over-
  throw.
From virtue procure men to set their minds aside,
And wholly employ it to all sin and pride.
Let thy new-fangled fashions bear such a sway,
That a rascal [may] be so proud as he that best may.
 New. Tush, tush, that is already brought to pass,
For a very skipjack[1] is prouder, I swear by the
  mass,
And seeketh to go more gayer and more brave,
Than doth a lord, though himself be a knave.
 Lu. I can thee thank,[2] that so well thou hast
  play'd the part ;
Such as do so, shall soon feel the smart.
Sith thou hast thus done, there remaineth behind,
That thou in another thing show thy right kind.[3]
 New. Then, good godfather, let me hear thy
  mind.
 Lu. Thou knowest I am both proud and arrogant,
And with the proud I will ever be conversant ;
I cannot abide to see men, that are vicious,
Accompany themselves with such as be virtuous
Wherefore my mind is, sith thou thy part canst play,
That thou adjoin like to like alway.

---

[1] [" A dwarfe, dandiprat, little-skipjacke."—*Cotgrave.*]
[2] [*Can* or *con thee thank*, give thee thanks—a common
expression.]
[3] [Nature.]

NEW. I never loved that well, I swear by this
　　day.

LU. What, my boy ?

NEW. Your mind is, sith I fast three meals
　　every Good Friday,

That I eat nothing but onions and leeks alway.

　　LU. Nay, my mind is, sith thou thy part canst
　　play,

That thou adjoin like to like alway.

　　NEW. Tush, tush, godfather Devil, for that have
　　thou no care :

Thou knowest that like will to like, quoth the
　　Devil to the Collier.

And thou shalt see, that such match I shall make
　　anon,

That thou shalt say I am thy good-good sweet-
　　sweet godson.

　　LU. I will give thee thanks, when thou hast so
　　done.

Here entereth in the COLLIER.

NEW. Well, godfather, no mo words but mum !

For yonder comes the Collier, as seemeth me.

By the mass, he will make a good mate for thee.

　　　　　　　[*The* DEVIL *walketh aside.*

What, old acquaintance, small remembrance ?

Welcome to town with a very vengeance !

Now welcome, Tom Collier, give me thy hand :

As very a knave as any in England.

　　COLL. By mass, god-a-marsy, my vreend Nichol !

　　NEW. By God, and welcome, gentle Tom Lick-
　　hole !

　　COLL. Cham glad to zee thee merry, my vreend
　　Nichol.

And how dost nowadays, good Nichol ?

　　NEW. And nothing else but even plain Nichol ?

Coll. I pray thee, tell me how dost, good
    vreend Lick-hole?
New. It is turn'd from Nichol to Lick-hole
    with Tom Collier.
I say no more, Tom, but hold thy nose there.
    Coll. Nay, hold thy tongue, Nichol, till my
    nose doth come,
So thou shalt take part, and I shall take some.
    New. Well, Tom Collier, let these things pass
    away;
Tell me what market thou hast made of thy coal
    to-day?
    Coll. To every bushel cha zold but three
    peck:
Lo, here be the empty zacks on my neck.
Cha beguil'd the whoresons, that of me ha' bought;
But to beguile me was their whole thought.
    New. But hast thou no conscience in beguiling
    thy neighbour?
    Coll. No, marry, so ich may gain vor my
    labour,
It is a common trade nowadays, this is plain,
To cut one another's throat for lucre and gain.
A small vau't[1] as the world is now brought to
    pass.
    New. Thou art a good fellow, I swear by the
    mass:
As fit a companion for the devil as may be.
Lo, godfather Devil, this fellow will match with
    thee.   [*He taketh him by the hand.*
    Lu. And good Tom Collier thou art welcome
    to me.
    Coll. God amarsy, good Devil, cham glad of
    thy company.
    Lu. Like will to like, I see very well.

---

[1] [Fault.]

New. Godfather, wilt thou dance a little, before
    thee go home to hell?
Lu. I am content, so that Tom Collier do agree.
Coll. I will never refuse (Devil) to dance with thee.
New. Then, godfather, name what the dance
    shall be.
Lu. *Tom Collier of Croydon hath sold his coal.*
New. Why then have at it, by my father's soul!
      [*Nichol Newfangle must have a gittern or*
             some other instrument (if it may be);
             but if he have not, they must dance about
             the place all three, and sing this song
             that followeth, which must be done also,
             although they have an instrument.

The Song.

Tom Collier of Croydon hath sold his coals,
    And made his market to-day;
And now he danceth with the Devil,
    For like will to like alway.

Wherefore let us rejoice and sing,
    Let us be merry and glad;
Sith that the Collier and the Devil
    This match and dance hath made.

Now of this dance we make an end
    With mirth and eke with joy:
The Collier and the Devil will be
    Much like to like alway.

New. Ha, ha! marry, this is trim singing,
I had not thought the Devil to be so cunning;
And, by the mass, Tom Collier [is] as good as he:
I see that like with like will ever agree.
    Coll. Farewell, Master Devil, vor ich must be
    gone.   [*Exit.*

Lu. Why, then, farewell my gentle friend Tom.
New. Farewell, Tom Collier, a knave be thy
  comfort !   [*Exit* Tom Collier.
How say'st thou, godfather ? is not this trim sport ?
Lu. Thou art mine own boy ; my blessing thou
  shalt have.
New. By my truth, godfather, that blessing I
  do not crave ;
But if you go your way, I will do my diligence
As well in your absence as in your presence.
Lu. But thou shalt salute me, ere I go doubtless,
That in thy doings thou may'st have the better
  success.
Wherefore kneel down and say after me :
            [*He kneeleth down.*
When the devil will have it so, it must needs
  so be.
New. What shall I say, bottle-nosed godfather,
  canst thou tell ?
Lu. All hail, O noble prince of hell !
New. All my dame's cows' tail[s] fell down in
  the well.
Lu. I will exalt thee above the clouds.
New. I will salt thee, and hang thee in the
  shrouds.
Lu. Thou art the enhancer of my renown.
New. Thou art Hance, the hangman of Calais
  town.
Lu. To thee be honour alone.
New. To thee shall come our hobbling Jone.
Lu. Amen.
New. Amen.
Lu. Now farewell, my boy, farewell heartily,
Is there never a knave here will keep the Devil
  company ?
New. Farewell, godfather, for thou must go
  alone :

I pray thee come hither again anon. [*Exit* LUCIFER.
Marry, here was a benediction of the Devil's good
    grace :
Body of me, I was so afraid, I was like to bestench
    the place !
My buttocks made buttons of the new fashion,
While the whoreson Devil was making his saluta-
    tion.
But, by mass, I am so glad as ever was madge mare,
That the whoreson Devil is joined with the knave
    Collier.
As fit a match as ever could be pick'd out,
What sayst thou to it, Jone with the long snout ?
    [TOM TOSSPOT *cometh in with a feather in his hat.*
But who comes yonder puffing, as hot as a black
    pudding.
I hold twenty pound it is a ruffian, if a goose go
    a-gooding.
    TOM. Gog's heart and his guts, is not this too bad?
Blood, wounds, and nails ! it will make a man mad.
    NEW. I warrant you, here is a lusty one, [and]
    very brave :
I think anon he will swear himself a knave.
    TOM. Many a mile have I ridden, and many a
    mile have I gone :
Yet can I not find for me a fit companion.
Many there be, which my company would frequent,
If to do, as they do, I would be content.
They would have me leave off my pride and my
    swearing,
My new-fangled fashions, and leave off this wearing.
But rather than I such companions will have,
I will see a thousand of them laid in their grave.
Similis similem sibi quærit, such a one do I seek,
As unto myself in every condition is like.
    NEW. Sir, you are welcome ; ye seem to be an
    honest man,

And I will help you in this matter, as much as I
  can,
If you will tarry here a while, I tell you in good
  sooth,
I will find one as fit for you as a pudding for a
  friar's mouth.
  TOM. I thank you, my friend, for your gentle
  offer to me :
I pray you tell me, what your name may be.
  NEW. Methink, by your apparel you have had
  me in regard ;
I pray you, of Nichol Newfangle have you never
  heard ?
  TOM. Nichol Newfangle ? why, we are of old
  acquaintance !
  NEW. By my troth, your name is quite out of
  my remembrance.
  TOM. At your first coming into England, well I
  wot,
You were very well acquainted with Tom Tosspot.
  NEW. Tom Tosspot ? *Sancti ! amen !* how you
  were out of my mind !
  TOM. You know, when you brought into England
  this new-fangled kind,
That Tosspots and ruffians with you were first ac-
  quainted ?
  NEW. It is even so, Tom Tosspot, as thou hast
  said.
  TOM. It is an old saying, that mountains and
  hills never meet ;
But I see that men shall meet, though they do not
  seek ;
And, I promise you, more joy in my heart I have
  found,
Than if I had gain'd an hundred pound.
  NEW. And I am as glad as one had given me a
  groat,

That I have met now with thee, Tom Tosspot.
And seeing that thou wouldst a mate so fain have,
I will join thee with one, that shall be as very a
      knave
As thou art thyself, thou may'st believe me :
Thou shalt see anon, what I will do for thee.
For you seek for as very a knave, as you yourself
      are ;
For, like will to like, quoth the Devil to the Collier.
   TOM. Indeed, Nichol Newfangle, ye say the verity,
For like will to like : it will none otherwise be.

Enter RALPH ROISTER.

Behold, Tom Tosspot, even in pudding time [1]
Yonder cometh Ralph Roister, an old friend of
      mine !
By the mass, for thee he is so fit a mate,
As Tom and Tib for Kit and Kate,
Now welcome, my friend Ralph Roister, by the
      mass.
   RALPH. And I am glad to see thee here in this
      place.
   NEW. Bid him welcome hark, he can play a
      knave's part.
   TOM. My friend, you are welcome with all my
      heart.
   RALPH. God-a-mercy, good fellow, tell me what
      thou art.
   NEW. As very a knave as thou, though the best
      be too bad :
   TOM. I am one, which of your company would
      be very glad.

---

[1] [A tolerably early example of the use of this saying,
which may have taken its rise from the custom of having a
pudding as the first dish on the table, and may consequently be equivalent to *betimes.*]

RALPH. And I will not your company refuse of
   a certainty,
So that to my conditions your manners do agree.
   TOM. It should appear by your sayings, that we
   are of one mind,
For I know that roisters and tosspots come of one
   kind ;
And as our names be much of one accord, and
   much like,
So I think our conditions be not far unlike.
   RALPH. If your name to me you will declare and
   show,
You may in this matter my mind the sooner know.
   TOM. Few words are best among friends, this is
   true ;
Wherefore I shall briefly show my name unto you.
Tom Tosspot it is, it need not to be painted :
Wherefore I with Ralph Roister must needs be
   acquainted.
   NEW. In faith, Ralph Roister, if thou wilt be
   ruled by me,
We will dance hand in hand, like knaves all three :
It is as unpossible for thee his company to deny,
As it is for a camel to creep through a needle's
   eye.
Therefore bid him welcome, like a knave as thou
   art.
   RALPH. By my troth, Tom Tosspot, you are wel-
   come with all my heart.
   TOM. I thank you that my acquaintance ye will
   take in good part.
And by my troth, I will be your sworn brother :
   NEW. Tush, like will to like : it will be none
   other.
For the virtuous will always virtue's company seek
   out :
A gentleman never seeketh the company of a lout ;

And roisters and ruffians do sober company eschew :
For like will ever to like, this is most true.
    RALPH. Now, friend Tom Tosspot, seeing that
      we are brethren sworn,
And neither of our companies from other may be
      forborne,
The whole trade of my life to thee I will declare.
    TOM. And to tell you my property also I shall
      not spare.
    NEW. Then, my masters, if you will awhile abide
      it,
Ye shall see two such knaves so lively described
That, if hell should be raked even by and by in-
      deed,
Such another couple cannot be found, I swear by
      my creed.
Go to, sirs, say on your whole minds,
And I shall paint you out in your right kinds.
First, Tom Tosspot, plead thou thy cause and thy
      name,
And I will sit in this chair, and give sentence on
      the same.
I will play the judge, and in this matter give judg-
      ment :
How say you, my masters, are you not so content ?
    RALPH. By my troth, for my part, thereto I do
      agree.
    TOM. I were to blame, if any fault should be in me.
    NEW. Then that I be in office, neither of you do
      grudge ?
    BOTH. No, indeed.
    NEW. Where learn'd you to stand capp'd before
      a judge ?
You souterly [1] knaves, show you all your manners
      at once ?

---

[1] [Clownish or rude, like a cobbler, from *souter*, a cobbler.]

RALPH. Why, Nichol, all we are content.

NEW. And am I plain Nichol? and yet it is in
　my arbitrement
To judge which of you two is the verier knave.
I am Master Nichol Newfangle, both gay and brave;
For, seeing you make me your judge, I trow,
I shall teach you both your liripup[1] to know.

> [*He fighteth.*

TOM. Stay yourself, sir, I pray you heartily.

RALPH. I pray you, be content, and we will be
　more mannerly.

NEW. Nay, I cannot put up such an injury;
For, seeing I am in office, I will be known therefore:
Fend your heads, sirs, for I will to it more once.

> [*He fighteth again.*

RALPH. I pray you be content, good gentle
　Master Nichol:

TOM. I never saw the like, by Gog's soul.

NEW. Well, my masters, because you do intend
To learn good manners, and your conditions to
　amend,
I will have but one fit more, and so make an end.

RALPH. I pray you, sir, let us no more contend.

NEW. Marry, this hath breathed me very well:
Now let me hear, how your tales ye can tell.
And I (master judge) will so bring to pass,
That I will judge who shall be knave of clubs at
　Christmas.[2]

TOM. Gog's wounds, I am like Phalaris, that
　made a bull of brass—

NEW. Thou art like a false knave now, and ever-
　more was.

---

[1] [A word of somewhat uncertain meaning and of obscure
origin.　See Halliwell *v. Liripoops.*]

[2] [This is an allusion worth noting; the editor does not
recollect to have met with it before.]

TOM. Nay, I am like Phalaris, that made a bull
   of brass,
As a cruel torment for such as did offend,
And he himself first therein put was :
Even so are we brought now to this end,
In ordaining him a judge, who will be honoured as
   a god,
So for our own tails we have made a rod.
   RALPH. And I am served as Haman, that pre-
   par'd—
NEW. How was he served, I pray thee, do me tell?
RALPH. Who I speak of? thou knowest well,
NEW. Thou art served as Harry Hangman,
   captain of the black guard.
   RALPH. Nay, I am served as Haman, that prepared
A high pair of gallows for Mordecai the Jew,
And was the first himself that thereon was hanged :
So I feel the smart of mine own rod, this is true.
But hereafter I will learn to be wise,
And ere I leap once, I will look twice.
   NEW. Well, Tom Tosspot, first let me hear thee.
How canst thou prove thyself a verier knave than
   he ?
   TOM. You know that Tom Tosspot men do me
   call ?
NEW. A knave thou hast always been, and ever-
   more shall.
TOM. My conditions, I am sure, ye know as well
   as I.
NEW. A knave thou was born, and so thou shalt
   die.
TOM. But that you are a judge, I would say unto
   you,
Knaves are Christian men, else you were a Jew.
   NEW. He calls me knave by craft, do you not see ?
Sirrah, I will remember it, when you think not on me.
Well, say what thou canst for thine own behoof ;

If thou provest thyself the verier knave by good
    proof,
Thou must be the elder brother, and have the
    patrimony ;
And when he hath said, then do thou reply.
Even Thomas-a-Waterings or Tyburn Hill [1]
To the falsest thief of you both, by my father's will :
    RALPH. I pray you, sir, what is that patrimony ?
    NEW. I pray you leave your courtesy, and I will
        tell you by and by.
If he be the more knave, the patrimony he must
    have,
But thou shalt have it, if thou prove thyself the
    verier knave ;
A piece of ground it is, that of Beggars' manor
    do[th] hold,
And whoso deserves it, shall have it, ye may be
    bold—
Call'd Saint Thomas-a-Waterings or else Tyburn
    Hill,
Given and so bequeathed to the falsest by will.
    TOM. Then I trow I am he, that this patrimony
        shall possess,
For I Tom Tosspot do use this trade doubtless :
From morning till night I sit tossing the black
    bowl,[2]
Then come I home, and pray for my father's soul.
Saying my prayers with wounds, blood, guts, and
    heart :
Swearing and staring, thus play I my part.
If any poor man have in a whole week earn'd one
    groat,
He shall spend it in one hour in tossing the pot.

---

[1] [The two places chiefly used for executions, after the
discontinuance of the Elms in Smithfield]
  [2] [The leathern drinking vessel, generally called *a jack.*]

I use to call servants and poor men to my company,
And make them spend all they have unthriftily ;
So that my company they think to be so good,
That in short space their hair grows through their
    hood.
    NEW. But will no gossips keep thee company
    now and then ?
    TOM. Tush, I am acquainted with many a woman,
That with me will sit in every house and place :
But then their husbands had need fend their face.
For when they come home, they will not be afeard,
To shake the goodman, and sometime shave his
    beard.
And as for Flemish [1] servants I have such a train,
That will quass and carouse, and therein spend
    their gain.
From week to week I have all this company ;
Wherefore I am worthy to have the patrimony.
    NEW. Thus thou may'st be called a knave in
    grain ;
And where knaves are scant, thou shalt go for
    twain.
But now, Ralph Roister, let me hear what thou
    canst say.
    RALPH. You know that Ralph Roister I am
    called alway,
And my conditions in knavery so far doth sur-
    mount,
That to have this patrimony I make mine account,
For I entice young gentlemen all virtue to eschew,
And to give themselves to riotousness, this is true.
Serving-men also by me are so seduced,
That all in bravery their minds are confused.

---

1 [The Flemings or Dutch (for the two seem to have been
pretty generally confounded) had a great reputation here,
like the Danes afterwards, for habits of excessive drinking.]

Then, if they have not themselves to maintain,
To pick and to steal they must be fain.
And, I may say to you, I have such a train,
That sometime I pitch a field on Salisbury plain.[1]
And much more, if need were, I could say verily :
Wherefore I am worthy to have the patrimony.

 NEW. He, that shall judge this matter, had
  need have more wit than I ;
But, seeing you have referred it unto my arbitre-
  ment,
In faith I will give such equal judgment,
That both of you shall be well-pleased and content.

 TOM. Nay, I have not done, for I can say much
  more.

 NEW. Well, I will not have you contend any
  more.
But this farm, which to Beggars' manor doth
  appertain,
I will equally divide between you twain.
Are you not content, that so it shall be ?

 BOTH. As it pleaseth you, so shall we agree.

 NEW. Then see, that anon ye come both unto me.

 RALPH. Sir, for my part, I thank you heartily :
I promised of late to come unto a company,
Which at Hob Filcher's for me do remain :
God be with you, and anon I will come again.

 TOM. Farewell, brother Ralph, I will come to
  you anon.   [Exit TOM.[2]

 NEW. Come again, for you shall not so suddenly
  be gone.

---

[1] [Salisbury plain was formerly one of the resorts of foot-
pads, who infested the place in small bodies, and waylaid
travellers.]

[2] [The entrances and *exits* in this piece are so imperfectly
marked, that it is often difficult to be sure about them. It
seems to be Tom Tosspot who goes out now ; but if so, he
soon returns, though his re-entry is not recorded.]

Here entereth HANCE *with a pot, and singeth as*
followeth.

See ye not who comes yonder? an old friend of yours:
One that is ready to quass at all hours.

> [*He singeth the first two lines, and speaketh*
> *the rest as stammeringly as may be.*

Quass in heart, and quass again, and quass about the
> *house-a :*
And toss the black bowl to and fro, and I brinks[1] *them*
> *all carouse-a.*

Be go-go-gog's nowns, ch-ch-cha drunk zo-zo-much
> to-day :
That be-be-mass, ch-cham a-most drunk, ich da-da-
> dare zay.
Chud spe-spe-spend a goo-goo-good groat :
Tha-that ich cud vi-vind my ca-ca-captain To-To-
> Tom Tosspot.   [*He setteth him in the chair.*
> NEW. Sit down, good Hance, lest thou lie on
> the ground,
He knoweth not Tom Tosspot, I dare jeopard
> twenty pound.
> TOM.[2] He will know me by and by, I hold you
> a crown.
How dost thou, servant Hance? how comes this
> to pass?
> HANCE. Ma-ma-master To-To-Tom, ch-ch-cham
> glad by-by mass—   [*He drinketh.*
Ca-ca-carouse to-to-to thee, go-go-good Tom.
> NEW. Hold up, good Hance, I will pledge thee
> anon.

---

[1] [Drink.]

[2] [Tom seems to have gone out and returned, as observed
above.]

RALPH. Well, there is no remedy, but I must be
    gone.
HANCE. Ta-ta-tarry, good vellow, a wo-wo-word
    or twain :
If tho-tho-thou thyself do-do-do not come again.
Bi-bi-bid Philip Fleming co-co-come hither to me,
Vo-vo-vor he must lead me home, now ich do ze.
RALPH. Then, farewell, Hance, I will remember
    thy errant :
He will be here by and by, I dare be his warrant.
                        [*Exit* RALPH ROISTER.
NEW. Farewell, Ralph Roister, with all my
    heart :
Come anon, and I will deliver thee thy part.
TOM. Now, Hance, right now thou drank'st to
    me,
Drink again, and I will pledge thee.
HANCE. *Omni po-po-po-tenti*, all the po-po-pot is
    empty.
NEW. Why, Hance, thou hast Latin in thy belly
    methink :
I thought there was no room for Latin, there is so
    much drink !
HANCE. Ich le-le-learned zome La-La-Latin,
    when ich was a la-la-lad :
Ich ca-ca-can zay *Tu es nebulo*, ich learn'd of my dad.
And ich could once he-he-help the p-p-priest to say
    mass :
By giss, ma-man, ich ha' been cu-cu-cunning, when
    'twas.
TOM. I knew Hance, when he was, as he say'th :
For he was once a scholar in good faith ;
But through my company he was withdrawn from
    thence,
Through his riot and excessive expense.
Unto this trade, which now you do in him see :
So that now he is wholly addicted to follow me ;

And one of my guard he is now become.
Well, Hance, well, thou wast once a white son ! [1]
   NEW. Now, so God help me, thou art a pretty
      fellow, Hance ;
A clean-legged gentleman, and as proper a paunch,
As any I know between this and France.
   HANCE. Yes, by-by-by God, ich co'd once dance.
   NEW. I speak of no dancing, little-bellied Hance ;
But, seeing thou say'st thou canst so well dance,
Let me see where thou canst dance lively.
   HANCE. Tha-tha-that ca-ca-can I do vull trimly.
         [*He danceth as evil-favoured as may be de-*
           mised, and in the dancing he falleth
           down, and when he riseth, he must groan.
   NEW. Rise again, Hance, thou hadst almost got
      a fall :
But thou dancest trimly, legs and all.
Body of me, Hance, how doth thy belly, canst thou
      tell ?
By the mass, he hath beray'd his breeches, methink
      by the smell.
   TOM. I will help thee up, Hance, give me thy
      hand.   [*He riseth.*
   HANCE. By-by mass, ch-ch-chwas almost down,
      I think ve-verily.
   NEW. Wast thou almost down, Hance ? marry,
      so think I,
But thou art sick, methink by the groaning :
He grunts like a bear, when he is a-moaning.
Hark, how his head aches, and how his pulses do
      beat :
I think he will be hang'd, his belly is so great.
   HANCE. Go-Go-God-amercy, good Tom, with all
      my heart :

---

[1] A term of endearment. A commoner form is *white
boy.*

NEW. If thou canst not leap, Hance, let me see
    thee drink a quart,
And get thee out abroad into the air.
    TOM. Tush, he had more need to sleep in this
    chair.
Sit down, Hance, and thou shalt see anon,
Philip Fleming will come to fetch thee home.
        [HANCE *sitteth in the chair, and snorteth, as*
         though he were fast asleep.
    NEW. I pray thee, Tom Tosspot, is this one of
    thy men?
    TOM. He is a companion of mine now and then.
    NEW. By the faith of my body, such carpenter,
    such chips,
And as the wise man said, such lettuce, such lips.
For, like master, like man : like tutor, like scholar ;
And, like will to like, quoth the Devil to the Collier.
    TOM. It is no remedy, for it must needs so be ;
Like will to like, you may believe me.
    [PHILIP FLEMING *entereth with a pot in his hand.*
    NEW. Lo, where Philip Fleming cometh even in
    pudding time !
    TOM. He bringeth in his hand either good ale or
    else good wine.

      PHILIP FLEMING *singeth these four lines*
        following :

Troll the bowl and drink to me, and troll the bowl
    again,
And put a brown toast in [the] pot for Philip Fleming's
    brain.
And I shall toss it to and fro, even round about the
    house-a :
Good hostess, now let it be so, I brink them all
    carouse-a.
    PHILIP. Marry, here is a pot of noppy good ale.
As clear as crystal pure and stale.

Now a crab in the fire were worth a good groat,
That I might quass with my captain Tom Tosspot.
What? I can no sooner wish, but by and by I
    have!
God save mine eyesight, methink I see a knave.
What, captain! how goeth the world with you?
Why, now I see the old proverb to be true;
Like will to like, both with Christian, Turk, and
    Jew.
Marry, Philip, even as I was wont to do:
    PHILIP. Ralph Roister told me that I should find
      Hance here,
Where is he, that he doth not appear?
    NEW. I hold twenty pound the knave is blind.
Turn about, Philip Fleming, and look behind.
Hast thou drunk so much that thy eyes be out?
Lo, how he snoreth like a lazy lout.
Go to him, for he sleepeth sound:
Two such paunches in all England can scant be
    found.
    PHILIP. Why, Hance, art thou in thy prayers
    so devoutly?
Awake, man, and we two will quass together
    stoutly.
    HANCE. *Domine, dominus noster;*
Me-think ich a spied three knaves on a cluster,
    NEW. Stay a while, for he sayeth his *pater noster.*
    HANCE. *Sanctum benedictum,* what have I
    dreamed?
By Gog's nowns, chad thought ich had been in my
    bed.
Chad dreamed such a dream, as thou wilt marvel
    to hear,
Me-thought I was drowned in a barrel of beer.
And by and by the barrel was turned to a ship,
Which me-thought the wind made nicely to skip.
And I did sail therein from Flanders to France:

At last ich was brought hither among a sort of
    knaves by chance.

NEW. Lo, Hance, here is Philip Fleming come now,
We will go drink together now, how say'st thou?

HANCE. I pray thee, good Vilip, now lead me
    away:

PHILIP. Give me thy hand, and I will thee stay.

HANCE. How say you, Master Nichol, will you
    keep us company?

NEW. Go before, Master Lick-hole,[1] and I will
    come by and by.

Mates matched together, depart you three;
I will come after, you may believe me.

      [*They three are gone together, and* NICHOL
          NEWFANGLE *remaineth behind, but he*
          must not speak till they be within.]

NEW. Ha, ha, ha, ha, ha, ha, ha!

He sings.

Now three knaves are gone, and I am left alone,
Myself here to solace;
Well done, gentle Jone, why begin you to moan?
Though they be gone, I am in place.

And now will I dance, and now will I prance,
For why I have none other work:
Snip snap, butter is no bone meat:
Knave's flesh is no pork.

Hey tisty-toisty, an owl is a bird,
Jackanapes hath an old face;
You may believe me at one bare word,
How like you this merry case?

---

[1] [Nichol had previously addressed the Collier as *Master
Lick-hole*; but as the Collier is not on the stage, it is clear
that he here applies the same bye-name, *rhythmi causâ*, to
Hance.]

A piece of ground they think they have found,
I will tell you what it is :
For I them told of Beggars' manor it did hold,
A staff and a wallet i-wis.

Which in short space, even in this place,
Of me they shall receive :
For when that their drift hath spent all their thrift,
Their minds I shall deceive.

I trow you shall see more knaves come to me,
Which whensoever they do,
They shall have their meed, as they deserve indeed,
As you shall see shortly these two.

When they do pretend to have had a good end,
Mark well, then, what shall ensue :
A bag and a bottle, or else a rope knottle,
This shall they prove too true.

But mark well this game, I see this gear frame :
Lo, who cometh now in such haste ?
It is Cuthbert Cutpurse
And Pierce Pickpurse,
Give room now a little cast.

Here entereth CUTHBERT CUTPURSE *and* PIERCE
PICKPURSE.

> [CUTHBERT CUTPURSE *must have in his hand a*
> *purse of money or counters in it, and a*
> *knife in one hand and a whetstone in the*
> *other ; and* PIERCE *must have money or*
> *counters in his hand and jingle it, as he*
> *cometh in.*]

CUTH. By Gog's wounds, it doth me good to the
    heart,
To see how cleanly I play'd this part.
While they stood thrusting together in the throng,

I began to go them among ;
And with this knife, which here you do see,
I cut away this purse cleanly.
   NEW. See to your purses, my masters, and be
      ruled by me,
For knaves are abroad, therefore beware.
You are warn'd : and ye take not heed, I do not
      care.   [*Aside.*
   PIERCE. And also, so soon as I had espied
A woman in the throng, whose purse was fat,
I took it by the strings, and cleanly it untied :
She knew no more of it than Gib our cat.
Yet at the last she hied apace,
And said, that the money in my hand she saw.
Thou whore, said I, I will have an action of the case,
And seeing thou say'st so, I will try the law.
   CUTHB. How say'st thou, Pierce Pickpurse, art
      thou not agreed
These two booties equally to divide ?
Then let us count the total sum,
And divide it equally, when we have done.
   NEW. My masters, here is a good fellow, that
      would fain have some.
   CUTHB. What, Nichol Newfangle, be you here ?
So God help me, I am glad with all my heart.
   PIERCE. Then, ere we depart, we will have some
      cheer,
And of this booty you shall have your part.
   NEW. I thank you both even heartily,
And I will do somewhat for you by and by :
Are not you two sworn brothers in every booty ?
   BOTH. Yes, that we are truly.
   NEW. Then can I tell you news, which you do
      not know :
Such news as will make you full glad, I trow.
But first tell me this, Pierce Pickpurse,
Whether is the elder, thou or Cuthbert Cutpurse ?

PIERCE. In faith, I think we are both of one age
    well nigh.
CUTHB. I suppose there is no great difference,
    truly :
But wherefore ask you? I pray you, tell me why?
    NEW. I will tell you the cause without any
    delay :
For a piece of land is fallen, as I hear say,
Which by succession must come to one of you :
A proper plot it is, this is most true.
For thou, Cuthbert Cutpurse, was Cuthbert Cut-
    throat's son,
And thou, Pierce Pickpurse, by that time thou hast
    done,
Canst derive thy pedigree from an ancient house :
Thy father was Tom Thief, and thy mother was
    Tib Louse.
This piece of land, whereto you inheritors are,
Is called the land of the two-legged mare ;[1]
In which piece of ground there is a mare indeed,
Which is the quickest mare in England for speed.
Therefore, if you will come anon unto me,
I will put you in possession, and that you shall see.
    CUTHB. I cannot believe that such luck is
    happen'd to us.
    NEW. It is true, that I to you do discuss.
    PIERCE. If you will help us to this piece of
    ground,
Both of us to you shall think ourselves bound.
    NEW. Yes, in faith, you shall have it, you may
    believe me ;
I will be as good as my word, as shortly you shall
    see.
    CUTHB. Then, brother Pierce, we may think our-
    selves happy,

---

[1] [The gallows.]

That ever we were with him acquainted.
   PIERCE. Even so we may of a certainty,
That such good luck unto us hath happened.
But, brother Cuthbert, is it not best
To go in for awhile, and distribute this booty?
Whereas we three will make some feast,
And quass together, and be merry.
   CUTHB. What say you, Nichol?
   NEW. I do agree.

Here entereth VIRTUOUS LIVING.

But, soft, awhile be ruled by me,
Look, yonder a little do you not see,
Who cometh yonder? awhile we will abide;
Let him say his pleasure, and we will stand aside.
   V. L. O gracious God, how wonderful are thy
      works,
How highly art thou of all men to be praised:
Of Christians, Saracens, Jews, and also Turks,
Thy glory ought to be erected and raised.
What joys hast thou prepared for the virtuous life,
And such as have thy name in love and in awe;
Thou hast promised salvation to man, child, and
      wife,
That thy precepts observe, and keep well thy law.
And to the virtuous life what doth ensue?
Virtutis premium honor, Tully doth say;
Honour is thy guerdon for virtue due,
And eternal salvation at the latter day.
How clear in conscience is the virtuous life!
The vicious hath consciences so heavy as lead.
Their conscience and their doing is alway at strife;
And altogether they live yet to sin they are dead.
   NEW. God give you good-morrow, sir, how do
     you to-day?
   V. L. God bless you also both now and alway.
I pray you, with me have you any acquaintance?

NEW. Yea, marry, I am an old friend of yours,
    perchance.
    V. L. If it be so, I marvel very much,
That the dulness of my wit should be such,
That you should be altogether out of my memory.
Tell me your name, I pray you heartily.
    NEW. By the faith of my body, you will appose
    me by and by ;
But, in faith, I was but little when I was first
    born ;
And my mother to tell me my name thought it
    scorn.
    V. L. I will never acquaint me with such in any
    place,
As are ashamed of their names, by God's grace.
    NEW. I remember my name now, it is come to
    my mind :
I have mused much, before I could it find.
Nichol Newfangle it is ; I am your old friend.
    V. L. My friend ? marry, I do thee defy,
And all such company I do deny.
For thou art a companion for roisters and ruffians,
And not fit for any virtuous companions.
    NEW. And, in faith, art thou at plain defiance ?
Then I see I must go to mine old acquaintance.
Well, Cuthbert Cutpurse and [Pierce] Pickpurse,
    we must go together ;
For, like will to like, quoth the Devil to the Collier.
    V. L. Indeed, thou say'st true, it must needs
    be so,
For like will ever to his like go ;
And my conditions and thine so far do disagree,
That no familiarity between us may be.
For thou nourishest vice both day and night :
My name is Virtuous Life, and in virtue is my
    delight.
So vice and virtue cannot together be united ;

But the one the other hath always spited.
For as the water quencheth fire, and the flame doth
    suppress,
So virtue hateth vice, and seeketh a redress.
  PIERCE. Tush, if he be so dangerous, let us not
    him esteem,
And he is not for our company, I see very well;
For if he be so holy, as he doth seem,
We and he differ as much as heaven and hell.
  NEW. You know, that like will to like alway,
And you see how holily he is now bent:
To seek his company why do we assay?
  PIERCE. I promise you, do you what you will,
    I do not consent:
For I pass not for him, be he better or be he worse.
  NEW. Friend, if you be wise, beware your purse.
For this fellow may do you good when all comes
    to all;
If you chance to lose your purse in Cutpurse Hall.
But, in faith, fare ye well, sith of our company you
    be weary:
We will go to a place, where we will be merry.
For I see your company and ours do far differ;
For like will to like, quoth the Devil to the Collier.
  CUTHB. Well, let us be gone, and bid him adieu:
For I see this proverb proveth very true.
  PIERCE. Then let us go to Hob Filcher's house,
Where we will be merry, and quass carouse.
And there shall we find Tom Tosspot, with other
    mo,
Meet makes for us: therefore let us go.
Then, seeing we are all of one mind,
Let us three go, and leave a knave here behind.
      [*Exeunt* NEW., CUTHB., *and* PIERCE.

They sing this song [1] *as they go out from the place.*

Good hostess, lay a crab in the fire, and broil a mess
  of souse-a :
That we may toss the bowl to and fro, and brinks
  them all carouse-a.

And I will pledge Tom Tosspot, till I be drunk as a
  mouse-a :
Whoso will drink to me all day, I will pledge them
  all carouse-a.

Then we will not spare for any cost, so long as we be
  in house-a :
Then, hostess, fill the pot again, for I pledge them
  all carouse-a.

> [*When this is spoken,* V. LIVING *must pause*
>   *a while, and then say as followeth.*

O wicked imps, that have such delight,
In evil conversation wicked and abhoninable:
And from virtue's lore withdraw yourselves quite,
And lean to vice most vile and detestable.
How prone and ready we are vice to ensue ?
How deaf we be good counsel to hear ?
How strange we make it our hearts to renew ?
How little we have God's threats in fear ?
Saint Augustine say'th in his fifth book, *De*
  Civitate Dei,
Conjunctæ sunt ædes Virtutis et Honoris, say'th he ;
The houses of virtue and honour joined together be.
And so the way to honour's house is disposed,
That through virtue's house he must needs pass :

---

[1] [The song is divided between the three, each singing
two lines, and the division is marked ; but the name of the
singer in each case is not given.]

Or else from honour he shall soon be deposed,
And brought to that point, that he before was.
  But if through virtue honour be attained :
  The path to salvation may soon be gained.
Some there be, that do fortune prefer ;
Some esteem pleasure more than virtuous life.
But in my opinion all such do err ;
For virtue and fortune be not at strife.
  Where virtue is, fortune must needs grow :
  But fortune without virtue has soon the over-
    throw.
Thrice happy are they, that do virtue embrace,
For a crown of glory shall be their reward :
Satan at no time may him anything deface,
For God over him will have such regard,
  That his foes he shall soon tread under foot ;
  And by God's permission pluck them up by the
    root.
It booteth not vice against virtue to stir,
For why vice is feeble and of no force :
But *virtus eterna preclaraque habetur.*
Wherefore I would all men would have remorse,
  And eschew evil company vile and pernicious :
  Delight in virtuous men, and hate the vicious.
And as the end of virtue is honour and felicity,
So mark well the end of wickedness and vice !
Shame in this world and pain eternally,
Wherefore you, that are here, learn to be wise,
And the end of the one with the other weigh,
By that time you have heard the end of this play.
But why do I thus much say in the praise of
    virtue,
Sith the thing praiseworthy needs no praise at all?
It praiseth itself sufficiently, this is true,
Which chaseth away sin as bitter as gall ?
And where virtue is, it need not to be praised,
For the renown thereof shall soon be raised.

Intrat GOOD FAME.

G. F. O Virtuous Life, God rest you merry,
To you am I come for to attend.
V. L. Good Fame, ye are welcome heartily.
I pray you, who did you hither send?
G. F. Even God's Promise hath sent me unto
    you,
Willing me from you not to depart:
But always to give attendance due,
And in no wise from you to start.
For God of his promise hath most liberally
Sent me Good Fame to you Virtuous Life:
Whereby it may be seen manifestly,
God's great zeal to virtue both in man and wife.
For why they may be sure, that I, Good Fame,
From the virtuous life will never stray:
Whereby honour and renown may grow to their
    name,
And eternal salvation at the latter day.
V. L. God is gracious and full of great mercy
To such as in virtue set their whole delight:
Pouring his benefits on them abundantly.
O man, what, meanest thou with thy Saviour to fight?
Come unto him, for he is full of mercy,
The fountain of virtue and of godliness the spring:
Come unto him, and thou shall live everlastingly;
He doth not require thee any price to bring.
    Venite ad me omnes qui laboratis et onerati
    Estis, et ego refossilabo vos.
Come unto me, ye that travail (say'th he)
And such as with sin are heavily loden:
And of me myself refreshed you shall be.
Repent, repent, your sins shall be downtrodden—
Well, Good Fame, sith God of his goodness
Hath hither sent you on me to attend,
Let us give thank to him with humbleness,

And persuade with all men their lives to amend.
　　G. F. Virtuous Life, I do thereto agree,
For it becometh all men for to do so.

Intrat GOD'S PROMISE, *and* HONOUR *with him.*

But, behold, yonder cometh God's Promise, as
　　seemeth me;
And Honour with him cometh also.
　　V. L. Such godly company pleaseth me very well;
For vicious men from our company we should expel.
　　G. P. God rest you merry both, and God be
　　your guide.
　　HONOUR. We are now come to the place where
　　we must abide.
For from you, Virtuous Life, I Honour may not slide.
　　G. P. I am God's Promise, which is a thing eterne,
And nothing more surer than his promise may be:
A sure foundation to such as will learn
God's precepts to observe : then must they needs see
Honour in this world, and at last a crown of glory;
Ever in joy and mirth, and never to be sorry.
Wherefore, O Virtuous Life, to you we do repair,
As messengers from God, his promise to fulfil;
And therefore sit you down now in this chair,
For to endue you with honour is God's promise
　　and will.
　　　　[VIRTUOUS LIVING *sitteth down in the chair.*
　　HONOUR. Now take this sword in hand as a
　　token of victory,
This crown from my head to you I shall give :
I crown you with it as one most worthy,
And see that all vice ye do punish and grieve,
For in this world I Honour with you shall remain,
And Good Fame from you cannot refrain :
And after this life a greater crown you shall attain.
　　G. F. What heart can think, or what tongue can
　　express

The great goodness of God, which is almighty?
Who seeth this, and seeks not vice to suppress,
Honour, Good Fame, yea, and life everlastingly?
Thy name be praised, O Lord, therefore,
And to thee only be glory and honour!
Sith God's Promise hath brought honour into place,
I will for a while leave you three alone:
For I must depart now for a little space;
But I shall come to you again anon.

                        [*Exit* GOOD FAME.

    V. L. God's Promise is infallible, his word is
       most true;
And to ground thereon a man may be bold:
As Scripture doth testify and declare unto you,
On which foundation your building you may behold.
For virtuous rulers the fruit of felicity do reap:
And reward of fame and honour to themselves
      they heap.
    HONOUR. Seeing we have now endued him with
      the crown and the sword,
    Which is due unto him by God's promise and
      word,
    Let us three sing unto God with one accord.
    G. P. To sing praises unto God it liketh well me.
    V. L. And I also with you do thereto agree.
A pleasant noise to God's ears it must needs bring,
That God's Promise, Honour, and Virtuous Life
      do sing.

They sing this Song following.

Life is but short, hope not therein;
Virtue immortal seek for to win.
Whoso to virtue doth apply,
   Good fame and honour must obtain.
And also live eternally,
   For virtuous life this is the gain.
    Life is but, &c.

God's promise sure will never fail ;
   His holy word is a perfect ground ;
The fort of virtue, O man, assail,
   Where treasure always doth abound.
      Life is but, etc.

To thee alone be laud and praise,
   O Lord, that are so merciful :
Who never failed at all assays,
   To aid and help the pitiful.
      Life is but, etc.

                    [Exeunt omnes.

[Here entereth in NICHOL NEWFANGLE, *and
bringeth in with him a bag, a staff, a bottle,
and two halters, going about the place,
showing it unto the audience, and singeth
thus :]*

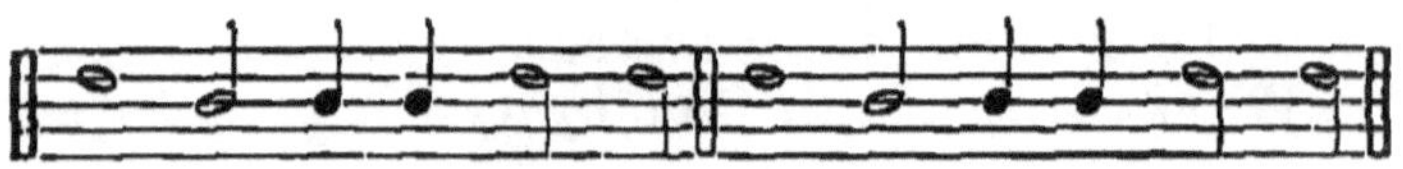

[He may sing this as oft as he thinketh good.]

Marry, here is merchandise, who so list for to buy
     any :
Come, see for your love, and buy for your money,
This is land, which I must distribute anon,
According to my promise, ere I be gone,
For why Tom Tosspot, since he went hence,
Hath increased a noble just unto nine-pence,[1]
And Ralph Roister, it may no otherwise be chosen,

---

[1] [*To bring a noble to nine-pence,* was a proverbial expression
for the idle dissipation of money.]

Hath brought a pack of wool to a fair pair of hosen.
This is good thrift, sirs, learn it who shall,
And now a couple of fellows are come from Cut-
    purse Hall;
And there have they brought many a purse to wrack.
Lo, here is gear that will make their necks for to
    crack.
For I promised Tom Tosspot and Ralph Roister a
    piece of land :
Lo, here it is ready in my right hand :
A wallet and a bottle; but it is not to be sold.
I told them before, that of Beggar's Manor it did
    hold,
And for Cuthbert Cutpurse and Pierce Pickpurse
    here is good fare :
This is the land of the two-legged mare,
Which I to them promised, and [to] divide it with
    discretion :
Shortly you shall see I will put them in possession.
How like you this merchandise, my masters ? Is it
    not trim ?
A wallet, a bottle, a staff, and a string,
How say'st thou, Wat Waghalter ? Is not this a
    trim thing ?
In faith, Ralph Roister is in good case, as I suppose :
For he hath lost all that he hath, save his doublet
    and his hose,
And Tom Tosspot is even at that same point ;
For he would lose a limb or jeopard a joint ;
But, behold, yonder they come both, now all is
    gone and spent,
I know their errand, and what is their intent.

[Here entereth in RALPH ROISTER *and* TOM TOSSPOT
*in their doublet and their hose, and no cap nor hat
on their head, saving a nightcap, because the strings
of the beards may not be seen, and* RALPH ROIS-
TER *must curse and ban as he cometh in.*[1]*]*

RALPH. Well, be as be may, is no banning ;
But I fear that, when that this gear shall come to
    scanning,
The land to the which we did wholly trust :
Shall be gone from us, and we cast in the dust.
    TOM. Gog's blood, if Nichol Newfangle serve
    us so,
We may say, that we have had a shrewd blow ;
For all that I had is now lost at the dice,
My sword, my buckler, and all at sink and cise ;[2]
My coat, my cloak, and my hat also ;
And now in my doublet and my hose I am fain to go.
Therefore, if Nichol Newfangle help not now at a
    pinch
I am undone, for of land I have not an inch.
    RALPH. By Gog's wounds, even so is it now with me,
I am in my doublet and my hosen, as you see :
For all that I had doth lie at pledge for ale.
By the mass, I am as bare as my nail,
Not a cross of money to bless me have I ;
But I trow we shall meet Nichol Newfangle by
    and by.
        *[*NICHOL NEWFANGLE *comes forward.*
NEW. Turn hither, turn hither, I say, sir knave,
For I am even he, that you so fain would have.
    RALPH. What, Master Nichol, are you here all
    this while ?

---

[1] [It appears from what is afterwards said in the piece,
that they do not see Newfangle, who has probably retired to
the back of the stage.]

[2] [Five and Six, a game at cards or dice.]

New. I think I am here, or else I do thee be-
    guile.
Tom. So God help me, I am glad that you be in
    sight ;
For in faith your presence hath made my heart light.
New. I will make it lighter anon, I trow.
                          [*A side.*
My masters, I have a piece of land for you, do you
    know ?
Ralph. Marry, that is the cause of our hither
    resort.
For now we are void of all joy and comfort.
Tom. You see in what case we now stand in,
And you heard us also even now, I ween,
Wherefore, good Master Nichol, let us have this
    land now,
And we shall think ourselves much bound unto
    you.
New. You know, that I this land must divide,
Which I shall do ; but a while abide.
All thy goods for ale at pledge be (*to Tom*),
And thou (*to Ralph*) say'st a pair of dice have made
    thee free.[1]
First, Ralph Roister, come thou unto me,
Because thou hast lost every whit at dice,
    [*He giveth the bag to* R. Roister, *and the*
        bottle to Tom Tosspot.
Take there this bag to carry bread and cheese,
And take thou this bottle, and mark what I shall
    say :
If he chance to eat the bread and cheese by the way,
Do thou in this matter follow my counsel,
Drink up the drink, and knock him about the head
    with the bottle ;
And because that Ralph is the elder knave,

---

[1] [*i.e.*, Destitute of money.]

This staff also of me he shall have.[1]
    RALPH. But where is the land, that to us you
      promised ?
    NEW. In faith, good fellows, my promise is per-
      formed.
    TOM. By Gog's blood, I thought that it would be so.
    NEW. This must you have, whe'r you will or no,
Or else fall to work with shovel and with spade ;
For begging now must be your chiefest trade.
    RALPH. Gog's heart, can I away[2] with this
      life ?
To beg my bread from door to door ?
I will rather cut my throat with a knife,
Than I will live thus beggarly and poor.
By Gog's blood, rather than I will it assay,
I will rob and steal, and keep the highway.
    TOM. Well, Ralph Roister, seeing we be in this
      misery,
And labour we cannot, and to beg it is a shame ;
Yet better it is to beg most shamefully,
Than to be hanged, and to thievery[3] ourselves frame.
    NEW. Now, my masters, learn to beware ;
But like will to like, quoth the Devil to the Collier.
    RALPH. O Lord, why did not I consider before,
What should of roisting be the final end.
Now the horse is stolen, I shut the stable-door.
Alas, that I had time my life to amend !
Time I have, I must needs confess ;
But yet in misery that time must be spent :
Seeing that my life I would not redress ;
But wholly in riot I have it all spent :
Wherefore I am now brought to this exigent.
But the time pass'd cannot be called, this is no nay.

---

[1] [The 4to of 1587 reads, *thou shalt have.*]
  [The 4to of 1568 has *way.*]
[3] [The 4to of 1568 has *the every.*]

Wherefore all here take example by me :
Time tarrieth no man, but passeth still away ;
Take time, while time is, for time doth flee ;
Use well your youthly years, and to virtuous lore
    agree.
For if I to virtue had any respect,
This misfortune to me could not have chanced ;
But because unto vice I was a subject,
To no good fame may I be now advanced.
My credit also is now quite stanched.
Wherefore I would all men my woful case might see,
That I to them a mirror might be.
    TOM. O all ye parents, to you I do say :
Have respect to your children and for their educa-
    tion,
Lest you answer therefore at the latter day,
And your meed shall be eternal damnation.
If my parents had brought me up in virtue and
    learning,
I should not have had this shameful end ;
But all licentiously was my up-bringing,
Wherefore learn by me your faults to amend.
But neither in virtue, learning, or yet honest trade,
Was I bred up my living for to get :
Therefore in misery my time away must vade ;
For vicious persons behold now the net.
I am in the snare, I am caught with the gin ;
And now it is too late, I cannot again begin.
    NEW. This gear would have been seen to before,
But now, my masters, you are on the score.
Be packing, I say, and get you hence ;
Learn to say : I pray, good master, give me nine-
    pence.
    RALPH. Thou, villain, art only the causer of this
    woe ;
Therefore thou shalt have somewhat of me, or ere
    I go.

TOM. Thou hast given me a bottle here ;
But thou shalt drink first of it, be it ale or
    beer.
      [RALPH ROISTER *beateth him with his staff,
        and* TOM TOSSPOT *with his bottle.*
RALPH. Take this of me, before I go hence.
TOM. Take that of me in part of recompense.
NEW. Now am I driven to play the master of
    fence.
Come no near[1] me, you knaves, for your life,
      [*They have him down, and beat him, and he
        crieth for help.*
Lest I stick you both with this woodknife.
Back, I say ! back, thou sturdy beggar !
Body of me, they have ta'en away my dagger.
    RALPH. Now, in faith, you whoreson, take heed,
      I you advise,
How you do any more young men entice.
    TOM. Now, farewell, thou hast thy just meed.
    RALPH. Now we go abegging, God send us good
    speed !
      [RALPH ROISTER *and* TOM TOSSPOT *go out,
        and* SEVERITY, *the judge, entereth, and*
        NICHOL NEWFANGLE *lieth on the ground
        groaning.*
SEV. That upright judgment without partiality
Be minist'red duly to ill-doers and offenders !
I am one, whose name is Severity,
Appointed a judge to suppress evil-doers,
    Not for hatred nor yet for malice :
    But to advance virtue and suppress vice.
Wherefore Isodorus these words doth say :
Non est Judex, si in eo non est Justitia !
He is not a judge that Justice doth want,
But he that truth and equity doth plant.

Fully also these words doth express,
Which words are very true doubtless.
Semper iniquus est judex, qui aut invidet aut favet :
They are unrightful judges all,
That are either envious or else partial.
　　NEW. Help me up, good sir, for I have got a fall.
　　SEV. What cause have you, my friend, thus
　　　heavily to groan ?
　　NEW. O sir, I have good cause to make great
　　　moan ;
Here were two fellows but right now,
That (I think) have killed me, I make God a
　　vow.
I pray you, tell me, am I alive or am I dead ?
　　SEV. Fellow, it is more meet for thee to be in
　　　thy bed,
Than to lie here in such sort as thou dost.
　　NEW. In faith, I should have laid some of the
　　　knaves in the dust,
If I had had your sword right now in presence ;
I would have had a leg or an arm, ere they had gone
　　hence.
　　SEV. Who is it that hath done thee this injury ?
　　NEW. A couple of beggars have done me this
　　　villainy.
　　SEV. I see, if severity should not be executed,
One man should not live by another.
If such injuries should not be confuted,
The child would regard neither father nor mother
Give me thy hand, and I shall help thee.
　　NEW. Hold fast your sword then, I pray you
　　　heartily.　　　　　　　　　　　　　　[*He riseth.*
　　SEV. Now, friend, it appeareth unto me,
That you have been a traveller of the country
And such as travel do hear of things done,
As well in the country, as the city of London.
How say you, my friend, can you tell any news

NEW. That can I, for I came lately from the
    stews.
There are knaves abroad, you may believe me,
As in this place shortly you shall see.
No more words, but mum, and stand awhile aside :
Yonder cometh two knaves ; therefore abide.

Intrat C. CUTPURSE *and* PIERCE PICKPURSE.

CUTHB. By Gog's wounds, if he help not now,
    we are undone :
By the mass, for my part, I wot not whither to run.
    PIERCE. We be so pursu'd on every side
That, by Gog's heart, I wot not where to abide.
    CUTHB. Every constable is charged to make
    privy search ;
So that, if we may be got, we shall be thrown over
    the perch.
    PIERCE. If Nichol Newfangle help us not now
    in our need,
We are like in our business full evil to speed.
Therefore let us make no delay,
But seek him out of hand, and be gone away.

    SEVERITY *and* N. NEWFANGLE *come forward.*

NEW. Soft, my masters, awhile I you pray ;
For I am here, for whom you do seek ;
For you know that like will never from like.
I promised you of late a piece of land,
Which by and by shall fall into your hand.
    CUTHB. What, Master Nichol! how do you to-day?
    PIERCE. For the passion of God, Master Nichol,
    help to rid us away ;
And help us to the land, whereof you did say,
That we might make money of it by and by ;
For out of the realm we purpose to fly.
    NEW. Marry, I will help you, I swear by All
    Hallows :

And will not part from you, till you come to the
    gallows.
Lo, noble Severity, these be they without doubt.
On whom this rumour of thievery [1] is gone about,
Therefore, my masters, here is the snare,
That shall lead you to the land, called the two-
    legged mare.
      [*He putteth about each of their necks a halter.*
  SEV. My friend, hold them fast even in that
    plight.
  NEW. Then come, and help me with your sword;
    for I fear they will fight.
  SEV. Strive not, my masters; for it shall not
    avail;
But awhile give ear unto my counsel.
Your own words hath condemned you for to die;
Therefore to God make yourselves ready.
And by and by I will send one, which for your
    abusion,
Shall lead you to the place of execution.
  NEW. Help to tie their hands, before ye be gone.
               [SEV. *helpeth to tie them.*
  SEV. Now they are bound, I will send one to you
    anon.   [*Exit.*
  NEW. Ah, my masters, how like you this play?
You shall take possession of your land to-day!
I will help to bridle the two-legged mare,
And both you for to ride need not to spare.
Now, so God help me, I swear by this bread,
I marvel who shall play the knave, when you
    twain be dead.
  CUTHB. O cursed caitiff, born in an evil hour,
Woe unto me, that ever I did thee know.
For of all iniquity thou art the bow'r;
The seed of Satan thou dost always sow.

[1 The 4to of 1568 has, as before, *the every.*]
VOL. III.   Z

Thou only hast given me the overthrow.
Woe worth the hour, wherein I was born !
Woe worth the time that ever I knew thee !
For now in misery I am forlorn ;
O, all youth take example by me :
Flee from evil company, as from a serpent you
　　would flee ;
For I to you all a mirror may be.
I have been daintily and delicately bred,
But nothing at all in virtuous lore :
And now I am but a man dead,
Hanged I must be, which grieveth me full sore.
Note well the end of me therefore ;
And you that fathers and mothers be,
Bring not up your children in too much liberty.
　　PIERCE.　Sith that by the law we are now
　　　condemned,
Let us call to God for his mercy and his grace ;
And exhort that all vice may be amended,
While we in this world have time and space.
And though our lives have licentiously been spent,
Yet at the last to God let us call ;
For he heareth such as are ready to repent,
And desireth not that sinners should fall.
Now are we ready to suffer, come when it shall.

Here ent'reth in HANKIN HANGMAN.

　　NEW.　Come, Hankin Hangman, let us two cast
　　　lots,
And between us divide a couple of coats :
Take thou the one, and the other shall be mine.
Come, Hankin Hangman, thou cam'st in good
　　time.　[*They take off the coats, and divide them.*
　　HANKIN.　Thou should'st have one, Nichol, I
　　　swear by the mass,
For thou bringest work for me daily to pass ;

And through thy means I get more coats in one
    year,
Than all my living is worth beside, I swear.
Therefore, Nichol Newfangle, we will depart never:
For like will to like, quoth the Devil to the Collier.
    NEW. Now, farewell, Hankin Hangman, farewell
      to thee.
    HANKIN. Farewell, Nichol Newfangle: come
      you two with me.
        [HANKIN *goeth out, and leadeth the one in his*
           right hand, and the other in his left,
           having halters about their necks.
    NEW. Ha, ha, ha! there is a brace of hounds,
      well worth a dozen crowns,
Behold the huntsman leadeth away!
I think in twenty towns, on hills, and eke on downs.
They taken have their prey.
So well liked was their hunting on hill and eke on
      mountain,
That now they be up in a lease : [1]
To keep within a string, is it not a gay thing?
Do all of you hold your peace?
Why then, good gentle boy, how likest thou this
      play?
No more, but say thy mind :
I swear by this day, if thou wilt this assay,
I will to thee be kind.
This is well brought to pass of me, I swear by the
      mass :
Some to hang, and other some to beg :
I would I had Balaam's ass to carry me, where I
      was ;
How say you, little Meg?
Ralph Roister and Tom Tosspot, are now not
      worth a groat,

---

[1] [Leash.]

So well with them it is :
I would I had a pot, for now I am so hot ,
By the mass, I must go piss.
Philip Fleming and Hance have danc'd a pretty
　　dance,
That all is now spent out.
And now a great mischance came on while they
　　did prance :
They lie sick of the gout.
And in a 'spital-house, with little Laurence louse,
They be fain for to dwell :
If they eat a morsel of souse, or else a roasted
　　mouse,
They think they do fare well.
But as for Peter Pickpurse, and also Cuthbert
　　Cutpurse,
You saw them both right now :
With them it is much worse, for they do ban and
　　curse ;
For the halter shall them bow.
Now if I had my nag, to see the world wag,
I would straight ride about :
Ginks, do fill the bag : I would not pass a rag
To hit you on the snout.

The DEVIL *entereth.*

　LU. Ho, ho, ho ! mine own boy, make no more
　　delay,
But leap up on my back straightway.
　NEW. Then who shall hold my stirrup, while I
　　go to horse ?
LU. Tush, for that do thou not force !
Leap up, I say, leap up quickly.
　NEW. Woh, Ball, woh ! and I will come by and by.
Now for a pair of spurs I would give a good groat !
To try whether this jade do amble or trot.

Farewell, my masters, till I come again,
For now I must make a journey into Spain.
         [*He rideth away on the* DEVIL'S *back.   Here*
            entereth VIRTUOUS LIFE *and* HONOUR.
    V. L. O worthy diadem, O jewel most precious,
O virtue, which dost all worldly things excel :
How worthy a treasure thou art to the virtuous ?
Thy praise no pen may write, nor no tongue tell.
For I, who am called Virtuous Life,
Have in this world both honour and dignity :
Immortal fame of man, child and wife,
Daily waiteth and attendeth on me.
The commodity of virtue in me you may behold,
The enormity of vice you have also seen :
Therefore now to make an end we may be bold,
And pray for our noble and gracious Queen.
    HONOUR. To do so, Virtuous Life, it is our
        bounden duty ;
And because we must do so, before we do end,
To aid us therein, Good Fame cometh verily,
Which daily and hourly on you doth attend.

Here entereth GOOD FAME.

    G. F. Virtuous Life, do what you list :
To pray or to sing I will you assist.
    V. L. O Lord of hosts, O King Almighty,
Pour down thy grace upon our noble Queen !
Vanquish her foes (Lord), that daily and nightly
Through her thy laws may be sincerely seen.
    HONOUR. The honourable council also (O Lord)
        preserve,
The lords both of the clergy and of the temporality :
Grant that with meekness they may thee serve,
Submitting to thee with all humility.
    G. F. O Lord, preserve the Commons of this
        realm also ;

Pour upon them thy heavenly grace ;
To advance virtue and vice to overthrow,
That at last in heaven with thee they may have
 place.
AMEN.

A Song.[1]

Where like to like is a-matched so,
That virtue must of force decay :
There God with vengeance, plagues and woe,
By judgment just must needs repay.
 For, like to like, the worldings cry :
 Although both likes do grace defy.
And where as Satan planted hath
In vicious minds a sinful trade :
There like to like do walk his path,
By which to him like they are made.
 So like with like reward obtain,
 To have their meed in endless pain.
Likewise in faith, where matches be,
And where as God hath planted grace :
There do his children still agree,
And like to like do run their race.
 Like Christ, like hearts of Christian men :
 As like to like well-coupled then.
Therefore like grace, like faith and love,
Like virtue, springs in each degree :
Where like assistance from above
Doth make them like so right to be.
 A holy God, a Christ most just :
 And so like souls in him to trust.

---

[1] [This song is divided by a paragraph-mark between
Virtuous Life and the other speakers; but the names are
not given, and the mode of distribution is consequently
uncertain.]

Then like as Christ above doth reign,
In heaven high our Saviour best :
So like with him shall be our gain,
In peace and joy, and endless rest.
If we ourselves like him do frame,
In fear of his most holy name.
To him be praise, that grace doth give,
Whereby he fashioneth us anew :
And make[s] us holily to live,
Like to himself in faith most true.
Which our redemption sure hath wrought :
Like him to be most dearly bought.

FINIS.

END OF VOL. III.